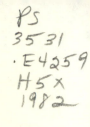

THE
HISTORY
OF
R O M E
H A N K S
and Kindred Matters

Joseph Stanley Pennell

SECOND CHANCE PRESS
RD2, Noyac Road
Sag Harbor, N.Y. 11963

To
E. S.P.
who is dead
AND
T. H. B.
who is alive

Originally published in the United States 1944 by
Charles Scribner's Sons, New York

Republished 1982 by Second Chance Press,
RD2, Sag Harbor, New York

Library of Congress Catalogue Card Number: 81-85726
ISBN 0-933256-32-9 (Clothbound)
      0-933256-33-7 (Paperbound)

Printed in the United States of America

Note to Reader

All anachronisms are conscious, as the narrative is filtered through the memories and desires of several narrators who may be either ignorant or untruthful—or both. For instance, it seems a stretch of the truth that one of Wagnal's age could have been at Edinburgh when the body-snatchers were operating, for he was not an old man at Shiloh. Yet the legend of the Resurrectionists still must have been fairly green when it would have been chronologically possible for him to have been a medical student in the capital of anatomy.

The devices of omission of quotation-marks and the running-together of several characters' speeches in one paragraph are designed to make the narrative flow from one alembic without entailing either too much cloudiness or clarity.

J.S.P.

Now you may go, and never see me more,
For I am set upon by little things;
And you are that I knew you were before
You smiled—another wall for beating wings
To beat against, and never span the space
Between the false and true. Now you shall go!
My time, dimension and your lovely face
Remain irrelevant as fire to snow.
As blood forgets its content in the dust—
As atoms dissipate—as chance sorts life
To waste and seed—and moves it all with lust,
I shall forget our little while, in strife.
For you I cannot lift a broken voice,
Because there is no love nor any choice.

J. S.P.

THE HISTORY OF ROME HANKS

AND KINDRED MATTERS

You awake, Lee thought, in the vast night of all the years. You awake somewhere in the vast night: Everything is around you, all time forwards and backwards and all space. At night, in your bed, you see everything that has been or will be. And you awake at someplace where you never have been, nor ever will be: You awake at Gaines's Mill, lying in the hot, blood-reddened swampweeds with Tom Beckham, or you awake with Robert Lee Harrington, carpenter's bound boy, as he leaves Gadkin county, North Carolina, on his way to make coffins in Abilene, or you awake with Romulus Lycurgus Hanks and General Ulysses S. Grant as they stand in the rain on the night of April 6, 1862 at Pittsburg Landing, Tennessee. Or you awake lying on your own death-bed in a body you do not know. And you cry out: How could I have known? I tell you I didn't know! All right! All right, Goddamn it! I go back and look again and heed and look again and heed—

The compass, the clock, the calendar, the inevitable azimuth, day or night, summer or winter, things vernal or diurnal. Despite these eternal factors, my Grandfather Judson Wade Harrington, fine Southern Gentlemen was what he was. But I went back and looked again and heeded, forgetting why (Christa's face and hair and bored voice) I was looking and heeding. And, therefore, because perhaps celestial computation of direction begins with the North, I struck out into the mysteries of my Yankee grandsires: That is how I came to heed Gaines's Mill and Shiloh and Thomas Beckham and Romulus Lycurgus Hanks. . . .

CHAPTER 1

YES, Christa said. Yes; I'm sure your Grandfather must have been a fine old Southern gentleman.

She is bored, Lee thought. I have talked too much about him and those smooth words are a bored dismissal of the subject. What do I really know about Grandpa Harrington except that he spoke with a Southern accent and that Aunt Cornelia said he was in Pickett's charge at Shiloh with a regiment from North Carolina—or was it Bull Run? All I know is that he kept cows and delivered milk in Fork City and that he bound Papa out in North Carolina to be a carpenter. They came to Kansas when Papa was fifteen and Papa made coffins for John Swinton at Abilene (that was when he ruptured himself) until he got a horse and wagon and camera and went around the little towns taking pictures of babies and children, sometimes on ponies. What was Grandpa Harrington in North Carolina? He always wore a slouched brown hat and a little black tie like a Confederate general—but he always looked shabby and smelled of horses and cows.

Christa could be expected to doubt: Almost anybody with Southern ancestors had had a grandfather at Shiloh or Bull Run in that charge —and who was always a "fine old Southern gentleman." Well Grandpa hadn't had much weight in Fork City. But what sort of people squatted in Fork City anyway? They all sold each other wheat and bacon and corn and beef and farm machinery and squeaky shoes; they all talked in the same Goddamned flat, nasal voices about the same Goddamned trivial things day-in-day-out-year-after-year—eating, sleeping and growing more rustic and pompous and proverbial (as if the secrets of Life with a capital L were to be found in the saws mouthed over a corner rail or a gutter: You kin ketch more flies with molasses than you kin with vinegar. Where there's that much smoke, there must be some far. First ketch your rabbit. Time is money.) They begat their kind, hating each other because of the no-privacy of the place, stunned because of the dulness of the virtues they felt obliged to wear, beckoned at and tempted by the rich vices that each kept each from enjoying except in deep, painful secret . . .

And now here he was, Lee Harrington, sitting across the table from the most beautiful and proudest girl he had ever seen. Maybe she would

3

be his, if he could impress her, so he was telling her about Grandpa Harrington being a Confederate officer in Pickett's charge at Shiloh in the cavalry and Grandpa Beckham being a Yankee, thinking it would make her "love" him. He did not even think that the war was fought for something besides the arms of a tall blonde girl. He did not know how it had been fought; he did not know that neither Grandpa Harrington nor Grandpa Beckham had understood what they had been fighting for—and that when they had finished fighting and marching and starving and shaking and squittering and had gone home (to places that were not home then) they had not, even then, found out that what they had supposed they had been fighting for (what Jefferson Davis, Abraham Lincoln, Harriet Beecher Stowe and all the principal propounders of the Confederacy and Union said the war was about) had evaporated and become something else. Lee did not think: Now I will use that old spilt blood to fertilize my love. Rather he thought: It will add to my stature in her eyes. She was what he wanted most in the world. What harm if a couple of dead grandfathers charged each other in more richly gilt uniforms than the North or South ever saw on its more foppish and drunker brigadiers at any stage of the war? What matter if he made Grandpa Harrington into a hell of a great Southern gentleman—more than Grandpa ever thought of trying to be, even though Aunt Cornelia said he had been the best-dressed man in Gadkin county?

But it didn't seem to matter to Christa one way or another, Lee thought. Yes, I'm sure your grandfather must have been a fine old Southern gentleman. She said it coldly as if it made no difference at all, sitting there in the crowd of the department store lunchroom in a smart, tweed suit, looking like the sweet Vassar girl she was, only something more—something with the look of pride and angels, something that made you believe that real nobility was not just made in the College of Heralds in London, or in Paris, or in Berlin, or in Elsinore, or in Provence, or in Camelot—or that it was only a physical look that Fra Mendel, or Charles Darwin, or any good American stockbreeder could, with proper dames and sires, make in two or three generations.

Yes, your grandfather must have been a fine, old Southern gentleman.

Lee looked at the photograph and the four sonnets he had pulled out from under the desk drawer. Years ago I did not tell it so well as

I think it now but my voice was more vibrant and I could beat harder on the pine of the table in a beerjoint. I could have believed then that I was the Prince at Elsinore, that I was Dante standing by the bridge in Firenze as Beatrice Portinari walked past him in a crimson dress and turned her eyes to him. I knew I could have been a great minor poet and transubstantiated Christa into another Beatrice. This dusty space under the desk drawer is hardly the sala de' Gigli—neither am I dead. But I *am* an exile—an exile, Goddamn them all to hell!

CHAPTER II

God help me, boy, I'm old and Katherine is dead and Dick's dead at Savage's Station and Clint Belton's dead in New England and Unc caught pneumonia in a topless Worth gown and died in Washington. Here, he said, pouring more whiskey into the communion goblets, have a drink.

So many are dead that were young . . .

MY MOTHER, Lee thought, would have had me a preacher or a banker or a smalltown school superintendent. She would have preferred me in a blueserge suit stretched over a generous belly, my feet laced up in those old-fashioned half hookup shoes. It would have delighted her to have heard me as I walked and paused on Pawnee street, repeating the country proverbs. Time, as the fella says, is money.

Years after her anger against Sinclair Lewis had abated—when he was no longer sharp and timely—she began to read his books at the behest of a Fork City preacher and "Psychologist" who had begun a "study class" in what he called "social problems," in her church. Long ago, I had advised her to read the same books. She had said she would never read what "that man" wrote—and told me sharply that I did not know what I was talking about. Is it true, Lee asked himself, that all middleclass smalltown women distrust their own men and worship the blueserge professordoctorsuperintendent?

When my mother used to say regretfully that I would have made such a fine minister, I always mentioned old Wagnal. Lee unfocused his eyes from the time and place. I can hear her say "minister" now—

she said it with a caressing respect—a lovesome awe—in her voice, in just the same tone that she said "God" or "Doctor."

Most women in such villages use the same tone. Let a great booby with the handle of Reverend or Doctor on his name deliver himself of some arrant nonsense, some Goddamn' tripe, some witches' brew and your village woman will roll over and swoon with love and respect.

If you were not born in a smalltown, you do not know how women there love the degrees of Divinitatis Doctor, Medicinae Doctor and Philosophiae Doctor. You do not know how they love the rustic bedside manner of priest and physician—how the chance phrase of a little Biblepounder or a fusty homeopath with a vandyke becomes a perpetual household word: I'm just like Reverend Horseley was when your Papa died; or that's what Dr. Southern always said—he said, you know, Mrs. Harrington, the thing of it is—and then the remark, paradigm or apothegm or saw, fatuous and final but never final—would be repeated again. You know it by heart; you see it rising to the tonguetip again; you feel that someday you must do something to free yourself from these unctuous little fools who have left their stale saws in your women's minds.

But Old Wagnal was something else. Oh, he was the Rev. Mr. Thomas Wagnal, D.D. all right. He had a pension from the Protestant Episcopal church—everybody knew that. The storekeepers got to know when it was coming. Once a month they raised prices on everything he loved. They got nearly all the money as soon as it came, so that there were three weeks out of every month when he starved and smoked cigar butts.

His physiognomy was Johnsonian—although rather more handsome —and he was six feet four in his stocking feet. He had to stoop to get into his house which had been either an old Union Pacific caboose, or a thresher's cookwagon, or a caravan, or the long-discarded backyard studio of one of the Prentiss "girls" who "painted" and married a Florentine nobleman. It was partitioned in the middle for his bedroom and kitchen and smelled of coaloil lamps, cheap tobacco and a certain oldman stench. We sat in splitbottom rockers for perhaps ten hours.

He said: Shiloh—Shiloh? A beautiful name. No; I have never been there, though one day I shall go to the Holy Land. And then he understood me. Pittsburg Landing, he said. The *battle* of Shiloh. Why yes, yes of course, young man. A bloody field. Yes, of course. The Hundred and Seventeenth *Ioway*? He rolled it out in echoing cellartones. Yes;

that was my regiment. I was regimental surgeon. We had our work cut
out for us too.

A kit from Savile Row, a monocle screwed in his eye above his
shaggy cavalry moustache, and you might have thought he was sitting
in his London club talking about some long lost incident of the Khyber
Pass. But that was not it exactly, Lee thought softly. He was something
else.

Yes. Our work was cut out for us too. People used to sing a song
in Edinburgh—I've heard it even in Tanner's Close near the place
where Burke and Hare lived:

> *The body-snatchers they have come,*
> *And made a snatch at me;*
> *'Tis very hard them kind of men*
> *Won't let a body be!*
> *The cock it crows—I must be gone!*
> *My William, we must part;*
> *But I'll be yours in death, although*
> *Sir Astley has my heart.*

That was not the tune he sang, Lee said to a younger Lee. And his
voice was deep bass. He was faraway then when he sang that and he
said softly in a sibilant retired-don sort of a whisper: It's Hood, I fancy,
or a corruption of him. Ah, sir, those were great days. The city was
dirty and I can see the rain now and the poor harlots in the streets—
and many's the one of them found her way under a lad's knife with
whom she'd lain. There was dear Dick Ames who uncovered a poor
cadaver in the dissection theatre—a great wit he was in those days.
No doubt he had some jest on the tip of his tongue, but not the grim
one he made when he looked down and saw the face of the stiff and
the poor mole on its belly. Suffering Christ, he said, and a bloody crown
of bloody thorns! This isn't from a crib. We all saw it was poor Red
Mary who'd been swyved by every medical in the town. Suffering
Christ, no more rent on this bloody beef. She's ours for good and all.
A little piece for you boys and he lopped off Mary's left titty and threw
it to us.

Wagnal was all at sea now, Lee said aloud. He took one of those
old-fashioned pound sacks of tobacco—strong and dry, the kind you
used to buy at crossroads where there was a stove and a sawdust box

and outside a Bull Durham billboard—and loaded up a long cherry-stemmed pipe, spilling dark shards of dry tobacco—perique probably —on the faded blue jeans that stretched across his big, loose wenlike belly. There was another song, he said, and stared across the cracked willowpattern cup at an old Dr. Pierce's Almanac that hung on a nail near a Ladies Home Journal print of The Night Watch. *Bols* in stone bottles, he muttered—there was another song—another one. And then he sang out in a fine Scotch burr—as if heather were moving in a gentle wind:

> *Up the close and doun the stair,*
> *But and ben with Burke and Hare.*

Fie! he said. I can remember no more. But don't you fret—it will come back. Many's the night Dick Ames and other lads and I have roared it out till dawn in a pub. Great lads we were, no bloody fear of death—and great anatomists.

Shiloh, I said. Ah, yes, he said, the s's hissing. Ah, yes, Shiloh. We came to Shiloh at nightfall, where for three hundreds years the Jewish Ark and Tabernacle had remained. There Abijah, the prophet, lived and thither came the wife of Jeroboam to consult him. I was there: May third, eighteen hundred and ninety-four, *Anno Domini*. There were two ruined buildings. Men were making photographs—Americans. Brady perhaps.

Pittsburg Landing, I said—the Hundred and Seventeenth Iowa.

Ah, he said, another Shiloh. Ah yes—your great grandfather, Captain Hanks.

You know St. Louis? he said. You know the river? The levee where the Eads bridge is now? I shan't forget the day we marched through those dingy little streets of warehouses to the boat. We weren't long out of Keokuk, and we expected something more than we got in the way of a sendoff. We had a regimental band of sorts. The drum-major, a Viennese, I think, struck up a Strauss march—but it was no good. There was hardly a dwelling house along our way—narrow streets and high buildings, wet cobblestones, puddles and not a single mean balcony from which a beautiful young girl could wave a snowy-white handkerchief—a square of lace and finelinen—if there was anybody in that district but broadfaced underbred brewers' daughters. When the music stopped we stumped along silently, but for the officers' orders and our own footsteps and the shoes of the colonel's horse and the coughing. We were coughing, for the air was full of fog and soft coal smoke. The boys, who had put on clean white collars to please the beautiful young St. Louis princesses who would lean over the wrought-iron balconies in silk and laces and blow kisses, must have been disgusted. The musketbarrels began to sweat and the Belgian muskets—we'd only got them the day before and had never fired a shot with them—dug into our shoulders.

Somebody swiped a boy in the rear rank with a bayonet—Clint Belton, the major, had insisted on marching with all those wicked meat-pins skewered into the smoke. In any case, the boy in the rear rank of your grandfather's company got his cheek laid open—and I had to sew him up after we got aboard the boat. We were little more than an armed mob then—and damned poorly armed at that. Belgian muskets! Some with curved barrels. I've known them to burst and blind a man, and they always came little short of throwing you down when you fired them. Those who stayed in the fight long at the Landing had lame shoulders the day after. But we didn't have those muskets long I can tell you. When Beauregard retreated the boys picked up Enfields and Springfields. One man got a breechloader of some kind—a fowling piece with a fancy chased frame—but Clint Belton wouldn't allow him to keep it. Clint took it himself, saying it was not soldierly to have a weapon so far from regulations—the only regulations I ever knew in those days of the war were a gun's a gun. Perhaps the only man in the regiment who didn't get a new musket—even I picked up a magnificent Enfield with a beautiful curly walnut stock and carried it clear to Atlanta—was a boy who jerked out both his front teeth with a mandolin string on the night of April sixth. He said his teeth had been blown out—but they were found still in the wire, the blood dried on the roots—and a goodish piece of gum-meat on them.

Oh I can understand now how the boy felt when he ran under the bluff and pulled those teeth out. God in his mercy knows there were enough men behind that hill—and some swimming the river and some dug into the ground lying there quivering with their pants full—many of those who, on the day before, had thought war was such a bully sport. I had a bad moment under the bluff myself.

Oh, no; I wasn't cowering, though I wanted to bad enough. I needed a few more men to help me get my stretchers and medicine chests off the *Die Vernon,* our packet, and I went over to see if I couldn't shame a few of the lads into helping me and the bandsmen. What I knew about surgery in the field was damned little and gleaned out of monographs on Waterloo (where most were left to fester and die) by two-bottle Britons who might as well have still been painted blue. Saw-bones with dundreary whiskers in pillbox fatigue caps. Even now I lie awake nights and think of the poor dead leg of Shuball York that landed in the tub with such a bloody thump. Sir, I am against the uses of inscrutability. I affirm again, as I did many years ago from my pulpit, that, alone, God must make no masked flank movements, create no diversions to carry us for glory. Why should He send a boatload of young rustics from Ioway down the Tennessee to a tanner from Illinois to be killed, mangled and disgraced by a pack of timberwolves from the woods of Georgia and the hills of North Carolina and Virginia, when few or none had any notion of what they were fighting for?

That be as it may, however, I saw your grandfather beneath the bluff. Oh, no. I never knew a braver man. He was trying to gather a few of his company and take them back where they could fight. The boy who had pulled out his front teeth lay on the ground beside him moaning, and Captain Hanks had a great hulking fellow named Sleepy Bates by the front of his jacket. Now Bates, Rome said, you're going back with me, and let me hear no more, sir, about seeing the major run behind the bluff. We'll pick up muskets and powder and ball on the way back. Any of you men who wish to follow me, may, regardless of your regiment. But I tell you, Mr. Hanks, Bates said, I did see the major, and he was a-running here to hide like a bat outa hell. That will do, Bates, Rome said. The boy without the teeth moaned again and flattened himself in the mud. I asked Rome to get me some men to help carry the medicine chests, and I remember he said, yes, Thomas, quite gravely. He was a gravefaced man with dark steady eyes and the sleekest black beard and moustache I ever saw—not handsome as we think of it, but well-favored. There was a superstition about him—and his name was Romulus you know. It was said that once as a young man in Kentucky an old overseer had seen Rome as a boy standing in a patch of timber patting a vulpine—and the animal was in turn muzzling his hand. And there was a legend about his father, Mordecai, and a great she bear: Mordecai's dogs had run the bear to earth, and Mordecai had been about to kill the bear with his knife—but he had changed his mind and spoken to it. The bear at once grew tame, and

Mordecai allowed it to follow him home. And Rome was a cousin of Mr. Lincoln's.

There were a good number of people from Kentucky in Ioway before the war, and there were those who remembered and told me about Rome. He had been ever a mystery, boy and man. His Pa (they always spoke of their fathers thus) had given Rome a squirrel rifle on his tenth birthday.

But and ben with Burke and Hare—

Wagnal said musingly—I wish I could recall—

CHAPTER III

IT WAS perhaps about four o'clock in the afternoon then, Lee remembered, and Wagnal lit the coal oil lamp then and brought the whiskey from his bedroom and two communion goblets.

Lee said to the spider above the desk: There was a rising dust in the air around the lamp and I thought it was cosmic dust. You know how it is: suddenly and noiselessly motion ceases in the world. Everything is egocentric; and you have stopped and the world cannot go on. There it was four o'clock in the afternoon of a spring day, gray as a dead rat with a coal oil lamp burning and an old man, who looked like the bust of Dr. Johnson in the oriel window of my college library, telling me what my great grandfather had done at Shiloh.

Shiloh is an old and obscure battle already—as old as Thermopylae now. The Civil War is so old a war to us Americans—a war so long gone. Shiloh is so old, Lee repeated softly, so long gone that even photographs taken at the reunion in 1889 with the women in broad skirts and legomutton sleeves and a brash little boy in tight knickerbockers standing, feet planted wide apart in front of a pavilion where Encampment No. 39 Band of the Grand Army of the Republic had paused in the generous battle-forgetting gesture of blaring Dixieland (I wish I was in de land ob cotton), that even the broadbrimmed black and gray oldsoldier hats and the lingering campaign beards of the veterans of the Army of Tennessee—not yet quite old (and most of them just oldstyle professional pension-hunting lugs like any today) seem now as mysterious as what you see in breathtaking depth (deeper than space) when you look through the eyewindows of a stereoscope at a pair of pictures labelled, Recent Excavations, Pompeii, and try to fill the wheeltracks in the cobbles with carts and chariots, the apothecary's stall with the leering apothecary, and, most mysterious and sweetly vicious of all, try to pick out and people the Pompeian bawdyhouse where the sixty-three positions of love were done in frescoes on the walls—some say ninety-eight.

The sound, Wagnal said, reminded me of some gargantuan thundershower in summertime over the hard ground of a stubblefield—with an occasional metal crackle like the shaken-tin thunder which frightens the vicariously stormbeaten sitters in an opera house as they watch a melodrama. I could not get one man to help me and the bandsmen with the medicine chests, so I started back to the steamer when I saw Rome bending over a man in blue who lay flat on the ground near a clump of bushes. It was Clint Belton all right, pale as your shirt, his face wet and splotched with sandy mud from trying to shove it under the ground. Come along, Clint, Rome said. Come along! It can happen to anybody—it's only a bad day. Colonel Shaw's hit bad, and we need you. Here—Rome pulled a bottle from his hip pocket—here, Clint, this'll help. Clint Belton grabbed the bottle and took a long swig that ran down into the bluish beginnings of the beard he was nursing and from the corners of his mouth. I remember that it was the only really human thing I ever saw Clint Belton do. He got up and brushed the sandy mud off his long uniform coat. I was ill, Rome, he said. I knew it, Rome said. I thought I got out of sight without them seeing me, Clint said.

Up on the Landing near the log house two of my bandsmen were pointing toward the road, My God, there's a dead man! Yes, there's some more! they were saying. Somehow, four bandsmen and I got the big chests of medicine, a case of brandy, stretchers and leather buckets off the *Die Vernon*. We had a good wagonload—and there were about five hundred wagons and teams on the Landing then and more coming back every minute, the drivers lashing their horses like hell. I saw Rome stop one driver who had a bit of wire in the end of one of his lines. He was out in front of the horses beating them across the eyes with that wire. The eye of one was knocked out and hanging all bloody below its socket. Rome grabbed the man by the scruff of the neck and turned him around in the mud. The man cut at him with the wire end of the line. Rome pulled out his sword and beat the man across the back with it, and the man ran screaming for the bluff. Some other teamsters helped Captain Hanks unhitch the horse and get him out of the road. I saw Rome shoot him with the Colt's Walker he had carried in Mexico. Then he walked down the road passing the stragglers and the walking wounded who were coming back, his long coat open, his high boots sucking up and down in the reddish loblolly.

The five of us got some dressings and brandy and folded stretchers spread on two open stretchers and set out to find the regiment.

There was a major in a mudspattered broadcloth uniform and a Mexican war medal standing beside the muddy road yelling what I thought was, Remember Buena Vista! Go back and fight! at all the men who came past on the trot heading for the bluff or the river. They had a fixed look in their eyes like a dogfrozen rabbit and didn't pay any attention at all to the major who stood there cursing and waving a sword. Before we could get past him and down the road, he dropped the sword and doubled up like a prizefighter punched in the belly. By the time we stopped and set down the stretchers, he was dragging himself along in the mud like a turpentined dog. Both his hands were in his crotch, and there were streams of blood coming through his fingers. We tried to lift him and straighten him out—and one of the bandsmen fetched a bottle of brandy and some bandages. But the major didn't look at us or let on we were there. He tore open his trousers and bent over the bloody place as if he were a Buddhist contemplating his navel. Then, as if he had made a quick mental note, he shook his head and jerked a navy six from his officer's sash. He put the muzzle in his mouth and let a bloody thumb slip off the hammer. We didn't hear a damned thing *more* in that rain-on-the-stubble thunderstorm, but when we saw smoke rising from what was left of his head, the boy who had the brandy took a swig and picked up the major's gun, wiped it on some grass and stuck it in his belt. We picked up the stretcher and walked on. How we expected to find the regiment, I don't know.

We started that tramp of ours by trying to ask every live soldier we saw where the Hundred and Seventeenth Ioway was. Those that stopped to answer said they'd never heard of the Goddamn' sonsuh-bitches—and did they belong to the Rebels?

There was the most extraordinary collection of uniforms: red zou-ave's trousers, short blue artillery jackets, an infantryman with a pair of leather-lined cavalry trousers and a man in a little Scots highland cap with a rosette on it—he was lying in a little depression digging in the mud with his fingers, like a dog. I leant over and yelled in his ear, but he didn't hear or see me—or let up digging.

We bandaged up one or two lads and I cut away the hanging right arm of a young leftenet who was sitting on a stump holding the bloody butt of his arm with tears rolling down his dirty cheeks. I gave him a drink of the brandy before he would let me cut the arm away—and when I got it loose, he grabbed at it and began to cry more, holding it in its old place as if he were trying to put it back on. He was still sitting there when we went on. We were in the timber now; and one of the musicians kept pointing to the way the bark was peeled off the trees. I thought I could hear the balls going through the branches. But I don't know. Perhaps it was about that time we came to the clearing with the tents in it. It was low ground, muddy and full of puddles. All down the middle was a windrow of blue soldiers, dead and wounded, lying in the puddles. They looked familiar, as if I had seen them asleep in the same attitudes before. Lying about were caps, hats, cartridge boxes, muskets, tincups, bibles, packets of letters, newspapers, books and even a piece of pink-frosted cake trodden into the mud beside a copy of *Uncle Tom's Cabin*—and a frightened snake. Something stirred in the thick center of the blue windrow. It was a man's hand lifted up towards us and pulled down with the palm towards the earth. We could see it well, for it caught a slanting beam of the sun which filtered through the trees. We went on toward the line until one of the band boys threw out an arm and fell flat, his face splashing in a puddle. We understood the hand then and put down the stretchers. We crawled and wriggled the rest of the way to the hand. It was Captain Hanks's hand.

Lieutenant Hanks then, I said.

Leftenet or Captain, Wagnal said, it was Rome.

Did they call him Rom or Rome? I asked him.

Rome *and* Rom, he said, pouring some more whiskey into the communion goblets. There was a phrase among a small faction of the men —after the affair at Pittsburgh Landing and never to his face—who wished to elect him colonel of the regiment over the leftenet colonel's and major's heads—the grandeur that was Rome. And there was one old sergeant who told wild tales about the Crimea, who said, by Jesus Christ and on a bloody stack of bibles the Captain had been suckled by the she-wolf, and no bloody buggering question about it.

My grandmother said they called him Rom sometimes in Kansas, I said.

Rome or Rom, Wagnal said, it makes no odds. The sergeant from the Crimea, as callous a devil as you'd find in a brigade of mercenaries, an old regular, mind you—Rome was a volunteer—repeated over and over again that it was a bloody f—ing shame that Rome wasn't Colonel of the regiment at least. This from an old soldier who would do almost anything for money or tobacco or a drink of liquor—and during the time that Clint Belton was keeping him in Havana cigars and sutler's brandy to campaign among the men for the colonelcy. That began at Shiloh in May and lasted until July at Corinth when Clint got the colonelcy. The Crimean, after all that electioneering for Belton, it was said, voted for Rome, who by that time was captain of the company—

But what about under the bluff? I said. Wasn't Belton branded a coward? How could the men elect—

He looked up again at The Night Watch. Under his papery skin some color was creeping: his great nose was reddening like some swollen, cavernicolous berry, its black, dirt-clogged pores, the seed.

Ah, he said, nobody knew that but Rome, the boy without the teeth, Sleepy Bates and me. Belton only suspected that *I* knew and I don't think he knew that the boy without the teeth knew for some time—and you must remember that we had just stepped off the boat, a gang of young yokels, into what was—until Antietam, Chancellorsville, Gettysburg, the Wilderness, Spottsylvania—the worst and bloodiest battle the world had ever known. If a man had been under the bluff at Shiloh, was it likely he would point a finger at another and say: You are a coward, sir—I saw you under the bluff? Oh, no! No; not at all. And any way you look at it, coward would hardly describe Clint Belton. I can think of other unpleasant names for him, but he was hardly a coward—at least not a military coward. In comparison with Rome—but then there was no man who could have been compared with Rome.

We never questioned what Rome told us to do after the musician had let go of the stretcher and flopped face down in the mud. He lay down dead and we lay down alive and wriggled on our bellies up to the breastworks of bodies that Rome and Sleepy Bates, Evarts Haley, Don Trott, Rufus Lamb, Shuball York, the Crimean and Newton, the color sergeant, had made. Shuball York was badly hit with a minié ball in the shoulder, and he lay there in a puddle biting cartridges for the toothless boy who was letting off a musket at the trees and tents as fast as he could load and pull the trigger. I remember the green looked deep and quiet and unnatural—even with all the noise. They had a pile of cartridge-boxes emptied on the spreadout jacket of one of the dead. All but the toothless lad were firing slowly.

Rome had told him not to fire until he could see something, but it was no use. Hero, now't he don't bite, Sleepy Bates said. The toothless boy began to blubber a little, and Rome said: No more of that, to Bates. Bates made a face. The Crimean said, Mind the leftenet's orders! and patted the toothless boy.

Whatever the Crimean was, he was an obedient soldier—and he had a great admiration for Rome, perhaps because of the British officers he had known. At first he tried to trim his beard like Rome's and walk and talk like Rome, but he could not conquer his barrack-room billingsgate. And then there was the other thing, of which I shall tell you presently.

God! Lee thought. Christ! From Crimea and Edinburgh to Shiloh! The old bastard, Wagnal, was a doctor and a preacher both!

Lee thought: Oh, he was both all right. He had seen too much and done too much and one day after his wife had died, he went after the organ-pumper. There was a little room at the back of the church where they kept the surplices for the choirboys and bread for the communion—they didn't use those pressed wafers then. Ed Carter was pumping the organ for two bits a Sunday. I suppose it was damned uneven and wheezy, for Ed was thin and languid and did the pumping just for the two bits, not because he hankered after heaven. Ed saw him come in the little gothicpanelled door and go over to the breadbox that sat on the table under the tablet to General J. E. B. Stuart, who was one of the founders of the church while he was still a lieutenant in the Union army at Fort Davis. But Ed didn't have any idea what was going to happen, until the sharp breadknife, used to cut bread for the communion before they got the patent wafers, was against his throat. The old man held him against the wall and told him if he didn't pump the Goddamned organ properly, it wouldn't be a neat incision. Ed told his father. His old man said, by God, that was a hell of a Goddamn' joke—scarin' the holy livin' piss out of people's children—and him a rector too. Maybe, by God, it wasn't a joke. After that people began to say that he had put his hands on their daughters' asses.

One Sunday night the young people's association—or whatever they called it—met at the rectory to play whist. A young girl pulled down the front window shade and giggled. Wagnal got red in the face and put it up again. Never, said he, never sneak, my child. Only Christ may come as a thief in the night. He talked to them a long time; and they watched him, not listening. When they were not watching him, they stared at the dim filament loops of the old carbon lightbulbs and his painted college oar on the wall and the Flemish prints, particularly The Anatomy Lesson and the pine woodwork and the hollow golden-oak newel post with the bronze maiden holding up some fruit and the books under glass in the Globe-Wernicke sectional book cases and the transmitter snout of the wall telephone. All this in that dimyellow carbonlight, the strange and familiar, and the cellartoned voice going on about hypocrisy was hard going. He saw them staring at The Anatomy Lesson; and hastened to tell them about the rain in Edinburgh and the spring guns and mortsafes on the graves of the Scotch bourgeoisie to keep away the body-snatchers. He had got to the operating theatre when Marian Fuller stood up, tall and blonde and less afraid than the wide-eyed oafs of boys, and said: It's terribly late, Dr. Wagnal, and my mother expects me. Of course, my dear child, he said looking at her fine breasts with a warm eye. It's been an awfully nice game, hasn't it? (They hadn't played.) I'm so sorry Katherine wasn't able to join us tonight, but I insisted she keep her bed. (She had been dead a long time.) They looked toward the newel post and then away quickly and back to the carbonbulbs. They got up and began stammering about what a good time they had. It was cold and clear outside; and everything was hard and distinct in the moonlight. The snow glittered where there were no shadows of trees and houses. But the boys walked home fast and stayed together as long as they could after they had taken the girls home.

The whiskey looked like dirty water with oil on it—in the lamplight, Lee thought. Rain was coming down on the roof of the old caboose or backyard studio now like a soundeffect in a moviehouse and there was a growing drop on the magazine papered roof above the print of The Night Watch. Wagnal looked up at it as if it were all time or a peepshow to the past.

As I see it now, he said, a strong and curious bond grew on us that day at Pittsburg. Oh, I know you're thinking that there is always a strong bond among those who have been in battle together—and there is. But this was strange. There was the Crimean who intrigued for Belton's colonelcy, but voted for Rome; the toothless boy whose sphincter muscles had been useless in the morning, but who came into that fire because of Rome; Shuball York, who had given up a commission in a cavalry regiment to come with Rome as a private; Newton, the colorbearer, who began from that day on to stick to Rome and stuck from there to Atlanta; Sleepy Bates, who, for the remainder of his short time, followed Rome like a great hound—though he admired Belton for a while; and the rest of us who took it as our special charge to make Rome as comfortable as possible. We were even jealous of each other. And for a long time we could not understand how Belton got the colonelcy, even though Rome was appointed to count the votes. Perhaps, at that time, just before Corinth, the other nine companies did not—could not have known well as quiet a man as Captain Hanks.

Besides his revolver, Rome had picked up a Springfield musket. He had it looped over his shoulder; and when I first wriggled up he had the Colt's Walker and his sword in his hands. Among the tents, which had been some Illinois regiment's that morning, we saw a burst of orange flashes and then blue smoke choked the company street down which we were looking. I saw a man in browngray running toward us. A blood red flag was jerking slackly along in the air so that only now and again could you see the blue St. Andrew's cross and the stars. I saw Rome put his sword in its scabbard and saw it was red as it slid sandily in. He took the Walker in his right hand and rested the barrel between two brass buttons on the jacket in front of him, keeping both eyes open. Shuball, he said, before the front sight of the pistol flew up in his hand, tell them to aim. Then the Rebel flag went down for a second and came up again jerking toward us. Rome cocked his pistol again. He had that flag up and down three times before he emptied the gun and put it up in his holster. A Rebel officer had the flag then. We could see that he was screaming like a Shawnee as he ran toward us. Aim, Rome said, and unslung the musket from his shoulder. He put the stock up and laid the barrel across the dead man's belly. We saw the Rebel officer's face splash the water in a puddle. They kept on coming in small numbers—and we kept on firing. I had picked up the Enfield—which I lost at Atlanta—and one of the bandsmen was using the pistol he had taken from the Mexican war major who did himself in. Somebody began firing at us from a tree. The minié balls rocked and shook the dead protectors we had in front of us. When the Rebels would start for us they would scream. A good many of them were just fuzzy boys in hickory shirts with a wild indignant puzzled look in their eyes, as if they were about to lynch a nigger.

Rome put his head down beside Shuball's ear and shouted: We've got to fall back. Crouch and run to those trees and take cover. Pass the word along. I'll signal with my hand. Gather up the powder and ball. We got back to the trees—and then fifty yards further. Shuball was bleeding badly. I gave him a swig of whiskey with a little morphia in it and cut out the squashed minié ball. He kept biting cartridges, for the boy who had pulled his teeth, all the while I was probing. There was a little ridge on the ground there, and, with another of the bandsmen who had got it and several dead Rebels we made another breastworks. Newton stood up to plant our flag. The staff broke in his hand and blood spurted from the palm. I saw him pull out a thick sliver two inches long. The boy cut a sapling, tied the flag to it and shoved it in the ground with the lead flying all around him. The Crimean let out a high scream of defiance; we all cheered; and some Rebels near the tents yelled and fired their ramrods. We could see them quivering like featherless steel arrows in the sunlight through the trees.

I heard the Crimean begin talking to the breastworks as he fired and bit cartridge, and, in the gaps which were beginning to open in the musketry, I heard the breastworks answer in a weak voice—I remember thinking at that moment that it was proper for a breastworks to answer. Gawd's sake git that Tait offen me. Ah cain't ketch mah breath. How did you get 'ere? the Crimean said. They war a shootin' off a cannon oveh thar an Cunnel Neill says go git 'em— The second dead bandsman's foot was on the man's belly. Take that man out of there! Pull him down! Rome said. But the breastworks, Leftenet—the Crimean said. Rome stood up in the Rebel fire and pulled the man back into shelter. How long have you known this? Rome said. Not over ten minutes, sir, the Crimean said. Thomas, Rome said to me, do whatever you can. Git that Tait offen me, the man kept saying. He had a stubble of red beard and long black hair, very dirty and full of lice and white scurf flakes. The beard around his mouth was full of powder grains. His eyes were already beginning to glaze. Where're you hit? I said. Lead in my bellybutton, he said. Drink— I gave him a drink of water and then a little brandy. He was hit in the belly all right—but there were three balls in the right side of his carcass where it had been presented to the enemy. When he tried to swallow, blood bubbled from the

corners of his mouth into the powderclogged beard. Twenty-third
Tennessee, he said. So's that Tait. Lives a pieceways up the branch.
Cunnel Neill says, Gahddammit gentlemen, go git that batt'ry. Cain't
have them bastards a-shootin' us up thisaway. His eyes glazed over
completely and the crotch of his homespun jeans got wetter. Didn't
know who he was talkin' to, the Crimean said. Mind if I take him
back? A fly settled on the open left eye as the Crimean pulled him up
on top of the second bandsman. The toothless boy turned his head and
began to puke. It smelt warm and pissy in that timber—if it hadn't
been for the powder smell, it might have been a backhouse in Ioway.

We couldn't see any more live Union soldiers around us, for the
smoke and trees and undergrowth. The toothless boy wiped his mouth
and kept crawling around and fetching back cartridge boxes. Each of
us kept a little pile of cartridges beside him and some in his pocket—
and each stuck a ramrod in the soft red mud near to his hand. Rome
fired less than anybody, but it was easy to see he was aiming at something every time he pulled the trigger. The toothless boy used both
hands to pull back the heavy hammer of his musket, for he was weak
and stringy. Crime helped him as much as he could.

The sun lowered and the vistas of the thin timber burnt with shafts
of sunset light in which smoke and spiderweb floated. Alma was beer
and bleeding skittles to this, the Crimean said, sitting up. Yes, Rome
said, Buena Vista was child's play. It's quiet, the boy without the front
teeth said. Christ a'mighty it's quiet. You don't have to holler to be
heard no more. You sound purty funny without them ca'tridge biters,
young fellah, one of the bandsmen said. How'd you git 'em out? Yeh,
Sleepy Bates said. They was reg'lar hoss teeth. Bet he called the hoss
doctor. The boy's fuzzy, pimpled face got pink and he tried to pull
down his short upper lip over the black toothgap. Quiet, Rome said.
And stay down till we look about. Rome and the Crimean and I
walked around the position. Somewhere in the woods, I heard the
boardy clucking of artillery wheels and the snap of whips, but I must
have walked a quarter of a mile to our left without seeing anything but
dead and wounded. Gradually I became aware that the woods were
moaning—they moaned all that night and for three days and nights.
They smelled like piss and powder at first—and then they began to
smell different. I had only just got my ears attuned to the moaning
when I came to a two gun section of Napoleons with a litter of Union
and Confederate dead and dying sprinkled around it. It was the outfit

Colonel Neill had told his men to go and git. One of the guns was spiked with a ramrod, and a man in brown homespun with a spike still in his hand lay across the trail of the other. There was a letter sticking out of his pocket with Cass Tait, Twenty-third Tennessee on it. I went back and told Rome that I had found the guns.

The Crimean had been an artillerist for Her Majesty once, so we decided to go back and work the unspiked gun—if anything more happened. We put Shuball York on one of the stretchers along with some of the brandy and bandages.

Not like Alma, no bloody fear, the Crimean said. Well, Crime, Shuball said from the stretcher, what was Alma like? Crime! Sleepy Bates said. Ain't he a Crime! From that time on nobody remembered the Crimean's real name. Well, Crime said, we stood up in bloody formation so that the bloody Rooshin buggers could shoot us easier— and the buggering subalterns hollering: Foller me! And don't a bloody one of you turn 'is blahsted back fer 'er Grycious Majesty wouldn't think you'd died shipshape. Was you hit? Sleepy Bates said. Four buggering times, Crime said—and left for bloody dead! Sir Colin Campbell, the old sod, comes up on his blahsted 'orse, and sez 'e: Me lads, it's inter action you goes. And remember this: 'ooever is wounded must lie where 'e falls until the bandsmen come to attend him. No soldiers must go carryin' ahf wounded men. If any soldier does such a thing 's nyme'll be stuck up in 'is parish church. Ayn't got no buggering parish church, thinks I—and nobody knows me under this nyme. Make me proud of me 'ighland Brigyde, Sir Colin sez. 'Is 'ighland Brigyde! me arse! I was near the ruddy colors and the bleedin' flag sez: Egypt, Corruna, Orthes, Fooentz Daughnor, Pye-rennes, Nivelle, Nive, Toulouse, Peninsula and Waterloo. Every one a bad enough show fer the lads in it. And all at once I sez to meself, if I come through this show, 'er Majesty can go bugger off. And me not even a Scotsman, standin' there in a kilt like a bloody fool for a bloody bob a day and a gill of rum when we bleeding got it. 'Ow did I get 'ere? I sez to meself. Me knees bare! But it wasn't like this. This is more like the Mutiny. What mutiny? Sleepy Bates said. Why, the Great Indian Mutiny, Crime said. What tribe? Bates said. Not the redskins, Crime said, the wretched 'Indoo buggers. The Braymins objected to bitin' ca'tridges like the boy there, but they didn't pull no teeth. The Mutiny was bloody awful.

Sleepy Bates pushed the dead Tennesseean off the trail of the gun and sat down on it; the boy without the teeth began to unbuckle the

sword of a tall bearded corpse with a smashed face and a Confederate
colonel's uniform. Crime looked at them contemptuously. Rome saw
the look and said: Now, look sharp! Crime's in command here while
we man this gun. You, Toothless, Crime said tenderly, get away from
Colonel Neill's sword! No pillaging now, laddie. You can rob the
buggers when it's safe—but look out you ain't pillaged yourself.

We dragged the dead to one side; and I gave one or two of the
wounded water and brandy. Rome himself was on the rammer; Bates
fetched up the first charge of spherical case in the tongs; the toothless
boy stood by with powder; and I waited with another charge of case.
Crime made the rest and a major from an Ohio regiment act as infantry
supports. Shuball York was to bite cartridges. There were maybe three
or four on either side of the Napoleon: Haley and young Lamb and a
bandsman piled the dead Confederate colonel and some of the dead
Union artillerymen in front of them and Trott and Newton and Lamb
got behind a swollen dead horse. Shuball decided he'd bite cartridge
for Trott and Lamb and Newton. We hadn't any more than got set
when it started again. There was that stage thunder and then the
thundershower of the musketry. Crime had the lanyard in his hand;
and everybody was still and quiet. The lads behind their new breastworks squatted and looked into the timber. The smoke got thicker
again; and the minié balls cut and whined in the underbrush. Crime
must have thought he saw something moving, for he held up his hand
and jerked the lanyard. The ragged weeds in front of the muzzle lay
tight to the ground and there was a great flash. The wheels lifted and
fell back in the mud. I saw Rome put his hand to his left ear before he
dipped the spongestaff into the leather bucket. Crime shoved in the
silk powderbag and I hefted up the loaded ball in the tongs. Rome
rammed them back in the gun. Crime depressed the piece and looked
along it after he had shoved in another primer. It was while he was
pointing that Clint Belton rode up on a cavalry horse. He had a bloody
rag around his forearm, and he was yelling and waving a sword. I
couldn't hear what he was saying, but I could see his face. I saw it
change as he caught sight of Rome and Bates. They did not smile or
scowl. Bates blushed and Belton—a high-colored man—got a white
fixed expression. Belton turned to Rome and, leaning over, yelled: I'll
see what's in your front. Then without waiting for an answer, he
kicked the horse in the belly and rode into the brush directly in our
line of fire. We could see the horse shy and stumble. Hold your bloody

fire, Crime said. It's the major! We held our fire for a minute or so until Clint came back—on foot—backing towards us firing his pistol into the timber. They got my horse! he yelled in Crime's ear. There's a regiment over there, if there's a man. But I got *one*, I know. He pointed to the red blood gutters in his sword. I thought I heard Sleepy Bates say: Horseblood. Crime pointed the Napoleon at the patch Belton had indicated. We worked the gun at it for five rounds. Don Trott saw them coming from the left to flank us. There were a good many of them, and, from their faces, they all looked to be screaming. This lot had gray uniforms and gray kepis with patent leather visors. We wheeled the gun around. Crime nipped off the fuse close in the next charge of spherical case. I'll be buggered, he said. Damned if they ain't trying to march in close order. Cadets, I'll bet. We could see an officer with sword on his shoulder—and see his lips moving in the commands. They think they'll carry us, Crime said—or they ain't seen us.

Rome rammed home and stepped back. I had the next round ready. Crime jerked the lanyard. Ha! Crime yelled. We could see the thing explode and see the officer close up the gap. He closed it three times— and kept them marching straight towards our gun. He may have been going to give us a volley. We got the gun primed again; and Crime was ready to let them have it when he saw Clint Belton running towards the officer. What was left of the column was firing at Belton. I saw Belton fire his revolver at the officer and the officer fire at him. Then Belton fired again and the officer went down like a sack of meal with Belton pushing his sword into him. Belton fired at what was left of the ranks a couple of times and ran back to us. We hadn't fired even a musket shot while this was going on. Crime and I looked at each other; and I knew that he had been wishing the same thing that I had—that the Rebel officer would get Clint. I got him, boys! Clint yelled. Crime pulled the lanyard again, and when the smoke lifted, they weren't coming on any more.

Our ears were ringing when Crime dropped the lanyard. It's Jesusly quiet, Bates said. I wonder who's licked, the toothless boy lisped, us, or the other feller? We ain't lost the battle have we, Mr. Hanks? The toothless boy lived in Knoxville, Ioway, where Rome ran a livery stable. His mother ran a young ladies' academy that never had more than two pupils. She had let him go to war only because he was going with Mr. Hanks. He couldn't keep from calling Rome, Mister instead of lieu-tenant—a good many of them couldn't. I beg your pardon, sir? Rome said, cupping his hand over his left ear. You're shot, Mr. Hanks, the boy howled.

Shot? Rome said and put his hand up to the ear. It came away with dried crusty blood on it. In the ear, the toothless boy whined. Not shot, sir. I saw it 'appen, sir, Crime said. The Leftenet, sir, was too close to the muzzle when we fired the first time. Broke 'is eardrum, sir. Saw it once before at Lucknow. Drum-major workin' the spongestaff. Couldn't 'ear a bleedin' thing on 'is 'orf side. Buggered up 'is band a good deal I can tell you. I swabbed out Rome's ear with brandy and packed it with lint. I hope this doesn't disable you, Rome, Belton said. Nonsense, Rome said. Well, Belton said, Lieutenant Hanks you will bivouack here and the rest of the regiment will form on you. I'll be off to find them. He looked sharply at Sleepy Bates and walked off toward the Landing.

'Ows fer a swig of that brandy, Leftenet, Crime said to me. The toothless boy was already pulling at the Confederate colonel's sword. I gave Crime a swig. We all sat down about that time—tired out.

Bates came back from the place where the men in kepis lay with a West Point cadet sword in one hand and three wallets and a packet of letters in the other. In his trousers' band he had a duelling pistol. He laid the other things down on the ground and sat down with his legs over them as if he expected someone to snatch them away from him. Then he pulled the pistol from his belt. He waved it around in the air. Ain't it a beauty? he said. Ain't it bully? It had an octagonal barrel, with engraved plates, a dolphin shaped hammer and a pine-apple end on the butt. There was a monogram in the silver on the grips. It had an old swivel ramrod, and the top of the barrel was marked W. Bond, 50 Lombard Street, London. All but Rome and I had gathered around him. That officer had it, Sleepy Bates said. The one the major got. Out of a pair, Crime said. Out of a bryce of duellin' pieces. Gentleman's blahsted firearm. One f—ing shot. No bloody good against a Colt's. You'll get tired packin' it around and throw it away. In pillage, me lad, it's money and flahsks that counts. Let's just 'ave a look inter them wallets. Bates's lower lip hung down sulkily, but he picked up the wallets. There was a lock of black hair tied with a pink ribbon, an ivory miniature of a woman with her dark hair parted in the middle and slicked tight to her head and ten dollars in Confederate bills. The letters were addressed to Third Lieutenant Charles Farquhar, Louisiana Grays, Fair Grounds, New Orleans. 'Air! Female 'air! and two bloody quid in Rebel shinplasters, Crime said. Spoils o' war! Now some of them Rooshins 'ad got gold on their sword pummels. You better try again, me lad.

Crime and Newton got the flys of a Sibley tent; and we put them up on stakes and laid Shuball and a couple of the Louisiana Grays under it. One of them had a piece of his brainpan knocked out—I suppose by our spherical case—and you could see the gray matter. I never understood how he lived until the next morning—in the rain too. The other one died in a few minutes. He had a broken back—a shell fragment through the belly. Crime and I and Rome and the bandsmen picked them up.

It was almost dusk then—and I kicked something. I picked it up before I saw that it was a young golden-haired head with its blue eyes open. Even after Edinburgh, I almost dropped it. Crime saw it. Looks as if 'e was blowed from a gun, Crime said. Blown from a gun? I said. Right you are, Crime said. Punishment for sepoys. It was at Lucknow, if I recall correct, sir. Ole Sir 'Enry 'Avelock sez to the gunner captain: Can you blow a man from a gun? Well, sez the cap'n, it ayn't in the curriculum at Woolitch. Cap'n, sez Sir 'Enry, I asked you a question. I expect an answer. I can try, sir, says the cap'n. We unlimbered and come to action front and they brought out the sepoy—as fine a lookin' feller as I ever saw out in Hindier. We made a wrist fahst to each wheel and I depressed the muzzle until it pointed right above 'is nyvel. The cap'n says: 'Ere, all you get away from the bloody gun except you, damn' yer blahsted eyes. You tyke the port fire. The buggerin' sepoy didn't let out a bleedin' whimper—'e just looked at me standin' there with the port fire. I didn't 'arf like it because we 'adn't put any shot in the gun. Wot, thinks I, if it only burns the poor bugger's belly? The Cap'n run back about five yards and hollered, Fire! And I put the port fire to the touch hole. She kicked like old bloody 'ell and smoked liked a bad flue. It burnt the poor bugger's belly aw right. When the f—ing smoke had cleared awy, all there was left was a bryce of legs lyin' in front of the gun.

Abaht six or eyt seconds after the report, the 'ead fell down at the cap'n's feet. It was a little powder burnt, but 'ardly chynged—except it 'adn't got no body. Must 'ave gone stryte up. I grinned at the cap'n gettin' the 'ead, and 'e made me blow the 'ole bloody lot of 'em—'arf a blahsted regiment. But I never got 'arf so good a shot as the first one.

Crime grinned at me, and I nearly dropped the head. Beginner's luck, I said. Then, casually, I tossed the head aside. I was still young then.

Crime picked it up again and opened the mouth. The jaws worked like the jaws of a chicken head I once had picked up when I was a little boy.

I knew a sergeant, Crime said, as used to be a resurrection-man. 'E always looked into their mouths after a brush—especially the officers. Said the bloody gov'ment ruined a good perfession. Dentists wouldn't buy teeth no more—but, says 'e, the poor dead buggers don't need their gold canines. I see him foller a gold-toothed subaltern fer weeks. He threw the head down and grunted. Too young fer gold, he said sadly.

Newton built a little fire, and we fried some sowbelly and had some brandy and coffee. After that Rome and I lay down on the stretchers—we put the handles on two logs. It seemed years had gone when I woke up soaked to the skin. I tried to bail some water out of the stretcher with my hat. Thomas! I heard Rome say. I'm going up to the landing. Coming with me? Yes, Rome. I couldn't be wetter, anyway, Rome said.

Once I fell down and put my hand in the mouth of a corpse. It was cold and full of water, and I could feel it trickling out of the corners. Rome helped me up; and we went on, our feet slipping on the side of a little gulley. The ground all around us was moaning under the long steady swish of the rain. We walked like blind men on ice, putting one foot cautiously in front of the other, two hands holding each other and two held out before us. When our toes felt anything soft above ground level we said look sharp or watch out and veered off or stepped light and high. When something came between us, we didn't let go of each other's hand until we spoke. We had just groped around a cannon and stepped high over several bodies when we heard the neighing. Rome must have put his hand out against it, for there was a swish in the air. Steady, boy! Rome said. Steady, boy. Stand still a moment, Thomas. Rome put both hands out and felt all over the horse. He's standing up, Rome said. But he doesn't feel just right. Tck! Tck! Tck! Rome's tone changed. He's all open in the belly—hanging down.

Back away a little bit, Thomas. There, old boy. There, Rome said. I could hear him patting the wet hide. I heard the click, and the horse neighing weakly again—and Rome talking to it more softly. There wasn't much flash, for Rome had put the barrel against the head, but I saw the horse's filmy eyes as he sank down on his knees. We joined hands again and walked on through the cold rain.

Something plucked at my heel, Rome, I said. Squat down and feel,

Rome said. My matches are wet. We squatted down and felt. Don't touch me there, the voice said weakly. Got any tobacker? Chawin'? I've got a cigar, I said. Put it in my mouth—up here. Don't for God's sake try to move me. Some fellah drug me around and took my money and my watch and tobacker a little bit ago. Don't try to move me! His voice had risen to a low scream in the rain. I felt for his mouth and tried to put the cigar in it. What's your name and regiment? Rome said. Fiftieth— What? Rome said. I leant over the mouth—tried to find a pulse. Might have been fiftieth anything, Rome said.

We could tell that we were climbing up a slippery grade. And then we saw the lights of the transports—a long line of them, maybe thirty. The *Die Vernon* must have been there—and I thought that only yesterday Don Trott was trying to teach Sleepy Bates to sing The Girl I Left Behind Me on the deck of that boat. Now we could see the rain falling steadily and stubbornly on the decks, and the soldiers moving about in the dirty weather—soldiers going in and out of the log house on the Landing. Rome and I sloshed down to the door of the cabin. The surgeons had taken a couple of reflector-lamps from some steamboat and put them up on the wall. As Rome and I went in, a huge winged shadow jerked over the walls and across the faces of the two men who stood over a bloody pine table in the middle of the room. A big powdery moth flew into my wet face. I blew and beat at him knocking him to the floor. Thank you, sir, one of the men at the table said. You have rid us of the angel of death. John Simpson, Rome said. It was Simpson all right. He had a bloody scalpel in his hand; his cuffs were bloody— and his eyes were bloodshot. He had a black ring of powder around his mouth.

But, John, Rome said, I thought you signed up as chaplain. I did, Rome, but I learnt this trade before I put on the cloth. And today I have handled the musket, I believe, sir, as tellingly as anybody. Since dark, sir, I have cut out some twenty-odd minié balls and made thirteen amputations of mortal limbs—in company, of course, with Surgeon Raith here. Dr. Raith let me introduce Lieutenant Hanks and Surgeon Wagnal of my regiment, the Hundred and Seventeenth Ioway. Raith bowed. Hanks? he said. Hanks, did you say, Simpson? That's it, sir, Rome said. An unusual name, Raith said. It's possible. Excuse me, Rome said, but what's possible, Doctor? There's a man lying in the corner there, Raith said. See if you know him, Rome, Simpson said.

Rome walked to the corner, stepping on the little clear spaces of puncheon floor between the legs of double and single-legged men. He stooped over and waved a fly off the face. Buhloom! Buhloom! I turned in the doorway as two wide fringed streaks of fire shot up over the river. Rome was kneeling when I turned back.

Raith was using the bonesaw; and there was a high, thin steelsong as Rome looked up and moved his head. I picked my way to the corner where he was leaning over a big man with a beard. It was a boy's face in the dirty fringed circle of hair. The eyes were blue and sunken in the dark shiny flesh. It was a face trying to be Rome's face. It's my little brother, Ream, Rome said. Remus. But not my twin. Remus looked thirty and over six feet.

Buhloom! Buhloom! Bloom! Buhloom! came from the wooden gunboats on the river and the exploding shells in the woods.

Are you hurt bad, Brother Rome? the man on the floor said. What do you think? Rome said to me. I'll talk to Raith, I said.

A hospital orderly was picking up a tub of arms and legs preparatory to carrying them out and two more hospital pimps—as we used to call them—were taking a lone-legged man from the bloody pine table. Raith was wiping his hands on a gray uniform coat, leaving it smudged with red. Eh? he said. Oh, him? The ball went in the belly and took out two vertebrae just above the coccyx. Can't move his legs. Don't know why he's alive now. Got it early this morning. His regiment was one of the first hit. Rome looked up, and I shook my head.

I heard there was more Ioway troops comin', Remus said. I was a-going down to the landing when they hit us. I thought you were in a Kentucky regiment, Brother Ream? Rome said. I am, Brother Rome, Ream said. The Seventeenth—first lieutenant, Company B—it's Union or was, if there's any left. They shot us in bed. A fellow run a cannon muzzle up in one tent, they said. Where's Brother Lucius and Granny? Rome said. I think Loosh is with a Tennessee regiment and Granny's with a bunch called Morgan's Lexington Rifles. They're Secesh. He stopped and Rome brushed a fly from his face. Ma's dead, Brother Rome. He coughed and a bubble of blood came from his mouth. I joined the Yankee side, because I knew you'd be on it. Is it like the Mexican war, Brother Rome? Yes, Ream, just like it, Rome said. I'm a lieutenant. And a good one too, I'll bet, Rome said. You going to stay for a while, Brother Rome? It's raining outside. Sure, Ream. Sure, honey. I read Livy and Suetonius and Shakespeare and the story about Romulus and Remus and the she-wolf— The mouth did not close to make another consonant, but the eyes still pointed up at Rome's face. Mr. Simpson, will you keep him here until daylight? Yes, Mr. Hanks, Simpson said. His papers? Eh? Rome said. Oh, yes, I was forgetting. There was a watch that Rome had given him, still in the chamois case of the Ohio watchmaker; three photographs of himself in full uniform taken in Savannah, Tennessee, one of which was in an envelope addressed to Romulus L. Hanks, Knoxville, Iowa; a photograph of a softfaced blonde girl with a cameo on the bosom of a black silk dress. He was your brother, Mr. Hanks? Simpson said. My youngest brother from Kentucky, Rome said. He has gone to his reward, Mr. Hanks, Simpson said dourly. Never forget it, Mr. Hanks, his reward. I'll get him at daylight, Rome said.

In the door there was a pinkface and a short brown beard held up by a pair of muddy crutches. The dark slouch hat was shiny and dripping. Good evening, Rome, I haven't seen you since we was in Mexico. I smelled the whiskey through the smell of piss and powder and rot. Good evening, sir, Rome said. Why, it's Lieutenant Grant, the man with all the horses. That was a fine pony you had, Grant said. But you wouldn't sell him. Rome was remembering young Grant the horse fancier—Beauty Grant, Desdemona to Lieutenant Porter's Othello— and the day in the chaparral when they both had seen the captain's homeless tongue lolling in the air after the roundshot. A voice lost in blood: Eighteen Forty-six, Eighth May. I could see Grant remembering. It's a long time, Rome said. Bloom! Buhloom! The flashes of the Columbiads on the wooden *Tyler* and *Lexington* paled the black behind the leant-forward roundshoulders of the man on crutches. Simpson was lifting his scalpel. Good God, not *that* leg! Not that one, Goddamn' you! a scream said. Sixteen years, Grant said, a frown coming from the scream. How have you been, Rome? Very well, thank you, Rome said. I have a wife and family and a livery business in Ioway. Ah, horses, Grant said. How is it with you, Lieutenant Grant? I don't know, Grant said. I don't know. The man on the table keened, and the bonesaw began again. The rain dripped from Grant's hat. You were hit today, sir? Rome said. My horse fell on me before the fight, Grant said. A torchlight flared up and soldiers began moving across a gangplank into the mud of the Landing. Buell's troops, I calculate, Rome said. What happened today? Who was in command? Then it must have come to him. By the way, Lieutenant, he said, are you any kin to General U. S. Grant? Grant turned his roundshoulders awkwardly on the crutches. I am General Grant. Excuse me, General, Rome said. I did not connect you with the initials U. S.—I remembered you as Sam. My youngest brother just died in there. It has been a bad day. There is no offense, Rome, Grant said. Come to see me tomorrow. I'll be aboard the *Tigress*. Good night, Rome. I am sorry about your brother. Good night, General. Grant pegged away in the rain, his crutches working like punt poles.

Buell's regiments were slosh-slosh, slish-sloshing up the plateau. The officers kept saying, close up! close up! in hoarse vexed whispers as if that were all they knew of the English language. The rain poured off Rome's hat into his eyes and beard. He did not look back at the log house. He did not want to be near Little Ream dead. He did not want to see or think of anyone dead. Let us find a thick tree, he said. I'll bury him in the morning. No use trying to find our camp.

Someone unloading a battery from a boat began to curse the horses and the soldiers. Bloom! Buhloom! The shells from the gunboats shrieked and boomed again somewhere in the woods. A flurry of rain caught us coldly in our faces. We found a thick tree and sat dozing with our backs against it until dawn. But I heard the guns on the gunboats all night, and the swearing and the slish-slosh of Buell's regiments —and some regimental band playing selections from Il Trovatore on the deck of one of the steamboats. Rome did not speak. But I knew he was not sleeping.

CHAPTER IV

WE FOUND a tin cup and two bayonets and dug under the tree where we had spent the night. It was not deep enough, but Rome said: I'll mark the tree and come back. We cut an X on it and started to find Crime and the gun. The plateau was full of soldiers hunting their commands and of soldiers rising from a muddy sleep and of wounded and dead. The air still smelled like powder and piss. Rome and I wandered a good while before we found the camp. The faces of the Rebel dead had begun to turn black, but the Union dead lay pallid and cold as marble angels in the light. Something in their diet perhaps. The blackhearted sons of bitches turn black as their negroes, a sergeant from an Illinois regiment said, and, leaning over a Union corpse slit open a trousers' pocket with a barlow knife.

All the way back to the gun there were pillagers, some shamefast and furtive, others brazen. In blue, a Union boy with the beginning fuzz of a military beard looked up from a dead man's pockets as Rome and I came up to him. It's Brother, he said. I'm a-goin' to take his watch to Ma. We was in the same regiment. The dead man was dressed in gray, but he may have been a Union man.

All through the timber there were wandering wet soldiers looking for friends or their companies. The ground still moaned with wounded; bleeding soldiers were walking, being helped, being carried on stretchers back toward the Landing. We crossed a creek—probably Owl or Snake creek—that we had not seen the day before, and came upon our camp from a strange side.

The breastworks of bodies were still there; the windrow of dead gray cadets lay in the path of our Napoleon—some ants were at the fairhaired head. All the brandy bottles were lying empty about a little patch of ashes. The Crimean was sitting on the stock of the gun, and facing him, sitting on the soggy loose head of a tall drum painted with an American flag and the number of an Indiana regiment, was a boy of about thirteen dressed in a blue uniform and a little leather-visored kepi. The boy was slim then, except for his face which was plump in the cheeks. He had blue eyes and deep red full lips. He was the drummer boy of an Indiana regiment all right.

Crime got up unsteadily and stood to attention. He was still pretty drunk. Good morning, Leftenet, sir, he said. 'Ere's a lad as 'as adopted us, sir. The boy simpered at Rome. Good mornin', Lootenet, he said.

Shire Newton came over to us. Oh, Mr. Hanks, Shire said, we was afraid you and Dr. Wagnal was lost. Shuball's bled bad this mornin'! I went over to the flys of the Sibley which were still supported by the bushes we had hung them on. Shuball was lying there pale as hell with a black powder-ring still around his lips.

The bandsmen and Rufus Lamb and Sleepy Bates came, staggering and slipping in the mud, from the direction of the dead cadets. The toothless boy was tagging after them giggling. They had their pockets full of wallets, watches, a flask or two, jackknives, lucky charms, cards, photographs and home-knitted socks. All but the toothless boy had pistols of one kind or another—he had a scabbardless, homemade home-ground sword. Bates had a liquor bottle in his hand when he saw Rome and me. He threw it down like a big guilty child and tried solemnly to straighten up. The toothless boy twittered. Bates began to unbutton his trousers, began to piss and then straightened up.

Howdy, Mr. Hanks, Bates said. Howdy, Rome said. Sergeant, Rome said to the Crimean. Yes, sir, the Crimean said. Take the men and put the camp in shipshape order. Rufe Lamb said: I won't! I don't care a damn' how the camp looks. I joined up to fight. A bottle grin came over his face.

Crime lined them up and made them count off. Lamb stood at a tipsy attention, grinning fixedly at the ground, his head wagging loosely. Suddenly he put his hand in his pocket and pulled out two horsey human front teeth. Lookit! Take a squint at the missin' ca'tridge biters. They was in the young rooster's britches. He pointed at the toothless boy who first giggled, then turned pale and began to blubber. Rome was with me holding Shuball's arm while I probed for another ball I had missed. He looked across Shuball at me.

'Shun! Crime yelled. No more talkin' in ranks or I'll flay yer bloody 'ides! He took the teeth on the wire from Lamb and came to meet Rome. I've got a stout belt, Crime said, saluting in the British fashion, and if the Leftenet wishes— No, Rome said. I'll talk to them, Sergeant. Give me those teeth. It was a mandolin string. The boy had been trying to learn the mandolin at Keokuk—until he found it smashed to pieces under his bunk one morning. Rome put the wire and the teeth in his pocket and walked over to the squad of men. He looked at them gravely. You and I and the sergeant, he said, fought together yesterday. I know you all to be brave men. The toothless boy and Bates looked at Rome like a pair of spaniels. Even Lamb straightened up.

The bodies were tidied up into better breastworks. (The dead horse had swollen so that he gave several inches more cover.) The guns were put in as good condition as possible—Crime got the ramrod out of the vent of the spiked one. He made the men throw up some breastworks of earth.

But we didn't fire a shot that day. Rome would not move forward without orders. There were not enough of us—and Belton did not come back with the rest of the regiment.

Towards nightfall of the third day Rome came back from a reconnaissance and said he'd found the rest of the regiment. They weren't far away. We carried Shuball there on a stretcher. The tents were full of holes, for they were the tents of one of Prentiss's captured regiments,

I think. We hadn't yet unloaded ours from the *Die Vernon*. Shire Newton got a new staff and put the flag up in front of the headquarters
tent. I put Shuball in an empty tent with only one hole in the roof.

You did not now notice the odor of high, sweet decomposition,
except when a sudden gust blew it out of your nostrils, and then the
gust dying away, it seeped back in again shocking your olfactory nerve
briefly with the mysterious sweets of death. A gust blew up the company street as Rome and I walked through the mud to Clint Belton's
tent. We saw the flap come up and the Crimean emerge smoking a
cigar. He took it from his mouth and gave us the British salute.

As the Leftenet is in command of the company now, sir, I've just
asked the major to have the drummer boy transferred from the Hundred and Seventh Indiana. Does it suit the Leftenet's pleasure, sir, to
'ave 'im as drummer to 'is company, sir? Well, Sergeant, as long as
you'll be responsible for him, Rome said. Yes, sir, thank you, sir, Crime
said eagerly.

Rome lifted the flap of Belton's tent, looking curiously after the
Crimean. Ah, Rome! Belton said. Wagnal! Belton had a coldgray eye.
Years later, in the regimental history, when the whole web had been
woven and the flies caught, some simplehearted man, who had enlisted
after Vicksburg as a lad of eighteen, had written that General Belton's
was the eye of Mars, to threaten and command.

Drink, Rome? Wagnal? Thank you Clint, Rome said. You'll be
company commander, Rome, Belton said. I'm in temporary command
of the regiment until we hold a ballot. Of course, Clint. You, Wagnal,
will be acting surgeon—at least until Beeston's found. And now, Rome,
I must write my report. You gentlemen will excuse me. The coldgray
eye, the eye of Mars, did not meet Rome's eye. Why, yes, Clint, Rome
said, getting up. And, Rome, see that the men keep clean—especially
their mess. We want no disease. Why, yes, Clint, Rome said.

We left our drinks and walked out into the company street. The
slight change brought the high sweet stench to us again. Well, Rome?
I said. Well, Thomas? Rome said. I don't see how, I said, after under
the bluff— Until I read Mr. Darwin's book, Rome said, I was puzzled
about the inscrutable ways of God. Now I am not troubling about such
large things any more—smaller things puzzle me just as much.

Clint Belton began to issue orders. The first was put up on a bulletin board outside the headquarters tent perhaps two days after the
battle: Attention of the officers is called to the arms of the regiment. No

man may have in his possession any breechloading rifle, musket or fowling piece—or any musket other than that of the prescribed calibre. Only commissioned officers may wear the ceremonial *arme blanche*.

It was probably on the day he issued that order that I saw him walking down the company street with the chased fowling piece. Often, after that, I saw it in his tent. It had as fine a breechloading mechanism as I'd ever seen and a lovely curly walnut—a fine heavy solid gun. I saw it in his tent from Pittsburg Landing to Goldsboro, North Carolina. It followed the regiment in the Crimean's wagons.

Special orders began to appear daily. The companies were rated on the cleanliness of their pots and pans and tents. The Crimean was put in charge of the regimental punishments. The first two men he got in toil, he made to get some packing cases and build two high saw-horse-like arrangements with a thin top bar. Then he made them crawl up and mount their own horses, after which their hands were tied behind them and their legs tied underneath the slim wooden belly of the horse. Sometimes prisoners were left on the horses for a day and a night—and new horses were added to Crime's stable as he thought he needed them.

Between Corinth and Grand Junction, I found the toothless boy hanging head down by the ropes on his feet—or it may have been Holmes Plantation. I cut him down and put him to bed. He walked with a spraddled limp for a week. Toothless got the clap from a nigger wench, they hollered at him. Toothless got a change of luck. What'd it cost, Toothless?

I told Crime if he put the men on such an apparatus again and left them there too long, I'd see that he was broken. Colonel's orders, sir, he said grinning. Tyn't bad punishment, sir. Now out in Hindier I 'ad a cap'n as bloody well flogged us—and on top of that would tyke our pay.

I didn't say anything more to Crime. One day I watched: Well, me fine rooster. 'Ow'd you like a nahce ride on the 'orsie? You look as 'ow you'd make a fine bareback equestrian. Hup you go! There were mounting steps on the legs now; and when the man got up, Crime told the drummer boy from the Indiana regiment: Now, Honeybun, make him fahst. The plumpfaced boy climbed up and tied the man with the knots Crime had taught him. It got so I never reported anybody for an untidy mess.

Rufus Lamb was sitting tied to one of the horses one day at Shiloh.

It was an ironcold day—and Rufe had the dysentery. When I saw him sitting there in the company street, I knew it was going to rain, for it rained coldly that year in Tennessee—but hail did not occur to me. I did not think of him again until a stone ripped through my tent. I cut him down myself and took him to his own tent. He was knocked out; and his head was bleeding. He had wronged his trousers both ways— he couldn't have done otherwise. He nearly had pneumonia.

Rome and I went to Belton. Now, Rome—and you, Wagnal—he said, we've got to keep discipline. We can't win a war without it. But I'll see what I can do. The sergeant has helped the regiment no end. Why General Halleck mentioned us in his reports the other day. I know, Clint, Rome said, but we can't kill these boys. Nonsense, Rome, kill 'em, or cure 'em!

It was true that a good many of the regimental camps were not as tidy as ours. Arms and legs sticking up out of the ground, even in the middle of a company street, were not a startling sight—for the rains had besoddened everything and washed away much of the loose soil that the burial parties had thrown in the three and twofoot graves. Probably nobody got his promised six feet of earth but the Texan Colonel.

Shire Newton fell face down at night in a burial trench just outside the camp of an Indiana regiment and flopped around like a chicken with its head cut off in a mass of putrefying flesh. One regiment had knocked together a little band pavilion near a dead mule which they took as a mascot.

I thought time and again of the waste at Shiloh. What a fine glut of subjects for the anatomists. Why, with a fast ship and ice and formaldehyde, Surgeon's Square could have had many a fine specimen—and all the smashed and incomplete ones need not have been given a thought. How *does* that song go?

> *Up the close and doun the stair,*
> *But and ben with Burke and Hare.*
> *Burke's the butcher—*

But, Lee said to the photograph, he couldn't remember it. He poured us another drink of the oildark whiskey into the communion goblets. It's a wonder your great-grandfather survived the war, he said. Oh, he was hit by bullets enough; and his health was thoroughly broken— but that is not what I mean.

CHAPTER V

A GHOUL, a necromancer, Lee said aloud. No, not exactly that. You must remember that he had looked a good many places for something he had expected to find, and never found it: Yale College and Edinburgh; medicine and Pittsburg Landing and Vicksburg and Atlanta and the March to the Sea. He had heard all the cheer, boys, cheer stuff; and heard the wildfaced hillbillies and rickety poorwhites who never owned even a brokendown fieldhand in their lives ask: Whut ah you'uns comin' down heah to take ouah niggahs away from us foh? Perhaps he had some ideas about human slavery—but I've no doubt they sat pretty lightly on him while he was a regimental surgeon. When the battle of Shiloh was over, and the Army of Tennessee was tidying itself up on that miasmal whistlestop on the Tennessee river, he had some time to think over the uses of man as a firstrate absurdity. He knew what was called the states' rights argument; he had heard Southern friends of his at Yale talk sententiously about the Sons of Ham and their bondage; he had read old Greeley's crap in the New York *Tribune*— What was Greeley's crap? Lee posed the question to the spider. I thought he said go west, young man and grow up with the country. Abolitionist crap! *That* was after the war. The G.A.R. was organized by that time old Greeley started hollering about the west. And out in the Black Hills or in Cheyenne or on the plains bearded men would pause with the cradle or the brandingiron or the spikehammer and say: Well, I'll be a son of a bitch! Was you at Shiloh? Nineteenth Indianay, eh? Hunderd and Seventeenth Ioway? Why, I was in the Seventh Ioway myself. Well, I'll be Goddamned! They had forgotten everything: the cowering under the bluff, the smashed bodies, the rain and hail, the seas of sandy mud, the stink of their dead friends and the mess of a disorganized mob of rustics, whose remnants were just becoming an army when they reached Columbia, South Carolina.

Oh, it was fine all right, if you knew how to get along. Why, when thousands of those boys got back home to Ioway and Indiana and Ohio—some of them sporting goldbraid shoulder straps—they had travelled. They knew a thing or two. Some of them married the village banker's daughter—a thing they would have never aspired to do, if they hadn't been to and come back from a war.

Pittsburg Landing was a strange charnel house that spring, Wagnal said. The dogwood trees were in blossom; and when it wasn't raining, Rufus Lamb and Shire Newton used to tramp through the timber hunting wild onions and come back with johnny jumpups in the buttonholes of their jackets.

Crime used to send out burying details: Watch the ruddy vultures, he'd say. When you see those gentlemen swoop bloody down, you'll have your job under your bloody noses. The boys hated the burying detail, not because of any sensitiveness of heart or sight or smell—for, in a week, they began to care nothing for death and decay. And stenchless air would have amazed their noses—but it was hard work and the gnats and greenflies stung hard. And it was a lush year for the buzzard and the blowfly.

The new dress hat—a hard black beaver, turned up on one side and trimmed with feathers and gilt wire—and the sash must have come down with the new silk flag made by the Ladies Club of Keokuk. Some newspaper correspondent or somebody with the Sanitary Commission must have brought it on a packet.

The afternoon that the flag came Clint Belton went the rounds of the camp himself (after he had posted the order on the bulletin board) and told all the officers and most of the men that he wanted the regiment to be shined up in tiptop order. He wanted to be proud of it; he wanted good old Ioway to be proud of it. You'll button your coat, won't you, Rome? Why, yes, Clint. And you, Sergeant, let us see some of that famous British smartness. Let us see that the pipeclay and tallow tells. Yes, sir, Major Belton, sir, Crime said. He saluted in the queer childish wooden-soldier manner of British military ceremonials. Clint tried to return his salute with the casual authority of a General the Duke of Soandso doing his job for the Empire in the best Eton and Woolwich manner. I will say that it was fair too. He had a certain grace and address; and Harvard had given him a manner of speaking. Nevertheless, he couldn't hit the casual air of authority. It never really comes to Americans. You've heard them in the theatre playing Englishmen. You know the accent is right, the mannerisms good, but there is something strained between the conception and the execution. They can't even wear English clothes like Englishmen. The Crimean grinned as Clint walked away from him. Don't mistake me, Clint wasn't one to be laughed at. He was feared enough, respected enough, hated enough, perhaps even admired enough by some of the men. And most women—well, they nearly swooned in admiration.

We lined up in company front the next day, Clint singing out the commands, and the staff and line officers taking them up pretty smartly for volunteers from the country. It was May but the sky was a sort of a deep indigo-lead color—and it was raining and misting in fits and starts. The sweet corpse-stench was still on us; and we had to march carefully, on the little clearing Clint had chosen, to keep from going down into the mushy twofoot graves. We had been told not to cough or snuffle; we had been instructed to stand to attention like the young war eagles—those were Clint's words in the order—that we were. Clint himself inspected Shire Newton's uniform.

Oh, we looked smart enough—smart as any volunteers. Crime had made some little pipeclay crossbelts for the drummer boy and flanked him with two other drummer boys and a couple of bandsmen who played the fife. We passed in review before Clint and the lieutenant governor and adjutant general of the state—and some sort of a committee. Then we stood to attention for what must have been almost half an hour while the committee, the adjutant general and the lieutenant governor made speeches about how proud the governor was of us—and of all the boys of Ioway who had laid down their lives for the Union. Then the color guard marched up, slapping in the mud with the fife and drum corps—Crime marching along as a sort of major-domo.

Clint made a speech of acceptance during which the toothless boy fainted and wronged his trousers again—and Halleck rode up and watched us. We gave the prearranged three cheers for the new Ioway flag while he was there. He later complimented Clint on the regiment. Two of us fell out to get the boy back to camp—and that night Clint issued an order concerning the proper conduct of soldier on parade. The toothless boy got a day on one of the Crimean's horses.

Clint got himself elected to the colonelcy all right. We held the balloting just before Corinth was evacuated. We all had dysentery by that time; and most of the soldiers were so tired of old Halleck's making us dig in the ground every few paces that they hated our glorious cause. We had four desertions in one week. Clint caught one boy and made a point of not having him shot, for it was before the men had elected him to the colonelcy. I believe we cast our ballots in Rome's hat one morning; and that evening the gold leaves were off Clint's shoulders and the silver eagles perching there. Rome became captain of the company that day.

We began to become accustomed to the country and the smell and the dysentery. Those squirms on our belly in the mud that we made toward Corinth with old Halleck in command and what was later called the siege of Corinth became a laughing matter. The very officers and the very unlicked rookies in their ridiculous regimentals who had gone about saying: Hit Rawlins on the head and knock out Grant's brains! began to wish for Old Sam Grant before he came back to them (Good Old Unconditional, they said!).

Clint Belton had become one of Grant's greatest detractors as soon as he heard Halleck had come down from Washington. But when Grant got back in the saddle, Clint made it a point to look him up and talk about Grant and his father being in Mexico together. Clint Belton was a suave man. His beard was longer now and he kept it well-groomed. His uniform was always neat; he was free with the cigars he always carried in the wagons.

He knew when to speak to the men and when not to speak. Even the punishment horses which Crime had devised had little effect on his popularity. The colonelcy was already nothing to him: the day after he got it he was thinking of a brigade. Every day there were officers from other outfits—none ever below a leftenet-colonel and some as high as major general—in his tent. He had Crime to pour the whiskey and the drummer boy to pass the cigars and lift the tent flap as the generals passed in and out to relieve their military bladders. The political brigadiers—most of them jackleg lawyers from the West—left Clint's tent impressed. Bully whiskey. Bully cigars. Clint Belton was a coming man all right.

And he did distinguish himself. Oh, without a doubt. At Corinth he drew enough fire for a brigade—while still suffering from wounds sustained at Pittsburg Landing, according to the report of one of his brigadier friends—and had another horse, a poor one, not his parade horse, shot out from under him. These antics—it was still the period of the war when infantry would make a frontal attack on a well-tended battery firing grape or canister—got him a good deal of notice.

The cigars and whiskey, the exposure to fire and the military neatness which he enforced, by the use of Crime's horses, on the gang of rustics who called themselves a regiment were having their effect. He was a welcome visitor at Grant's headquarters, and it was said that

Grant's brains, the great Rawlins, was listening to our charming colonel, of whom the regimental historian, the poor lad who had enlisted after Vicksburg in sixty-four, had said: He had an eye to threaten and command, the eye of Mars.

Well, General Rawlins (I actually heard him say it one day), the poor general has been so harassed in this campaign I feel I ought to send him something. Do you think, sir, he would like some of that excellent Bourbon and some of those Havanas. The cigars, Colonel, Rawlins said with that stern, solemn, smalltown look of a steelengraving frontispiece, the cigars—not the whiskey. The general does not drink. He has promised me, sir, not to drink during this campaign. Clint looked at him, simulating warmth with that coldgray eye. Ah yes, of course, General Rawlins. It'll be the cigars, sir. Why, you know, sir, I can't understand how you've got the general through this heartsickening campaign—a man in his position, with Washington as it has been. It has been very hard, Colonel, Rawlins said modestly. You could see the look of satisfaction in the bleak solemncomic face of Rawlins.

Crime would load up the wooden horses, and the men who paid him twenty-five cents to slip their latrine-boxes on the wagons—the dysentery was getting worse—would pay up and we would move on. We got a couple of steamboat rides, but most of the time we fought mud and dust and heat on foot. Corinth, Iuka, Memphis, Yockena, Holmes Plantation, Haines Bluff, Warrenton, Vicksburg, Fox's Plantation, Big Black River.

At night Crime and the drummer boy used to sleep under the same blanket which he and the toothless boy had slept under; and every half hour they would wake each other to sit side by side on a doublebarrelled latrine box. Nights in bivouac sounded like the turn-on of a thousand hoses. Bloody flux, Crime said, bleeding, bloody flux. He used to sing My Luve's Like a Red, Red Rose to the drummer boy as they sat squittering in the moonlight—or in broad daylight, for that matter.

I had a photograph of the regiment once, and in the background— out of focus—there sat a man on a soapbox. You could not see that he had his pants down except by looking carefully. A man called White made it that spring at Corinth. I don't know who the man on the latrine box was, but he was undoubtedly answering the call of nature. Later the same photograph got into the *Photographic History of the Civil War*. White had a gallery at Corinth, and we used to watch his prints a-printing in the sun. I suppose more than half the regiment had their portraits made there with their head in an iron headrest— and a glassy stare in their eyes. I used to own the whole lot of *Cartes de Visite*: Crime with a Victoria medal on his Union coat—he won it in the Indian Mutiny; the drummer boy, the toothless boy with his short upper lip pulled down tight over the tooth gap, Shuball York with his arm in a sling, Clint Belton in the black beaver dress hat with the plumes and the silver spreadeagles on his shoulders—and even Sleepy Bates with a thick churlish stare on his face—God rest his phlegmatic soul.

He came to me at two one morning with a flesh wound in his shoulder. You're on picket, aren't you? I said. You shouldn't be off your post. I sent Rufe Lamb, he said. Say, he said, whispering heavily, say, the colonel taken a shot at me. He had that britch-loader he taken away from Billy. Oh come, Bates! I jist squatted down to tie my shoe— I jist begin to squat when it hit me. I seen him in the timber. It's too dark, I said. You look out, Bates said, you kin read a noosepaper—you kin damn' near read bible printen. You mean Colonel Belton? Yes, cross my heart, by Jesus Christ, I hope to die, I mean Colonel Belton! Are you sober, Bates? I hain't had a drink since we was workin' the cannon—but I need one now. Well, I said, if it was the colonel—but, of course, it wasn't—he thought you were a Secesh. Secesh, hell! He could see easy it was me. They hain't anybuddy taller'n me in the regiment. You look outside.

You could see the grains in the sandy mud and all the ropes on the Sibleys in the company street and sharp blueblack shadows on the ground. We went back in my tent and I dressed Bates's shoulder by the light of a candle. When he had the commissary whiskey down, I said: You go back and send Rufe to his tent. Stay your trick out and don't mention being shot at. Understand me, Bates? Yes, Doc. No God-damn' fool yarns about being shot at by the colonel. Nobody would believe you. I don't. Yes, Doc. But wasn't he under the bluff at the Landing that day Mr. Hanks— What bluff at what landing? If he was under any bluff, he was trying to drag you boys out as Mr. Hanks was doing. No; by Jesus! Bates said. No! He was a-layin' with his mush in the mud—and when he got up I seen him look me in the eye. He was a-scairt as me. I bet he shit his britches. Don't be a fool, Bates. You'd best keep your trap closed. It couldn't have been the colonel, under-stand!

That must have been before Corinth, because Bates saw Clint out in front of the regiment drawing fire that day in the hell-for-leather way that he had adopted after his first horse died under him at Shiloh. He was getting used to being shot at. Bates got hit by a spent ball at Corinth. We were supporting a battery where some damn' fool Texans, full of liquor and bragging about honor and marksmanship no doubt, charged. Their colonel looked right into the muzzle of the twelve-pound cannon and kicked his skinny horse in the ribs and said: Come on, boys! We'll show the fourflushin' bluebellied sonsuhbitches. And the regiment hollered high and wild and bared their teeth like dawgs and came in shooting with six-shooters. They showed us bluebellies all right. Rome got shot in the knee and there were about three wounded and one killed in our regiment. But there were mounds of dead and broken Texans in ragged gray lying in front of the battery—practically the whole fire-eating regiment was piled up like a stepped-on cockroach.

They ate fire all right. You would think that men from a state which developed such a murderous proficiency with Samuel Colt's small arms would have been shrewder. But that was still sixty-two. Well, Bates had seen Clint riding that condemned cavalry hack around in front of all those maniacs from Texas. Maybe, you was right, Doctor, he said. That couldn't a-been the colonel that taken a shot at me. He couldn't a-been under the bluff. Maybe you seen him out in front there today. He was shootin' his pistol too. It musta been somebody else. Rome was sitting on an old cane-bottomed chair waiting for me to dress his knee. I looked toward him, but he seemed not to have heard Bates. By God a-mighty, Bates said as I finished his bandage, the colonel's a hunkydory soldier, ain'ty, Mr. Hanks? Rome looked up at Bates with an engrossed expression of curiosity in his eyes. Why, yes, Harold, he is.

Clint got permission to give the Texan colonel a funeral with full military honors. Crime was detailed to get the grave dug; and Rome's company had to furnish the firing squad. Some chaplain made a moral sermon on the bravery of our enemy (old Simpson would not do it). Rawlins and the political brigadiers and colonels stood around with their hats off. It had been discovered that the Texan colonel was a Freemason, so a half dozen brigadiers trooped past the grave and threw sprigs of evergreen—or something which served as such—in the grave. After the salute, Belton took the brigadiers and colonels to his tent.

One or two of them rolled a little when they came out. I heard the latest one say—from the other end of the company street—Yes, sir, Colonel Clint Belton, that was a great and honorable ges'ure.

When I got up later to relieve my dysentery, I saw Crime and the drummer boy coming out of the tent. Good night, sir, Crime said. Good night, Sergeant. The tent flap fell and Crime threw his arm around the boy's shoulder. Not so much whiskey for you the next time, me love. I'll do as I like, the drummer boy said sullenly, ducking out from under Crime's arm. Nah! Nah! Honeybun, Crime said— Oh, f—— you, the drummer said, and ran lightly from Crime, giggling.

God, Lee thought. There were the sands of Shiloh and the steamboats on the river and the silverbellied fish floating dead on the yellow waters of the Tennessee near the *Tyler* and *Lexington* on Monday morning and the smoke drifting away through the blasted oaks. And all the boys from Ioway and Illinois and Ohio lost on a riverbank in Tennessee. And the sutler's cigars and the commissary whiskey and the political generals already counting the votes. And the broken Napoleons lying in the mud which would later decorate leading articles in the Century in dead dry linecuts for little boys lying on their bellies in front of the glasspaned Globe-Wernicke sectional bookcase with *The Doctor Book* and *The Lives of Illustrious Americans* and *The San Francisco Disaster* and *The Assassination of President McKinley* in it to stare at and imagine about. Everything was tidied up at last, and the debris of two armies served as the colophons and initial letters of several thousand books: *The Blue and the Gray, The Picket Off Duty Forever, The Charge, An Affair of the Pickets, Fighting the Mud in the Wilderness, Going into Action, Sherman's Bummers, Burnside's Bridge, The Bloody Lane, The Hornet's Nest, The Guns that Held, An Outpost, A Scene in Devil's Den.* Yes, sireebob. We sure licked the Secesh, didn't we, boys? Speak up you old coffeecoolers!

And all those lads with cowlicked hair who lay shivering under the bluff at Shiloh. And when old Grant and Buell sent the cavalry to ride them down and send them back to death they climbed the bank of the river, clinging to the roots in the sandy soil.

I have lain under the banks at Shiloh on the morning of April sixth, eighteen hundred and sixty-two and talked to the pale major from Springfield, Illinois and heard the boy from Fairfield, Iowa blubber. I worked Webster's guns on the landing and lay wounded all night on the banks of Owl creek freezing in the spring rain beside a boy named André from Baton Rouge who went to General Sherman's academy. I am the soldier who never fired a shot, never marched a mile, never bled a cubic centimeter that freedom might not vanish from the earth—or that I might go home to Vincennes, Indiana, and marry the banker's daughter. I buried no dead, carried no lock of female hair in my wallet, ran no guns up to the enemy works by hand, and never stained my lips with bitten cartridges. Yet because of something that happened before my grandfathers came to Kansas, I know these things. I know my great-grandfather's silky beard, before he had the scurvy at Andersonville prison, and his brother Remus, whose grave was lost when the bark was blown off a tree at Shiloh—and how their father was killed by the Shawnees in Elizabeth county, Kentucky one morning in 1830. I know that Romulus Lycurgus Hanks, then ten, brought his brother, Remus, to the log house and shot down the two Shawnees who had killed his father with an old Brown Betsy maybe picked up at King's Mountain. Romulus fired a new squirrel rifle stamped E. Kirschbaum, Danville, Pa. on the long barrel. And Anna di Montorya Hanks loaded the gun with powder and ball while Remus passed it up to the loft of the cabin.

Di Montorya? Spanish? How the hell'd she get that name—my great-great-grandmother?

It's on a page of the family bible, that I saw once. There was an *y* something too that I couldn't make out because it was so old and dirty. Her sister and husband sailed from New Orleans for Europe in 1842— and the ship was never heard from again.

CHAPTER VI

WHO knows? Lee thought. I remember the corner of a table in a Los Angeles beer parlor. Pine or fir from Oregon or Norway. It stood on a point in Latitude and Longitude. Who has seen it as a sapling? The iron that cut it down was mined in Pennsylvania; and the jack that swung the axe was born in Sweden. It stood, beer-ringed, before me in a Los Angeles suburb waiting to become a hencoop in Van Nuys.

Why, I have walked daily across the same stones on which Percy

Bysshe Shelley and Sir Walter Raleigh must have walked. I have loitered in the same gateway where young Sam Johnson is said to have amazed his fellow students. I have stood on Mrs. Bracegirdle's grave in the Abbey and walked down Olive street in St. Louis with a battalion of whores hailing on the windowpanes and beckoning through the windows.

Ah! That's it! Lee said aloud, a battalion of whores. He smacked his lips over the phrase. A lost battalion of whores.

And bloody lost they were too! Those houses—the sixty years abandoned mansions of the bourgeoisie. Stiff and straight and high they were, with curlicues. Dark hallways and marble fireplaces. Brick, painted and repainted. St. Louis moved westward, leaving its most respectable warren to the whores. Ah, yes, Lee said, bloody lost.

That was during the depression—thirty or thirty-one or two it was. And you couldn't say that they were St. Louis whores or Olive street whores (though perhaps some of them had been born there). They were just anonymous women who had rented these empty former houses in Olive and Locust streets and in little cutoff, choppedout streets near Grand avenue. Former what? I was going to say of the bourgeoisie again, but let us say just former houses. Maybe it would be better to say that the women along that street were first former women and then former whores. They were hard put to it in these years to eat; and those houses weren't much shelter—broken windows, leaky roofs, bleak and sooty in the streetlights. It was as if Doré had turned Lunapark operator to show the bourgeoisie—who had moved farther west into halftimbered houses out by Washington University or even into the county—what they had escaped by having got money.

There were two or three miles of slumproperty—not all filled with whores, for how many could buy an orgasm then—even at fifty cents a crack? Occasionally there would be a swapshop or a surgical appliance shop with Venus-in-a-truss—or Love Lies a-Ruptured, in the window, or a radio repairshop—or four or five to a dozen houses just bloody empty.

Three stories most of them were and damned high impressive stories too, with overhanging brick and sometimes falsestone pediments—the kind with false stone designs in pressed tin. They had been built, no doubt, in provincial imitation of the bleak brownstone fronts of Fifth Avenue, for all American cities are footling and imitative.

After seeing them drawn and printed in linecuts in the civic guides of the seventies and eighties, neat and private and secret (more secret than now because the mind was more secret) and stiff, with gentlemen in stovepipe hats and frock coats standing on their cutstone steps and victorias standing at the kerb—and perhaps a woman in hoopskirts and a bonnet being handed into a victoria or a maid opening a door—after seeing them so, frozen into a flat tranquil picture labeled, A Residential District, or Fine Homes in the City, you could not believe that they had ever had any true function as houses. They were meant only for linecuts in early Americana.

Then, after the whores had moved into them, they seemed huge scenic flats painted by some artist more false than Doré and set up for an extravaganza produced and directed by someone such as the Great Barnum.

Olive street, along the blocks I'm thinking of, is a wide boulevard. Anyway, Lee went on, his voice droning to himself in solemn rhythm, the cars swish past, going fast toward where it's not so smoky. They swish past twice a day in thousands. After seven at night they thin out, but they keep swishing.

Those that stopped there at night were cars that looked as if they might have passed through the hands of a dozen finance companies—and as if they weren't wearing the license plates that were issued for them. But few stopped. Nor were there many walkers along that street—and those that did walk were far apart and furtive. The intermittent hail on the windows led them down the street and turned their heads. On most nights paper and dust rattled neurotically in city winds, scraping the sidewalks; but on still nights everything was still and dead and you could remember that inside the houses were marble fireplaces with rank oilstoves set in them and tencent incense burners made in Japan burning jasmine beside a brassbed with a maroon or mauve fancy bedspread that would be turned down finally when there was not another nightwalker visible in the streetlights or the dirty dawn.

You could remember, if you ever knew, that General Sherman lived in such a house—and that Grant, when he was out of the army and fumbling along trying to be a real estate agent, must have walked along there towards a home humbler than these. And you could think that now inside these houses, huddled around other oilstoves near the dirty cracked windows—rubbed clean in a spot to display a bright-painted face in the glow of a neon billboard outside—were women born in San Francisco, or Atchison, Kansas, or maybe Davenport, Iowa, or Memphis, Tennessee.

One with a key or a ring or a pair of scissors making a little hail-storm on the window, saying, no soap, if the walker passed, or get the door, you, if he turned up the steps. And after he went to the maroon or mauve covered brass bed with the woman, watching through the window again, and saying to the woman on the other side of the stove: Topeka's a railroad town, ain't it? Or I've got a cold. And then putting the bright-painted face up to the window again and moving the key or the ring and beckoning and saying, go on, Goddamn you! Two in ten minutes!

Further on towards Grand they became more like real whores. There was one tight-shuttered house with Venetian blinds. The women sat at the windows there in silk shorts with satin waists like tapdancers in a cinemahouse chorus. They lifted the corner of a curtain cautiously and sent a quick sharp short machinegun burst at you. And there were potted plants in the windows as if they had not yet quite given up the idea of moving to the westend with the bourgeoisie—and living in a halftimbered house maybe with a rayon dressed doll over the telephone.

And one I remember at the very brink of Grand avenue on the edge of the brightlights, stood well-painted with a curling lip in an open doorway at the foot of a dark staircase in a pair of velvet shorts and a blue satin dancing shirt. She was well made up, and she spoke with a profane and evil indifference.

I should have had her, for she was not like the others—whether it was in degree of parish-hood or not, I don't know. But she would not have said that a pinkfaced baby on a slick magazine cover was cute, or daydreamed of a little house with a lug coming up the frontwalk and a rayon-dressed colonial doll with a powdered wig and a beauty spot over the telephone or sitting on the made-up bed. Almost any of them will do that. Jazz or French, baby? they'll say and even then they'll be thinking of the stuffed canary under the belljar and the rose-bud loops that held back their mother's cretonne drapes in Alton, Illinois. They'll read True Confessions and a good many of them will go to church. They'll think the woman who has a little house or an apartment and an oaf who comes up the front walk or scratches at the keyhole is just one of God's more fortunate children who got the breaks.

But that one near Grand avenue was all bitch and bitter. A bird of prey. Two dollars was two dollars; and a squirm or a manipulation or two on a bed was merely something that would make something happen to a man that he needed to happen. Just a hunk of meat, tough, medium, rare, lying on a plate before him so that he could go back tomorrow to the ditch, or the office, or the bowling alley to toss out the dirt, transfer the figures from one column to another, or set up the silly bounding pins to be knocked over again by some fool.

The two-dollar woman is a pieceworker who can get no contract— she is one of the reasons why the middleclass women in so many small-towns, from Wichita to Riverside, wear the unionbadge of lumpy clothes and potshaped hats in dull colors—and purse their lips a certain way when they walk past drugstores and beerparlors and poolhalls. What they're saying is, well, anyway I am not cheap. I'm a good sub-stantial medium-priced article, let by contract only. I'm not a cheap woman. The middleclass woman has long had her labor union—her sister of the piecework is no more than a bloody scab.

In any winter St. Louis seems an inescapable hell of darkness. Living there gives you a special claustrophobia whether you are indoors or out. It is as if you were locked in the smoky glass trainshed at Lyons with a thousand deaf mutes. It is as if you were lost in the catacombs of a dimenovel unable ever to see the sun. It is a scabrous, diseased city, looking like a peepshow with dirty lenses in a penny arcade. I chose to go to Saint Louis when I finished college, Lee said.

It was there that I was to find my entrance into the Great World. There I was to step onto the stage after having studied my part and loitered in the wings. I was to step into the Great Drama of Civil Life and work myself up into a Responsible Position. I could have chosen any one of a number of other cities, but there were the words Missis-sippi and Mark Twain and Old St. Louis—and besides I knew people in Kansas City—people to whom I did not want obligation, people I did not really like. I did not wish to be watched while I Made Good.

Oh, I found a job all right. I found a good many. I found Christa— and I finished with St. Louis. I wiped it off the map of my Great World.

But then, Lee thought painfully, I had not even vicariously lain under the bluff at Shiloh. I did not know what to expect. You read in a book: He was educated at Harvard; and, as it did to many young New Englanders of his day, the Great West beckoned. In 1851, he settled in Terre Haute, where he hung out his lawyer's shingle. There

you have it—nearly two decades of a man's life; a period of walking
in and out of dreary academic doorways, a good many books, weekend
visits to Boston to see his parents, meals, baths, evacuations of his bowels
and bladder, women, several stagecoach and steamboat trips and perhaps the sight of buffalo and Indians on the plains—and most of all
the terrible deadening sight of Terre Haute, the hencoop shambles of
a miningtown, a sort of a disciplineless concentration camp of hope
as it must have looked to a young Harvard Bostonian of 1851, no matter
how willing his hands, how resourceful his brain and how sanguine
his nature. There you get it: the Great West beckoned, and, in 1851,
he hung out his lawyer's shingle in Terre Haute. It tells you nothing at
all. Suddenly he had a diploma from Harvard College, and he was
saying goodbye to Adams, his classmate and friend, and then he was
on a train with open coaches, and then a steamboat, and then a stage
coach with a driver who said something about the f—in' injuns, and
then there he is in Terre Haute hanging out his bloody shingle: Francis
Charles Cabot Lowell, Att'y. At Law.

What I knew about Life and the Great World was not as much as
you know about Francis Charles Cabot Lowell's Harvard years and his
magic-carpet jump to Terre Haute. I thought he got there just like
that—just as the motion picture camera cuts from Singapore to San
Francisco, or lets you lie flat on the ceiling face downward and see
between the halfnaked dugs of the mistress of your dreams while you
are sitting quietly in a loge next to a little bucktoothed beauty operator
in tears.

So, in St. Louis, I began to know what had been kept from me by
men who had written: the Great West beckoned; he hung out his
shingle. Slowly I began to know what to expect. And now I am beginning to know something not only of what has happened in the Great
World, but how it happened and how the people looked to whom it
happened.

I was drunk every time I walked up and down the length of Olive
street to listen—hardly daring to look—to the hailstorm of glasstaps on
the windows.

I began to be lonely and to know what filled the long gaps that are
pushed together into one sentence of the biographer and novelist—
telescoped on gravestones as a little dash between two dates: The opening and closing of one door to one room perhaps one thousand times
a year, the pulling back of one set of covers and opening of one window,

the walking down the same street so many times that you know a passing but unknown girl's face and legs and buttocks and breasts without
ever speaking to her—that you know the scars on the stones of the
church and the cracks in the paving under your nose. The eternal cold-
comforting of yourself with fantasies which always follow the same
pattern. Thus I would be driven to prowl Olive street at night—oh,
I'd whored before, all right, but that was in Paris and in the Rue de
Persil in Brussels and that was in camaraderie and a light enough spirit.
But this Olive street whoring was solitary and furtive. Indecisive too,
for it was a long time before I could bring myself to make the double-
backed beast with an Olive street whore.

    You walk along that street alone and come to a wind-harried corner,
and a bell on a stoplight rings and red changes to green and wind
rushes through. A piece of newspaper rakes down the empty sidewalk;
you walk beside a neon billboard in a bluesick light, looking directly
at the windows of the houses now because along that place there is a
half block of empty houses. Dust blows on before you with the paper-
scrap. You look up at the overhanging tin pediments. And then you
come to some houses that do not stand flush with the sidewalk but
have meager gray plots of tightpacked earth in front of them and a
stonewalk to the door. Most of them are empty, but you know that at
the end of the block there is a window with a lace curtain and a face
with a two-bit piece or a key or a ring—and you feel secret and evil
and afraid, but not lonely any more. The curtain's edge lifts and a sharp
burst of glasstaps hits your ears. You look full at the window and there
is a white face, redlipped and cheeked in a flashlightbeam, and a hand
beckoning above a lowfront dress. The old oak door alligatored by many
paintings resounds to a boltboom. The hall is dark and vault cold with
a dim yellow light in the stairwell and you think of the four-candle-
power hylo in the hall in Fork City. Hello, baby. Nice night, huh?
Wanna go upstairs? How much? Two dollars. Strip and play around a
while and a good jazz, huh? She shivers a little; the top of her breasts
are bluish for there is nothing below her loose whoredress. Then she
stands to you, bumping the three roundcuts of flesh against you and
wriggling. It's too much—a dollar's all I've got. Okay, baby, good night.
Strickly a two-dollar house. The door opens and you go down the street
again behind the rattle of dust and paper and beside the long spreadout
swishes of the cars.

    Look, Lee said fiercely to the blank wall. Look! One night when I

was drunk—so drunk that I didn't remember anything but dim dis-
embodied faces and eyes, floating cornices and windows and glasspanels
in doors—I walked the whole length of the street going in and out of
all the houses, the empty houses and the brothels. One had a locked
glasspaned door. I couldn't open it, so I rammed my fist through the
glass. But there were lights in it, and I walked through the rooms with
a handkerchief held around my bleeding wrist. There was a marble-
manteled fireplace in every room. Plaster had fallen on the floors—and
it seemed that in the next room always—perhaps in the next house, for
the houses seemed to join—there was somebody—a beautiful young
whore perhaps and someone drinking. How I got out of the house
before the cop on the beat picked me up, I don't know. And why were
there lights in an empty house? I woke up the next morning in my
room at the Y.M.C.A. Years later it frightened me. I knew no one in
the town then: I might have been picked up and thrown into jail for
breaking and entering—or I might have cut my wrist deeper and bled
to death. How many nights I spent burrowing in the debris of the
city, I can't remember. I used to try new streets and nigger houses,
looking furtively into doorways, saying nothing, but talking with myself
in a language I did not know, trying to think whether I had been in
this doorway before or walked through this street before—and finding
myself, at daylight, on board a streetcar with negro housemaids going
to work and milkmen and laborers. And the streetcar would perhaps
turn through a little spurstreet where in a little triangular park a man
would be waiting—standing underneath a scrub elm on the gray flat-
packed earth beside a waterplug. And over all this there would hang
a dampcold earlymorning fog. The passengers would look at me
queerly, maybe because they knew I had not got up sluggishly from a
bed to scurry through a mazeroutine as a rat scurries through a scientific trap to prove something for a psychologist because his ratmind is
on the grubend of the maze. They looked at me with reproachful suspicious eyes, because they could not place me in their day, because they
had no idea where I had come from or where I was going—and because
my object in getting on the car was not just the ration of grub at the
end of the mazetrap, but something unknown and not suitable to be
seen in the smoky morning air of a streetcar bangclanging toward the
work of a middlewestern city. I've no doubt that they felt much as my
mother would have felt had she walked into her wellshaded-against-the-
sun-on-the-wilton-carpet parlor to find the hooded head of a *hamadryas*

swaying above her favorite fern in the baywindow. Order must not only be preserved but worshipped; and the man who eats breakfast at six *post meridiem* and dinner at six *ante meridiem* must needs be a Dogberry or a locomotive engineer to preserve the respect of his fellowman.

Now, Lee said, his voice falling to a soft chant, I am afraid of cities when I am walking along alone at night; now I am the same as the smalltown housewife who fears the disgrace of dust on her floors, the romantic evil of the newsprint sexfiend leaping on her humdrum carcass from behind the lilacbush in her frontyard, the slight of her name's omission from the village societycolumn, the unwed pregnancy of her daughter, the chance display of her petticoat in the street—or a too cheap funeral in her family. I fear cities at night in the same quailing manner. For tell me, oh God, where there is love or light or freedom in the world?

CHAPTER VII

BUT there was never any doubt, Wagnal said, drawing at the long pipe with a fryingsound, oh, there was no blessed doubt at all that the regiment was a credit to Clint. He got to be known throughout the brigade, the division and the Army of Tennessee for his Havanas and his liquor and his regiment, and after a while he had, not only the political brigadiers, but a good many West Pointers who had a nose for the spoor of advancement eating out of his hand.

It was said, in the ranks before Atlanta (strangely, the news having taken that long to filter down), that the night Vicksburg fell he had engaged the women from a brothel of the town and given a champagne party for his friends—and that even Grant and Rawlins had looked in at the backdoor. Apocryphal perhaps.

Even then his brigadier-generalship must have been before Mr. Lincoln for a good while.

It was after Corinth, maybe it was before Vicksburg, Wagnal said, Holmes Plantation or that place in Georgia—an ill-proportioned Greek temple made of wood, all white, brummagem and lofty, deserted and all torn to hell with an uneaten skinny chicken or two roosting on the grand piano which was choked with flour and molasses and a painting over the mantel in the drawing room that looked like a Joshua Reynolds—maybe it was there that Sleepy Bates came to me again. He wasn't frightened this time; he merely thought it his duty.

It didn't whine like no minnie ball, Doc, Bates said. An' it wasn't like any damn' Rebel gun ever I heard—and besides the only Rebs I seen hide ner hair of round here ain't takin' pot shots down our company street. Maybe outa officers' tents. Well, Bates, I said, he didn't hit you this time, did he? And besides how do you know it was an officer's tent, as you say? What officer's tent? There aren't many. You know what I'm a-talkin' about, Doc. Why, lookee here, I ain't nervous any more. I ain't been a-scairt since we come to Pittsburg Landing, but I don't think it's jist right to be shot at thataway. What way, sir? Rome said. He had raised the tentflap and come in quietly, for we shared the tent. I hope, he said, I didn't intrude upon a private conversation. No, Rome, I said. Mr. Hanks, Bates said, I was a goin' to tell you too: I been shot at again. We'll all be shot at a good bit more, Rome said. God send we aren't hit. You look whole, Rome said. Hell, Mr. Hanks, I never got hit—and I don't mind bein' shot at, but this here wasn't a Reb. Oh, Rome said. The shot come down the company street. Possibly one of the men shooting at a squirrel. Squirrel *now*, Mr. Hanks? They hain't as good eatin' as sidemeat and hardtack—and they hain't any game to speak of here. I don't mind bein' shot at, but not thataway. I don't know what he's got agin me anyway. He oughta know there's things that's forgot. Who? Rome said.

Now, Mr. Hanks, you ain't a-going to tell me you don't know who's got the tent at the top of our company street. They was smoke there too. That's nonsense, Bates, Rome said. It was a strayshot from a hunter or a man targetshooting. With me for a target, Bates said. Anyway, he can't shoot for Jesus—he didn't hit me good the last time. Looka here, Mr. Hanks, I don't wanta believe it, but by God I thought it was him when we was at Corinth. And I seen him look at me funny many's the time—and Toothless too. We seen him at Pittsburg—

Bates, Rome said, you go on about your business now. That was a strayshot. I'll see you don't get hurt except at the hands of the Rebels— that I can't help. But I ain't afraid, Mr. Hanks—honest to God, I ain't! What I reelly come here for was to ask you and Doc to see that Ma gits my money and Pa's watch I got with me, if I was to git drilled. You may have confidence in us, Harold, Captain Hanks said. Thank ye, sir, Bates said. How is Missus Hanks and Myry, sir? Remember

me to them, sir. Why, Rome said, they're firstrate, thank you Harold.
Indeed, they asked me to remember *them* to all of you boys in the
company.

Bates got up and went to the tentflap, halfturned, as if he had more
to say to us, then reconsidered and went out. Rome turned and looked
me squarely in the face, with the mild honest look that all his friends
knew so well. It is not so, Thomas, he said, as if it were half a wish. I
looked down, feeling as if I were a child caught in a lie, though I had
not answered. Still, Rome said, I shall not believe it. I shall not believe
it yet.

Anyway, I said, there's no proof. And what could we do if there
were? Nothing, Rome said. Even if his value as an officer—he broke
off. Nothing.

Rome was sitting there in the halflight of the tent drawing figures
in the sandy soil with the scabbard of his old Mexican war sword.
Thomas, he said, curiosity is a great thing—simple curiosity—but it
should be directed toward the more general scientific studies in inquisi-
tionless times, or, as Sir Walter Raleigh directed his own—after he had
closed his barndoor too late—toward a history of the world in general
terms.

Oh, God help me, Wagnal said, I can remember Rome now as if it
were yesterday; the sword scabbard in the dust on the tentfloor, his
jacket open and a dirty hickory shirt showing, his black hat pushed
back on his forehead so I couldn't see the ring of sweatclung dust
around the band where it was frayed, but could know it was there. The
tarnished captain's bars on his old coat and the proud crinkled life of
his black beard and the steadfastness of his eyes, I see them all now.
And I can hear his low smooth voice—not suave—for suavity came then
from the old country—but strong because of the miles he had gone
since Kentucky and the rivers he had forded and the rifles he had fired
and the books he had got and read and the things he had thought in
Kentucky, revised in Mexico and Indiana and Iowa and brought back
with him down the rivers of the South.

He must have been strong to carry those things so long a way, for
he was not a man to put down his burden. And his burden then was
full enough of blood and doubt.

He looked up from the tracing in the dust on the tentfloor and said:
No, Thomas, I shall not give sanctuary to suspicion, for it eats the
bowels like a slow acid.

CHAPTER VIII

When I began to know him, Lee thought tenderly, it was as Grandpa Beckham. There were only a few black hairs left in the beard which had been inspired by that of the surgeon, Ames, who took the minié ball of Gaines's Mill from Tom's thigh at Savage's Station. Nevertheless, he walked (perhaps it would be better to say he tramped, for there was always a certain marching aspect in his carriage—and he would sometimes turn to me and say, Take care, don't tramp on the toad, he eats potato bugs, or don't tramp on your Grandma's clean floor with those muddy shoes, or don't let the horse tramp on your toe) with a firm upright carriage, his head held high still, as if he had never heard those saws which every Polonius is eager to tell us all and which every circumstance endeavors dully to emboss upon the hides of all men. And the beard, even in the quietest air, seemed always to be blowing backward a little (it resembled motion caught in sculpture), as if it were the beard of a jolly defiant satyr. I rarely saw his face when its expression was tired, or cynical, or in despair, but I conjecture that weariness, cynicism, defeat and despair must have eaten at the edges of him as they eat at the edges of all.

MAYBE it did not take much imagination, Lee thought, to board a ship at Liverpool when there was the shabby darkness of Manchester in the early nineteenth century to get away from. The factories and mills and smoke and fog closing over them as a cataract closes the eye of an old woman. Three generations of them were already mouldering one on top of the other under the sootstained stones of a Manchester graveyard where they had been buried because it was, Where We Are Buried.

Their rickety sisters walked through the long streets—where even the most squalid shops would have broken the bricked monotony of the houserows—to the gaslit brickboxes where they crawled for fifteen hours tending looms which maybe were weaving cotton from dear old Dixie. They did that because that was to do where everything was lint and smoke but your own hearth and the corner pub—and not at your own corner at that.

Thomas Beckham may have dreamed of being a Lord with a Great house and a park like Lord Stamford's. He might have died—not like my great-great aunt who drew a cart on the seventh level of a lord's coalmine of broken wind and a ginhardened liver—but from the boredom of the flatbrick streets, the monotony of wishing for the lipsalved Lady with the viciousdashing look on her in a Paris Worth gown whom he saw stepping haughtily from a carriage once. He might have died still envying the wellfed beauty of the redcoated Guards' subaltern he saw once in London when he went to town in his yokel's clothes and tophat Pa's brother had made himself but was not like the ones the toffs wore in Old Bond street.

He might have died from the lint and gas and smoke and fog in his lungs and the absence of light in his eyes and from the friction his thoughts made following the same course in his brain—and when he was buried on top of his great-great grandfather, the old man, not having been a tanner, would have been found to have mouldered away. But he didn't. He had some imagination. He didn't escape into the Guide Bridge Chapel. He didn't do charades in his brains. There were ships at Liverpool, and he was not a rickety lad. He would not stay in those bricked up sooty lanes until it got so that it seemed there was a brick ceiling between him and the sky.

He took two brothers with him, Ralph and John. After six weeks of semi-starvation, five burials at sea and a touch of scurvy, they disembarked at Boston. They had forty guineas among them. Thomas was twenty-five, John twenty-two and Ralph (it was always pronounced Rafe in the English fashion) forty. They were hatters.

Thomas had a letter in his pocket from a friend in Philadelphia; and the three of them went by coach to Philadelphia in the year Eighteen hundred and thirty-three. They had never seen such rich fields and deep green woods, for they had seldom been outside the brickedup shambles of Manchester. Things were large: fields and barns and distances and the forests of Penn's woodland. Thomas and John began to breathe more deeply than ever in their lives before. Things were not so neat, it was true; and the primitive North American accents startled and puzzled their Lancashire ears. The absence of their solid tradition made their simplest move a dangerous adventure. But Thomas and John were pleased. Ralph kept his silence throughout the long (as it would have been reckoned in England) journey, and looked at the woods of Pennsylvania and the big barns with glazed unfocussed eyes.

Thomas and John did not notice their brother's eyes until they got to Philadelphia and found that the friend was not there, nor a trace of him. Then they saw that Brother Ralph was ill, that he was eating hardly any of the highly-seasoned American victuals, that he walked up and down the light roomy Philadelphia streets with a dead lacklustre stare. They were standing beside a nocturnal oysterbar, when Thomas, seeing Ralph's eyes in blue flare, said:

What's the matter, Brother Ralph?

Yes, Brother Ralph, John said. Are you ill?

I don't know, Ralph said. I don't know.

They were all hatters: they made the tall hats that Englishmen of the time considered as essential as a head. That night at their inn they decided that they would hat Philadelphia. Beckham Brothers, Ltd., Hatters.

But, Ralph said, your brother, John, is a rougher, and you are a rougher, and I am a rougher. Not a one of us can finish a hat.

We can find a finisher, Thomas said. We can fetch Samuel from England.

Yes, Brother Ralph, John said. We can fetch Brother Samuel.

Too long, Ralph said. Too bloody long.

Thomas looked at John and John stared at Thomas.

Thomas, Ralph said, give me my share of the money. I'm a-going home to England. I do not like it here.

Thomas and John knew then: Brother Ralph was homesick. He was homesick, Lee said, for the stinkingest, drabbest, darkest, cruelest industrial town in England. His mind could not abide the tenantless air and the flowers and trees, air around the houses in Philadelphia— the light hurt his eyes. Forty years of Manchester and Audenshaw had got into him. He ate little, and, the next week he took the same British packet for Liverpool and the dirty skeleton streets of Manchester.

Thomas and John stayed in Philadelphia—or rather at its edge— but they did not hat. No Main Line head ever knew a Beckham Brothers' topper. They became boatmen on the Schuylkill canal, and, in 1837, when John died of a consumption he had brought from under the sooty brick of Manchester, Thomas was left sole owner of two barges and a small freighting business.

John's intended wife, a milky, anaemic millhand girl, died in a Manchester whorehouse in the arms of a mulatto girl from the docks of Liverpool two days before John. Word came from Ralph six weeks after John was buried. But John had known she was lost. Maybe that was the reason he died so soon. Anyway the freighting business went to Brother Thomas and thus to the nephews Thomas had already got him: John and Samuel Beckham, boys of five and three who had been mothered by an Ohio girl whose father came from Lancashire.

Thomas now lived in a fair-sized frame house in Manayunk, and, by 1842, when young Thomas was born, he had acquired a store and a parcel of lots besides. The panic of 1841 kept him from being a rich man. And the background and inclinations of a Manchester tradesman had not fitted him to climb into the Main Line families of Philadelphia which made a show of being more aristocratic than the county families of England.

Nevertheless Thomas had become a power in Manayunk. There the name of Beckham had become a household word; there the people knew his (now) Philadelphia tophat and his ivoryheaded walking-stick which had been sent from Manchester; there they knew the log-chain on his heavy hunting-case repeater; and his proud firm step in their little hilly cobblestoned streets. Thomas was an American among Americans—already a man of family and tradition. Three fine sons. Not many, but he would soon have a family worth mention.

Not the oldest was named Thomas. It was the third son, a fiery blue-eyed lad, even in his cradle proud and independent, who was given his father's name. It was the third son who would perhaps carry the malacca walking stick which was for the Thomases of the family. He was my grandfather, Lee said tenderly to the sonnets.

But young Tom was a disappointment to his father—and he never carried the walking stick. Oh, he got it all right, Lee said. But, by God, to carry a cane would have been a badge of infirmity. As a boy he was wild and proud and wilful. He was the smallest of nine brothers. On his sixteenth birthday he thrashed John soundly because John had tyrannized over him when he was too small to fight back. He was always leading Joseph, who was born a year after him, into trouble. He would go pub-crawling; he would make bets he could carry a hundred and fifty pounds of flour on his back ten miles. And by God, he would win.

So you see, you would expect him to go to war, though he knew nothing about the niggers or the Union. Perhaps he did see Mr. Lincoln raise the flag on Independence Hall at six o'clock in the morning of February twenty-second (Washington's birthday), 1861 and perhaps he heard the cannon in salute and something about the new star in the flag for Kansas. Maybe that was it.

When he enlisted in the three-months' regiment, his father said: Well, sir, you've 'listed in this war, sir, and now you'll go if I have to horsewhip you all the way to Washington.

But, Pa, I'm a-going. I calcalate to—

I have nothing more to say to you, young man. Old Thomas's transplanted face, the liberty over the red phlegni, fringed Gladstone whiskers, blunt-nosed and hardblue-eyed, stared coldly at Tom for a second from his tallness in the door of the warehouse in Canal street. Maybe he thought: Was it for this I left Manchester? The squareset tophat nearly raked the top of the doorway. One of my brothers went with the Duke of Wellington, and never came back. Your grandfather even went to Belgium. This isn't your quarrel, sir— Tom's father's broad thumb hooked across his beetling belly under the wide gold logchain, fished up the repeater. He looked at the dial, but did not see the time. His shoulders shook a little, and he raised the ivoryheaded, malacca stick. You'll go now, sir! he said again.

The stick hung above Tom's head in the duskair of a sleepysuburb —a suspended smalltown movement in time and space. Resolution paled again.

Tom stood stubborn and straight. Pa won't hit me, he thought. But he's no bloody right. The stick lowered, trembled down from the sleepy air. Pa's voice was dead level. Yes, sir; you'll go now.

But, Pa.

Let us hear no more, Thomas, senior said, snapping shut the repeatercase. War! The ferrule of the stick came down on the worn pine of the threshold. The ivory smoothed against the hard palm. His father had brought it back from Brussels when he had gone for the brother. A little shop in the big market—the engraving of the Place Grande still lay in an album in the house in Manchester.

Canal street was darkening. A lamplighter rattled feebly at the panes of a streetlamp. Good evening, Mr. Beckham, the lamplighter said. A fine evening! Good evening, Tom.

From behind the warehouse, another boy, slender and taller than Tom and bonier, ran out shouting. His shirt was open and he was bareheaded. Watercurly his dark hair glistened in the newlit lamp.

Pa, he yelled. Pa, did Tom enlist? Frisking, he came up beside them in the street. Did he enlist? Did he join the war to free the nigger slaves?

The ferrule clicked sharply on the walk and the father stopped.

Joseph, you've been in that canal again. You'll go to bed without your supper.

But, Pa—did Tom join the rigiment?

Yes, young man, your brother has become a soldier.

Say, Tom, that's hunky dory. Can I go, Pa? I want to be a calvaryman.

You cannot. Now get home as fast as you can. And mind, you're to have no supper! Leave Tom and me sir.

Joe walked away silently. Tom watched a nail in Joe's shoe strike a little spark from the cobbles. A horse-and-carriage clopjingle floated dozily from the next street. A bird hopped along the weedy parking. Tom walked along beside Pa saying nothing; and Pa made no sound but the leather bootsqueak and the rhythmic tap of the malacca stick's ferrule on the stones.

A week later Tom found himself out of the volunteer regiment. He signed up for the regular army and found his place taken by a substitute bought by Mr. Missimer, the lawyer of Mr. Thomas Beckham, Sr. That same night he joined another three months' regiment with headquarters in Rittenhouse square. Its nucleus was a company of Main Line city guards, social soldiers. They were filling out with anybody. Tom joined. This time he got away to Baltimore before Pa found out. The next day Joe got into Rush's Lancers, another social regiment. Nobody ever knew exactly how Joe did this.

Tom did not get to first Bull Run. The regiment started from Baltimore on the double, but the battle was all over and the army straggling into Washington before the Philadelphia soldiers had marched fifteen miles. They turned back, their new gray uniforms sweated through, half of them limping with footblisters. A first sergeant died of the heat. In Baltimore Tom saw where the Sixth Massachusetts had been fired on by the Secesh mob. Why, the sonsuh-bitches, Tom said. Two dead were sent home on ice.

On that march toward Bull Run, Lee said, there was a lieutenant who had a pair of tight dress boots. Tom Beckham almost carried him for five miles. The lieutenant told my grandfather that he'd have a company when they signed up again and that he'd make Tom his first lieutenant. In those days—well maybe even until he died—Tom believed promises were kept. When the lieutenant told Tom that he was sorry but he had forgotten that he had already promised the berth to a friend, Tom clenched his fists which were big for his size.

Don't Tom me, you son of a bitch, Tom said. I wouldn't join your Goddamn' regiment now—I'd get me a tin bill and pick shit with the chickens first. The lieutenant hollered attention. Attention, my ass! Tom yelled. I'm not in your bloody regiment. Then he called me a name, Tom said, and let him have a good one.

The same afternoon he got a corporal's warrant in the Ninety-seventh Pennsylvania Volunteers, Drake's Zouaves, recruited not from Main Line families, but just from Philly boys. Some of them were firemen and one of them, Ramrod Jones, had been expelled from the Ellsworth Zouaves for horseplay on tour in Detroit. Oh, Zouaves were the thing all right. Before the war they used to come to town like a circus; and thousands of people used to come out to watch Lightning Zouave Drills. Musket and bayonet and knapsack, baggy scarlet trousers, little blue jackets with brass buttons, orange and yellow trimmings and little red caps! Why, Grandpa Beckham climbed a tree in Philadelphia in 1860 to watch the Fire Zouaves and the branch broke because there were already two boys on it: There were squares, human pyramids, crosses and human ladders, Lee said softly. All that was great stuff then—and by Jesus, Grandpa must have heard tell how a Zouave was a fellow who could climb a one-hundred foot rope hand-over-hand with a flour barrel on his heels, or balance himself head-down on a ladder while shooting, with pistols, wild pigeons on the wing.

Maybe Grandpa didn't know that after the French stole Algiers, they took the name of one of the Dey's tribes who wore those baggy pants and recruited a French-Colonial battalion to flatter the con-quered natives. Musical comedy light infantry they were—in Oriental costume designed to fight as skirmishers. They were given the same tactics as the *chasseurs à pied*. They didn't stay colonial long, Lee said tenderly. They became the crack troops of a nation of soldiers. All the bad boys, *les gamins de Paris*, the *mauvais sujets*, wanted to be Zouaves; non-coms from other regiments sacrificed chevrons just to be a private with baggy pants. They used to stop in the middle of a charge and throw down their muskets to applaud an enemy band playing their favorite air. Everybody kissed his fingertips to the Zouaves; and the generals said: *"C'est bien magnifique, mais ce n'est pas la guerre!"*

And in Paris they used to hire a tumble-down carriage and pile into it in squads, turning somersaults and balancing on the back of the horse. They knocked down the beggars with well-filled purses and tumbled madly with the *poules*—and they fought wildly and gayly amidst the snows of the Crimea and on the bloody field of Solferino.

Ah, by Jesus, Beckham said, they were tiptop soldiers all right. Why, Ramrod Jones could turn a summerset in a full pack and musket!

Pa took Tom to his own tailor (the best in Philadelphia) and had the Zouave's uniform made—even to the white gaiters. The jacket was a fine blue serge, Lee said—I've got it at home—cutaway from the collar to the waist, with a single line of small brass buttons on each edge. It hooked at the collar. The trousers were soft red worsted and very baggy, with pleats at the top. On the left sleeve was a great, sprawling goldbraid chevron.

Johnson, Pa said, make this young man some regimentals. He'll tell you what he wishes.

Thank you, Pa, Tom said. Thank you, sir.

But Pa was walking out of the shop, the ferrule of the malacca stick tapping on the floor. Pa turned quickly; his face moving nervously in the air, unlike Pa's face, was floating out of the tailor's shop past the piled bolts of goods.

Ah, yes, sir, the tailor said. Yes, sir, I know the uniform, sir. Hit's Colonel Drake's Zou-ay-ves. Like Colonel Ellsworth's that was killed first by the Rebels.

That's right, Tom said. Red pants, by Jesus. Bully regiment.

CHAPTER IX

Is it then so simple as this, Lee thought, staring beyond the desk-drawer with rapt eyes and a soft frown, that he had not been apprised of certain truisms of life with a capital L? Or was it perhaps that he had, at nineteen, been too subtly (or too subtly to mark his unique convolutions) apprised? Nor yet would that seem to have been true, for, later, through the vertical-cum-horizontal arc of his life, he was apprised—and that rudely—many times over of these truisms, but he could not, did not, or would not grant them a roosting place.

When I began to know him, Lee thought tenderly, it was as Grandpa Beckham. There were only a few black hairs left in the

beard which had been inspired by that of the surgeon, Ames, who took
the minié ball of Gaines's Mill from Tom's thigh at Savage's Station.
Nevertheless, he walked (perhaps it would be better to say he tramped,
for there was always a certain marching aspect in his carriage—and
he would sometimes turn to me and say, Take care, don't tramp on
the toad, he eats potato bugs, or don't tramp on your Grandma's clean
floor with those muddy shoes, or don't let the horse tramp on your
toe) with a firm upright carriage, his head held high still, as if he
had never heard those saws which every Polonius is eager to tell us
all and which every circumstance endeavors dully to emboss upon the
hides of all men. And the beard, even in the quietest air, seemed always to be blowing backward a little (it resembled motion caught in
sculpture), as if it were the beard of a jolly defiant satyr. I rarely saw
his face when its expression was tired, or cynical, or in despair, but
I conjecture that weariness, cynicism, defeat and despair must have
eaten at the edges of him as they eat at the edges of all.

I loved him well: his good firm tramp, his smile, his backblowing
beard and the way he cursed. Once I heard a young poolhall lounger
standing idly in Pawnee street refer to him as Old Man Beckham.
I only glared, but I wanted to kill this man who had no respect for
a special god. Thus, I discovered, but tried to forget, that to some, he
was Old Man Beckham.

In places, Lee now knew, the Chickahominy must have been hardly
more than a creek, but where there was little water—with floating
greenslime and the upthrust heads of moccasins, and, indeed, a bank
of variegated life as wonderful as Mr. Darwin's—there was mire.
Teams of horses, skilful nigger cooks, portable kitchens, cannon, squads
of men, so the stories went, had been sucked under it.

The bridge swayed over the green water in the static miasmal June
air. The Ninety-seventh, or what was left of it after swamp fever had
taken a hand, was moving for the third time. The log bridge swayed—
and maybe Captain Merril hollered, Route step, march!

Chickahominy! Jim Bland said softly. Chickashit!

Tom's face was thin and yellow. He shivered, his feet slipping on
the mireslick logs.

Moccasin bit one of the Goddamn' Pioneers yesterday—deader'n a
mackerel, Jim said. Lookee here, where's Harry Mullin? Why ain't
he here?

Swamp fever, Tom said. Like the clap—everybody's got it. Doc Ames calcalates the Rebels'll win with their Godforsaken swamps.

I never had the clap, Jim said. Did you, Tom?

Why, hell yes, Tom lied. A man ain't a man till he's had the clap.

'Tain't no more'n a bad cold, Wad Ferrel said.

The hell it ain't, Ramrod Jones said. The *Hell* it ain't!

Again Tom's foot slipped on the logs. Jim Bland grabbed his arm. What's ailing you, Tom? Jim said.

Maybe it's a bad cold, Ferrel said.

Thanks, Jim, Tom said. Damned if I wanta drownd in the Chicka-hominy. Why they call us the Army of the Potomick, I don't know.

A loud gundrumming filled the swamp. McClellan's Napoleons were in battery too late as usual.

Firing again, Tom said.

You still got the ague, Tom? Jim said.

Hell no, my foot slipped.

They're a-comin' back a-ready, Jim said.

The hatless boy they saw plodding in the mud looked as if he had no nose, only a bleeding hole, with blood running like little rivulets down his chin and neck. He began trying to run in the mud as they looked.

First we seen this trip, ain't it? Wad Ferrel said.

Nobody answered. A couple of hospital pimps slish-sloshed past carrying an armless man on a stretcher. An officer stopped them, said a few words in a low voice, pointed to the man on the stretcher and toward the sound of the guns. The stretcher-bearers tilted the stretcher and the man rolled limply off into the mud by the roadside.

He's done for all right, Tom said. Those sonsuhbitches thought they were bombproof.

The column telescoped in the mud before the company, haalt! floated back on the jellied air.

Ahead a whip snapped dully in the swamp. Somebody guffawed. Captain Merril walked his mare up beside Tom and Jim, her hooves suck-sucking in the pasty earth. Adown the muddy line he came, and catching sight of Tom's proud chevron, he reined up sharply. The mare dropped a spludgy mass of well-moulded, oaty dungballs in the mud. They did not smoke: it was too hot.

Corporal Beckham, Captain Merril said, looking down from the shiny mareback in his best West Point-Old-Fuss-and-Feathers manner,

have your squad stack arms and proceed to the aid of the battery mired
in the ford.

Tom, Zouave-proud and rigid, saluted across the Springfield muz-
zleloader. Yes, sir! he said with fine soldiership.

A weary snigger slid off the mudbased line.

Silence! Captain Merril barked martially.

Tom and his squad slopped forward in the tepid, mosquito-den.
They laid hold of the wheelspokes of the Napoleon. Quirrt-snap-flack!
the artillery whip said. They strained and lifted. The brass gun rose
from the water, and, stock dripping, the barrel jolting on its trunnions,
began to roll, the gunners sloshing after it. Curdles of red mud oozed
on the stock, spongestaff and trail. The wet gunners climbed wearily
to the caisson. A mudfaced Massachusetts boy looked at Tom patron-
izingly: Thanks, sonny, now how about a human ladder? he said and
began to sing in a sweet baritone:

> My love is a Zu-Zu so gallant and bold.
> He's rough, and he's handsome, scarce
> Nineteen years old.

Hell! Tom said, blushing. Wad Ferrel laughed.

Baggy red trousers dripping with watery mud, the white gaiters
invisible, they walked back to their stacked muskets, wiping their
hands on their jackets. Tom was thinking how good the uniform had
looked in Pa's tailor's shop.

Redfaced, Colonel Drake jigjogged along the roadside loblolly
aboard Miss Stowe, a pert, black mare.

We support the artillery in more ways than one, eh, Corporal? the
colonel bumbled in fiercehoarse geniality.

Yes, sir, Tom said, blushing again.

You and the Old Man! Wad Ferrel whispered.

He's loaded, Jim Bland whispered. Bet you could light his breath
with a match, like one of Pa's lamps.

Route steeep—maarch!

They slogged forward squish-squishing, feeling the swampwater between their toes.

I got a girl in Baltimore—I don't love'r any more, somebody sang.

They tell me that's where he got shot, a boyvoice said. And him
jist married. They said it'd been a hell of a lot worse if he hadn't
been thinkin' about his wife.

The numbers of walking wounded increased. Tom saw a man running—a horseman trying to stop him with the flat of a sabre. The man dodged and ran on; the trooper pulled a revolver and shot him down. Jesus, Tom thought, both Union men too.

The cannon shook the ground. A screaming floated through the woods on their right.

I saw a man who was at Beaver Dam Creek yesterday; and he said all of Stonewall Jackson's army got here—a million of 'em, Jim Bland yelled in Tom's ear. They must be in them woods now.

The ground grew firmer as they labored up to the top of the plateau. On the fringe of the woods Tom could see little men in lines moving; a heavy Parrot gun strained and jingled toward an unpainted grayish farmhouse, the sun glaring on the dark steel barrel. A squadron of cavalry galloped toward the Chickahominy. They were lancers all right, but he couldn't see whether Joe was with them or not.

Hurrah! Hurrah! he yelled, a quick warm surge of clanlove running through him. Wad Farrel stared at him. My brother Joe's with those cavalrymen! Tom said proudly.

Baaattery—forrr—waard!

He saw the Napoleon he rescued from the mud quicken its horses to a queasy farting gallop, and head toward the woods.

The warm, wet air was full of a boomthumping roar which excluded or drowned all small vibrations on the eardrum; the noise of exploding gunpowder destroyed all accord between the senses—as now, when a man sitting in a cinema, sees a soundpicture go suddenly soundless and sees exaggerated the grotesqueries of gesture and grimace in the actors, he is in a strange new world he has only half seen before. Wet with sweat and swampwater, weak and dizzy from malaria and the quinine with which Dr. Ames, the regimental surgeon had dosed him, pressed upon by the hot June miasma and the sharp odor of gunpowder, his eyes saw the humans and horses moving so slowly that he began to distrust his sight. How he would have liked to take off the sodden wool clothes and dive into the Schuylkill from his father's coal barge with Brother Joe beside him, getting out at dusk, cool and shivering, just in time to catch Jim Bland lighting the streetlamps for his father. His eyes turned to Jim who was walking along beside him with his eyes fixed on something in the distance. He touched Jim on the shoulder. Jim turned slowly: Wouldn't a swim be bully? he shouted. Jim shook his head; he had not heard. He jerked his head toward a man on a horse who was riding up and down the column swaying in the saddle.

It was Colonel Drake again: his rubricated face jiggled above the richly gilt illumination of his shouldereagles, its loose cheeks in the air not fifteen feet away. Tom could see the empty look in the watery eyes. Jim was right; the old man was drunk as a lord. His mouth was working so much that he drooled around his lips—and he was waving his sword. He looked pretty much of a damn' fool. Miss Stowe, the mare, was taking him along carefully. By Jesus Christ, Tom said aloud, though he did not hear his own words, that's no damn' condition for battle!

He could see the red-legs of zouaves lying around his path already as the regiment neared the woods. They were falling as if they had been suddenly boned. Maybe one or two who went down stayed on their knees and moved slowly and aimlessly. It was as if there were a great thick sheet of glass between him and the others, as if he were looking down on some charades performed in the Crystal Palace in London—the place his cousin had written to Pa about. He kicked aside a muddy kepi and stumbled over a musket.

In continuance of this extended and silent mummery of the battlefield, he saw the Massachusetts battery of Napoleons un-limbering, the horseholders leading the nervous horses back from the woods and a spray of small blue men marching and running back from the woods. All this he noted in the silence—for now that he could not sort the sounds which made the great swallowing roar in his ears, he was living in an artificial silence. It was unreal: nothing really happened.

He saw Captain Merril's signal, and, thinking proudly of the big chevron on his arm, muttered Spread out as he touched Jim Bland on the shoulder and made a pushing-outward gesture with his hard young hand. Jim passed it along; Ramrod Jones passed it along; the company spread out in front of the dark green, gleaming woods. By God, Tom thought, we're a-going in now—real battle. War. But he could not realize the difference between one moment which was not battle and another moment which must be battle.

In passing, he saw the muddy-faced Massachusetts baritone with a rammer in his hands, standing beside the Napoleon, which the squad had pulled out of the creek. He gripped his musket hard with sweatslick hands. He saw the Massachusetts lieutenant step back from the gun. He saw the gunners jump aside. The lieutenant pulled the lanyard, the gun jumped, the weeds around its muzzle bowed for a slow instant like a botanical minuet, white smoke encased the artillerymen. The man with the sponge-staff dipped it in the waterbucket and hopped back to the muzzle. Tom trotted forward precariously on the muddy ground and found himself in the woods.

Maybe it was Wad Ferrel among the wateroaks, but he could not be sure. Smoke trickled in lazy rivulets through the thick air, hung like steam over the hot day's kettle. A white tender spot would appear suddenly on a treetrunk—and a tree stood wounded in the wood. An amputated branch or leaf would float downward through the warm sunshafts. Tom still lived in an unreal silence. Feeling as if he were a graven image, Tom thought: now, if I did not have to prime and fire this musket, I could stand still peacefully and watch or lie down and go to sleep. I am so tired I would not even take care to watch out for the moccasins. A ballcut branch brushed his face. The lethargy breaking a little, he cocked the strong-springed musketlock and put the magnesium cap over the nipple. *They* were in the woods. Tom knew it. Maybe that was one moving in that little thicket.

Tom stopped walking and stood stockstill on the marshy ground. Pulling up his musket quickly, he looked along the barrel and jerked the trigger hard. It went off all right: he felt the steel butt-guard jam into his shoulder. His feet sinking in the mud, he fumbled a paper cartridge out of his box, bit off the end too close and got a mouthful of powder. He flung the impotent cartridge away, bit another and another, rammed them both home, replaced his ramrod, put the cap on the nipple and looked about him. It was as if he were alone in a swampy island. Where, in God almighty's name, had they all got to?

The artificial silence began to sort itself into single explosions. The bang-banging seemed to come from the left. Tom began walking toward the sound.

He had walked about fifty yards when he saw a bareheaded man standing partly behind a tree—sidewise to him and firing around the tree with a revolver. Watching the pistol jump in the man's hand, Tom raised his musket. But he walked on a few steps to get a better aim, and, as he looked down the barrel, he saw the man's blue zouave jacket and his shoulder straps. Well, Tom said, it's luck I saw that. Why, Christ a'mighty! it's Captain Merril. He walked up to the captain's side and stood looking in the direction the captain had been firing. There was nothing there now anyway. Where the hell are they, Captain? Tom yelled.

Merril whirled, shoving the pistol into the air before Tom's breast, then dropping it to his side. Oh, it's you, Beckham. His face was white; one of the cheeks was scratched and bleeding, the forehead clustered with little globes of sweat.

Where are they? Tom repeated.

Fell back, I think! Merril shouted.

Where are we? Tom said. Merril turned the white, scratched, puzzled boyface toward Tom. Company F, Tom said,—the regiment?

As they stood in the moment of puzzlement, there came a scurrying and a bellow in the brush behind them. Through the trees lunged Miss Stowe, her guts dragging in the weeds, the colonel reeling in the saddle. He fired his pistol wildly into the timber and howled, Come on men! Then he fired twice at Tom and Merril, threw down his pistol, dragged out his sword and rode at them. Merril jerked Tom behind a tree, just as Miss Stowe, a long dirty intestine flopping under her, swerved and bore the colonel past. The colonel hacked at the tree with his sword. They saw him tumble from the saddle and Miss Stowe drag him through the mud out of sight.

They found him lying with the crotch of his legs around a tree, with blood on his uniform frock coat. He had disdained the zouave uniform, for he had gone to the Mexican war—and this damn' zouave business had been none of his idea. Tom and Merril sat him up beside a tree without looking at each other. Part of the regiment—not Company F—came up beside them in two ragged ranks. Major Stubbs was yelling and gesticulating for them to halt when Tom saw that they were on a ridge next to what looked as if it were the Massachusetts battery of Napoleons. High and hysterical screaming cut the air. A lieutenant and two gunners were hauling one of the brass guns around to the left. Another gun was already pointing in that direction. Tom saw it belch and jump—jump as if it were a man hit with a whip—the weeds bow in front of it and turn bluegray, and the men hop like jumpingjacks to reload. Tranced, Tom bit another cartridge and tamped it down in his musket, and fixed his bayonet, for he saw that the other lads had the long steel gutspikes on their musketmuzzles. Somewhere more artillery had opened and again the great artificial silence had taken hold of his ears. A zouave next to him moved his lips; Tom shook his head. The other boy pointed.

They were coming up the hill in a long ragged line in front of the zouaves and behind them and to their left. Flanked, by Jesus Christ! Tom said. Flanked! It might as well have been a thought, for no one heard. Stubbs was pointing, pushing his sword toward the Rebels. A dozen of the zouaves followed him, then a few more. Tom saw one running back. He found himself following Stubbs. The line of Rebels was coming up the hill in long, leaping strides—still hollering a little. One was carrying a red flag which fluttered weakly with the motion of its carrier, for the air was too lifeless to flap out a banner. Tom brought up his musket and looked down the barrel at the jacket of the Rebel colorbearer. He felt the gun kick as if it were breaking his shoulder and saw the flag and man go down. The flag jerked up in the hands of another Rebel. Tom was sitting on the ground from the kick of his musket rubbing his shoulder—but he reloaded with two cartridges before he got up. That gets 'em, he said to himself. Two balls. He walked on watching his chance for a shot. He was only a few feet from the Napoleons when it happened.

He went over sideways, twirling a little, his left thigh numb. From where he lay, he could see the lieutenant trying to get a team of screaming, biting horses up to the gun. He saw him give up and hop aboard the caisson of a limbered gun. Another artilleryman gave a jerk at the lanyard of one of the abandoned cannon. Tom thought it was the boy who sang the Zu-Zu song at the creek. The lanyard broke in his hands and he pitched over in the weeds.

Grandpa Beckham, Lee thought, told me the line of Rebels—maybe it wasn't a line then, but just Rebels coming up the hill towards the guns the Massachusetts battery had abandoned—were not yelling then. They must have been saving what wind they had.

Tom hung onto his musket and crawled, dragging his leg, up to the breech of the gun. Near it, faceup, lay the baritone who sang the Zu-Zu song. God, Tom thought tenderly, his eyes hot, he's dead. Tom put his hand up toward the piece of lanyard and raised himself with the other hand on the guntrail. Maybe a minié ball or two hit the spokes of the gunwheels and spattered slivers and lead around him. He could see their faces coming on in the hillside air, and the black-powder around their mouths. He caught another glimpse of the bloodred flag just as he pulled the broken lanyard. The Napoleon thumped and Tom felt the trail jump as he hit the ground with the concussion. His ears rang loudly, and he could see now that the weeds under the muzzle of the gun had not sprung back straight after they had bowed in the powderblast, but stood at an angle, ragged and scorched and bleeding—some had even been blown out of the ground. He thought the Rebels would sure kill him after that, so he hugged the ground. He put his hand to his thigh and looked at his dirty, bloody fingers. He closed his eyes, thinking: the bastards will take me for dead. He lay that way for what seemed a long time, for the flies were not only at his thigh but at his face and hands. Jesus, they bit, Lee thought reverently. And he could hear them droning around his head in the gaps of musketry and cannonades. He could even hear the Rebels panting and talking in strange hoarse voices.

He felt something lifting one of his feet and opened his eyes in a small slit just about like a thin dime. There was a Goddamn' ragged Rebel in a brown woolen slouch hat with a chew in his mouth trying to unfasten one of his zouave's gaiters that Pa's tailor had made for him. I hefted up that Goddamn' musket, he said, and raked across his face with the bayonet and let him have the double charge in that Goddamn' dirty face of his. Well, sir, it knocked me flat on my back and took the wind out of me—this time I thought my shoulder was broke. And then a cold sweat broke out all over me—and the Goddamn' flies started in on my leg and face again. If it hadn't of been for the flies, I could have stood the wound better. A-laying there on that hot day I began to shiver and my teeth chattered. He fainted all right, Lee thought. Good thing he did too, or I might not have been here—or maybe it's worse.

Wad Ferrel said: Hell, he's dead.

But Tom opened his eyes all right.

It's Tom Beckham, Wad Ferrel said. Where you hit, Tom?

In the ass, Tom said. They sneaked up behind me.

You hurt bad? Wad said.

Not so bad, Tom said. If it wasn't for the Goddamn' flies—

They ain't eat so good in months, Wad said. But ain't you lucky. You'll get to go back to Philly.

Wad and some other zouaves, not from Company F, put him on a stretcher and carried him away from the gun. Wad said for Christ's sake to hurry, because those bastards from the Bowery couldn't hold 'em like the boys from Philly. Tom looked over the stretcher's edge and saw the shoe-stealer faceless on the grass, the weeds around him all splattered with blood, and the bloody pulp that had been a dirty Rebel face under a slouch hat—it lay bloody under his head —clustered with bright little green flies. Well, they *had* needed shoes all right. His bare feet were swollen and caked with old blood under the mud.

Holy Christ, Wad said. Tom, did you do that?

Well, Tom said roughly, he was a-trying to take my shoes. He thought: By God, that's a hell of a thing to do to a man for stealin' a pair of shoes a fellah can't even use to walk on. Well, I been in a real battle now, anyhow—you can bet your bottom dollar.

Wad and the other man took Tom off the stretcher and laid him down under a tree near a weathered frame house. Tom thought he heard someone crying and hollering inside the house. Wad said: It's a hospital. They'll get you and look after you in there, Tom; or they'll take you someplace where a sawbones can get to you.

Oh, there was plenty of sawing, all right, Lee said. Grandpa said he saw wagonloads of amputated feet, legs, arms, hands and everything which could be cut off a man lying around loose in front of houses and cabins. Amputation flourished in those sadistic days.

Sometimes the sawbones were cauterizers; they would whack off a leg and burn the new bone-and-meat end with hot oil or irons. Some amputated screamed, some fainted and some died of what surgery now calls shock.

They remembered how the bonesaw sounded and how the hot oil and iron felt, Lee thought, in the long heat-dazzled afternoons when they were old and looking down the smooth length of the cane which leaned, between their legs, against the chair on the hotel porch. Shiloh, Gaines's Mill, Gettysburg. It was a big brick house—and there was a big pile of arms and legs and guts outside. I remember the sun shining on the bubbly innards. And, by God! I'll always say there was a whole man in that pile.

He ain't a-going to do any sawing on me, Tom said.

Oh, hell no, Wad said. He'll jist wrap you up. How you feelin' now?

A number one, Tom said. Firstrate. His thigh felt as if a hot bellows was pumping in it, and, now that his cold sweat was dry, he began to burn as if the hot sand of a desert grave were falling on him. Maybe he had the idea that if he got up and screamed and ran, he could get away from the throb and the flystings and the noise and the hot sand falling on his burning skin. He beat both fists into the red damp earth and took a drink of warm brackish water from his canteen, wishing for some of the whiskey he had seen poured on the ground by the commissary men last night—wishing for a bath in the house in Manayunk and a clean shirt and some of his mother's chicken pie.

A column of men in flat straw hats were marching back towards the bridge. Tom thought it must be the Eighteenth New York. Some of the boys said they had joined the army to steal and they were already deserting.

The two-wheeled ambulance driven by the hospital pimps who picked him up for an excuse to get away from the million Rebels they knew were coming slowed **down beside a** brass Napoleon with a broken axle. The man's head was down between his knees and his back shook as if he were sobbing. The road swarmed with men in all kinds of muddy uniforms: red-legged zouaves from Tom's regiment and other zouaves with red fezzes, maybe those New York Firemen; shell jacketed artillerymen; New York infantrymen in straw hats; yellow-striped cavalrymen walking; Union men in gray. At the creek where Tom had helped the Massachusetts battery, he saw a man fall into the water and fail to come up. As the horse of the ambulance floundered in the soft creek bed, a man using a musket for a crutch shouted: Please! For God's sake let me ride!

But the driver and the orderly lashed on, the horse's hooves sucking in the mud until they hit the slippery cord-roy approach to the bridge. Then they pulled up the lathery quivering horse. A sutler's wagon, with baskets of oranges roped to the top stood crossways in the mud. Soldiers had grabbed the horse's bridle. The sutler, rage on his sweaty bearded face, stood cutting at some artillerymen with a whip. Tom saw he had a gray cast in one of his dark eyes. A burly, chevroned man leapt up to the sutler and swung the butt of a Colt's revolver on his head. As the sutler's knees gave way, Tom saw the blood trickling down his forehead. Stragglers swarmed over the wagon and into it, coming away with jars of preserves, cigars, cookies, cakes, hams, fish and whiskey. The oranges spilled off the top in a yellow cascade onto the muddy ramp of the bridge, rolling into the loblolly of the road from which soldiers scooped them up and began to tear away the muddy rinds. . . .

Who put you here? There's plenty of room in the tents.

I came by the train last night, Doctor. A couple of men took me off on a stretcher. See here, can I have a drink of water? Some son of a bitch stole my canteen.

Orderly! Ames said sharply. See that this man is put in a tent—and give him some water. Wash that wound. God Almighty! I don't know how anyone can ever live with this medical department. I'll come and see you shortly, Corporal.

Ames looked at the armless dead man on the ground beside Tom. These regular army surgeons would be sitting around a bottle of liquor somewhere gassing about anything from women to laudable pus—and letting these boys die. Not that maybe it wasn't better for them to die. Laudable pus—pus, *laudabile et bonum*. How in God's name could any suppurating thing be laudable and good? All this damn' foolishness of men shooting each other anyway. Ames sighed. Oh God! He wished he were back in Edinburgh listening to Old Bevis talk about anatomy and Boswell; he wished he were in a pub drinking with Tom Wagnal. Glory! Union! Niggers! He sighed again and mopped his forehead thinking of Red Mary, the Edinburgh whore, they had loved and dissected. A scream issued from the shed; a bone-saw rasped.

We're gonna git our pictures took. Look pleasant and watch the birdie! yelled a boy with a bloody bandage around his shoulder.

A little, knotty man with a big cavalry sabre strapped underneath a muddy linenduster was shading the lens of his camera tentatively as he prepared to remove the lenscap.

Colonel, the man said, in thickrich Irish tones, to Captain Ames, will ye ask the men to stay quiet whilst I photograph them.

Ames, still bending over Tom, said shortly: They won't move. They can't move very much. All right, men—can you keep still for a moment? Your picture's wanted for your sweethearts.

It's Brady and his Whatsit. I got my picture took at Bull Run, someone said.

I'll bet it was your assend runnin' like a bat outa hell, someone answered.

Tom rose up on an elbow and looked at the small Cork Irishman, the great Washington society photographer, the Lincoln-snapper, the Preserver of the Senatorial Stare, the Poser of the FFV's. Brady removed the lenscap, and, for a long instant, all was quiet and still: the instant was freezing in collodion as the light burnt the bromides and iodides of Brady's wetplate. Everyone within the eye of the lens had struck an attitude as if he were a statue in a public square of his home town. Wooden faces grew on the boyfaces, the beards petrified. The dead grew deader before Brady's camera. Tom watched the Irishman's lips silently tell off the seconds of frozen time. Time stretched to the breaking point like a bit of rubber; the buzz of thousands of flies only locked the paralysis of the minutes. Brady returned the velvetlined cap to his shining lens. The camera was blind again. But in 1912 the moment would be there even to the ladder against the house.

Thank ye, gentlemen, Brady said, putting on his battered brown strawhat which he had used to shade the lens. Time continued, men unposed—slipped down off the instant's edge.

When can we get one of those pictures, Brady? someone yelled. I want to show my girl how brave I am. But Brady was already on his way, trotting a phantom bog, toward the little tarpaulin-covered buggy to develop the wetplate, the sabrescabbard clacking against his heels. The flies whirred on, living out every moment of hypnotized existence in the sun.

Two orderlies picked Tom up and carelessly laid him on a stretcher. Tom grunted.

Ames looked down into Tom's whitedrawn face as the orderlies put the broken boy on a cot in the tent. The doctor's face was also white and drawn. He thought of how Bevis had known Knox, the man who bought bodies from Burke and Hare. And he thought of the rain in Edinburgh and how Bevis had been with the Scot's Greys at Waterloo and how he had told pretty tales about sabre-fighting to illustrate his lectures on surgery. Ames saw the man's eyes, remote and burning, as he spoke of the bloodgutters in the long, sharp swords of Napoleon's cavalry. Blood! Ames thought he would never escape it. He looked down at Tom Beckham's thigh, shuddered a trifle and slashed the zouave trousers with a scalpel from the clumsy leather U.S. surgical kit.

I never wanted to be here anyway, he muttered. And now when I can't get anything to work with, I'd rather be in hell with a broken back trying to eat soup out of a bottle with a fork. Tom watched the trousers sadly, thinking of the day Pa took him to Johnson.

Quinine and whiskey! Ames said sharply to the orderly. Now, son, he said as Tom looked up at his fierce black beard, we're going to pull that Rebel ball out of you. It'll hurt worse than when it went in.

Go ahead, Doctor! Tom said. You just go ahead.

An orderly brought a bloody sponge and a tin basin of water. Ames threw the sponge on the ground. He tore a strip from Tom's shirt tail and sloshed the wound. The red hole was bigger than a silver dollar. Ames hand struck something hard in Tom's pocket, and he fished out a bloody purse with a bent and cracked steel rim.

May have saved your leg, boy, Ames said softly.

Tom took the purse in his hand. The heavy rim was bent almost double. The minnie ball must have fetched him a hell of a wallop.

The orderly brought a paper packet of quinine and a bottle of commissary whiskey.

Take a good slug of this Moral Suasion, Corporal, Ames said. We're going to hunt that ball. Jesus, but the Rebels got a lot of my boys in the same spot.

I wasn't running, Doc. Nobody in the Ninety-seventh was running. They flanked us. By Jesus, they come up behind us and to the left and shot us in the ass—the dirty—

I know, Ames said. I saw 'em.

Ames took a bright probe in one hand and a pair of forceps in the other. Steady, son, he said. Tom watched, holding his face steady. The probe grated bone and struck lead. The flies gorged.

Ahhh, Ames said, nosing the bright forceps into the hole.

Tom's forehead beaded up with coldsweat. Then he saw that the doctor was holding up the red, squashed minié ball. It looked bigger than the hole from which it came; thread, flesh, a scrap of his zouave trousers and a sliver of his thighbone clung to it.

Slick as a whistle, Ames said. We won't bother the bone. It'll knit. You'll be back on duty in no time, marching into Richmond with General McClellan. He knew he ought to do a resection—that at the very least, Tom's left leg would always be shorter than the right. But there was nothing he would do—or could do here.

That's fine, Doctor, Tom said, as the black curtain came down, just fine.

The flies wouldn't go away no matter how much you brushed at them with your hands. Tom became so inured to their bites that he could lie for several minutes without brushing them off; he timed himself by the watch Pa had given him before he left Philadelphia the second time. The hospital orderlies brought him more whiskey and quinine, and he lay as if suspended in eternity with his ears ringing, under the tent which made him think he was inside a balloon blown up with foul air.

What were the orderlies doing? They were taking away the man who had howled for mosquito netting to cover the bandages around his bleeding belly and bringing in a boy with a shattered skull from the Thirteenth New York who still hung to his bloody straw hat. Someone brought Tom some stew, and he vomited it up in rancid chunks on the muddy tentfloor.

The Rebels got him at Savage's Station. But after he was captured he lay there for two weeks perhaps forming in his fevered head such images as a cool drink of water from his father's well and the breasts of the girl, Molly, who lived in the next street above him, as she stood of a summer night in the yellow light of the streetlamp on the cobble-stoned corner—the weak slow light of the streetlamp which Jim Bland had lighted for his father only an hour ago. Maybe he heard the dull sounds of a Philadelphia summer night pouring down the hilly Manayunk streets: a horse clopping distantly, a door slammed, some-body's shoes in the street, a dog barking, the wind in the trees. Maybe he thought of the night he and Jim Bland saw the firstrate girl in the light of a flare at an oyster-bar—a real Main Line Swell, and lively. Perhaps he thought of how they marched, singing The Girl I Left Behind Me, to Broad and Prime streets to get into the boxcars for Washington.

A Rebel girl, Grandpa Beckham said, came up to the wagon. I couldn't see her very well at first—it was pretty dark. They was a-taking us to prison; and the wagons stopped.

Was that in Richmond, Grandpa? Lee asked long ago.

Yes, Grandpa said. It was night. We was in the wagon—a line of wagons—a-going to the Tobacco Warehouse prison.

She came up beside the wagon in the light of a Richmond street, Tom was lying bruised, his wound throbbing beneath the dirty bandage, in the springless wagon. The lamp was dim, I think; and Tom raising himself saw the purple black hair in the sultry July night of 1862.

She had on a hoopskirt of some light stiffish material with a dark cameo brooch at her low collar. Maybe she smelled of lemon-verbena

—I don't know, Lee thought. Grandpa said she was a swell and a looker all right. I heard him say that many times—but he seemed always, as he said it, to make some almost forgotten reservation and to make it as if it were a reservation he had chosen to forget. Maybe she was evil, or he thought she was evil, but she was beautiful too and smelled good.

He had only the beginnings of the beard then; his shirt was dirty and his zouave jacket lying on the dirty straw in the wagonbox. He scrambled into the jacket so fast that he hurt his thigh, wiped his face with his hands, pushed the hair out of his eyes and pulled himself up on the sideboards of the wagon.

She may have been a little finicky about his looks. Not that she said anything. She just stepped back a little—but Tom understood. He knew how he must have looked; and, at intervals, his olfactory nerve, blown clean for a moment by some hot desultory breeze, gave him a shocking momentary précis of how he must have affected other olfactory nerves.

But the girl, by some alchemy of control which Tom had never noted before in any female, and which he associated with the word aristocratic, took herself in hand and moved forward as she lifted up a deadwhite face and lips as purple as her geometrically parted hair. She was asking in the puzzling soft-hard accent of the South about someone in a Virginia regiment. Tom never could remember the number later—perhaps he had never heard it, for the word Virginia would have been as far as he needed to listen.

Then he was explaining to her that he was from the Ninety-seventh Pennsylvania Zouaves and wounded at Gaines's Mill. Either she did not hear the word Pennsylvania or did not know that there was such a state, for she kept asking how the battle was going for us. Tom, his thigh paining him badly now, from holding himself in an unnatural position, explained that he was a *Union* soldier and that it was going all right for *us*. She seemed to disregard him, or not to listen to him, as, again, she began to ask about the man in the Virginia regiment, her brother.

But, Lee said, Tom didn't know anything. He may have thought of the Rebel whose face he had blown away, but all he could say was that there were thousands on both sides. Her dark mouth opened with the soft imperious petulance of an impatient female demanding a service of an anonymous inferior. It may have been given to her, at that moment, to see that Tom was hurt and feverish, or to have had a trembling phantasy of her brother in dirty bandages on the hard bed of a springless wagon. Perhaps that was where the pity which is akin to fear came from, for she called to the dusk beyond the streetlight and, Tom said, a nigger girl with a basket of cake and a silver pot of coffee came slowly to her. And she gave me some little spice cakes and coffee. Then her and the nigger walked away among the wagons a-looking for the brother. Maybe they never found him.

Tom didn't have anything to eat after that for two days, until he got to Belle Isle. There he got a half-loaf of bread and a few ounces of maggoty meat every other day. The lice, he said, was that thick, if you laid down in the tent you would find yourself carried out under a tree. They had louse inspection among themselves twice a day.

They died off at the rate of a dozen a day. And throughout the time he was on Bell's Island, as he called it, no doctor came near the Union soldiers. He dressed his own wound—that is, he took off the dirty bandage every day and brushed away as many of his friends, the maggots, as he could with his dirty fingers.

But worst—what Tom would never forget—was the day he found Ramrod Jones so miserable that he would not even allow them to pick the lice from him. The only way I knew it was Ram was by his voice. He had a bandage around his eyes—they were both blown out. And, by Jesus H. Christ, they were too! The Rebels took the bandage off before they took him away to bury him. They were *black* eyes like a man that'd been in a fight and festered shut with maggots at the edges and little green flies buzzing around 'em. I remember thinking that he wouldn't ever turn another summerset—and he was an Ellsworth man too.

In August, after Tom was exchanged at Harrison's Landing, and sent to the hospital at Point Lookout, Maryland, he wrote to his Sister Mary that when they saw the Star Spangle Banner it made us feel like new fellows. Even Camp Misery, the convalescent camp at Alexandria, a swampy culturebroth for contagion and discomfort, was not bad after Belle Isle.

His father had bought him out of the army twice, so it was Ma who came for him dressed in her best black silk. She brought him pies and cookies, but he couldn't eat much because of the squitters.

He was discharged at the convalescent camp because of disability. Ames had been right about the resection. He went back to Manayunk on crutches, a gaunt whitefaced boyghost with a new beard. His mother helped him up the hills. A black felt hat sat where his jaunty kepi should have been; a blue serge suit hung on him in place of his beautiful red and blue brassbuttoned zouave's uniform. His mother carefully wrapped up the little blue jacket which his father had had Johnson make. It was splashed with blood and already ragged. The red trousers were gone.

CHAPTER X

AH YES, *and I, Lee thought, my hospitable carcase has been host to many several bacteria, bacilli and parasites. I believe I have never known the healthful privacy of perfect brutemeat. My frame and walls have always squeaked and ailed. Look well—it isn't obvious: my father's coffinmaker's shoulders. Hmmm! Hmmmm! Slight lateral curvature of the spine, the doctors say. Hmmm! Hear that? A hole, a little suppurating cavern inside my left lung where various prefixes of the cocci dwelt rowdily. See that pit? Before my arm could be scratched with Jenner's cowscab, I lay pussed and pocked, greased with vaseline and whimpering in my crib. These shins are covered with a growth of invisible ivy, little cryptogamous plants, meat fungi, delicate parasites like the mistletoe—perhaps berrybearing. They strangle my far-from-oak limbs, and I itch as if I had need for the King to touch me.*

Before I was twelve I had bled more than a battalion of volunteers; before I was twenty I had lived—against the laws of chance—through ten personal plague years.

My cordial cadaver still puts out a hail-fellow-well-met hand to nearly every one of God's little micro-organisms; my tenement of clay is a cheap youth hostel for every invisible beast that divides its cells and whisks its tail in culturebroth; my darksome house is not contented only to stand and wait, it must constitute itself a Mermaid tavern for God's smallest wits.

I am like the middleclass housewife who drapes her house with plush horrors: I festoon myself with small beasts and give them to eat and suck and warm them. I am a truly generous mound of flesh. I daily lay down my life not for my friends but for those hungry little persons I have never seen. Stay, says my carrion, do stay and raise a bloody fine family—there's room for us all here and food for the children. Thus daily I am camped on, lived in and eaten. Your little fellows are your emperors for diet. Czars and Kings and Comissars have fed the fore-bears of my little laboratory pets.

I have a restless bivouac on my legs and several industrious shifts of blood miners in my lungs. Of late I had thought that the mine had been abandoned, but I note that the red production graph is rising again. And only yesterday my little bloodgrubbers sent up a fine grade of ruddyg ore.

Ah no; Lee thought, savagely hypochondriac. Nobody is his own man, but I have been such a big happy community of tiny fellows— sub-infinitesimal squatters—for such a long time that I do not know how to be anything else but a thwarted landlord. Oh, mind you, there were rentals: safe conduct through absence from dreaded schools, a bicycle, rollerskates, guns, cowboy chaps, model airplanes, erector sets, firecrackers—even women. But now there is nothing but repairs—and no chance of evictions.

I am a very slum, a bonetown, a ragtown, a hooverville, a wrong-side of the tracks for all the little aides of the M.D.'s. Soon, I hope, my beams will decay entirely and fall down with all my little tenants and cadgers. I'm so tired of not being able to see and hear my dwellers that I shall welcome the visible deathfly and the poetical worm as they march rhythmically in and out my halffleshed bones. Ho! ho! Lee said aloud, the bastard's full of bloody bacteria. But I'm not yet a spa for spirochetes, he answered. No; by God! No buggering spirochetes. I've got a jimcrow law agin' 'em. Ho! ho! he repeated crazily to the sonnets. A spa for middleclass spirochetes—

Quiet, you bastard! he cautioned himself. Now where was I? Oh yes, a politic convention of necrophile worms was at me. Well, it's some-thing to look forward to, he said slowly. You know where you are then.

Ho! ho! said the other compartment of himself. A bloody spa for bloody middleclass buggering spirochetes—

And bloody middleclass they are too these days. Long the secret-shame of the churchgoer and just retribution for the sins of the flesh, there is now an antiseptic middleclass crusade against the dear little borers. They are now mentioned halfaloud in the front parlor. Now that I think of it, Fork City was always full of them. Yenser must have shot the natives and shock troops full of colored water for years at ten dollars a shot, thereby rising from a diplomamill quack to the final

glory of an olefamily-doctor. The royal road to success watered down
with diluted sixohsix.

CHAPTER XI

THE BIG HOUSE at Messenger's Ferry was still white as drivensnow,
Wagnal said. It was the Old South to a T. It had formal boxwood
hedges on the grounds, and horses still in the stable. Oh yes, it was a
Plantation with a capital P. Magnolia and big oaks with some moss
hanging on them, brought, Rasselas told me, all the way from New
Orleans because the young mistress prized it higher than that which
grew thereabouts. A slave was killed when he fell against a tombstone
while he was draping the long damp trailers on a tree over the burial
ground. In the park there were a sundial or two, some good copies of
Greek statuary and a little summer house made of marble—a little
Greek temple.

Oh, it was an unusual place in more ways than one, but mainly
because—this was sixty-three, mind you—it had only just begun to
look rundown when we arrived there and pitched a camp a few miles
from it. Or perhaps the indefinitely shaggy look of the grounds was
the look it had worn since it was a new plantation in the late
eighteenth century. You know: A weed or two in the sundial, grass
wedging between the marble slabs in the floor of the little Greek
temple summer house, an arm from one of the statues lying in the
tallgrass around the slightly leaning figure of a Greek maiden who
looked at once to be a figure in an old churchyard and of a sort of
whorish *demimonde* of statuary—even a bit obscene, perhaps because
of the hot smell of the earth and the moss on the crumbling *mons
veneris* and the straybees and insects going about their ways of crea-
tion. Obscene not exactly as a Pompeian statute to aid seduction, but
in the same way by suggestion. All the paths which had been graveled
perhaps when the house was built were now spotted with weeds and
rankgrass and their edges blurry as if to say it made little difference
where you walked here, for in a timeless place there is no direction.

Except for two or three, the quarters—little whitewashed brick
cabins made of the same brick and whitewash as the house—were
empty. Nevertheless the two or three of some twenty, which sat in

two long rows some distance behind the big house, still gave the quarters a beating heart. The cabins glared in the sunlight; and the street between them was tightpacked loam—no grass. One day I saw a little black girl and boy making a little cabin out of sticks on the ground beside a white stone stoop.

Now, sir, Wagnal said, I'm not one to sentimentalize about the old darkies singing and the Swanee river, for I have heard no darkies sing ever except in minstrelshows, and the Swanee river I never saw— moreover, if there is such a stream, it is no doubt finicking and footling and used for nothing but sewage disposal. But even now I think of the negro quarters of that plantation; their abeyance in the sunlight, their simple peace at noon, their solidarity and laughter. Everything was there for man: food, drink, shelter and not a jot of responsibility, except to the earth.

The stables and the carriage house were long and low. There was an old colonial carriage and some rotten horse furniture—saddles, and saddlebags, antique saddleholsters and blankets—and the three horses. But it was unusual enough at that time in sixty-three to find even three horses in the stables of a large plantation. We soon knew, however, the reason—nay the reasons for the animals.

Clint Belton saw the house from the road. I was riding along with him that day: we had been told to guard Messenger's Ferry and given an Ohio battery. Clint had sent them on and told them to make a camp, while he and I sat in the tent of some political brigadier and drank bourbon waiting for Crime and the drummer boy to load up Clint's personal wagon with the supply of Havanas, brandy and whiskey, his uniforms, the pillaged fowling piece, tent and personal commode. By that time Crime and the drummer boy were hardly anything more than batman and bootboy to Clint.

A couple of new arrivals from Iowa, cowlicked yokels, sat in the back of the wagon with primed muskets across their knees, one of them leaning against the colonel's *cabinet,* but both on the alert for a potshot at a Reb. They all began like that. Crime generally let the boys draw straws to see who would guard the colonel's wagon, for, though it was an easy job, no one but a recruit liked it. Now few liked to be near Crime and the drummer boy—and the punishment horses which Crime had now come to be in the habit of carrying in the colonel's wagon, because, more and more, when they were entrusted to the wagon of an ordinary teamster, they were always broken or lost or knocked carefully to pieces and the nails thrown away. No one could ever be charged with these depredations, for there was never any evidence. Teamsters knew that they had forded creeks with stony beds, that their wagons had broken down on hills, that they had been fired on—but they never knew anything of the things that had happened to the Crimean's wooden horses.

So that sultry afternoon we made a procession along the road near Messenger's Ferry: Clint, in fine black jackboots and silver spurs, a bright colonel's frockcoat and a neat felt hat and buck gauntlets, astride his fine horse with his sword clinking against a sabretache. I? Oh, I was a bit of a dog too in those days and looked quite a fellow aboard the Arabian I had picked up in Tennessee. And with the wagon behind a pair of sleek brewer's horses that Crime had commandeered, with Crime and the drummer on the seat and the two yokel rookies dangling their feet from the wagonbox, anyone might have taken us for cavalry staff instead of a colonel of infantry volunteers and a regimental assistant surgeon.

The house was white all right and three stories high, but it stood back from the road in a thick park of liveoaks hung with that moss wherein were hidden the little Greek temple, the sundials and the statue of the Greek maiden with the mossy pubic hair. Oh, it was a big enough house. I should say it had some forty-odd rooms, including the storerooms and lumber-rooms and the roomy waterclosets with candlebrackets, low bookshelves and statuettes of Cloacina. In one doubleyousee there was a rococo piece of goldsmith's work, a ewer, attributed to Cellini and made entirely of small models of male and female genital organs both in states of excitation and repose and in many curious combinations. As I said, Wagnal said, his eyes focussing on the lumberrooms of his brain, the house was big, but it was far back from the road. We should not have seen it, had it not been for the fact that it was early afternoon and the sun glared in broken shafts on the white brick and the marble columns.

A Southern mansion, I said. Clint looked—nay, sniffed the air and looked. Ah! he said. Ah, yes! He took an Irish linen handkerchief—newly washed by Crime—from the tailpocket of his frockcoat, and—we had drawn our horses up in the shade of a roadside oak—carefully wiped his face and hands and the inner band of his hat free from sweat. I merely sat sweating on my horse. No handkerchief, Thomas? I understood then: I wiped my face and buttoned my coat.

By that time the wagon had come up opposite us. Gribble, Clint said to Crime, got that clothes brush handy? Yes, sir, Crime said. Does the colonel wish a brushup, sir? Yes, and be quick, Clint said. He didn't have it handy. It took him five minutes to find it in the tangled stock of the wagon—and Clint had to wipe the sweat from his face and hands all over again. You'll have to get down, sir, Crime said. Can't reach you, sir. His face was almost impassive and servile, but with what I have long since known was a sardonic look, Crime brushed him, wiped his boots with a bit of canvas, polished the horse furniture and the sword and sabretache. And the surgeon, sir? Crime said. Eh? Oh! Clint said. Yes, of course, Gribble—maybe it was Mibble. You should have attended him first. Yes, sir, Crime said. Right you are, sir. He went over my boots and the drummer boy from Indiana grinned down at us from the wagonseat. Clint saw and turned red. I looked away from him at a bumblebee droning through the hot golden air. That all, sir? Crime said to me. That'll do, Clint said. You will go on to the camp and pitch the tent—on a good high spot, mind you! And mind you, look to the floor. Yes, sir, Crime said. The yokels jumped off the wagon and saluted.

Only a little way back from the road were a pair of heavy wrought-iron gates with a device of griffins, lions and crocodiles—perhaps in the manner of Sir Francis Dashwood. They were the sort of thing that millionaires pay exorbitant prices for today. They were partly covered with vines and, though closed, were not locked. Clint leant over and lifted the latch and they swung silently open. Oiled, eh? Clint said. Probably a nest of Secesh. When we looked up inside the gates we saw a little brick lodge or gatehouse, and, spanning out from it and the gate on either side, an unfinished wall. Clint kicked the gatehouse door, but no one answered—and we turned our horses up a dark, gravel drive over which the Spanish moss hung down and showered our hats with vermin. For all the heat it seemed as if we were in an Edinburgh graveyard on a dank cold day. Clint shivered. I felt my sweat turning clammy. We rode on for perhaps half a mile, seeing, for the first time, the garden statuary and the little Greek temple and the blurry pathways, but not a living soul.

We passed what was obviously a family burial ground, a plot full of fantastic statues, wroughtiron fences, box tombs and a mausoleum. At the end the drive widened out and swept into a magnificent semi-circular arc of shining gravel in front of the house.

The porch or piazza or portico must have been seventy feet high. It was supported by six fluted columns of pinkish Carrara marble with Doric capitals. The wooden pediment was painted white. The floor of the porch was of marble flags. The great double doorway was an adaptation of Ionic in white marble with a fine leaded fanlight. A narrow balcony cooped in by a simple wroughtiron rail ran clear across the second story; french windows opened on it.

On the big door there was a wellpolished brass knocker and a bellpull. Clint slammed the knocker and waited while I tied the horses to a ring in the nose of a bronze blackamoor. Nothing happened. Clint slammed the knocker again, then pulled at the bellpull impatiently. We heard a tinkle. Still nothing happened. He took the wroughtiron door handle in his hand; it turned smoothly and both doors swung back. We stood looking into a blinding glare from a rectangle of light perhaps some eighty feet in front of us. It was thus that we did not immediately see the hallway or the great curving staircase. We were looking through what is commonly known as the dogrun of a Southern plantation house, but in that whimsical piece of bastard housebuilding, it was more of an arcade. After all, Clint, I said privacy—Privacy be damned, Clint said. It may be a nest of Secesh spies. A bloody big nest, I said.

And a pair of bloody intruders, a light, sweet voice said from above us. Well, gentlemen, the voice went on in a pleasant satiric tone, as our romantic novelists say, to what do I owe the honor of your unexpected visit? As the irises of our eyes expanded again we looked up, blinking over the curved baluster of the great staircase. She was dressed in blue silk, full without hoops—a slender girl of perhaps fifteen or sixteen but mature. Oh, well past puberty all right. Twirls of dark hair seemed stirring all around her small featured, always animated face—and the smile was amused and satiric. She was tapping her skirt lightcavalrywise with a riding crop. Will you remove your hats, gentlemen, and sit down?

We stood there shivering a little in the dark hallway, for we had cooled in the ride through the damp shaded park—indeed, compared to the sun of the hot road, the hall seemed chilly. And such meetings are always strange, Wagnal said. You got her scent, you felt her presence.

Consider, sir, that here were two men who had ceased to be semisedentary men in the professions and become campers-out in a land of miasma and rickets—become monitors in a great mob of child campers-out which had been rather foolishly trusted with firearms. Consider also, sir, that Shiloh was not yet neatly filed away in our memory and that the women we had seen had been the underbred poorwhites of Southern villages, negro wenches of varied shades, campfollowers and a few Southern Ladies who were, at best, poured into the same mould of swooning shallowness and strong predatory cunning. Consider these facts, sir, when I tell you that Katherine Theron and her sister, Una (whom we had not yet encountered), were the most extraordinary—shall we say the most fascinating pair of women I have met in my lifetime. They were not Southern Ladies. Oh, no! They remind me of all the wilful, dashing, malicious, perverse, intelligent handsome overbred women I have ever seen or read about in novels. I often think, sir, of the women between the lines of poor Jane Austen and the Brontë sisters and the poor incomplete girls of dear Miss Alcott—there, sir, are women—is woman—and however obscured the pictures are, by protective coloring, of the female, they are there. Even as Katherine stood on the steps that afternoon, I thought of her as making Jane Austen's remark about sonnets as antidotes for love.

She was smiling a little smile (for she could not, because of the smallness and fineness of her features, smile a big smile—though she had moments of heartiness and gusto)—shall we say it was a little grin, impudent and insolent at once, as we—the smartest colonel of volunteers in the Army of Tennessee and a regimental surgeon who was, though I say it myself, far from the run-of-the-mine country sawbones who served in the yokel regiments—stood as if we were the greatest of oafs, hats on, mouths a little ajar, staring confounded at a fifteen-year-old child who looked as if she might have danced at Almack's in London with Brummell, who watched us with wicked contemptuous delight, making us all thumbs and oxdumb.

Clint took off his hat with a clumsy sweep at which she gave a light chuckle that rustled up a dimple into her cheek and narrowed her small dark blue eyes into slits. This gave the impression that she was in the throes of a paroxysm of silent but gloating laughter. Clint blushed and tried to draw himself up and stand on his political and military dignity. I took my hat off quickly and stood still. My dear young lady, Clint said, in as good a colonel-lawyer voice as he could muster, this is an official call. We wish to see the master of the house.

She laughed again. And, gentlemen, she said, I've no doubt that he would be amused to see you. Well, Madam? (he did not call her young woman) Clint said. Come, come, General, she said, sobering her face slyly, and coming down the rest of the wide steps—she was a small woman, mind you—more stately than a great actress playing a great queen. Colonel, Madam, Colonel Belton of the Hundred and Seventeenth Iowa Volunteers, Clint said clumsily.

Iowa? she said. That's somewhere in the great west, isn't it? Madam, we wish to see the master, Clint said rudely. Sir, the girl said coldly, you will remember your manners, or I shall call my servants and have you thrown out. Or better still whip you to the gates with my crop—she fingered it lovingly— And take your hand off that silly bludgeon in your scabbard. You know quite well you couldn't touch a lady with cold steel, sir. This time she allowed herself a short light peal of laughter. Come, Clint, I said. Let us go.

Colonel, she said, do present me to your fellow officer. I beg your pardon, Madam, Clint said. Mrs.—Miss, she said. Miss—Clint said. Theron, she said. Miss Theron, Clint said, Lieutenant Wagnal, regimental surgeon of the Hundred and Seventeenth Iowa. Charmed and enchanted, Lieutenant Wagnal, she said in a most pleasant but sarcastic voice. And I, Miss Theron, am overwhelmed. It was plain to see, Doctor, she said. But how glad I am you are here. Percy's ill. I assure you, Miss Theron, if I can help, I shall be very glad to, I said. I'll take you to him now, she said. Will you come, Colonel, or will you amuse yourself here? There are books in there and decanters—brandy and *liqueurs*. She indicated a door with a toss of her head. But Miss Theron, if you don't mind, the master—I am as much master here as anyone, Colonel. Both my father and grandfather are away. My sister and I will talk to you presently. In the meantime, the surgeon has consented to see Percy—and that is most important.

I followed her out into the sunny clearing behind the house to my first view of the quarters, where I had the phantasy of peace for the first time. A few bright insects gauzed the afternoon air and dustmotes and spidersilk floated on the breezeless space. We stopped in front of the low stables, and the girl opened the door of a big boxstall. A handsome black stallion lay moping on the straw. Percy, darling, she said and put a hand in his forelock and one on his nose. Fever, she said. She stroked him while I felt his nose. He tried to bite me, but she paid no attention. Can you do anything, Doctor?

You must do something. He was taken ill this morning: he refused his favorite fence. She wasn't pleading. She was telling me what I had to do—and no foolishness. I never knew what was wrong with the stallion, but I went round the house to my saddlebags and got about twenty grains of calomel. She got it down him—I didn't. She shoved her arm clear down his throat. As it turned out the stallion recovered—and I became her friend.

She looked like Sir Joshua Reynolds's The Age of Innocence, but she was far from anything so nambypamby as that. If anything happens to Percy, she said, I'll kill you myself—and I'll love killing you. She smiled, but she would have done it. She rose from her squat beside the stallion and with bits of straw clinging to the blue silk of the bustle and the full skirt walked slowly out of the stable, never mincing a step.

In the library, which smelled of the calf and morocco and levant bindings that crammed all four walls to the ceiling and brandy and *liqueurs,* Clint was standing theatrically in front of a high gravestone mantelpiece which was carved with the same griffins, lions and crocodiles that we had seen on the gate. A tall girl sat straight but easily in an Elizabethan chair. Clint had a small Venetian glass with brandy in it in his hand; and the tall girl in the chair was rolling another of the same kind between her long fingers. Mind you that was Eighteen sixty-three in the South, where such a sharing of drink with the men was considered only a step removed from harlotry. I looked at the girl in the chair and saw that she had the same warm coloring as Katherine, but that her features were larger—but not large—and more angular—and that her warmth ended with the coloring.

Colonel Belton of the umpteenth Iowa, this is my sister, Miss Una Theron. Una, sweet, this is Colonel Belton. The Colonel and I have introduced each other, Kitty dear, Una said coldly. But—she looked at me. Oh, Katherine said, Lieutenant Wagnal, regimental surgeon, my sister, Miss Una Theron. How do you do, Doctor. How's your precious beast, Percy? Beast? Clint said. A skittish and dangerous stallion, my grandfather gave her in the spirit of malice, Una said. A horse? Clint said. I didn't know you were a vet, Thomas, he grinned. The horse, Katherine said, is a thoroughbred, Colonel—a creature of sensitivity and beauty. He's a mean-tempered villain, Una said. A murderous hack. Wild. My sister, Una, likes them docile so they won't disarrange her precious *toilettes*. She wears a Worth gown and a diamond tiara to

dinner in this godforsaken swamp even when there are no guests.
Katherine! Una said sharply. Please do not show off before these
gentlemen. Then do not patronize me—nor Percy. As for gentlemen,
they're damned Yankees from the Iowa Territory. Iowa is a state,
Madam, Clint said, drawing himself up like a senator. Is it? Katherine
said. Well, Colonel, so is Mississippi, but it's a dull and pokey hole
and I hate it. So does Sister Una, if the truth was known. We've
only three horses left--and the damned palateless soldiers have raped
the winecellar. They swilled *Bénédictine* and *fine champagne* in the
same gulps with that nasty moonshine Papa had for the negroes. And
they took our ham and the cheese he brought from France on the
last trip home. Miss Theron, Clint said, hereafter I shall see to it
personally that our men are kept from foraging here. Oh, Katherine
said, don't bother, Colonel. Besides it's not only your precious Yankee
crusaders, but the Rebels too. Why, I've no doubt that some of
Grandfather's own command have stolen from us.

You must excuse my sister, Una said. She is very young and quite
impulsive. Impulsive! Katherine said. And I had rather be impulsive
than be a coldblooded chunk of vanity such as you—you grow more
like Father every day, selfish and vain— But clever, my dear sister,
Una said, clever enough not to rattle the family skeletons before
strangers. Humph! Katherine said. Pish! Do excuse my impetuous
nature, Colonel, and you Lieutenant. Then, thinking to annoy her
sister, she added formally, You must dine with us, gentlemen, if you
can forego the pleasure of your no doubt convivial campfire. Yes,
gentlemen, Una said, smiling, you must. We must in some way repay
the doctor for his kindness to Katherine's child. Even then Wagnal
said slowly, time all around him, Una had begun.

Katherine only laughed showing her dimple and pulling the little
sliteyes into narrower slits. Her dark hair seemed always to be moving
around her face; and I can still see the childish texture of her skin.
(How tight and smooth young skin is over young flesh, Wagnal said
parenthetically. Why does it always give one the illusion that the mind
of youth is noble—that the person standing under the skin is as beautiful as the skin itself?)

Well, Katherine was standing there with the new yellow straw of
Percy's stall on the blue silk of the great fullskirt and bustle, dangling
a wineglass in her hand, the corners of her mouth denting into the
little rosy shadows of flesh—standing there incredibly small and fine,

sharp and tempered—and also young and lush and passionate as befits a woman. No, Wagnal said, she was never tidy in her appearance. She never dressed elaborately. She was small, but she was a Great Lady who did everything with an air. Oh, much more regal than Una, though Una could have outfaced a duchess. Those two girls could have played ducks and drakes with the designs of any woman. Una was truly evil—though evil, sir, is a word that has many meanings—and Katherine had been tempered at the springs of evil and remained neither good nor evil, but a strange thing in this world, a woman without jealousy of women, but only contempt and sometimes pity.

Una got up and pulled a longmusty tapestry bell-pull; and after a few minutes' wait, a gigantic black man in black satin knee breeches, a bottlegreen tailcoat with lace in the cuffs, walked into the room with solemn clumsiness, stopped and bowed. Rass, Una said, these gentlemen are dining with us. Show them up to the suite on Mr. Fulke's side. And Rass, Katherine said, see that the gentlemen have a hot bath and clean linen, if they wish. Turn back the bed in case they should want a nap. Rass bowed from the waist to each of them in turn, stiffly and ludicrously. Shall I rub the gentlemen, Miss Katherine? Come, Rass! Una said. You may, Katherine said, if the gentlemen wish it. Oh, Una said, to Clint, he's Father's. He used to travel with Father. He was at Balliol with Father. He was everywhere with Father, Katherine's voice broke in, and Father had him taught massage. A Swede in Paris. So that when Father drank too much— Katherine! Una said. Katherine smiled. Well, so you see, gentlemen, if you have any kinks or headaches, Rass will rub them out.

Follow me, gentlemen, Rass said. He had no negroid accent, but spoke as if he were a young Regency fop. In fact he minced his speech and drawled out certain words, making me feel—and Clint must have felt the same—as if we were provincials and crude. Then for the first time, I began to be aware of one of the things which had made the two girls seem unlike any Southern Ladies we had seen. They had hardly any Southern accent on their tongues, but spoke the same English that the servant spoke.

He led us up the wide curving staircase, the full three stories of the house, and opened the double rooms of a large sitting-room or study type of room. It was filled with leather easy chairs, leather ottomans, a great stone fireplace with iron andirons made in the shape of the same crocodiles, a rack of churchwarden pipes, big blue tobacco jars, a display group of Damascus scimitars—and again the walls were lined with books: great folios, quartos, octavos, bound manuscripts. Two more sets of double doors opened out of this room; and the negro opened them into great bedrooms.

Whichever you wish, gentlemen. They are much the same. I started for one of the rooms, and he followed me.

He pulled the long tapestry drapes and let in the light. Then he opened some wroughtiron framed casement windows and let in the air as he knelt on a leather covered windowseat. I looked out into the damp park through which Clint and I had ridden.

Here and there, pointing up the darkgreen afternoon secrecy of a forest, the gray or pinkwhite of the statuary peeped up at me behind the glare of the sun which fell on the gravel driveway. I turned blinking to Clint who stood, impatient, but fixed and fascinated, in the doorway. We both looked at the bed which was perhaps mahogany and five feet high with an empty canopyframe almost touching the high ceiling. It was carved with a good many coats of arms and had a patina of age. Beside it stood a strong little stepladder of the same wood. There were a fireplace, more books, leather chairs, and a cellarette of full decanters. Two doors, one padded with leather, led off somewhere from this room. Rass opened the padded one and showed us a spacious watercloset. The stoolbowl was made of figured pottery with the griffon, lion and crocodile device on it. The seat was shaped like an English saddle and covered with well-seasoned padded cordovan leather. Along the wall within easy reaching distance was a shelf of books and above the stool hung a bracket of glass-shaded candles. On top of the bookshelf sat the ewer attributed to Cellini, holding matches and an old flintlock powdertester.

Above, on the high wall, a semi-cylindrical pottery container rested on a pipe which led down to the stool.

Rass lighted the candles. The bath, he said, nodding at the other door, is there, sir. Now I shall look after the other gentleman and fetch your hot water, sir. He led Clint to the doors at the other side of the sitting-room. I, you may be sure, closed the door and sat down on the saddle of that watercloset with the most sensuous pleasure I had had in months of campaigning—with, indeed, the most sensuous pleasure I have ever had in relieving myself. As I sat down, I saw that, on one of the bookshelves, there was a tall pile of thin soft Japanese paper—and when I had finished, I discovered how to move the lever which held the water in the cylinder on the wall. It flushed as well as any modern stool I have ever seen. And as I went out toward the bath that Rass had filled for me, I saw the obscene little statue of Cloacina sitting in a wall niche.

The blackamoor had laid out a set of Irish linen underwear, a French linen shirt and a pair of socks on one of the chairs. Will you have a rub, sir? he asked. No thank you, I said. And is there anything else, sir? I told him no. He was still bowing when Clint broke through the door with the paper in his hands.

He held it up with a self-righteous expression on his face. Vicksburg *Sun,* the paper said, May 4, 1861. There, Clint said. There! What'd I tell you! A nest of Rebels. LIBERAL PATRIOTISM, the headline read. Col. Fulke Theron, a citizen of Warner County, has contributed $15,000 to uniform and equip our volunteer companies, and says that his whole estate, worth $5,000,000, if necessary, will be expended to maintain Southern rights, honor, and independence. This is what we call showing a man's "faith by his works." There are a number of others in our midst who will do likewise—and it went on for another paragraph about the patriots of the South, ending by saying that Col. Theron had been elected colonel of some Mississippi regiment and that the colonel's personal company had special shakos and pipeclay belts— And, Wagnal said, so help me God, the colonel had been an officer with Wellington at Waterloo.

Well? Clint said. But what did you expect, Clint? I said. This is a war. I know, Clint said,—but fifteen thousand dollars and this plantation and God knows how much more. The man's dangerous. He folded up the paper and put it in his pocket. I'll report this, he said. He did all right. He always bore all the tales he could to the right quarter. He had his eye on the White House even then, and he would have got there if it hadn't been for Una Theron—or perhaps he wouldn't have got as far along the way if it hadn't been for Una Theron.

And, my God, Thomas, he said, what a house! Have you got a privy like mine? The man who built this is not right. Clint tapped his head sententiously. He's a menace. He paced up and down the room like an actor playing a statesman. And that lovely daughter—that beautiful girl. Daughter? I said. Granddaughter! Even a subaltern at Waterloo would be crowding seventy. Eh? Clint said. Oh! He didn't say any more, but went into the other bedroom.

I pulled a copy of Hazlitt's *Liber Amoris* from the shelf and sat down in the living-room. *Liber Amoris,* or the *New Pygmalion,* the title page said and there was a little engraved picture of Sarah Walker, the serving-maid on it. When he came out to go downstairs, he had clean linen on. Didn't you change your shirt? he said. No, I said, I didn't want to— Impose, eh? he said. Well, my boy, this is war. And, by God, I must get a masseur like this fellow.

Rass lit the candles in the wallbrackets of the living-room and said: The ladies send their compliments, gentlemen, and they will receive you in the drawing-room at your pleasure, sirs.

Through the casement windows at the sides of the staircase I saw the air was filled with a bloodred dusk such as I have never seen before or after in my life—and, at one turn in the grandiose curve a window looked out on the park. I could see nothing but a dark green broth blotched with a few spots of stonegray. A cannon boomed and thumped somewhere on the Big Black river and some dogs yelped and howled. Perhaps it was Rome and the Ohio battery. I saw a stirring in the dark broth of the park and knew that a hot nightwind had risen and was blowing over the little Greek summerhouse and the broken statues and the burial ground.

For a moment at least, the house was empty and lifeless, stagnant as the ruins of the Parthenon, or some deserted and ruined Mayan temple full of nothing but lizards and the stone signatures of the long dead. Clint seemed to feel something, for, as we rounded the turn, and came into the blaze of candlelight that flowed up the stairway from the great crystal chandelier full of aromatic candles, I saw a perplexed, dumb look on his face. In their delicate glass chimneys the candles sputtered and flickered, making our shadows, which had never been cast on that staircase before, seem ancient and irrelevant to their casters. And as the faint hot current of the burning wax—how they still had wax candles in July, sixty-three, I never knew—came up with the light in our faces, I saw Clint's face in a light more evil than those in which Rembrandt painted his beggars. And I suddenly realized that he was jingling. Your sword and pistol? I said. I want them handy, Clint said.

Looking down on a beautiful woman in hoopskirts from a great staircase by candlelight is a sensual pleasure, sir, that few men but motion picture directors and sensitive travelers in the galleries of Union Stations have ever had these days—but looking down on Katherine

Theron in a pale blue lownecked gown, it all spread out about her like the petals of a dark-stamened flower, is a sight that few men will ever equal. We saw her come into the hall, the big skirt twirling and swaying about her. She walked quickly to the foot of the staircase before she looked up.

Good evening, gentlemen, she said, narrowing her sliteyes with a smile. I was about to fetch you. Sister and I have broken out some of the Amontillado sherry which has lain concealed from the brave soldiers for two years. Come into the drawing-room for your apéritif? Why, Colonel, you're armed? Really, sir, with only a pair of defenseless ladies— She laughed. Clint was all thumbs again. I only brought them down, Clint said. I thought— Here, Katherine said, give them to me. You can't eat in that harness.

Clint blushed as he took them off and handed them to the girl, who tossed them across the newel post of the staircase and dragged the heavy sword from its scabbard with a gritting sound. The blade was covered with rusty stains and sticky in the bloodgutters, for Clint, in his vanity, had not wiped it since Shiloh. Oh, Colonel, Katherine said lightly, wrinkling her nose a little, how brave you are! But it's a very clumsy weapon, she said, coming to the salute in foils' play. Give me a rapier any day. We have some fine ones here. I'll show you after dinner.

The cutglass chandelier in the downstairs drawing-room swung low from a false ceiling that was some feet lower than the hall. Though the French windows were open to the piazza and a clammy breeze stirred some tapestries of scenes at some court on the walls (Katherine said after the fire that they were Gobelins) the room was hot, close and chilly at once as if it were in the throes of a tropical fever. Though it was long, it was not very broad and had a striking character of intimacy, as they say of big theatres which create the illusion of the spectator sitting with the performers. It was Louis XIV for the most part, I believe, all gilt and color and spindly chairlegs with a few bright sentimental landscapes and the pretty portrait of an arrogantfaced young woman—all framed in ornamental gilt. There were several mirrors, large and small, a harpsichord with scenes of the *noblesse* pointing a minuet in a stiff formal woods painted upon it, and a good bit of ornamental china and bric-a-brac scattered around. Katherine led us in to Una, who was watching Rass set a tray of decanters and glasses on a small round marbletopped table. The big black, grotesque enough, with his kneebreeks and bottlegreen tailcoat, in the lofty rooms of the house where he had space to match him, looked like some servile and ill-at-ease Othello serving to Desdemonas to whom he could only bow and say: Shall I fetch the brandy, Miss? Yes, Miss. Thank you, Miss.

Una was dressed in a gown of dark wine which displayed as much breast as possible without showing the paps themselves. She wore a necklace of rubies. She had a fan in her hand; and she stood, I suppose, as queens have wished they could stand, before us. Sherry? she said. We managed to save this Amontillado. It's quite passable. The black poured—with all the ceremony of a famous *sommelier*—the sherry and passed it on a gold tray. Clint stood pretending to savor it more than he did, all the time looking almost lecherously at Una's breasts. Katherine, her eyes slitted tightly again, glanced from one to the other and then to me, her insolent, disdainful little face charged with suppressed laughter. I turned my eyes away, and she smiled and chuckled. Una had met Clint's ardent lechereye with a cold, provoking look of power—a taunt.

Strange, Wagnal said, strange how I can remember how that room felt that night. For I have felt it again and again—many times. With the windows open to the park and the forestrustle coming in and a large moth—like the one in the cabin on the Landing—fluttering around the hot chandelier, fluttering a huge shadow over the bright colors of the room and the things in the room standing as if they had been shut away from humans for a long time, or as if they had been roped off with ornamental plush ropes in a museum where they could be watched only. Katherine saw my eyes moving around the room curiously. It was, she said, a whim of my great uncle's, who built this house, he had a fondness which was, in a sense, French—she looked at the pretty painting. At least it was half New Orleans French—there was a lovely yellow shade in her that the artist, who was a good colorist but a proslavery man, chose to do an injustice. Katherine! Una said coldly.

Yes, dear Sister? Katherine said. Oh! I believe it was—still is for that matter—quite fashionable in New Orleans. They have a ball or something—and charade weddings.

Now, Una said to Clint, pray Colonel, tell me again how you repulsed the Louisiana Grays regiment with that one Napoleon. I do so admire tales of heroism. Clint coughed and I did not look his way

—but I was younger then and I felt myself turning red and found that when I was again cogent my eyes were focussed on the painted harpsichord. Do you play? I said fatuously to Katherine. With one finger, she said, and it's out of tune—but what fun.

We walked over to the little instrument which stood beside an ornamental screen, and, as she sat down, I thought of the screenscenes of Restoration comedy and all the cruel cold Wit of the World. Wagnal seemed to capitalize the words as if he were speaking a Restoration prologue himself. Katherine, he said, twanged out a light fast merry little tune and wagged her head delightedly. Something like Ha! Ha! Ha! You and Me! She sang some words to it that I can't remember. I could see Clint talking to Una, and Una leaning forward in simulation of intense interest. And as I looked I smelt the faint clean lavender that Katherine had scented herself with and I heard the candles sputter a little above us in the chandelier.

Already I had begun to feel sticky in the little room. Let us, I said to Katherine, have a breath of air before dinner. I know, she said, this room is hardly bearable in the summer, but Una likes it. She thinks it sets her off. But outside at night in the summertime it's almost like the grave, and there are lights hovering in the park over that old burial ground. No negro but Rass would ever venture near the park at night. And Messalina's—our cook's—mother who has no name but Mammy says it's full of spirits. Uncle and the woman in the picture are buried in the burial ground. I'll show you the graves sometime—but let us not go out tonight.

Dinner is served, Miss Una, Rass said. He was standing in a double door; and beyond him we could see a heavy silvergleam on a dark table. Grandfather told me, Katherine said, that there was a tobacconist's daughter at Oxford who thought that Rass was an African prince up at Trinity. She was a terrible, milkypretty thing with insipid blue eyes like one of those girls that man Dickens writes about. Rass never told her he wasn't a prince; and the undergraduates at Balliol said there was a black baby with blue eyes and golden hair. Grandfather said it cost him five hundred pounds, but he thought the laugh was worth it —though he said that he'd be damned if he owed the girl anything. For after all, the little black was at least half his. If the mother wanted it, he really ought to have made her buy out his interest.

She told me this in a low voice as we loitered after Clint and Una into the dining-room where the ceiling was high and beamed with carved beams. This is the great hall of the castle, Katherine said. Grand-father had dogs lying on the floor for the bones, but he took them with him. Dinner is not elaborate, Una said. Sumptuous, Clint said. Fit for a king. Or a colonel, Una said, smiling coldly. Katherine looked at me squarely and again the about-to-laugh expression rippled over her face as if she had said: Oh my God! Do my ears deceive me?

It was good to come into the high room after the French drawing room which smelled like a woman too heavily scented and too delicate and nervous. Nevertheless, there was a tenseness in the dining room. The grub was excellent: a great ham, spiced and seasoned, all stuck with cloves and bathed in wine; chicken brown and crisp; a rice curry such as I have never eaten before or after; and yams, a garden salad, a sweet with a light winey crust and a heavy inside—all of it seemed cooked in a way that was peculiar to the house. The wine was a still burgundy, not too heavy. Rass served it all as unobtrusively and easily as a ghost. No; it was not too heavy for the hot night. It was not that at all. For the meal was far from phlegmatic, having been cooked with a touch.

It was the scene, the circumstances, the big house off the track of civilization—of, shall we say, light and air and sunlight. It was Clint Belton fawning upon Una; Katherine sitting—though perfectly poised —like a wilful child, a bored queen of Egypt at the table. And it was Una, who was already planning the evolution of an imperial purpose to satisfy the cold perfect pattern of her geometric vanity. The war? Tiresome, Una said. If only the soldiers would leave us alone. You may count upon the Union soldiers leaving you alone—and *I think,* the Rebels, Clint said.

I'm sure it was a Rebel who killed the mastiff grandfather left us, Katherine said, frowning like fire. And he was beautiful. A great hulk, Una said. He tore a Worth gown trying to hug her, Katherine said. He liked her face. She smiled, the fire leaving her face for a moment.

Well, Clint said, you may count on protection now. I'll send a guard— And have the guard steal us blind, Katherine said. Rass can protect us. Can't you, Rass? Rass bent forward from the waist in a silent and profound bow and smiled tenderly—the only time I ever saw him smile. How civil of you, Una said to Clint. We accept. The heavy silver English candelabra flickered out soft lights and the candle-wax ran down into the cups.

Now I know that Clint sat there weaving the things that he and

Una would do after the war; how he would walk her and drive her and promenade her in theatres and at receptions before the pothouse political senators in Washington who had been the political brigadiers of the Army of Tennessee. He knew how she would arouse the covetousness and lechery of a thousand men who had smacked palateless mouths over his (now modest) brandy and Havanas in the tents from Shiloh to Columbia, South Carolina.

We'll leave you now, gentlemen, Una said. Coffee will be in the drawing room. Oh come, Katherine said, let us have brandy with them. Come, Kitty, Una said, using the pet name with faint derision. Stiff, Katherine said. Bloody stiff! Like dear Vicky. Oh well. She got up smiling and left Clint and me to the brandy. Rass brought cigars that made Clint's Havanas mere weeds. We have port, Gentlemen, he said, but it is not too good. I do not recommend it. The colonel would never drink it. No thank you, Clint said as if he were a judge. Then he appeared to think a moment, and turning his fine Greek statue beard to the negro said: And what do you think, Rass? How would you like to be free? What do you think of President Lincoln? I have nothing against President Lincoln, sir, Rass said. He seems honest—but I am a free negro already, I have been legally free for ten years. Now in France —but I beg your pardon, sir. Ah! Clint said fatly. Ah, yes! He picked up his brandy and awkwardly sniffed at it. A fine bouquet, he said to me. Rass walked out silently.

To think of Miss Una, he said, his eye glittering, at the mercy of that big overeducated blackamoor. And Katherine, for that matter, I said. Eh? Oh! he said. But there's no danger; he's been their dog since he was a youth—he loves them. There's a trust between them, I said.

Yes, Clint said. By God, he's a big, handsome bucknigger, isn't he, Thomas? Biggest buck I ever saw. I'll bet the old man used him for a stallion. What a stud fee he would command. You know, Thomas, I can't understand the kind of a man who would go off to war and leave those two girls here—especially as lovely a woman as Una. And this house. Why, by God, that statue in that fancy privy upstairs—that Goddamned frippery Louis Quatorze drawing room for a New Orleans Quadroon! I can't understand such a man. He's—they're stark mad. I'll report that piece in the paper and see that Stanton knows— Remember Clint, I said, the lovely Una. But Clint said: It's for her own good.

CHAPTER XII

ALONG the rivers, somewhere in the darkness of the deep South, Wagnal said—and it is deep and dark still, for there are thousands of empty houses down there sitting like the castoff skins of cicadas beside roads that are no longer roads, houses whose people have never been told about, houses long dead but unburied on a battlefield of time and hate and envy and indifference—somewhere there was a little musketry and some fast hoofbeats on a plank road perhaps. Beating up some pickets, Clint said. We'll be in Vicksburg before the month's out. By God—

What ails you, Clint? I said. The shelling, he said. They've ceased firing again. Last night we could see the sky lit up from the mortars. He got up and went to the window of the dining-room. You're looking the wrong way, I said—and besides you couldn't see from here anyway. Too low, too many trees. They're still in their caves and cellars down there, I'll bet, Clint said. The place looks like an open grave. By God, Old Sam made 'em burrow. Ten dollars it's fallen, Thomas. Say, what's the date? The date? I said. Why, let me see—it's the fourth of July. Bully! Clint said. Ten dollars it's fallen. You don't know these people, I said. Twenty it hasn't. Shall we join the ladies?

Katherine was nervously picking at a high key on the harpsichord, and Una was saying: Do shut up, Kitty. Nothing's happened to Grandfather. Nothing could. He's too vicious and contrary. You worry about that old man when I—we haven't heard from Father in months. That vulgar old— Una saw us in the doorway. Ah, Colonel, she said. Coffee will be along. Doctor, Katherine said, the vexed fiery frown coming over her face, there's something wrong tonight, I *feel* it. There are more cannon firing, or perhaps the sky is lighter.

Before I could answer, Clint said with a foxgrin: There are no cannon firing, Miss Theron. I have just laid a wager with the lieutenant that Vicksburg has fallen. That's it, Katherine said. The quiet. That damned rumble and then the quiet. Here, she said, her voice tight and words fast, here, Colonel are weapons. I fetched them in from the armory. On a sofa lay a long sheaf of old rapiers, with gold, silver and jewelled hilts. She whipped one up from the sheaf and quirted it in the air. It sang like a whip. Look, look, Colonel, what can you do with this? She pointed to the half-inch tapestry head of a French court dandy on the sofa back, assumed the on guard, holding the silver hilt lightly, her short fingers almost languid under the engraved figure eight guard of the sword, and lunged. The sharp point punked through the threadbrains of the dandy and out the back of the sofa. Katherine! Una said. This is my furniture, you little— Katherine pulled the rapier from the wounded head and a tuft of hair stuck out the hole where the eyes of the courtier had been. Dead and scalped, Katherine cried and threw down the sword. Dead. Grandfather's dead! Be still, Una said, nothing could kill Grandfather. He's dead all the same, I know it, Katherine said staring at the hole in the sofa, her darkblue eyes wild.

Rass brought in the silver coffee pot and the cups and set them on the marbletopped table. Rass, Katherine said. Rass, saddle Niobe and ride to Grandfather—find Grandfather fast! Yes, Miss Katherine. What shall I say to him? Do nothing of the kind, Rass, Una said. We don't know where he is—

A bell jingled and someone beat upon the front door. Katherine ran out of the room, the big black following fast. Coffee, Colonel? Una said. Cream? Lieutenant? She was smiling with marble disdain. Ah, yes, thank you, Clint said. I was listening for the doors. I heard them and then voices in expostulation: No, somebody was saying, but I'm not— Bring him in here, Rass, Katherine's voice said. We'll soon see.

Katherine came in first, dragging the drummer boy by the ear. He looked pinker and prettier and more sullen than usual. Rass had the Crimean by the scruff of the neck and was bending one arm behind him. Drop it, you bloody bugger! Crime said, trying to reach the British non-com's sword he was wearing in defiance of one of Clint's Special Orders. No bloody nigger's— Sergeant! Clint said, sharply pompous. Colonel, sir, Crime said. Let him ¿ o, Rass, Katherine said. I suppose they're his men. Crime shook himself. The drummer rubbed his ear and scowled. What are you doing here, sir? Clint said. And you? I thought I told you to pitch the tent and make ready. It's pitched, sir— But I've told you never to follow me—and you, young man! But Colonel, sir, Crime said. If the colonel pleases, sir, hi come to tell the colonel the news, sir. Yes? Well, sir? And also, sir, there's another matter— What's the news? Well? Vicksburg's fallen, sir. General Pemberton surrendered last night; and the garrison marched out this afternoon. You owe me twenty, Clint said to me.

But colonel, sir—if the colonel pleases— Una made a move to go Please, Clint said. We'll just step into the hall. Come, boy, he said to the drummer. Katherine and Una and I watched them silently for a moment. Oh, Lieutenant, Clint said from the door. I excused myself and went with them.

Beggin' your pardon, sir, Crime said, they said they was paroled and was bringing the bloody body home. Casualty? Clint said. He wasn't killed in battle, sir—'e was shot in a dool. Come, Mibble, who is he? One Theron, sir, Crime said, a buggering Rebel brigadier. They got 'im on a caisson wrapped up in a blahsted Secesh banner. Dressed like a proper toff 'e is too—pipeclay belts and a bleedin' shiko, like a 'ero with a buggerin' milit'ry hescort. They let them past the regiment? Clint said. Who did it?

Captain 'Anks done it, Crime said. 'E said seein' as 'ow they 'adn't got no weepons but a sabre or two and they'd been paroled, it couldn't do no 'urt to fetch the old gent 'ome—'im bein' dead. Killed in ar haffair dahner 'e was over a lidy. 'E's a 'ero all right. Crime grinned. How the hell do you know, Mibble? Clint said. Straggler come along from Vicksburg and sees the caisson and sez 'e: That's the old fireeater as got plugged in a dool over gittin' inter bed with the wrong wife, aint'y? A young Rebel leftenet pulls out his sword and yells: Shut your filthy Yankee mouth.

How long Katherine had been standing in the doorway of the drawingroom I don't know, but she said: That's Grandfather all right. Her face was stone still, and her voice was low. Go tell them, she said to Crime, to fetch him in. Yes, Miss, Crime said, bowing. At once, she said. Yes, Miss, Crime said backing away as he bowed.

Hadn't you better let us handle this, Miss Theron? Clint said. You could send a servant to make sure. Perhaps it is not your—

Dear Colonel, Katherine said, I knew my grandfather was dead— I know this is my grandfather by the way he died. I'll tell my sister. Una was coming through the door with Rass following her. Grandfather's dead, Una, Katherine said. They've brought him home wrapped in a flag. She smiled. He was killed in a duel over a woman.

It must have been an accident, Una said,—I mean his being killed. Yes; it must have been, Katherine said. Rass, fetch the lanterns.

Miss Theron, I cannot allow— Clint said.

Katherine swung open the double doors; and the yellow perfumed light of the candles in the great glass chandelier of the hall flowed over the pink marble slabs of the porch to the edge of the gravel drive. The park remained dark and unpenetrated, until we saw a light swinging in its depth.

Rass had come with two lanterns. Katherine took one from his hand. Come Rass, Katherine said, we'll meet him. She did not hold up her skirt but dragged it down the steps of the piazza, the blue silk, ghastly now in the lanternlight, sweeping a trail in the drive. Rass followed her. The lowswung lanterns pointed up little snowy crystals in the gravel. Their feet plunch-plunched. Katherine held her lantern high; and I could see the Spanish moss hanging, like an inert and poisonous fog, in the damp forest air.

Cold mossfronds brushed my face; and I could feel small things crawling on my skin as we walked toward the light in the park. I could hear the peculiar cumbrous rattle of the caisson and the jingle and creak of the horsesoldiers riding at a walk in the night. After a while we could see them through the cavelike curtain of moss. There were only three of them: one riding the lead horse of the caisson and one on either side of the caisson. Their shoulders were hunched forward—even the man who held the smoky pinetorch did not hold it high.

The hungry cadaverous horses were hardly moving—but all three men had fine smart uniforms (brought in by the father and sold to the grandfather at a handsome profit), only a little dusty. The caisson lumbered to a stop and stiffly one of the men got down from his saddle and walked—with his shoulders thrown back hard—toward us. He halted a pace in front of Katherine and swept off his black plumed shako as if he were a matinee idol. Have I the honah of addressing Mizzus Theron? Katherine was holding the lantern high: before he bowed I could see he had a white lank face that had once been plump with an ill-cultivated set of short whiskers: He looked hungry and nervous and sullen. His black hair was straight and long, and, in the lanternbeam, seemed greased with tallow. As he bowed a sprig of moss brushed his face, but he did not raise a hand. He's my grandfather, Katherine said.

Then I have the honah—the man began all over again. Katherine Theron—Miss, Katherine said. Then, Miz Theron, it is my unpleasant duty to inform you that your grandfather, Brevet Brigadier-General Fulke Theron, died while performing his duty— Yes, Katherine said, his duty to womankind. But, Miz Theron— And to whom have I the honor of speaking, sir? Katherine said. Lieutenant Cady Ocamb, late of the Okalona Rifles, and now—up until today—attached to the staff of General Theron. Well, Lieutenant Ocamb, my sister and I are grateful for you bringing my grandfather home. Will you and your men accept dinner and a rest here? But before we go near the house, tell me what happened.

Miz Theron it was duty— I have already heard, Katherine said. Well, Miz, the Lieutenant said, there is—was—a man at Vicksburg who keeps a gambling house; and Gen'l Theron tried to stop him preying on the soldiers. It was his duty, ma'am— Who was the woman? Katherine said. There was no— Who was she? Katherine said. Well, Miz Theron, there was a female that some said was the gambler's wife. Ah, Katherine said. What was her name? Bonnie, the lieutenant said. Bonnie what? I'm suah I don't know, ma'am. I nevah heard her called anything else. Pretty, I suppose? Well, ma'am, I suppose you would say— I know, Lieutenant Ocamb. Now we'll go to the house—but how was it my grandfather was killed in a duel? They used the gambler's pistols, ma'am; and the one your grandfather had missed fire. Careless! What is this gambler's name? Katherine said. I can truthfully say, ma'am, I nevah knew what his name was. Oh, Katherine said. Who did that? Well, ma'am, I had my own brace of pistols with me and when I saw the charge and priming of your grandfather's weapon— I see, Katherine said. Didn't you exchange cards? Well, ma'am, aftah that pistol bein' found like it was, I didn't really considah that the man even desuhved— Oh, Katherine said.

Except for the creak and lumber and crunch of the caisson and the feet and hooves, there was nothing but silence in a macabre and perambulating ring of light canopied by the shaggy moss trailing from the liveoaks. As we passed what seemed to be the burial ground in the outer ripples of our light, Katherine said suddenly:

Where are the dogs? Dogs? the lieutenant said. Grandfather took two mastiffs to the wars. Oh, Donne and Huhbut, he said. Yes, Donne and Herbert, Katherine said. They were lost, ma'am. Lost? They never get lost. What happened? Well, ma'am, people were hungry in Vicksburg.

Damn you! Katherine said. You didn't eat— No, ma'am, he said. No! Then what in the name of God— Well, ma'am, many of the soldiers weren't buried deep, there bein' nobody to dig much but caves, and—well, the dogs were shot a month ago. The gen'l almost had the man who did it shot himself. Oh, Katherine said. The gen'l had *them* buried deep, Ocamb said.

Una was standing on the porch with the light from the open doors behind her, her perfume all around her in the stagnant air. The couch in the library is ready, she said. As Rass and two soldiers and I were taking him in the red flag flopped back from his face. It had already begun to blacken—like the faces of those boys at Shiloh. But Katherine fell upon it with both her arms and kissed it wildly.

Before Clint and I and Crime and the drummer boy left for camp that night, Rass and I put old Fulke Theron in a long Elizabethan clothes press—and Rass went to the burial ground with a shovel and a lantern.

You could hear the river and see the candleflames in the bayonets licking the nightair, for the men had rolled up the tentwalls in spite of the mosquitoes and bugs. The Ohio battery had a gun unlimbered near a ford; and the cannoneers were playing poker by bayonetlight. Somebody was singing obscene words to Dixie on commissary whiskey.

Rome was in his tent writing to his wife and daughter, Myra, back in Knoxville. A guard had been mounted around the tent which Crime had pitched for Clint—and a guard around Crime's wooden horses. Rome had written only, Vicksburg has fallen, when Clint came to our tent. Gentlemen, Clint said, I want to talk to you. Will you come to my tent and have a drink? Why, yes, Clint, Rome said. And before I forget it, Captain Hanks, I have asked Washington for that majority of yours—and your captaincy, Dr. Wagnal. Why, thank you, Cl— Colonel Belton, Rome said gravely.

Crime had the candles lighted in Clint's tent and the cigars on the table. Brandy, sir? he said as if he were a stage butler. Lend an ear to this, Clint said and began reading an order praising the regiment. Where each performed his duty so well, it would be invidious to particularize, the order said. It mentioned neither Rome nor me and ended with a description of the Theron place, a quotation of the clipping from the Vicksburg sun and a recommendation that the male Theron still alive be prosecuted as a traitor when caught—apprehended, Clint had written.

CHAPTER XIII

WE DIDN'T have as much dysentery and misery and as many rashes as the Rebels had, Wagnal said. And we had houses back home with suits of civilian clothes in them and perhaps a book we hadn't read and the copies of *Harper's Weekly* accumulating fatly week by week in our minds and closets to say nothing of our leftbehind traps and trinkets and the girls we knew and the trees and hitching posts along the streets. We could think of those things and how new they would be to us— and think how easy the life at home would be after sloshing around bayous and swamps and rivers with a bellyache and a hot forehead and the squitters. But *they* could not think that way: they could only lie awake and wonder if the damned Yankees had got to their hometown or their plantation or their cabins and burnt their houses, dosed their mulattoes, put molasses in their pianos, taken their horses and their books and their pictures—and even their women and girls. They could only hope that they wouldn't be turned wrongside out by the bloody flux before they got a minié ball in the gizzard or a decent meal instead of greencorn.

We kept following them and pushing them along a little way at a time. And Old Joe Johnston would turn around and scratch us like a wildcat and slink away. But we never had anything more like Shiloh.

We went home—the whole regiment—in the Spring of sixty-four. The home guard met us at the boat with a brassband. It wasn't like the time we marched down to the levee in St. Louis to go down to Pittsburgh Landing. Oh no; everybody was there—and we marched through the streets with bayonets fixed, proudshabby uniforms brushed and Clint at our head on a black mare which the city gave him riding beside the mayor and waving that black Jeff Davis dresshat that had come down the river for the flag presentation after Shiloh.

Rome's wife and daughter, Myra, came to meet him and stayed until Rome had gone to one of the banquets the city gave for us. Some judge, a Black Republican friend of Clint's who had failed to get a colonelcy, made a redundant speech in the square. It was all about coming back a little weary, not vanquished, not despairing of the Cause, not unwilling to make greater sacrifices for the salvation of Your Country, but coming back battlescarred veterans, brilliant in deeds of heroism. He bore down hard on that; and I saw Sleepy Bates and the toothless boy squaring their shoulders and strutting even as they stood at parade rest. He said we came to rest a little at our own firesides and the bosom of God and our own kith and kin.

Ah, now, Wagnal said, I remember. He swung out an arm and let his voice drop low, the judge. He was the kind of a man that every farmer and housewife in Kansas would call a good talker—just a dandy talker. When he dropped to that low, thrilling, confidential tone, the soldiers, the firemen—lined up with their red hosecarts and their brass-bound engines—the young girls in frilly hoopskirts and ribands and bonnets all felt the cold crawl on their spines and their tear ducts let loose.

I refer to the battle of Shiloh, the Judge said, in which your major, now Colonel Clinton Belton of the Hundred and Seventeenth Ioway Volunteer infantry—a veteran regiment—and we look for him to go much farther both under the glorious flag of our Union as a soldier and under its re-united stars as a statesman—was stricken down after acts of Spartan heroism in which he vanquished nearly singlehanded and with only one cannon the furious attack of a vaunted Rebel regiment of Louisiana Grays.

I could see the set sardonic face of Crime beside Shire Newton who was holding the colors; and I could see Rome look down to the dust in which he stood, before the crowd broke into cheers as the judge's voice gathered volume and thundered to a period. Bates and the tooth-less boy were looking down too. Clint responded as modestly as a young virgin. He talked of our training at Keokuk and how a friend-ship had sprung up between the citizens and the regiment. He thanked the ladies especially for all the kindness they had done us (two soldiers had gone to Shiloh with the clap) and ended by praying God to reward those who had not returned with us for laying down their lives in their Glorious Union's defense. Then I saw him signal Crime, and Crime hand his musket to the drummer boy.

Nah! Crime yelled at us: Three cheers for the good people of Keokuk!

Well, there must have been a good deal of underbreath oaths wasted, for few liked Crime by that time. Everybody knew that the wooden horses were waiting in the wagons parked in Mississippi; and besides there were a good many of us who had bought things in Keokuk for four times the right price before we left. But the regiment cheered. By God, Wagnal said, you can always get a regiment to holler—and most of the lads had their eyes on those girls in the frilly dress and ribands, so all the heroism they could grab was needed toward the tumble in the grass—or maybe even a regular wedding night.

After the cheers for the townspeople, Crime had them yell for the judge and Clint. And then a fire chief, who had two front teeth missing just like the lad in the regiment, crawled up on top of the brassfunnel of the engine and yelled three big cheers and a tiger for the brave boys of the Hundred and Seventeenth Ioway! He lisped; and some of the boys put their fingers on their cartridge-biters and winked. But the crowd yelled: Hooray! Hooray! Hooray! Wheeeeeee!

Clint had the regiment dismissed and went about shaking hands with all the city fathers and the women from the Sanitary Commission and the knitting club women. They were all voters.

Before the banquet, or supper, as they called it, a committee of women came to me and asked me to present Clint with a bouquet of roses, as I was then surgeon of the regiment, and, I suppose, at that time had a voice and a beard as imposing as my frame. I prefer now not to remember the remarks I made about beauty and chivalry—but I can see Clint getting up, the tasseled end of his silk sash dragging over the white tablecloth in the Estes House. His fine sleek curly beard and his Greekgod head and his eye of Mars, calculating and cunning. He paused, took the flowers reverently in his arms and put his face into them and inhaled deeply.

Ladies, he said, I accept these in the name of my—of our—brave men still on active service—and those finally mustered out. I accept with alacrity these lovely tokens from lovely hands, for it is such moments as this that help us to walk into the Valley of the Shadow of Death Down There. I can say no more but that we all thank you from the bottom of our souls—and I am sure that I speak also for those who have answered the last long roll but are, I know, gathered here in spirit.

Clint held a pause—a long one—, Wagnal said, the waitresses in the Estes House didn't dare move—nor did they want to move. For Clint was another of the tribe of men to whom women will listen with awe and remember long and quote much as wise, until, three generations later, his political euphemisms will still be echoing: It's just like Grandma used to say about those that have passed away are gathered here in spirit. Oh, Clint was shrewd: When he finished the pause, he broke the silence softly, his voice almost crooning: And now I'm going to ask a hero to pronounce the benediction, Chaplain John Simpson.

Old Simpson got up and looked around him. Since Shiloh he had been surgeon to another Iowa regiment, for he had had enough of praying impotently. His face was long and dour, with shadows in the creases. It looked like a relief map of the soul of St. Paul. Women used to use his name to frighten their children into obedience. As he rose in the kerosene lamplight of the Estes House, I saw him with the bloody scalpel in his hand and the blackpowder ring around his mouth and the bloodshot eyes under the moth shadow—and I heard the guns of the *Tyler* and *Lexington* on the Tennessee and heard Grant saying, sixteen years. Ah, horses! And then I heard Buell's regiments slish-sloshing up from the Landing. And I remembered how I helped bury Rome's brother in the morning with a tincup and a bayonet. Your great granduncle, boy.

God grant health and sun and peace, Simpson said, to all the wounded. His voice vibrated with something like rage. Almighty God grant that this war will soon be over and that all may go back to their homes. But most of all give us to know the truth without slaughter. Amen.

Now there *was* a pause. You could feel the charge of embarrassment in the air of the Estes House diningroom—feel the disapproval of the women straining at their faces and vocal cords. You could hear the oil-lamps sputter and the foot of a waitress on a creaky board. He had not mentioned Our Great Cause, or the regiment, or the city fathers, or affirmed for God which side He was on. But I could see a good many of the boys thinking, by Jesus, he's right. Ole Simpson's right. It don't make a damn' just so's the thing's over—for it ain't like I thought it was.

I saw Clint nod to the Crimean again, and the Crimean get up and yell: Three cheers for the ladies! There were three for the ladies and three for the colonel and three for the chaplain and three for me and three for General Crocker, who commanded the brigade, and then three for the Army of Tennessee and, finally, three for General Grant. Then someone probably a little drunk started: Yes, we'll rally round the flag, boys! We'll rally once again, shouting the battlecry of freedom!

By the time they had got to, Down with the traitor, up with the star, all the women had joined in and were singing with cruel, determined, righteous looks on their faces. It wasn't any battlecry to the soldiers, but it was to the women. To the soldiers it was just a song with words to roll over their tongues. Down with the traitor might as well have been tiddy-um-dee-dee.

The soldiers who weren't catching the train to go home and take off their shoes and lie still and eat and look at their traps and the streets and their front yards and the hometown girls and the streetlamps and the grocerystore and maybe the books they had not read and some that they had read, strolled out of the Estes house with girls, still humming bits of war songs. Rome and Mrs. Hanks and Myra said goodbye to me; and, as they left, Clint came up to me. Well, Thomas, Clint said, I'm going early on the way back. Way back where? I said. Back South. I'm going to stop in Mississippi—Messenger's Ferry. Are you coming with me? Katherine Theron's young and has much to learn, but the family's an old one and a good one. I don't think she has so much to learn, I said. Ah well, Clint said, not so much style as her sister, but— I beg your pardon, Colonel, I said, she has more. Ah! Clint said. So the fair Katherine has laid siege to your heart, young man? Are you to be my brother-in-law? Perhaps you're to be mine, Clint, I said before I thought. I saw the hard glitter of his eyes under the Jeff Davis hat and heard him say: Well, sir, I am staying here at the Estes House for a few days, and then I shall go to Davenport—and thence to Mississippi. Let me know, Thomas, if I can expect your company.

He walked away quickly as I saw Sleepy Bates coming toward me with a pretty ovalfaced girl in a ruffled, ribboned dress, her mouth red and primped as smalltown girls used to do—and her hand on his arm. My! My! Harold, she was saying. You don't say! It ain't reely so. Sure is, Bates said. Well, I hope you get all those awful Rebels killed good and quick, she said. Oh, they ain't so awful, Bates said. We shoot at *them* too. Yes, she said, but they're reel mean and keep niggers and wanta break up the Union and kill everybody. But you sure whipped 'em, didn't you?

They passed without seeing me and struck out under the big elms and maples which were just budding. The street wasn't paved; and there were stone hitching posts in front of the houses. Everything looked as if men with names had put it there—not as it is now: the paved streets and the electric street lights all made in great quantities by men who have no names but such-and-such, inc. And the quiet trees and the grass saying, we used to be hosts here long ago—but now we're unwelcome guests even in little towns.

Ah, Wagnal said, I didn't much like the wind and the rain in Edinburgh when I was a young medical, but I would go back to that now, if I could be young. For even in Auld Reekie then, you could turn a corner out of a wynd and find a plot of green or a tree that was still a tree. God! You could feel young and green and your thoughts could creep around all the things of the world in an instant and you could love and sing and go into a pub and drink a dozen pints and argue loud and long with Dick Ames.

God help me, boy, I'm old and Katherine is dead and Dick's dead at Savage's Station and Clint Belton's dead in New England and Una caught pneumonia in a topless Worth gown and died in Washington. Here, he said, pouring more whiskey into the communion goblets, have a drink.

So many are dead now that were young. Why, God, there was the young artillery lieutenant from Ohio who got a fleshwound before Atlanta. Young and sharp, with eagle-eyes and a sweet smile. That's what I'm going to do, he said to me when I bandaged his wound. As soon as this is over I'm going to Baltimore and study to be a doctor—and maybe I'm going to Edinburgh. They say that's a good place. Do you know anything about it, Doctor?

There were minié balls clipping the trees all around the end of Peach Tree street. You could hardly hear and it was hot as hell and we were all weary with the heat and sweat and dust—but we two stood there and talked. And I told him about Dick Ames finding Red Mary's corpse that many of us had swyved many's the time and what a beauty she was and how gay and dashing; and all about the middleclass bereaved who bought spring guns and mortsafes for the graves of their smug dead. It's black and smoky and it's raw and it rains like hell, but you'll love it, I said. And he said: By God, Doctor, I can see it now. I think I'll desert now and learn to use a scalpel instead of a spherical case. It's neater. Why, I never saw that boy again—and I never knew his name—but I can still see his face and the brass 45th Ohio on his collar and the mole on his triceps and a garnet ring he wore on the little finger of his right hand and the battledirt in the wrinkles of the cuticle and the dried blood.

I can see it. It is as if I could take time as one takes a telescope and close it tight again, leaving only a little space between the ends. Oh, I can see the boards in the breastworks and the mudcovered wheels of the Napoleons that the Rebels had left behind at the end of Peach Tree street and the springless wagon in the street and the old man with the ox team and the bank with the top off it after the fire. And I can see the morning in a quiet street with trees and white fences, where few, if any, shells had fallen—a street where there were no soldiers lying on the grass, a street that was cool for a few moments before dawn and secret and serene as the streets of a little town in America used to be long ago—not long ago in time, but long ago in some obscurity. There is the antiquity of Greece and Rome and Egypt; and to prove it there are stones that still stand and grasses that grow between them and lizards that lie upon them. But there is the antiquity of little American towns at night that is the antiquity of a wilderness, which is the lone· liness, the secretness, the obscureness of the earth. The little towns were strange at night and every house looked out upon the earth, the grass and trees, that for twenty thousand years had heard no mournful engine whistles, no long trains of freight cars which, at the empty streetends, sound like running water. Every house was closed and there were wooden fences and stone barns and cows and horses sleeping. And in the parks there were wooden bandstands and captured guns from Shiloh or Chickamauga or Chancellorsville or Gettysburg—and later from Cuba. And the towns slept most of the day under the sun or the snow or the rain, but at night they did not really sleep, for their terrible ancientness and obscurity were abroad in the night; and the wind in the trees was a sly ghost wind. And all time was in the houses in the little towns—the houses that had not been built a half a century.

Boy, Wagnal said, everything is strange: You sitting there on that kitchenchair; that wellcut suit you're wearing. Who made it?

A tailor in London. Jermyn street, I said.

God, Wagnal said. A tailor in London. Jermyn street. Is it not strange that you are sitting here in Fork City, Kansas, in a boxcar house, talking to a mad renegade preacher, a foolish old soldier, an anatomist who knew Knox in Edinburgh and walked in Tanner's Close where Burke and Hare, who killed the meat, lived?

Is it not strange that all over Tennessee, Mississippi, Alabama and Georgia are buried pieces of men that I hacked away from them— arms, legs, fingers and toes—even a nose and two left ears. Some I shouldn't have cut off. God, there are men even now living in Des Moines or Keokuk or Salina who wake up at night and think: Jesus Christ it's funny: part of me was buried down on the banks of the Tennessee river in the Spring of 1862. Part of me is already doornail dead, mackerel dead, beef dead, stone dead—bled like a stuck pig. Maybe, by God, the bones are still down there under the dirt, clean and white. *My* armbones and my hand bones. *My* meatless hand and arm that used to have such good hard muscles—that I was so proud and vain of. That I figgered ways to get the girls to feel and ways to let them see. God, it's funny: I've got a hand in Tennessee. I can remember how that saw sounded.

I knew a man once that had a funeral for his arm that they cut off in the hospital and buried it with a head- or would you say an armstone. And there was that Rebel officer who had his leg taken off by a cannonball. He lay there on the stretcher bleeding despite the tourniquet which the surgeon-general of the whole Goddamned Confederate army had put on him. And he said: Here, give me my leg. This here leg's been my friend a good many years. I stood on it a long time and now I'm gonna stand by it. They gave him his leg and he took the poor bloody thing and hugged it to him as he lay there—and they carried him off the battlefield huggin' it to him like it was a baby.

Yes, Wagnal said, it's a strange horrific world and while it hurts it fascinates. One considers too curiously; one gets to think of not only poor Alexander stopping the bungs, but of all the strange things in the world: such as how at night there are so many persons sleeping on the earth's surface, so many two feet above it, and so many fifteen feet above it, and so many any given number of feet above it. And bullets, he said, his old eyes focussing on the dim alley of an obscure thought. Bullets: Hollywood cemetery in Richmond is full of squashed minié balls. Every cemetery in every little town in America has a minié ball in it. Bannerman's Arsenal and Museum in New York City is full of muskets, Napoleon guns and shot-riddled logs from Spottsylvania, Chancellorsville and the Wilderness—and minié balls fired and unfired.

And how many eyes glazed and died looking at these things? And how did the eyes look? What color? What temper? What humor? And what had the eyes beheld in the moment before the smoke, and the ground coming up to meet them? Was it the burning trees all around them in the Wilderness or the rain at Shiloh? And the eyes that lived: after four years *they* said it was the greatest war the world had ever seen. And the eyes were flattered. They went back home to sit and think of it and think around it and carry that minié ball under the scalp or in the thigh. And every little town in America had a post of the Grand Army of the Republic or of the United Confederate Veterans. And they all wore those oldsoldier hats, blue or gray. And every little boy said: My Grandpa was in the Civil War or the War between the States; he's an Old Soldier. Was your Grandpa? And the answer was: Sure, everybody's Grandpa's an Old Soldier. And there were two days one for the North and one for the South when the Old Soldiers marched to the cemeteries of the nation. And when there was a military post near, the commandant sent a firing-squad with breech-loading rifles or a battery of three inch breech-loading cannon. And the Old Soldiers looked at the guns and the metal they threw and said: By Jesus, if we'd a-had them at Gettysburg Pickett wouldn't a-got off Seminary Ridge. By God, if we'd a-had them at Shiloh, Grant would a-been drownded in the Tennessee with his whole Goddamned army. You don't have to chaw them ca'tridges. Oh, they was a few britch-loaders all right, but I never seen none—and don't you fergit it! Many's the mouthful a-powder I got a-bitin' a minnie ca'tridge.

Yes, Lee said aloud, it is strange—damn' strange. He looked at the sonnets with warm, hypnotized eyes. Strange, he said, strangely.

CHAPTER XIV

YES, Wagnal said, I went back to Mississippi early with Clint. For, standing there, that night after the banquet in the Estes house, in the street full of trees and stone hitching posts, and smelling the smell of young girlflesh, and hearing the young girlvoices and the rustle of sweetsummer clothes under the nightwind's rustle in the leaves, and seeing the ovalface with the primpedmouth beside Sleepy Bates in the lamplight, I longed and lusted for Katherine Theron—and I longed for love and loved love; and my heart was wellnigh to bursting because it was so full of the sound of silly girls at night on a smalltown street. Quite pastoral it was and bucolic as a rustic masque, but not in a deca-dent way; there were your Colins and Chloes and Strephons and Cor-nelias, but they were not the decadent people who had appeared in verses like bad tapestry.

They walked through the summer streets with a lust that was as finetextured and elastic as their beautiful young skins—their young breasts and fine long thighs. The stray curling hairs around the girls' eyes and on their Venus' mounts and the golden freckles on their noses and the delectable curves of their throats. Sir, Wagnal said, even now in my senility, the time when a man's passion is said all to be spent, I tell you that I can feel an ache which I can not tell now from the sweet ache that I felt in my youth beneath the trees in Keokuk. *Penis erectu:*

conscientiam non habet—no. He has, sir. For he remembers, with senile and satyric regret, all the girls he did not meet.

I stood under the whispering trees then and saw the pert face of Sleepy Bates's primpmouthed, silly little girl, smelt her as she drifted past and her frilly clothes shook out showers of the near sicksweet lilac perfume on the warm nightair—and in my mind's eye I saw each skirt and underskirt and corset and corsetcover fall to the floor one by one until she stood naked to the navel, nipples and parts before me—smiling and acquiescent and smelling hot as a bitch in heat—and ready for it. And in a moment she was not Bates's girl, but Red Mary in Edinburgh, naked as I had seen her many times in life and finally in death as Dick Ames stood over her with the dissecting knife—and in the end it was Katherine Theron down in Mississippi standing, naked and inviting, on the staircase of the plantation, her dark hair stirring around her satiric little face, her nipples hard and her lips upturned and swollen for a hot kiss.

I walked through the streets of Keokuk for a long time that night, for the moment's soporific peace of the quiet street had left me. I found a woman in the Estes house—a broad country girl, who gave me a rather tasteless ride that finally let me sleep. I had her in my bed for three nights handrunning—but at the end of that week, I told Clint Belton that I would return early to the South and go to Messenger's Ferry with him to visit the Theron girls, if he could arrange an invitation. Clint laughed at that. He reached inside the hot, officer's frockcoat and pulled out a ragged but once fine London envelope.

And, dear Colonel Belton, on your return trip to join your regiment, you must stop to see us. Please bring Lieutenant Wagnal—is it not Captain now? Katherine joins me in hoping you will honor us with a visit. Our father may be with us this summer.

We took—rather Clint took—the Crimean and the drummer boy with him and crawled down to the South, though I suppose the journey was fast enough for those days. The steamboats were full of soldiers going to and from furloughs and whores following them about and sutlers and profiteers—and a few women going to fetch soldiers home from Southern hospitals, or what had been soldiers back to their home earth for burial. And there were delegations of longfaced old sisters from the Sanitary Commission bringing through consignments of lint and bandages. Everybody was hot on the steamboats and trains; and the insects bumped their feelered heads against the hot oil lamps on the walls and ceilings over the aisles. The trains screeched and chattered; and you looked out of the dingy windows with eyes that felt as if they were lined with sandpaper to see passing flatcars full of Napoleons and howitzers and regiments of conscripts in shoddy piling into boxcars.

And you could hear such things as: Yes; at Gettysburg. He was never found. Father went there and went over every inch of the battle-field with a finetooth comb. He even paid a man to dig up a grave, but they was too many in it—and you couldn't of told. Yes; Ma found him: there was a photoguffer making a picture after the battle of Shiloh. He was a-lying there with his arms all out like he was asleep—like he used to lay in the grass by the big tree in the front yard. Even with his eyes closed. Ma waited till the photoguffer was through, and then she said: If you please, sir, I want one of them pictures. That's my boy—right there. Oh, ma'am, I'm sorry, the picture man said. He took Ma's name and address and said, I'll send you one to Ohio direct I git 'em done up ma'am. No. He wouldn't take any pay at all. It was a long time but it come jist the other day—and it looks like he was asleep under the big tree—jist asleep. If the dog was there in the picture, it'd be jist like any day at home when he was a little boy. That's what Harriet said too—the girl he was a-going to marry—jist like he was asleep, like a littlebittovaboy. Ma cut off all the other dead soldiers and burnt 'em up. Some of them was swollen so bad from the sun. She said, if *they* ain't there, I can think of him asleep peaceful-like under the tree like when he was a littlebittovaboy.

I remember the girl who said that after all these years—she was in the same coach with me for ten hours. I never spoke to her—but she was a beautiful whiteskinned girl in a pokebonnet. She looked at me once or twice, long and soft. And I loved her and strained forward in my seat to get to Mississippi the sooner.

As we traveled Southward, Wagnal said, the old stink of soldiers rose up again in the steamboats and cars. Having been on furlough, we had had our nostrils blown out with the clean air of Iowa. Now we were returned to a land where even in the open and miles from where the human hunt was going on—a land miles from where any shot had been fired—you might suddenly smell the track of war. The sweat and urine spoor of long marched-in uniforms and the foxden smell of soldiers whose very ears had begun to sharpen up to points—whose motions had taken on the aspects of cunning economy which one sees in carnivores.

We went by train to Corinth, Wagnal said. We thought it would be quicker—and Clint said he had to execute a government commission there. It was a government commission all right: It was to deliver a pass to get some cotton through the lines to a New England mill. The cotton was bought under the name of a Belton cousin, a war department clerk in Washington. I found this out by chance—standing outside a window of the Tishomingo hotel as the two were eating. And later, Crime, who was privy to the manipulation (not by design of course, but by virtue of his sly pocket-Machiavellian nature) dropped me a hint. For he had begun even in sixty-two to cultivate a petty hold over Clint. He began to know too much about Clint at Pittsburgh Landing, having been his wardheeler, so to speak, throughout the regiment. From that time on he continued to gather information, like a packrat, about Clint's actions. I believe he knew about the minutes under the bluff at Shiloh. He began to know so much that Clint grew incautious about him.

Well, Crime saw that this little deal in cotton was a pretty careless thing for an ambitious colonel of volunteers to be conniving at in the summer of sixty-four when he was waiting to be commissioned brigadier and he told Clint what he thought of it. Clint always listened to Crime. That was one thing about Clint: he could recognize wisdom and use it to his advantage. With twenty dollars, Colonel, sir, Crime said, the colonel can get mentioned in the dispatches—after the cotton has gone through and the pass destroyed. It was at Atlanta that he got that particular mention in the dispatches. I shall tell you of it presently. It was at Atlanta that he became Brigadier-General Clinton Belton; it was at Atlanta that Rome and I found poor Sleepy Bates dead of a bullet in his back in a place where there had not yet been any fighting on both sides of the breastworks as there was in many places that day.

Clint finished the business with the cotton man and came out on the veranda of the Tishomingo hotel just before dusk. Crime and the drummer boy—dismissed after serving dinner to Clint and his guest—were walking along the loose rusty rails of the Mobile & Ohio; a wilderness of empty porkbarrels and mealsacks lay in a jumble beside the little station across the road from the hotel; an old negro, who had come from Africa in the late eighteenth century prodded a single scrawny ox, yoked to an old empty springless wagon, through the powdery dust. The ribs of the beast made deep slashshadows on his sides.

Above Clint and me, the wooden upperdeck of the veranda of the

Tishomingo hotel sagged wearily. A rickety poorwhite, his barefeet
gray with dust, sneaked past. The tavernkeeper, a fat man in a dirty
yellow brocaded silk waistcoat, stood in the doorway fanning himself
with a copy of a last year's New York *Tribune*: Vicksburg Has Fall,
a headline said, a tear holding the statement in suspension. That was
only last year—only last year, the day I had first seen Katherine Theron
—but it was an ancient newspaper, ancient as some hieroglyphics in a
tomb at Gizeh. And even then—that was back in sixty-four, boy, Wagnal said in a fiercedeep voice—the damned Tishomingo hotel was old,
then the town was dying, a town that was grandiosely named, by some
pompous men in shabby frockcoats with a little classical-romantic learning, after an old Greek city rapacious and cunning and, but for seven
broken Doric columns and a fragment of a pediment, dead. Corinth,
Mississippi, Wagnal said, his voice deepening and quietening—Athens,
Corinth, Thebes, and a thousand other little towns in the South named
out of Classical Literature. And tens of thousands of Greek columns
holding up the wooden pediments of the great verandas of the South—
all beginning to decay before the Yankees came, many never quite finished but good enough for the stage set that the Southern Gentleman
had built for his charades.

But perhaps, I said to Wagnal, Corinth of the huge rock, Corinth-
on-the-Isthmus was the same. Maybe it was a sorry pushing place that
aped another city which lived white and beautiful only in the minds of
those men who dragged their ships from one sea to another complain-
ing that the currants were not good this year and the wine would be
sour as the new crop of girls around the temple. Ah yes, Wagnal said,
I was forgetting. Of course, sir, Corinth, Athens, Thebes, exist, odor-
less and white and cool with a gentle breeze blowing through them and
stunning Companions beckoning in the street, only in the brain. But
there even the beggars are picturesque—and the slaves and whores exist
only to complete a rich picture. The very vices themselves are colors
for the artist. The odors, the lepers, the halt and blind, the defective
sewers, the brothels, the slavemarket, the hot days, the insects, the
masters, the cheats and the cheated are all no more than a flat picture
on a well-lighted wall—a fume on the mind. Corinth, a great, rich,
commercial city of ancient Greece—Corinth, a little town in Mississippi,
which would have been nothing more than a flyspeck on the map of
North America, had not General Albert Sidney Johnston rounded up
an armed rabble there in 1862 and marched them over to Pittsburgh

Landing in the mud, is again nothing more than a flyspeck. For who knows anything about either Corinth now? A few fusty theologians, pedantic classicists, and historians who sweep the years into the general dustpan. Mummies, dust, spinsterskin, a Doric capital or two, a clerical-scholarly protest against the Greek Companions cancelled out by a night in a Kansas City whorehouse, a tribute to the courage of a Texan, drunk with something or other, who rode up to a redhot wellfought battery and did not live to tell us how it was in the muzzleblast—except through the photograph in which he lay unburied and goggling at the sky. They stole his boots—for surely a colonel, at that stage of the war, had boots—and buried him with full military honors so that a regiment might be paraded before a general. The fat, yellowvested tavernkeeper fanned himself with Vicksburg Has Fall— And Clint said: Let us go on tonight—tomorrow—as soon as there is a train. But we rode horses.

It took two weeks or more to get down through the shabby country to Messenger's Ferry. We rode a good many different decrepit nags, ate sidemeat and cornpone, and, once, some collard greens in a negro cabin smaller than this. As we drew deeper into Mississippi it grew shabbier and more weathered and old to the eye. I kept thinking that it was all miasma and mystery. I saw, in weathered fence-corners, the ruins of mills and houses, the deadened trees, a sloven shiftless evil. Under the rich ground I thought I could hear the larvae of a million eyeless hookworms massing for attack. And though I saw but a few, my mind was full of sinister serpent-infested bayous and secret moss-hung swamps.

Every time we passed a big house, I looked at it as if it would draw the eyeballs from my head, asking myself: How did that place come to be here? Why, in the name of God, all those toplofty columns? To impress the neighbors, or the negroes, or God?

When we came to the road which had first led us past the Theron house, Clint and I did not recognize it. Crime said: Would the colonel, sir, and the surgeon, sir, like a bit of a brushup before presenting themselves to the ladies, sir? It was no wonder we didn't see it, for the moss on the live oaks was thicker and the weeds on the roadside—and, this time, the luxuriance of the trees concealed the house almost entirely. Crime and the drummer boy started to brush Clint's clothes, but Clint —he was sometimes extraordinarily sensitive in matters which touched his vanity—said sharply: Captain Wagnal first! Yes, sir, the Crimean said grinning.

Crime brushed my clothes and hat and the drummer boy, pouting his redlips like the girls I had seen in Keokuk, knelt to my boots. I did not again forget to use my handkerchief. The gates creaked a little more than before and the wall and lodge were nearly buried under vines. Our horses' shoes crunched on the weedgrown gravel. It was early afternoon, but it was almost dark—and more clammy than before —in the park. I could see none of the garden statuary. When we came into the semicircular sweep of the drive, we were blinded momentarily by the sun on the house. I was struck once more by the great height of the columns which stood glowing pinkly—and felt the warmth fall gratefully on my dampcold hands and cheeks after the dark mossraked ride.

If the father's here, Clint said, we must take him. Take him? I said. Yes, he's a blockader. He has a base in Nassau. But—I said. I'll include your name in the dispatch, Clint said. I'd rather you wouldn't, I said. Oh, very well, Clint said.

We heard the horse; and Clint took his Colt's from the holster and cocked it. Katherine came riding Percy around the side of the verandah. She had on a black silk habit with ostrich plumes in her hat. She laughed, looking at Clint with a luminous, sardonic expression. He put the Colt's away and took off his hat. How extremely pleasant to see you, Captain, Katherine said—and you, Colonel. Percy's in fine fettle since you attended him, Captain. I'll call Rass, and he'll take you up to your rooms. My sister is occupied trying on the things my father brought her from Paris. I trust we shall meet your father, Miss Theron, Clint said. I've no doubt you will, Colonel.

She had no need to call Rass, for he had opened the front door and was standing in it with a cocked and primed musket in his hands. Put that down, Rass, and fetch these gentlemen to their rooms. See them bathed and made comfortable. And these, she said, looking at Crime and the drummer boy, put them in the quarters. The quarters, Miss? You heard my instructions Rasselas! Rasselas? Clint said. The Prince of Abyssinia—Dr. Johnson. My great grandfather knew the insufferable old pedant well, Katherine said. They used to lounge in the gate at Pembroke and slide in Christ Church meadow. Christ Church meadow? Clint said. Meadow, Katherine said. Oxford. Oh, yes, Clint said blushing. Yes, Katherine said, my grandfather gave him those shoes he so cholerically threw down the towerstairs at Pembroke. And, Katherine said, my father is a very cold and calculating man and not a little bloody. He has not, shall I say, the warm heart which led my grandfather into the bravado of duels over women. He is not as interesting as my grandfather was, but he is logical and ruthless. My dear child, Clint said. My good man, Katherine said, do not patronize me in that politic tone. I know it too well from the politicians my grandfather used to bring here for his amusement. They used to quote him Latin tags—and quite incorrectly—, praise his worst brandy and tell him they knew a gentleman and a judge of good liquor when they saw one. What spunk! What fiah! they said when I objected to their chucking me under the chin—when I would not play Lydia Languish for them. Why, suh, the little lady's a veritable Amazon!

Ah, Clint said. I beg your pardon, Miss Theron. He smiled, but I could see the cold glitter in those eyes of Mars that the replacement boy who came out to the regiment too late had described. Clint never had any love for Katherine Theron. Granted, Colonel, Katherine said smiling. I think you will get on with my father who preserves a certain highflown manner to disguise his cold acquisitiveness. And it will interest you much to know that my dear sister, Una, has found in you, sir, her *beau idéal,* and the passion of her life. I see all the signs. Clint was red in the face. The horses, sir? the Crimean said to him. Around the house, Katherine said. You'll see the stables. Take Percy too—the open box stall. Yes, Miss, Crime said, almost grinning while the drummer boy pouted. Thank you, Miss. Rass, Katherine said, show the gentlemen up to their rooms. Take the colonel, Rass, I said. I can find my own way. How dirty you are, Captain, Katherine said. You will have to wash your magnificent beard. It's quite like a statue of Zeus in that dust—like marble. How have you been? What was the Iowa Territory like? And how many rustic maidens did you charm?

Yet perhaps, Wagnal said, that was not what Katherine said. Perhaps she said nothing except with a warm look from underneath the hair which was like dark violets around her face. Mind, sir, I do not wish to picture for you something that was not a woman—something that never lived except in the lines of some self-styled poet who hewed to his own form. I tell you she was standing there in the hot enervating sunlight of a Mississippi afternoon of 1864. I could see her breathing and examine closely the fine white texture of her skin—and see the moist red membranes of her lips cling and part over the words she said or did not say. And I could smell the lavender she had scented herself with. And I knew that, if I put out my hand and laid it on the black silk riding-habit, I should feel a warm solid flexible woman within, sensual and wayward and yet fastidious.

Katherine, I think, reminded me of Sappho. Perhaps because I could then and now always close my eyes and see her walking at dusk in a cool island grove—always young and sensual and wearing saffron and purple. No, not always, for perhaps it was later that I conceived her thus. Then, in 1863 and 1864, my life—my mind was a collection of things without focus: Everything from Dick Ames singing in an Edinburgh pothouse to the Crimean handing me the young Rebel's head on the field at Shiloh—or my love for your great-grandfather, Romulus Lycurgus Hanks. And how was it possible to think then, confronted by the dust and mud of the roads, the miasma of the swamps, the sweet putrefactive odors of dead soldiermeat, horsemeat and mulemeat—and a thousand other phenomena which accompany the process of a gravitation of power?

In all those collisions of life going deathward and death coming lifeward, such as Shiloh and Vicksburg and Atlanta, there was little time but for frantic concentration: a fascinated beating-off of death, a rapt rush into his arms, a cunning wriggle through his bloodslippery fingers. Always in such extremities there must be concentration: the gun, the sword, the dirk, the poison must be brought to bear hard upon the seat of life—life itself must bear hard and strain upon the blade, the wound, the venom to die. Be still. Let me die! Without war, a man must concentrate for seventy years to die—and sometimes. when his blood runs high, he cannot die sooner with war.

Whose fools are we, sir? Wagnal said, picking up the whiskey bottle again. Bacchus's? Fortune's? Venus's? He poured the communion cups full again. Society's? Jesus of Nazareth's? St. Mary the Virgin's? Islam's? Well, sir, of the infinite variety, I should prefer to be my own —or, at least nobody's. But I fear I am not. I fear that I am the fool of an infinite impractical joke with little humor and less wit. My God! Me, down in Tennessee sweating in a dirty blue coat, not because I had any convictions, any hatred, or even any political ambition, but because of the vanity of a little goldbraid which soon tarnished and a few yards of cloth which soon grew ragged and foul-smelling.

And Clint Belton. Well, Clint knew what he was doing. His one spontaneous act during the War Between the States—perhaps during his whole life—was his crawl to shelter under the bluff at Pittsburgh Landing.

CHAPTER XV

GOD forgive me, Wagnal said, I have always loved women for their most whorish artfulness. I am wooed by lipsalve and cunning hairdress, the soft folds of silk which cover them and the artificial scents with which they anoint their fair tight young skins. I like them to be a fair blaze of passionate color both in flesh and mind; I like them animated; I like to think of their soft clothes sliding free against the smooth skin which is made to touch and hold and feel. None of your milky pastel maidens for me—none of your twitterers. No, nor none of your exuberant country goochers.

I like them to be of bright color and unabashed—to know what they are doing when they lie down with you. I like them to be cool and crisp with the latent fire shining roselike from the skin—I like them to be everything the Greeks said their most famous courtesans were— which they were most probably not. But nevertheless, young man, Katherine was all these things to me. And I might have had her then, in the summer of sixty-four, not for the asking, but the bare taking. And I am sorry that the taking was not in me then. Now, I would take all of Katherine I could get. For, as I have said, she was no Southern Lady, to contract carefully for her mawkish bed and drive her husband to breed mulattoes in the quarters. Such a woman living in Mississippi in Eighteen hundred and sixty-four sounds dubious—but she was true. Oh, for that matter, the whole family was incredible enough, and, with the exception of Katherine, not a tribe to have around—but you shall see presently.

Though it will wreck the sculpture, Katherine said, you must wash your fine beard, Captain. Her face crinkled up around her small eyes, and again she seemed in a silent paroxysm of great godlike laughter. Then come down to me and I will give you some sherry—and, if it's light enough, I'll show you around the grounds. I can see her now, standing there under that tall falsegreek portico, her eyes in amused slits, her dimples up— Wagnal paused now looking back with a diffuse look in the old bloodshot eyes. He picked up the communion goblet and gulped the whiskey in a great pachydermatous gulp, a tear splashing his pale hairbacked hand as he did so. He flicked the tearwet hand openly and swallowed—not the whiskey, for it had already plummeted down his gullet, but the old particular lump in his throat which God had been making him swallow for those many years. Katherine, he said. Oh, Katherine!

Everything was as it had been in the upstairs sitting-room, except that there was a pile of new leatherbound books on the floor, and, on the chairs sheaves of magazines: Copies of Blackwood's, The London Illustrated News, Punch. I flipped through several numbers of Punch and saw Mr. Lincoln's large face most grossly caricatured, before Rass came in and said: Your bath is ready, sir. Before I bathed, I sat again in the cordovan seat of the porcelain watercloset. The Cellini ewer, the statuette of Cloacina, the Japanese paper were still there. A new book about Paris by Taine and Grain d'Orge lay on the shelf beside the blazoned stoolbowl; and, if I had not been so excited and unstrung over the proximity of Katherine, I should have thoroughly enjoyed my latrine duty.

The bath was porcelain also—with a high back. It was of a piece with the closetbowl, though there were more and larger griffons, lions and crocodiles on it. And at one end of the tiled room on a high stand, there squatted a stuffed, glasseyed crocodile, his mouth open as if he were about to amputate the tender leg of a baby. I got out, dried myself on several large, thick linen towels and went over to the stuffed reptile, looking curiously at the several rows of teeth, the fine well-cared-for state of the hide and the long heavy tail, cunningly flexed to counterfeit life.

When I had dressed, I found Clint sitting with a copy of Punch open on his knees staring at a cartoon of Mr. Lincoln and Jefferson Davis or the South playing billiards. The Southern figure was saying: Hurrah for Charleston! That's another one for me. The face of Mr. Lincoln was a depraved, boorish face. How, Clint said piously, can they do such things to such a great and noble gentleman? Clint, I said, I'm going down now. Ah! he said. The beautiful Katherine! Yes, Clint, I said slowly with no levity in my voice, the beautiful Katherine.

As you can still see, sir, I am a big man. And as you have perhaps heard through village gossip, that I am a crazy hotheaded fool. It is known here that I am insane, is it not? If it were not that I am such a Character, I should be sent to an institution—though they do not love me as they did Daft Jamie. Is that not the size of it? His eyes blazed coldly through the rivermaps of red veins. You do not need to deny it, sir! Speak up! Let us not have this thrice Goddamned village nonsense between us. We are not a pair of superstitious smalltown wiseacres. We are men of the world. You are sitting there in a wellcut suit from Jermyn street. Speak up!

Then suddenly the cold light left his eyes and the wattles of his neck hung down the more slackly, Lee remembered. I beg your pardon, sir, he said. That I should embarrass you so in my own house! Do not reply. That I have unpacked my heart to you as I have done must be proof enough that I regard you in the light of a man of understanding. I wished only to point my remark to Clint, to say that in those days I was a bigger and more impetuous man than I am now. It took me a long time to realize how dangerous I was considered to be. But I was not thought insane then, for I was still young. But for all my impetuosity, I did not take Katherine that summer in Mississippi— Katherine who was ripe, on the topmost bough, for the taking.

She had on a new blue silk dress and, with the lavender, some other perfume. She was standing in a sunshaft at the foot of the big staircase, looking up. As I rounded the curve, I could see that she had several little curls at the nape of her neck, and, when I had turned, I saw that she was not smiling—and the dimples were gone and her slit eyes were wideopen and there was a straight frownfurrow between them.

As God is my judge, Captain, she said, I am sick to death of this place. It is dead. It seems to me that all over the world—everywhere but here—things are happening. Since Grandfather was killed there is nothing to look forward to. A negro came in the front door last night. He was about to tear down one of those tapestries in the Louis Quatorze room when Rass picked him up and threw him out the back door. Rass would have killed him if I hadn't been near. Aside from that there's been no excitement. The battles always give this place a wide berth— You would not like battles, I said. They are cruel and dirty and you cannot see much. You could not see the flag waving and the men clashing forward as it is in the pictures of battles. And the blood is a dirtier color than in the paintings. But, Katherine said, the wideopen sliteyes burning, battle is dangerous—you know you are alive. It has got so, even when I take a high fence with Percy, I do not know I am alive. I believe I could shoot the enemy for sport. I saw now that her darkblue eyepupils were dilated. I had as leave take one of Grandfather's guns and take my chances in battle as die because I do not know I am alive. I could shoot for sport—I know I could shoot down that gambler in Vicksburg without a qualm. I should love to see a redspot grow on his white fussy shirt and see his eyes roll upward with that silly sanctimonious look a dead man gets. I do not know what I shall ever do.

I was so distracted by this cold bloody passion of Katherine's, that, to take her mind from the morbidity of such things, I said: That is a fine stuffed crocodile you have. I did not know there was a zoologist in your household. Zoologist! Katherine said. My grandfather used to shoot them because of the funny way they pirouetted and whirled and jumped high in the air when the bullet penetrated their eyes. He used to say that they had more *ballon* than all the prima ballerinas in St. Petersburg—and were a damned sight more graceful. He called the one in your bathroom Tamara, for he said she reminded him of a fine ballet wench who used to cross herself as she pirouetted before every entrance she made and who ran away with him to London pursued by a whole regiment of Imperial Guard's officers. When he shot the beast, he said, it jumped exactly like Tamara—the same grand lugubrious, lovable, flatfooted style that threw all the Tsar's young men into very ecstasies of love and yearning. He always kept Tamara the crocodile in the bathroom so that she would remind him of his ballerina as he lolled in the water like a Roman. I did not see her the last time, I said. Rass covered her up—not through any delicacy for your feelings—only because he had the notion that vulgar eyes must not look upon Grandfather's love. Now, I believe he has ceased to regard your gaze as vulgar.

Yes, Katherine said. Grandfather loved Tamara, the crocodile. He said the movements of her tail were very fantastic after the bullet hit her—endearingly comical. They grew more comical and endearing each time he described her deathdance. He added an extra pigeonwing each time he told it. It was he who added her to the griffons and lions. Are there crocodiles near here? I said. Not such splendid ones, Grandfather thought.

That was when we used to go to New Orleans. One year I made Rass get me a peek into the quadroon ball—and they were lovely. Grandfather shot Tamara in the big bayou near Lake Pontchartrain. There was a young man in New Orleans who amused him—an oaf named Jabez something, whom he used to foist upon my sister, Una— here Katherine's eyes drew into slits again and her dimples came up —and with whom he had a crocodile-hunting friendship.

The same day Grandfather shot Tamara, Jabez shot one he named Parson Judas. Colonel, Jabez said, see that gentleman gaping over there under the cane branch? Looks like Parson Judas from Kentucky that came psalm-singin' to Ma's last week. Same jaws—same white waist-coat! Here's for the white weskit! The parson ain't decent from the way he exposes his belly. I beg your pardon, Reverend. I fear I've spotted your white waistcoast. Grandfather used to tell it well, Katherine said. He was a fine mimic and could get the same unpleasant expression into his eyes that Jabez had. He could almost make his cheeks bulge and redden and his nostrils swell like Jabez'. Grandfather pretended to like him, but I don't think he did. The oaf was as tall as you, Captain, but his frame was covered with solid, motionless flesh like a stunned bull's —and when he drank, his breathing was heavy, and no one cared to go near him. He used to rush drunkenly out of a pub on a stormy night. I am not a dog to stay indoors and sleep on straw, he would holler. One night he walked to the riverside and got into his boat and steered out into the river where big treetrunks were rushing down swept by the mad water. Grandfather said he was magnificent—oh, magnificent, steering his boat, in lightning flashes, with the strength of Hercules. Nobody thought he would ever return, but he came back in the morning, fresh and good-humored as if he had been a great deepsea beast. He had been to the Mexican war too: one day he just left his stuffy English—well, not *so* stuffy, for there were a lot of Creole things in it—house, going on horseback, with carbines, pistols, hounds and a compass, straight through the woods. He came back after six months. People said that there was no doubt that he had covered a couple of thousand miles and killed at least a company of Mexicans and several Indians. His hounds foraged for themselves in the woods —and they were so savage when they came home with him that he had to shoot them.

Oh, he was popular enough. All the rich young men of New Orleans idolized him because of his daring. And Una, well, the only reason that Una did not encourage him more was because he was not likely to make her a duchess or a princess or install her in the White House. I believe she secretly thought him quite dashing, for his mother was a French Marquise from an old family. The Marquise had had him educated as well as possible and brought him up in the manners of the ancient *noblesse*. You know, Captain, that in the Creole society, Yankees pass as impudent tradesmen—mere grocers. But Jabez—oh, he was the cynosure of all eyes—had a fine carriage and fine horses, a parcel of smart well-whipped negroes and the usual pretty quadroon mistress who was not too faithful to him. The shopwomen thought he was a very devil, but I've no doubt they would have smiled on him fast enough had he given them the chance.

Once when Grandfather and I were stopping in New Orleans before the war, Grandfather and he went to a barroom. It was an awful day —so hot that several men and horses had fallen sunstruck in the streets. And the mosquitoes came up in clouds from the river. A heavy miasmal breeze came up towards evening, just before he and Jabez went into the barroom. Jabez had been bitten by a good many mosquitoes and was morose and sulky—besides he had caught his quadroon with an Irish dock laborer whom he had beaten with a crop while standing off a dozen of the man's friends with a pistol.

Jabez yelled arrogantly for a glass of rum and drank it with a grimace. Some gimleteyed old customers were standing up to the bar shifting their tobacco quids, picking their teeth with their knives and staring at the elegant and offensive cut of Jabez' white trousers. Jabez looked at them as if they were vermin. Grandfather, who had a morbid love for such situations, said that the air was full of feeling running high, and that any moment he expected something to stir the sluggish blood. The gimleteyed customers he thought to have been Kentuckians, of the more rough and ready fire-eating type, in New Orleans to sell their cotton and tobacco and get drunk and enjoy the town's large supply of vari-colored women—half-castes, quadroons, *et cetera,* Grandfather said. But the high moment, as Grandfather often called it since, came in a guise he had not foreseen. It seems, in that bar, Jabez had a favorite waiter, who was busy serving the gimleteyes. A match! Jabez said. But the waiter went on shoving sandwiches across the bar to the Kentuckians. Jabez called him three times, each time his voice growing more hoarse and his face getting more purple. The waiter, poor wretch, was beset on all sides. The Kentuckians were not going to allow this man in the elegant white trousers to take their due service from them; and Jabez, who regarded this waiter almost—though the man was white, or at least half-caste—as one of his own bought-and-paid-for negroes, was near to bursting not one, but all his blood vessels. The heat, the mosquitoes, the miasmal breeze, the uncouth Kentuckians (no better than poor white trash) and then this disloyalty of an old servant—the last straw had fallen. The waiter, afraid, kept saying: Right away, sir. He fearfully gave the Kentuckians their last sandwich and ran past Jabez for the match. Jabez, with a mesmerized look on his bovine face, pulled out his bowie knife and stabbed the waiter so hard in the back that

Grandfather heard the spine crack. The man fell on his face choking. He raised himself on his elbows and got out the words, right away, as he stretched out his neck to catch the air. He hiccoughed, vomited gouts of blood and died.

The knife stuck in the wound, Grandfather said; and everybody, including the gimleteyed customers, stared at it without moving from their places. Jabez also stared—he stared as if he were in a trance until someone brought a policeman. And then, morose and docile, he went away with the policeman. All New Orleans began to talk.

I heard a negro say: Well, Young Massa call de po' white fo' time. He don' come. Young Massa got a right to sen' him to de rewahd, Dat's whut de book say.

The young fellows who idolized Jabez for his spectacular feats of bravado thought that he ought to have caned the waiter—with a cane the fellow should have had a couple of dozen blows. He should not have been honored with the knife—and the knife made it awkward. Jabez would have to go to Europe for a couple of years—and they would miss his society.

The Irish dockhands and the shopkeepers held meetings and quoted Thomas Jefferson and swore to stop the aristocracy fattening on the poor people. They said if Jabez wasn't hanged by law, they'd hang him themselves. The dockhands began by cracking a gentleman's head or two. Grandfather forbade me to leave the hotel, but I saw one or two of the brawls. For he would leave me alone, not being able to stay off the streets when there was such a chance to view some dramatic bloodshed.

The judge in the case was an old French sea captain, who, Grandfather said, was too bloody honorable. He confused the law with God and God with power, not understanding, Grandfather said, that money was the only power. Though the judge did not love the lower classes, he said that he would show no partiality. All murderers were for the gallows—and he would follow the verdict of the jury. He was poor, but when a friend of Jabez called on him one morning with a packet of $50,000 in greenbacks, he pitched him downstairs into the street. Grandfather, in spite of the barbarous heat, the mosquitoes and dust, enjoyed the comedy more and more. He told the judge that he was trifling with his own life, but the judge only went about armed to the teeth under a bodyguard of five faithful negroes. Once the judge got a carbine ball in the shoulder; another time he was cut across the ribs with a bowie knife. The only reason he survived for the trial was every laborer, poorwhite, dockhand and shopkeeper in the town made it his business to protect him. Several young aristocrats were sniped to death in the streets and a pair of the judge's negroes was found strung to a tree, badly roasted. Grandfather would not tell me all the things that happened to the people in that fracas.

The trial came off, but Grandfather, though he went himself, would not let me go. Jabez would not speak. Grandfather said he acted as if he were a bull—a haughty, morose bull. They tried to prove he was drunk, but two dozen witnesses knew he had had but one glass of rum. The people began to yell. Kill him! String him up! He's a Goddamned mad dog!

It was a jury of shopkeepers and blacksmiths who thought that murders were bad for business. They brought in a verdict of guilty soon enough—and the judge put on the black cap for hanging. The fashionable young men were up in arms: they held councils. Hanging was fit for only Yankees and negroes! Jabez' mother put two hundred thousand dollars—all the family fortune—under the jailer's nose. He took his big family bible and spent the night reading it and praying—in the morning, with a pale pious face, he refused the money.

Laborers, singing as they worked, were already digging holes for the gallowsbeams, when a couple of hundred young aristocrats with carbines attacked the jail. A colonel and his regiment, who had been set to guard the jail, were conveniently inspecting Lake Pontchartrain. True, they had left twenty soldiers but these knew the better part of valor. The aristocrats brought files, axes and a battering ram and went to work on the great jail door. But it was too strong—or the dandies were not strong enough. They had to pile logs against it and set them afire. This worked, but the battering-ram and the flames had warned the Irish dockhands. They came up from the river flourishing crowbars and pickaxes and knives—they wanted to see the Englishman hang.

It was early morning, Grandfather said, and the Paddies had all had their whiskey. The aristocrats fired into the mob and brought down several—but the Irish closed in with their bowie knives. Jabez' friends ran—those who could.

I sneaked out of the hotel and saw part of this from a carriage. During the next week the fashionable young gentlemen began to appear in the streets furtively with bandaged heads. There was one fashionable funeral—for a young man who died in a fall from a hunter.

Grandfather said a man with a telescope had watched Jabez pacing about in his cell, his mouth open, his eyes staring as if he were still looking at the dead waiter.

All the gentlemen of the town were a little drunker than usual during that week—and there were many shots at night and in the early morning. Grandfather fought a duel with a man because he had said that he could hardly blame the laborers and shopkeepers for wishing to see Jabez decorating a gibbet—but he shot him only in the shoulder. Oh, Grandfather often said that he considered the duello a childish practice, but, since he wished to be feared, he had to do a certain amount of wounding and killing. That is the reason I cannot understand why he was so careless in Vicksburg. But I must finish the story of his companion crocodile hunter.

Jabez had one day left when his mother got permission to see him. She came to the jail in a carriage bringing another woman who was heavily veiled. She gave out that the veiled woman was Jabez' cousin of Natchez, whom the archbishop had given a special dispensation to marry him.

The two women stayed in the jail an hour—and when they came out the cousin was hunched over with grief and looked very queer. On the day of the hanging, the jailer and Jabez' quadroon mistress were discovered in the jailer's apartment. The pious jailer was dead drunk—and the quadroon was mother-naked. His clothes—including the elegant white trousers, now very dirty—in which he had stabbed the waiter, lay in disorder on the floor of Jabez' cell.

They locked the quadroon and the jailer up in separate cells. Many versions of how Jabez escaped spread over the town like wildfire. The Irish and the shopkeepers and the poorwhites all combined now. This time they had carbines. They howled for the blood of the jailer and Jabez' nigger winch, as they called the quadroon. They went to Jabez' mother's house, but she was gone—only two old negroes were left. These were soon hanged, shot and burned. Then the mob went to the jail. The regiment had gone, for there was no reason to guard a jailer and a quadroon—and there was only a makeshift door now, no guards and no young men of fashion to interfere, so they had little trouble in bringing out the quadroon—still stark naked—and the jailer, more white and pious than ever with remorse and fear. They

took them near a bayou—and when as many of the shopkeepers, dockhands and poorwhites as craved had done what they wished with the
quadroon—they stripped the jailer and tied him to the wench in a
position which I leave you to guess, my dear captain—and hanged
them with one rope. They came back to town singing righteously
with parts of the jailer swinging on the pickaxe of a Paddy.

Nothing was ever done to them. For no one cared about the pious
jailer, except his wife, who did not dare open her mouth because of
a *bourgeois* shame for his actions with the quadroon. And no one
brought up the subject of the quadroon, though I suppose many who
had enjoyed her favors—Grandfather, the fashionable young men,
a large black bush negro who was her choice, and even the lynchers—
must have had their moments of regret, for she was a beautiful golden
wench who was really made for lechery, Grandfather said.

In any event, the honorable judge shortly died of blood poisoning
from one of his wounds and the whole thing blew over. Lately, I have
heard stories about Jabez' exploits in the war. He is supposed to have
run a gun, by hand, up to a Union tent at Shiloh in the early morning
of April sixth and fired the first shot of the battle point blank into half
a dozen sleeping Yankees, of a Kentucky regiment, blowing them to
little bits and so terrorizing their camp that he took it singlehanded
while many ran to hide under the bluff; he is supposed to have killed,
with a bowie knife, the man who shot General Albert Sidney Johnston;
and he is thought to be the André du Bois of the New Orleans Washington artillery whose bravery is talked about by all the Creoles and
who has been mentioned many times in General Beauregard's dispatches. Parson Judas, the other crocodile, is here, Katherine said.
Would you like to see it?

I did not ask to see the other crocodile, Wagnal said. When she
finished the tale, we were walking along a grassfringed gravel path in
the park and had come to the little Greek temple of a summer house,
the stones of which already appeared as old as some I had seen in
Athens and Crete. Beside the temple stood one of the little statues—
perhaps of Venus—with the little mat of moss on its *mons veneris*.
One of Grandfather's embarrassing little jokes, Katherine said. The
moss. He delighted to shock middleclass morals. I am never embar-
rassed—and Una is such a cold creature that she can ignore it without
blushing. Look, she said, the little temple was built as a ruin—and that
grass growing up there among the figures on the pediment was care-

fully planted. It's a temple of Venus. Grandfather told me he wished
he could surround it with handsome Greek hetæræ from good families
to serve the goddess as they did in the old days of Greece.

I stood still, looking at Katherine, who again, in the soft light of
the park looked as if she were in the throes of that silent paroxysm of
laughter. I must have been blushing, for I had been put off my stride
by this girl who said such lewd words to a man. Even though I had
had to do with a good many trollops of all descriptions, especially in
my student days, I did not expect such realism from one who was
supposed to be a lady—at least in America. In England, I had heard
of a lewd young duchess who went naked in her garden and who
was thought a dashing and wicked eccentric, but to hear Katherine
Theron talk so in Mississippi in that time was startling.

And, sir, Wagnal said, his voice dripping sibilantly as the outworn
lechery of his youth came back to him, it was not only that it was
aphrodisiac—it was so powerful an aphrodisiac, that though I wanted
Katherine madly, I was so paralyzed by what her actions and speech
did to me that I could not move to seize her. She walked into the
summerhouse temple of Venus with a look of invitation on her face—
she told me, years afterwards, that it was calculated. But I stood rooted
to the ground, perhaps because of awe before her youth, perhaps because I knew no precedent for this girl who spoke, with unashamed
calmness, words which, if they had come from the mouth of a young
man to strike the ears of almost any Southern Young Lady, would
have sent her father and brothers—indeed the whole countryside of
Southern Knighthood—howling down upon the slayer with visiting
cards. And there would have been no rest until the blot upon Fair
Womanhood had been washed out in blood—a process which, I have
no doubt, was enjoyed to the dregs by Southern Young Womanhood
while watching her honor defended. It was a species of sexual cruelty
which ladies could comfortably enjoy; a genre of drama which must
have tingled in the dainty guts of many a fine Daughter of the Old
South to give her a sense of importance perhaps a little beyond that
of being born a viscountess. But it pleased Katherine little. I think
she enjoyed bloodshed but little, no matter how solemn and courteous
and formal it was. But, as I said, I stood still awkwardly, paralyzed
by desire and love when she ran into the temple. When I was able to
move and speak, I said a most regrettable thing: Have you marked
your grandfather's grave? I remember the night— Her eyes opened

widely, the slits disappearing slowly. She seemed to be looking at me in amazement as the straight, vexed frownline appeared. Grandfather's grave? she said. We weren't talking of graves, Captain—not that sort of beds!

She ran out of the summerhouse, her blue dress flashing in the dark green park, her dark head brushing aside the lowest trailers of moss. When I was alone, the temple and the statue and the hot forest damp of the park lost all the feeling of gayety that it had had—I knew then—while she was there. The temple, the statue, the manner in which they had been, so to speak, antiqued—now that I knew—became distasteful to me. The musky smell of life, the insects winging the dark air and a little snake—whose licking tongue and beady eye caught my eye—squirming down the pediment of the summerhouse temple of Venus all conspired to make me feel as if I were a guest in a poisoned wood where all life was evil—where I myself had recently designed to join forces with evil and got nothing for it but guilt. I am an awkward ghoul, I said aloud to myself. Here was the moment which I came away from that pleasant nightstreet of girls in Iowa—in a little town with clean trees—to catch. Here was the empty vision which drove me a thousand miles in a wartime summer, almost filled and alive. Here was the incarnation of my holy lust—and I had done nothing.

I walked through the park on the little blurry paths brushing the moss with my head, seeing here a mossy minotaur, there a greengray satyr leering out of the swampgrass at me. Turning a little curve in the path I came upon the place where Rass had dug the grave that night in eighteen sixty-three when I helped put old Theron in the Elizabethan press. The mound had sunken; and moss had started to creep greenly across the damp reddish soil. The grave was marked with a little phallic obelisk of red granite which looked to me ancient and Egyptian. There were ponderous box-shaped tombs or sarcophagi, weathered and cracked, some of them inscribed in academic Latin. And over all there was the smell of old death. One sarcophagus was of the mediaeval type which one sees in English abbeys: lying on top of it was the lifesize image in staring stone—with the eyes closed—figure of a man in armor with a long sword girded on, a casque in the crook of his left arm, a mastiff lying at his feet and his head pillowed on a lion *couchant*. Aethelstanus Theronus: MDCCLX—MDCCCLII, his tomb read pompously. Beside it was another more flamboyant tomb, probably rococo Italian in style, with the stone figure of a woman—hands clasped in prayer—in long flowing robes lying upon it: Marie Chatelaine, I. H. S., In Pace Requiescat—no dates. I looked at the stone face of the woman in the growing dusk, remembering the portrait of the beautiful quadroon in the Louis Quatorze drawing room.

Around these tombs were four small graves decorated with the neglected remnants of glass or bead flowers and wreaths: Aelfric, Odette, François, Toussaint. The mausoleum, another small Greek temple, had no inscription on it but a lion and a griffon. There were some other graves marked with headstones and several eroded box-tombs—Claudius, Elizabeth, Ovid, Pitt. Around the two sarcophagi was a wrought iron rail—it seemed newer than the tombs—with the griffon lion and crocodile device worked into it.

I walked back to the house, my hands and forehead clammy from the summer chill of the park and the graveyard humor. Glad to come into the sun of the gravel driveway, I was twice glad when I saw Katherine standing beside one of the columns leaning her small hand in the curve of a fluting. She was smiling as if nothing had happened—and truly what had happened was one of those events of life which seem, afterwards, as if they had almost occurred, or to have occurred only as a real-seeming and vivid dream, which, one can remind oneself with recurrent relief, was unreal and, therefore, something that carries no responsibility. But I am not sure: Perhaps in this monstrous world one is responsible even for one's dreams—or for nothing at all.

Captain, Katherine said, I am so sorry I left you rudely. It was my own lefthandedness, Miss Theron, I said. But it was not, I am sure, she said with perfect courtesy and gaiety, which I would have exchanged for a tantrum—for that, at least, would have been warmer. She stood looking at me with her small smile and all her bright colors —like the colors of the young girls who are paid, now, to pose for these color photographs. And I thought: Oh, God help me, I am lost. For I shall never be able to gobble her up, to absorb her whole, to ravish her, to bind her to my heart. And God did not help me, sir—and I never was. Wagnal sobbed a little—like distant thunder, Lee thought. And I sobbed with him. For I loved Katherine too—as I loved Christa and Anne and love when I was young, Christ help me. Last year I found the story of Jabez and the crocodile in Grain d'Orge.

CHAPTER XVI

God is the lifeboat, the insurance policy, the fire-extinguisher, the lastditch, the magnesium flare, the parachute, the trumpcard, the comforter in the sorest and uttermost need, the vaccination, the gasmask, the fortress. And He is Love. . .

That is how I came here, Wagnal said. And Stuart, Goddamn his foppish soul to hell, Goddamn his sanctity and his success and his plumes and his horses and his banjoman, Sweeney, and his Prussian dragoon, von Borcke and all his fire-eating heroics—even his death-wound at Yellow Tavern— Goddamn them all to hell, Wagnal said quietly, his old voice whistling on the sibilants. He was dead and rotting away, but I'll venture to say that a million women still prayed for him—still prayed his ghost into their beds before they fell asleep to dream of those plumes, that beard, and that black stallion-charger of his and his comicopera escort—all jackboots and horsepistols and sabres and beards and firegilt buttons going along the turnpike to the tune of Lorena on a minstrelshow banjo. And Stuart with his Goddamned knee crossed over the saddle, singing. . .

WAGNAL SAID: In a wartime summer—in any summer of the earth, but more in a wartime summer—a young man feels that he is missing something every instant that he lives. A young man feels that the narrow edge of the summer minute where he is perched watching the bumblebee on the wild verbena and the blue air all around it are meant to do him out of his right to see everything in the world. One young girl walking beside him in diaphanous fluffy clothes with a comic opera picturehat full of rambler roses and a little bowedup red mouth—walking with him near the lilac bushes and the redbud trees and the dogwood—can make him wish for a thousand girls, from the nakednaveled Egyptian dancers to the wellpainted, wellexercised girls of Hollywood and the debutante ad models, the sleek ghosts of Everyman's bed, who keep their legs crossed except to the men with the big cameras and the big money.

Not only girls, but all things: Katherine was there beside me, but Grant had left the Army of Tennessee. And that summer he was in

the Wilderness racing Lee to Spottsylvania Court House. In the summertime of Eighteen hundred and sixty-four a young man marooned
in a great Mississippi plantation house—no matter how much he did
not like war—was missing action. Portentous things were transpiring.
The shells set the woods on fire: men were dying roasted, trapped in
the woods. Old Sedgwick was killed. They ran a battery right up
to the breastworks at Spottsylvania; the Rebels didn't put the butts of
their guns to their shoulders, but reached them up, poking the barrels
above their heads over the breastworks to pull the triggers so that the
muskets stung their hands and almost jumped free of their grip as
they went off. The barrels got so hot they couldn't load—and it began
to rain, making the guns misfire. The Yankees went crazy with enthusiasm: Some climbed to the top of the Confederate works to fire
one shot down within and topple over dead. Some Rebs wanted to
surrender and climbed up to the top of their works, their hands in the
air, to come over to the Union line, but the shabby, bearded, starved,
squittery men of the Army of Northern Virginia let them have it in
the back, and they fell over into the piles of dead and wounded that
strengthened the works on either side. A tree, weakened by the minié
balls, began cracking one night and fell on them squatting there with
guns pointed at each other—and all floundering in the mud. In Paris
a man called Charcot was tinkering with the human mind. Everything
was going on in the world; nothing was stopping until I could finish
what I was doing and go see it happen, go take a part in it, go
everywhere and be everything.

Katherine, whose memory of a year had struck me, in Iowa, a
nightblow in a spring street and brought me through a thousand miles
of heat and discomfort, was near me. I ought to have brought my mind
and nerves and senses to bear upon her wooing; but even there, in the
Theron house near Messenger's Ford (or was it Ferry?), there were
books about things that had happened faraway and longago, papers
and magazines from London and Paris telling of our own battles and
things that had happened within the year—and objects from a score of
countries and a dozen centuries. I could not be still and love, though
I say to you, sir, when I detect that superior look of youth in your
eye, that you are wrong:

I am not, even now, different from you. I am as young and stubborn—except for a certain sclerosis of tissue and thought, except for
an overt appearance of the hide, which sags and flaps in the wind,

except for the bloodshot eyes and the dirty, careless dribblings of egg and whiskey on my shirt bosom and moustache. I am as young, sir, as you. I do not feel any different: I still desire—I still know the look of the rosy young flesh of a young girl. Men were young in my day, too, sir. Men were poets in my time, sir. And by the Almighty God, young fellow, they aspired to glory and knowledge and art for art's bloody sake just as much and with as fine a passion as any of you. Do not forget that, young man. We were just as dashing a set of young blades as any of you.

Forgive me, Wagnal said, stopping this spate of words. Forgive me! But you, who have already wandered a little, must already know what it is to ache and strain with love and lechery and ambition and curiosity and greed.

Before dinner Katherine brought me into the library where Una, Clint and her father were drinking sherry. He was a tall, slender man with a goldenbrown hide and elegant, neatly trimmed dundreary whiskers. He had an extremely steely blue eye and a long face, somewhat like a highbred horse or an Italian primitive. I never caught him with any expression on his face that was translatable into any word for an emotion or a humor. His smiles or frowns seemed always the conventional trappings for the character of his last remark—or the polite reaction to a remark made to him. Yet despite this blankness of physiognomy, I always felt that he had some emotions—and those strong. He was dressed in a white linen suit with a frock coat, a black cummerbund and a black silk stock—an outfit which he had got, perhaps, in the Bahamas, where his blockaders put in at homeport. His black boots were obviously made by a London or Paris bootmaker and elegantly varnished and polished.

Howjehdo? he said to me. Colonel Belton has threatened to seize me as contraband. I believe he has been disappointed because I have letters from Washington asking that I be protected as a subject of Her Majesteh. He smiled a coldlanguid smile, drawling out the Majesteh in a most fashionable Oxonian voice. Come, sir, Clint said, surely you see that I was only making a joke. I looked Clint straight in the eye, but his eyes did not drop, nor his expression change. The Colonel, Mr. Theron said, has innocently called me a blockader. That is understandable. Perhaps I am, in a sense. I have holdings in the Bahamas—and a vessel or two for the transport of my goods to England. Naturally, this war has made my situation embarrassing.

Oh, naturally, Mr. Theron, Clint said. I understood as soon as you explained. Let us say no more about it, sir, except for the tender of my abject apologies for my crude attempt at humor, which I now see was in extremely bad taste. On the contrary, Colonel, Mr. Theron said. I found it quite amusing. Katherine, ring for Rass. We must drink to Colonel Belton's wit. Yes, dear Father, Katherine said, her voice lightly sarcastic, her sliteyes smiling. Ah, Captain, Mr. Theron said to me, Una has told me that we are indebted to your medical skill, for the life of a fine thoroughbred horse. Are you a member of a horse regiment, sir?

No, Father, Katherine said, Captain Wagnal is a doctor of medicine of Edinburgh and a Fellow of the Royal College of Surgeons. Oh, but Miss— Do not be modest, Captain. In your relations with my father, the more of your honors he knows, the more highly he will value you. Ah, Mr. Theron said, very fine anatomists come out of Edinburgh, I'm told. A pity, sir, that our blackguard laws made it so extremely difficult for them to get in their—ah—subjects. Oh, yes, Father, Katherine said, Captain Wagnal knew the body-snatchers well, did you not, Captain? Well, of course—I said. Ah yes, Mr. Theron said, picturesque beggars, no doubt. Resurrectionists. Professional ghouls. Extremely unpleasant creatures and an extremely unpleasant way to eke out one's exchequer. A deal less pleasant than holdings in the Bahamas, and the Coolie trade, eh, dear Father? Katherine said. But somewhat akin.

Ah, Mr. Theron said as Rass came in, you did fetch that new Amontillado. You must try it yourself Rass—at your leisure—to see if it compares with that we had up at Balliol. Mettrefect, I got it from a merchant in the High. Indeed, Father, Katherine said, ignoring her father's flight from the subject, Captain Wagnal knew the notorious Burke and Hare, who delivered absolutely fresh subjects to the anatomy schools. Captain Wagnal often knew the subjects themselves. Did you not say you knew Daft Jamie, Captain? Really, Miss Theron, I am ashamed to think that I bothered you with the grisly tales of Edinburgh's dissecting theatres. It is a sad business— Ah, Captain, Katherine said, you admit then that it is a business, and, as a business, has as much right to a place in our conversation as holdings in the Bahamas —and the Coolie trade. Come, Kitty dear, Una said, do not mortify the Captain because he has been so injudicious as to tell penny dreadful stories to thrill the childish imagination. Grandfather often said

Katherine said blandly, still smiling with her sliteyes, that any sort of imagination was better than the absence of it.

The wellbred voices dropped into a little silence in which I saw Mr. Theron holding up the sherry to get the brown light through it. He was smiling slightly. To Colonel Belton's charming wit, he said. We sipped, and Clint bowed somewhat stiffly and said, holding up his glass, to your health. We sipped again. Mr. Theron began to talk of the last season in Paris and of the custom, in society, of staring at your fellowman, through glasses, at the Opera—of the custom, in America, of shying plates at the waiters at public dinners and drawing bowie knives when not served with dispatch.

We spent two or three days with the Therons. All the time Clint became more and more friendly with Mr. Theron, even in that short while, picking up an English milord's mannerism or two from our host—and polishing up the phrases that he had already acquired. It took little acuteness to see that he and Una had come to an under-standing about their subsequent marriage even then—and, I knew, from Clint's chance remarks, the important and portentous air which he now affected—I knew without Katherine's telling me that he and her father had entered into a business agreement.

Now, sir, Wagnal said, those few hours in a bizarre plantation house in Mississippi were Clint Belton's crossing of the Rubicon. His die was cast. He was bound to the course he took. The war was now a minor stepping-stone, a side issue—and nothing but his death, which did not come until the course was run, which I, somehow, do not believe could have come until the course was run, could have changed the course. Clint had got his lessons by heart now, he had grounded himself in all those fundamentals of life, that Rome, your grandfather, could never learn—and that I could grasp for a moment, but never master. Nevertheless, I left the Theron house in Mississippi that summer knowing that Katherine would come away from there with me when I was no longer a soldier, though there were no troths plighted, no banns published, nor promises made.

CHAPTER XVII

WE CAUGHT up with the regiment at Rome, Georgia, Wagnal said. From that time on we tramped along in the dust, dropping a man or two every day. The heat put one poor, silly lad—a bounty boy—out of his head, and he began crying: Mamma! Mamma! I have to pee pee. The others began to call him Pee Pee Blunt. I had to send him home as a disability because it got on his nerves so badly.

Rome made them let the toothless boy ride in one of the commissary wagons, for the lad was struck by the sun one day. The squitters came back to us full force—and we began to get on each other's nerves because of the bellyache. There was a lot of talk about the furlough time spent in Ioway—and about the girls in Keokuk and at home.

The Crimean's voice began to annoy me. Hello, Hunderd and Seventeenth, a voice would say on the road, or in camp at night—a voice through thick dust and the crawling membrane of heat. Didja have a good furlough? Oh, tollolish, tollolish! Crime's voice would say in a smug cockney-going-home-at-night-saying-goodnight-to-the-bobby tone. All the boys got to saying it until Johnston and Hood made them forget it at Kenesaw Mountain or Atlanta perhaps.

God, Wagnal said, Kingston, Georgia, Acworth, Georgia, Brushy Mountain, Georgia, Jawjuh! Jawjuh! Jawjuh! Kenesaw Mountain and Nickajack Creek, Turner's Ferry and the Chattahoochee river, Marietta, Cross Keys, and all of them little, common, shaggy and still asleep even with the Yankees on their doorsteps—all of them shabby and asleep and wild at the same time. And all along the way those Greek columns holding up the imitation porticos. Horseshoes and worn out human shoes in the streets, a nigger padding slowly through the dust —but ready to run. A hound dog, a dead mule—but seldom even a scrawny chicken.

He was not a brigadier until after the battle of Atlanta, Wagnal said, but Clint began to assume as much authority as he could lay his hands on as soon as he got back to the regiment. The Crimean had twelve punishment horses being ridden almost all the time while it was so hot that I have seen the strongest farmer boy keel over in the ranks. Often I have seen two men mounted face to face on one of the tall wooden horses. Sometimes, when it was not too hot to raise spittle, they played a game of spitting at marks on the ground, for their hands were tied behind them—a duty which the Crimean always allowed the drummer boy to perform. The drummer boy was now a corporal; and, since Crime picked him up at Shiloh, he had grown little taller but so much fatter that he was known as Drumbutt, behind his back. For no one dared incur the wrath of the Colonel's inquisitor. No one wanted to ride in Belton's Crimean Cavalry, as they named it when the new horses made their appearance.

I saw one man sitting on the narrow top rail holding up, with his shoulder, another who had fainted in the sun. I gave them a drink and threw cups of water over them both when no one was looking— and I know Rome did as much or more—but that was all we could do. Oh, the company cooks and the kitchen police scoured the pots clean enough, the lines were good, the muskets clean, all the buttons sewed on and the faces straight—too damned straight. And strangest to me then, the men admired and respected Belton for his hardness, though they now hated the Crimean. Belton's reputation was growing in the Army of Tennessee.

Where there was abandoned cotton—left unburnt in hope or hurry—there were always men following the army to wangle passes and send the cotton back through our lines to the North where it commanded contraband prices. While Clint was serving a short turn as provost-marshal of the corps, one night a Jew (sometimes it was an old Southern plantation owner and once I heard it was a German) came into Belton's tent. He oughta known better, they said. By Jesus the general sure give it to that Jew and/or Dutchy and/or Simon Legree sonofabitch.

Iss Brovust Marshal Pelton in? He is, sir, I am that officer, sir. Vell, I couldt denk der marshal vor ein bass do go oudside die lines. What for, sir? Ich vant to ged some goddon. Do you own the cotton, sir? Nein; bud tem Rebels burn id if I dond ged id. I do not give passes for such purposes, sir—especially to men who are too cowardly to shoulder a musket for their country at a time like this. Marshal, hier iss den tousand tollars vor ein sixdy tay bass. You damned thief and traitor, get out of here! If you are not gone in two hours, I'll have you shot. And, by God, the men said, the colonel taken him by the napa the neck and kicked his ass right outa the tent, where he didn't have any f—in' business anyway. Ain't ever seen hidener hair of that sonofabitch since the colonel worked on him. Why,

Wagnal said, as God is my witness, I heard that story all over again last year, from an old grayheaded man who joined the Crocker brigade in sixtythree and still draws a pension for a light case of dysentery he got cooling coffee in fence-corners.

But you can see now how Clint's star got into the ascending arc. He had built a reputation. The political brigadiers now sought him crawling. He sought very few men in the Army of Tennessee now, but Sherman himself. And Sherman, who preened himself a little on his wit, liked Clint well, for Clint arranged for Sherman to have said several good things which Sherman did not say.

One day before Atlanta, or at Peach Tree Creek, a young aide of Sherman's rushed up to the general, saluted and said: General Sherman, sir, two journalists have been killed in the action on our left. Clint, who was standing near knew how the general hated newspapermen, so he said: We'll have news from hell before breakfast, eh, General? Sherman laughed. Clint told the story that night in Sherman's presence to Sherman's staff, putting the remark in the general's mouth. After that it got down to the privates; and Sherman heard news from hell before breakfast so much that he came to believe that he *had* said it. But what was more important: that remark got Clint into the general's dispatches. It no doubt got Clint the call to speak to the New England Society and to the Reunion of the Army of Tennessee after the war, where the idea of Clint—this old friend who had sent him a box of Havanas—as a cabinet member must have entered the back of Grant's head.

But, Wagnal said, I don't believe I saw much of Clint in Georgia. I spent most of my free time, up to the battle of Atlanta, with Rome—and, if I ever saw a man gaunt down and sadden, it was your great grandfather. You must remember, my boy, that this was his second war and that he had had a youth of strife and hardship—and I think that his family back in Iowa had been forced to open a dressmaker's shop to help pay the taxes and keep themselves, though he sent them nearly all his captain's pay—when he got it. I believe that one Worsham Jones, whom he had left in charge of his livery stable was stealing the receipts and running Mrs. Hanks into debt. Besides these anxieties, he had one of the worst cases of dysentery I ever treated—and the general tone of his health was low. So I saw him sadden on the march through Georgia. Oh, he didn't give up. Don't ever believe, sir, that it was in Rome to give up. But the sadness grew deeper in him.

One day he said to me, at Peach Tree Creek, I think: Thomas, the boy without the teeth came to me today and told me Clint Belton had fired a pistol at him during the action. The boy thought it was only one shot. He said it looked as if the muzzle was pointed his way —and he sure heard the bullet whine. Do you think Clint is doing these things? Can it be that Bates and that lad are touched? Well, Rome, I said, what do you think of it! You pulled Clint and Bates out of the mud at Pittsburgh Landing—and Toothless too. Yes, Rome said, but that might happen to anybody.

The battle of Atlanta gave Clint Belton a fine total on the profit side of his ledger. His courage was high—he must have felt the luck in him that day. I am riding the crest, he said to himself. You know how that is: in a game of ball or cricket or tennis there are days when you are in fine form and fettle: when you wallop the ball you feel the good impact and you know as you swing and hit that this is a good shot, a beauty, which has already confounded your opponent and made him *hump* to no avail. Not that it was such a victory for the Union. It was a bad fight for us, a terrible fight. But for Clint it was a personal victory.

We were on the left behind some light works we had thrown up the night before. They opened with cannon about noon and pretty soon they were around behind us yelling that high Rebel screech and coming on like a bat out of hell. Oh well, Wagnal said, it seemed so. Perhaps they didn't really, for they were nearly all tired and hungry, and a good many of them were boys and old men. Why, I collared a boy who had his ma's butcherknife lashed to the end of a broomhandle. He tried to stick it in me, but it hit my belt buckle—and besides it was dull as butter and he was too weak. He cried with rage when I took the broomstick away from him and made him go behind our lines. He said you Goddamn' cowardly sonsofbitches of Yankees killed my ma with a shell.

I ought to have been with the wounded all the time, but I itched then to get out in front and get myself shot. That was how I happened to see Clint, on foot, running up and down the lines behind the works hollering for everybody to hold hard and give 'em hell. He had his Colt's revolver in one hand and his sword in the other—and, we'll give the devil his due—he had the eye of Mars and the beard of Zeus that day all right.

He had on his buck gauntlets and he was as dusty and dirty as all the actors who played the part of the dusty courier in all the melodramas about the War Between the States in little tank towns for years afterward. Once or twice I saw him wave his sword and take a shot at the Rebels over our heads. Sleepy Bates and the toothless boy were near me—and I saw Sleepy turn his head to look over his shoulder, with worship in his eyes, at the colonel. Clint was shouting and firing his pistol. I could see it kick in his hand.

Rome was standing beside Toothless taking aim with a musket he had picked up, when Toothless started beating him on the shoulder and pointing first to Bates, who was lying bellydown with his face in the redclay parapet of the works and then to Clint who was firing over our heads again. I saw Rome frown vexedly, try to hear what Toothless had to say and turn away to aim the musket again. I saw a red spot come up on Bates's back. When I looked up again, Clint was trotting toward another part of the line waving his sword. I think, if I recollect aright, Wagnal said, squinting his bloodshot eyes, that we had to hop over the works then, for they were coming up from the rear fast. After we got over I didn't see Rome or the Toothless boy again during the war.

I saw Bates later that day, or the next. Before I gave him to the burial party, I probed for the ball and pulled it out from where it had lodged behind the sternum. Somebody had taken his Pa's watch and his money—if he had had any. All there was left was a little soldier's diary with a lock of black hair tied with a cherrycolored ribbon— maybe from the head of that pretty ovalfaced, primmouthed girl who had walked with him at night in the quiet leafblown streets of Keokuk. Sleepy's diary made such statements as these: Have wrote to Ma and Pa and Tessie. Sent Tessie a Reb blet buckle and Ma 22 dollers. Got a lok of Tessie's hair and a pair nitted sox from her—wooll. She don't know it's hot down here this time of year. Ha! Ha! There was a Confederate shinplaster or two in the book—but I saw nothing of the pillage he had taken at Shiloh. I sent it all home to his mother, for there was no surname for Tessie—nor any address.

I wrote to Mrs. Hanks and told her that Rome was missing in action. Somebody else, I think, wrote to Toothless's mother.

But that was not all about the battle of Atlanta: Oh no. Clint became a hero that day. It was late, and they were desperate. We'd been on both sides of the works so much, I can't remember which side we were on when it happened. But we had plenty of muskets. Every time we beat them back, Shire Newton and Shuball York and some of the others would hop over the breastworks and pick up the good guns. There was a great lot of junk—flintlocks and shotguns and fowling-pieces—among the arms at Atlanta. For they were hardpressed, and nearly the whole city marched out with what weapons it could find in its houses. But the boys picked up only the good ones. So we were able to have relays of guns loaded every time they hit us.

I remember that line well. They were a set of the dirtiest, most forlornest, tiredest looking men and children I ever hope to see—some veterans and some recruits, but all tired and dirty and fought out, screamed out, marched out, squittered out and maybe starved out. We let them have three or four volleys and they went down like tenpins. The leader—he turned out to be colonel of the regiment, but you couldn't tell it from the getup he was wearing—seemed to be the only one who was shouting. He screamed right up to the edge of our breastworks and looked around. There were only six or eight men behind him—and they were standing stalk still, as if they were in a trance. Goddamn' you all to hell, for a passel of cowards, he screamed back at them. Come on! They didn't run; they just turned around slow and walked away.

The Georgia colonel was a little, old man with ratgray whiskers—nervous and stringy. He stood there on the parapet of our trench slashing the air with his sword—he didn't even have a pistol.

Suddenly I saw Clint jump up on the parapet and grab him by the seat of the trousers and the scruff of the neck and throw him back into the trench with us. Clint yelled: Don't curse your men! They're all dead! The Georgia colonel didn't say anything; he couldn't. He was knocked out cold. He didn't look as if he had anything to eat for a couple of days—and, to begin with, I doubt that he was ever fit for any sort of active duty. I noticed the sword he had in his senile hand was something like Rome's; and it later came out, in the various accounts of Clint's heroism, that the colonel was a veteran of the Mexican war.

Oh, yes, Clint's capture got around: That's the man who collared the Reb colonel barehanded, they used to say and point to Clint. He got a little scratch on his hand while he was grabbing the Georgian, and he wore the bandage around for days after it was useless. Sherman made him a brigadier on the spot, and, as usual, when he turned up the next day, the stars were shining on his shoulders where the eagles had perched. Some West Point colonel in the division resigned because of Clint's promotion over his head. But Sherman wrote a couple of fine warmhearted references to Clint into his reports, for he remembered how Clint could appreciate a major-general's wit. In that manner, my boy, Wagnal said, Clinton Belton began the first important leg of his political journey. Why, in a hundred books: *War Tales as Recounted by Our Heroes,* or *Under Both Flags,* or *The Blue and Gray,* or *Tales from the Campfire* which were sold by a thousand bookagents tramping the streets of all the little towns and are now turning up sadly on the shelves of cheap secondhand bookstores, you may still read how the gallant colonel of the Hundred and Seventeenth Ioway Volunteers became a brigadier at the battle of Atlanta, but few, if any, will tell you how the Georgian—though exchanged and back with his regiment—died perhaps of shame and loss of heart.

Wagnal's bloodshot eyes were staring into the oil-lamp now, Lee remembered. At sometime in their lives, Wagnal said, all men meet a god. Some meet him in death and some meet him at night in dark bedrooms and some in the light of pine torches in the woods to the tune of yelling in an unknown tongue and singing and a drunken man pounding a book and some while turning a wheel with a piece of paper on it in Tibet. And they meet God because He is part of them—because they've got to have Him. Because they created Him in their own image.

God is the lifeboat, the insurance policy, the fire-extinguisher, the lastditch, the magnesium flare, the parachute, the trumpcard, the comforter in the sorest and uttermost need, the vaccination, the gasmask, the fortress. And He is Love.

I forget, Wagnal said. I forget how it was then exactly. But take me back there to Atlanta, back to Bentonville, back to Columbia, South Carolina and let me try to find the streets and houses and feel how it was at night, and how it was on the turnpike at noon, and how it was at dawn. Oh, I would remember, all right. I would remember why Sleepy Bates and Toothless and Rome were gone and a thousand others I had known. Rome was dead for all I knew—and I had to cut off Shuball York's leg at Bentonville. And oh, there were thousands I had known or never known rotting away in the shallow graves and trenches of Georgia, Mississippi, and Tennessee. It may have been in

Georgia that I first met the Christian God. John Simpson's voice blurry with the Scot's burr on his tongue, praying for the dead—calling for God to take sides in this Armageddon of the world. John Simpson was a surgeon too—and I thought I had the call.

And indeed Abraham Lincoln was killed on a Good Friday.

CHAPTER XVIII

LEE LEFT his arsenic-colored room in the Y.M.C.A. and took a street car to Erma Memmiger's house in the West End, an Old English house with big new chimney pots like the little old ones on the colleges at Oxford. There were ivy vines carefully trained around the entrance and tall cedars and thicktrunked oaks in the grounds. There was an abbey-like entrance of gray sandstone against the dark red brick. The house and grounds looked like a set of flats in a theatre. The soil around the concrete stoop, bare in the sun of a mild January day, was rocky.

Downtown the air was full of gray smoke and soot; and the light in the aisles between the buildings was as if it were tinted with a weak solution of lampblack. Here Lee squinted in the sun of this lost January day which should have come in April.

Erma was yelling from upstairs about boots when the broadfaced German maid let him in. He told her he was Mr. Harrington and felt awkward as she looked at him suspiciously. Erma came downstairs—in ridingbreeches and boots which didn't fit very well—and said:

Hello, Lee, and took him in the drawing-room and began introducing him to the people who were going. After that she said wasn't it a beautiful day and they didn't get to use the farm much in winter and Daddy wouldn't do much about the farm now anyway because of the depression—and she heard he wrote poetry too.

Yes, Lee said, isn't it a beautiful day?

What're we waiting for? John Sheridan said glumly.

Christa, Erma said, getting up from a stool and a little wellbred annoyance in her voice. Ferris tried to pick her up, but she wasn't even home. The maid said she was out doing her social work. I'll bet she isn't even ready now.

Hell! Ferris said. She never is.

Well, by God, Erma said, she'd better hurry or we'll leave her and let her drive out by herself.

There were the sounds of a door flying open and panting laughter. That'll be her, Erma said.

Hello, Erma, darling! I'm awwful sorry, but I'm just congenitally late. Hello, everybody.

The voice was almost like an English girl's voice—only it wasn't as set and whinnying and cutanddried.

Hello, Chrissy, Erma said, smiling.

Lee lifted his eyes from a pagoda in the rugpattern and got up feeling clumsy. He was about to meet the famous Christa Schell: A tall girl in a light blue basketball sweatsuit and old tennis shoes had a foot up on a Duncan Phyfe chair pulling at a sock. Goddamn! she said. A great sheaf of bobbed hair the color of new straw with darker yellow stripes in it fell forward over her cheeks. Lee, standing awkwardly await, kept trying to think of the kind of a face that would go with the voice and hair and saying to himself that it wouldn't be the right kind of a face, even though he had been told that Christa Schell was beautiful. Christa tossed her head and threw the hair back a little from her cheeks. Lousy socks, she said. Ferris do give me a cigarette. Ferris gave her one; and she put it between her lips and allowed it to hang loosely while she pulled at the sock again. This gave her an amazing air of dash and evil. Ferris struck a match, and still pulling at the sock, she turned her head and drew the fire to the cigarette's end. Then she gave the sock another little pull. Nuts! she said and giving it up, stood upright, tossing the newstraw hair back off her face with a proud toss.

Miss Schell, Erma said. Mr. Harrington.

Perhaps something said to him then, as he looked at the face for the first time, that the end of seeing that face was a long time in the future —or maybe never. It was a white face; the pink on the cheeks was scarcely there. The eyes were dark brown with a little golden mote in one of them—the right—and the lips were lipsticked dark red, following the curled outlines of a child's lips. How do you do, Mr. Harrington, the child's lips said most impersonally and without question. How do you do, Miss Schell, he answered, not letting any expression come into his face at all.

She inhaled the smoke of her cigarette deeply and blew out a long blue stream. Christ! she said turning a little to Ferris as she lay back in a chair, her long legs stretched out, her body in a crumpled sprawl. Never live your life in a hurry, my lad—it's no sale.

Lee turned away from her after she had turned away from him, and feeling gauche, sat on the fenderseat around a large clean fireplace which looked as if it might have been a fireplace just built and waiting for its first fire in the reign of Henry the Eighth—perhaps in the hall of an Oxford college. Covertly, he watched Christa, for he had never seen a girl like her in his life. Her head was not so much tilted proudly, even when she sprawled, as it was fixed proudly to her shoulders. And, even in this pride of joining, her neck and the parts of her neck which became her chin and her breast had the soft curves of a lovely child.

I saw Miss Day, the producer, yesterday and tried to offer her my services for little or nothing to help her revolutionize the theatre. She said she was *awwful* sorry but she didn't care to revolutionize it—and she didn't want my services as an actress at any price.

Mr. Harrington—Lee, Erma said, was in Wilma Day's stock company, weren't you, Lee?

Yes, Lee said, watching the sheaf of Christa's golden hair tumble as she turned her face toward him again. It was very amusing, he said sterilely, under the cool haughty look she gave him.

Were you? Christa said, looking away. Well, you were much more fortunate than I. Erma had gone out of the room; and Christa left him marooned in his own silence.

He tried again, stiffly: Are you interested in the theatre?

Yes, but I don't seem to be able to do anything about it. She scarcely turned her head this time. For some reason that morning she had worn her haughtiest manner. Perhaps it was because she had been to Vassar, or worked on the *New Nation,* or had a member of the Royal Academy try to paint her back when she was fifteen, or perhaps she thought she was desperate.

Well, this was the first time I'd been on the professional stage wher I acted with Miss Day, Lee said.

Really?

Yes, I just happened to get the job—

Christa was not listening: Ferris and the girl named Elsie were talking to her about names Lee had never heard.

Hell, he thought, she can go to hell—old bloody hell.

One of the poses of the face in Lee's mind—one which he could never escape was her head laid back on the seat of the coupé. When she found out he "had been up at Oxford," she invited him to dinner at her house. He had promised himself that he wouldn't have anything to do with her because of that snub, but he forgot that promise quick enough. And he never could escape seeing her head laid back in the coupé.

It was March at night in the midblock darkness of the street in front of her house which had been a fashionable residential street when her father drove a buggy to the laboratory. There was a stunted elm just budding on the parking; and Christa was talking softly about the rocks on the Dalmatian coast and how she had hurt her foot on a walking tour in Provence. And Lee was talking—also softly—about the Isis and the Cherwell in the spring and the punts and the gramophones and undergraduates shouting: I say, have you chaps got a needle? in the long English twilight on the river.

Christa's eyes were halfclosed and her child's throat lay stretched back over the seattop and the great sheaf of newstraw hair with darker stripes in it spilled backward and fanned out on the little shelf of the coupé. By simple motions such as are never foreseen, Lee was kissing her with his arms around her waist and pressing her to him hard and smelling her clean, babyish smell of talcum and her cleanscrubbed American childhood with governesses and maids and private schools—and things a young girl must not do or read or think or see.

Christa was not kissing back, nor helping him to kiss her, nor being exactly passive, but lying there in quietness, her long body stretched out.

I'm sorry, Lee said, I didn't mean to do it—but you were so beautiful, I couldn't help it.

It's all right, Christa said. I was surprised you didn't kiss me before. People kiss each other.

But I mean I didn't want to kiss you because I'd decided I was through with love. And I decided I wouldn't see you again after that first day at Erma's because you were so damned haughty and didn't pay any attention to me.

But, darling, people kiss each other.

You've got stripéd hair, Lee said.

Christa laughed softly. Stripéd hair, she said. That's really lovely. That's one of the nicest things anyone ever said about me.

And, Christa, I love you—I love the hell out of you.

Christa laughed again: But it doesn't mean anything. I kiss people. People kiss me.

Who? What people? But it's none of my business, I suppose.

Sure, I don't care. John Sheridan kisses me and Vöder and lots of peeps.

But John's married—

Yes, I know, Christa said indifferently, but he kisses me just the same. He kissed me the first time out at Erma's that day. I was a little surprised.

What did you do?

Nothin', 'cept let myself be kissed.

Lee kissed Christa again, feeling her smoothtight cheekskin against his face and smelling her clean talcumpowder babysmell.

But Christa, he said, I loved you when I first saw you, even if you wouldn't pay any attention to me. I never saw anyone in my life who looked so really noble.

But darling, I'm just a blonde floozy.

Lee did not know where he was, nor what he was saying. He saw the lonely beam of the streetlight at the end of the block and the branches of the stunted tree, their green buds in shadow—and later he remembered the hunched shadowfigure of a young man going into the rooming house nextdoor to Christa's house and a cigarette tossed with a splattering of sparks into the street. A street away, but remote, an early morning trolley skreeked and clanged and bumped in its definite course.

He (who lived in an arsenic-colored cell in the Y.M.C.A.) sat with his arm around the girl who had grown up in the dark house. He knew then that the small living-room contained the pretty blue and gold and pink and gold watercolor of Christa in her teens (with her head thrown back and a wind in her hair and the childlike curves of her neck so accurately drawn that you would not have thought them true, if you had never seen Christa), a plaster cast of the Venus de Milo, a signed selfportrait of a famous German lithographer, her father's ashtrays, pewter and silver, engraved, like the one on Professor Whitehall's mantel in Lawrence, with the arms of a student corps at Heidelberg and crossed sabres commemorating his student duels, when he was a young Dane like the Prince from Elsinore.

Lee knew these things were there and he knew that when Brockdorf

Schell had driven a buggy to the laboratory and even later when he had driven his first motorcar—when Christa's mother had still looked like Christa looked now, a beautiful tall young girl not long out of Vassar —they were there except for the watercolor of Christa which was not painted yet. But it might as well have been there, for it was destiny that there be such a girl as Christa and such a picture of her above her mother's mantelpiece.

Christa called it the chocolatebox picture and said she didn't like the Goddamn' thing—and secretly, Oh puke! But it was still a very image of Christa—all white and pink and gold—definitive as the work of a fine cabinetmaker. And perhaps a truer likeness than a color photograph.

Lee had seen the watercolor and the Junker ashtrays and mugs and her father's shaved head and the ridges of scartissue not fresh and new now as they had been under the cap of the student corps. The house was not very large and had a porch like the smalltown house in which Lee had been born—but there were the Junker arms, the watercolor of Christa, the cast of the Venus de Milo—and Christa herself in a dress perhaps from Paris with no silk at all in it to cover the (fifteen year old, then) back that the Academy painter had followed from London to Nice to Cannes and from Cannes to Juan les Pins—and she saying about the dress: Jesus H. God, my two-year-old Paris frock! and treating it (though it looked new and much more distinguished than any in a roomful of rich debutantes) as if it were a troublesome clout of rags hanging onto her.

Waiting in the living-room of the house for Christa to come downstairs, he had looked long at the picture of her, trying to see her as she had been when she played in the garden at the back of the house and read *The Wizard of Oz* in English and Grimm's fairy tales in German —and trying to see her when she had quarreled with the other little girls—trying to see her when she hit that other little girl in the face and threw her down and rubbed her nose in the dirt—trying to see her as she moved, running, skipping, walking with dignity through the green spring streets of the city.

And the sooty snow of the smoky winter and the hot miasmal nights of the summertime: And then trying to see her, slim and straight, her straight, higharched feet in Educator sandals, sneaking away from the private school in the afternoons to see hot love pictures in neighborhood cinemas with smuggled powder and rouge compacts concealed between the breasts which were beginning to stand up firmly under the simple schooldresses which she never wore but allowed to come with her. And the city where she was born was always new and old and secret; and a place for discovery was always around the block.

Sitting in her living-room looking at her picture and at her father's ashtrays and the set of Goethe in German and all the small things scattered on tables (things which he knew were perhaps in the world, but things which were foreign to the house where he had been born), Lee could see her moving through the years of the city, of Vassar, of the Wisconsin summers in a cabin, of the times in Paris and on the Dalmatian coast and of that time in Provence. He could see her getting on trains in the Union Station and on a bicycle in the damp college green of Vassar. And he could see the gangling youths and the young fellows (Harvard and Yale and Amherst) who had kissed her or tried to kiss her or followed her around. But always above these images was the image of her proud face—the golden mote in her eye and the way her head was set on her shoulders—and her newstraw hair fanned out in the coupé. It was so painful that he could hardly bear it, yet he thought more and more of her and wanted to see her more and more. And she said:

But look here, my lad, you can't just play ducks and drakes with my social obligations.

Oh, to hell with social obligations, he said hoarsely, his voice profane with yearning. Holy Christ—social obligations!

Christa laughed. But you know, even if one doesn't like it, one has certain social obligations—friends. Peeps I've known all my life and who're pretty Goddamn' fine in their own quiet way.

They were getting out of the coupé at two o'clock in the morning in the dimlight of the cornerlamp and the nightsounds of the city; and Christa, turning her head as she stood under the stunted elm in the parking before her house, caught the light in her golden-moted eye. And Lee knew that she was thinking of a thousand things which did not concern him. And he knew that though he was thinking of other things (of home when he was a boy and other girls and Papa and the Lyric Theatre and the bicycle and Dee Given and Breezy Gortz and Grandpa Beckham and Grandpa Harrington and Mamma and the tin sword and Anne's house in Lawrence and Christ Church meadow in the spring) that all these thoughts were mixed with now and mystically changed by Christa, though they remained things that had happened as they had happened or as he had thought they had happened.

And he wished to say to Christa: I did not die once because of a three-speed bicycle which my father set beside my bed; and once I had a tin sword that I stuck in my eye and Mamma took it away from me and threw it in the privy; and Grandpa had white whiskers and fought with General McClellan at the battle of Gaines's Mill—and I knew a girl once who was like the music of a clavichord and said, with her eyes sparkling, It's so clear and crisp in wintertime! I love it!

I may go to South America, Christa said. I must go away to far lands. I can't stand this place. People squatting together! Ugh!

CHAPTER XIX

WHEN Christa came back after the publicity trip for the railroad company whose fat, middleaged publicityman sent her American Beauty roses at every whistlestop where the telegraph company and the florists' union could get them, she had a blue Virgin of Guadalupe waterbottle and stories about how she saw Sergei Eisenstein, the Russian film director, who had left Hollywood because they had wanted him to make Dreiser's *An American Tragedy* as if it were a set of newspaper clippings about any American murder trial.

He was making a proletarian film with peons and workmen as actors—and Christa went to see him shooting them in a few sequences. At the hotel there were a lot of comrades, Christa said, who were too amorous. And they said what the hell, weren't they all comrades together, and wasn't Eisenstein a great artist and hadn't he damn' well shown those Hollywood bourgeoisie rats he couldn't be bought?

And when she was in Mexico City, she climbed up on the scaffold and talked to Jiminez, the great proletarian muralist. And he was charming and made her stay all morning—until her Royal Academy back ached from sitting on the hard boards.

By God, she kept saying, I know they'll rise up and kill us all—and one can't blame them a damn' bit!

But Lee always saw her with her head held high and with the soft curves of her child's throat carrying a stately and arrogant pride. He thought of the Welsh queen Guinevere, and how she had been adulterous, and how often she had invoked dear Jesu, and how she had ended in a nunnery at Glastonbury.

You are like Guinevere must have been, he said to her, smelling the babyish talcumpowder smell of her nice young girlhood.

But I'm a whited sepulchre, darling, she said. And I'm not noble. I even talk like a floozie—and I have no reserve. My mother has almost completely despaired of ever making me a lady.

But you *are* a lady in the best sense of the word, Lee said.

And then that day at lunch when she said: Yes, I'm sure your Grandfather must have been a fine Old Southern Gentleman.

Lee didn't tell her any more about Grandpa Harrington, though he had meant to tell her that Grandpa Harrington had done no work in Fork City except to weed his mint patch for mint juleps. That wasn't strictly true. There were the cows and the little milk route—and anyway, there was never any liquor in the house—nor money for it—to make juleps with. And Grandpa Harrington sat and read *The Clansman* by Thomas Dixon, Jr. And Aunt Cornelia said it was Father's favorite book, because he knew all the characters in it—and if Lee would be a good boy and not call Grandfather Grandpa, someday maybe *Grandfather* would tell him about his Great Uncle Sion in Pickett's Charge.

Lee stopped talking, hearing his words fading and Christa's smooth Vassar voice saying what it did not finish, but what it put a polite unrounded period to. Yes, I'm sure he must have been. . .

But the waitress brought the check and he paid it and Christa said that hell she didn't want to go home. It would be just too bloody. By God, she was sick of 8899 Louisiana avenue and couldn't they go to a movie—one of those lousy movies on Pine street. She just loved lousy movies.

Why not? Lee said; and they went down into the dingy street which seemed bright and beautiful to Lee now. You could tell it was spring because of the soft, heavy air and the sun behind the smog-clouds. Grimm and Gorly's still had some gardenias at a dollar apiece, so he bought Christa one and said: And there stood Grimmie's Gorly ghost with a white flower in his hands. Beautiful, she said and laughed like her childlips.

They went in a fifteen-cent all night movie house in a light beautiful mood and sat in the balcony and watched a gangster picture with James Cagney in it. And Lee put his arms around Christa and kissed her and nobody paid any attention to them—except maybe to smile that kissing was the right idea. When they came out it was almost dusk and cooler and Christa said:

Oh, I'm perfectly wild about lousy movies.

And Lee said: I love you, Christa.

CHAPTER XX

There were about eighty of us after Pickett's Charge, Uncle Pink said. Oh, a few more came in afterward when we got back into Virginia, but I don't reckon we was more'n a hunderd and fifty when all was totaled up—and we had eight hunderd when we marched into Pennsylvania.

Why, hell, Lee thought, Uncle Pinckney was an old actor who luxuriated in talking like a hillbilly. How he loved the rich masculine quality of the word plowhannels! . . .

This ole feller talks in the tongues, don't he Jud said. No, Uncle Pink said, rubbing the tumefactive egg, the secret encystation of years of defeat and corruption, Jud always spoke better English than I. Even I spoke better than I do now. You may have noticed how I catch myself now. Why, I was considered a good scholar in Gadkin County in my time. Maybe Jud said: Old Cawdor's a fanatic, isn't he, Pink? He's what they call a Seventh Day Adventist, I said. Let's slow down and have a drink, Jud said.

MY GREAT UNCLE Pinckney Harrington lived—maybe still lives—up in the hills outside of Caldwell, near where my father was born, Lee remembered. No, he wasn't a hillbilly. Maybe it wasn't the hills—maybe it was just near the hills. His house was a house too—not a cabin. But it was not painted, and the pine siding had got the gray weathered look that all those unpainted houses get down there in North Carolina. The heads of the nails were rusting off, and the streaks of rust from them had run down the sides in parallel lines. The porch, which was on one side, had honeysuckle on it and sloped like a sloven toward a wooden stoop. Both the house and the porch stood on little piles of rock—added to now and again when they seemed to settle—so that there was a gap of about a foot and a half between the house and ground. There were a couple of fat brick chimneys built on the outside of the walls.

Inside there were a couple of fireplaces and a couple of mailorder house stoves. Two doors opposite each other—nearly always open— let air into the main room of the house, in which there was a long pine trestlelike arrangement with pine benches on either side of it. This was Uncle Pink's board: At this his family and guests—when anybody was passing that remote way—ate.

The house had bare pine floors, not very clean, a good many rooms of flimsy batten or wallboard partitions, windows with small panes—some broken and mended with yellowed newspapers and perhaps an old seed catalog or two. In the front of the house there was another door which led out on the rickety porch from a sort of parlor or sitting-room. In this was a pair of photograph-and-crayon portraits of my great grandfather and great grandmother in walnut frames and photographs of my father and grandfather. My aunt's organ and Uncle Pink's fiddle were there too; and a pineneedle pincushion souvenir of the Old North State from Blowing Rock was tacked to the wall. Maybe there was a stove in the center of the floor and a rag rug or two. I think there were some chairs called splitbottom—and a storebought or mailorder Morris chair with a tinbucket of the beergrowler type on the floor beside it for Uncle Pink to spit at while he sat in the bosom of his family as lord of the manor and patriarch.

The place was hard to get at: I drove there in a spring wagon, through a cool drizzle. The spring had been unusually rainy and the roads were thick with red sticky mud. Once my father had made a photograph of the old mill which you pass on the way to Uncle Pink's; and I remembered the old glossy print pasted in an old loose leaf photo album from my father's studio, marked Fort Davis Views. It was the same mill, though the image had gone through the rapid rectilinear lens of the old Poco Camera almost thirty years ago. But the unpainted pine boards were trousers gray now; and I could see the selfsame three knots in the double doors where the farmers had brought their corn to be ground into cornmeal and shared the meal with the miller for the grinding, in the days after the war when there was point to the story my Grandfather Harrington used to tell about the man who shot the squirrel and said to his wife: Well, Nancy, we-uns'll live high while we're a-livin'—we'll eat us a whole ham of this yere squirrel.

I looked at the old mill and the rickety wooden flume which had carried the water of a mountain creek, long since diverted to another bed, over the old overshot wheel, which now stood still and damp and green with moss, its iron shaft rusted—and probably stopped in the exact position those thirty years ago when the miller walked out of the mill with the last sack of meal over his shoulder, not even looking back at the millstone. I looked at the mill and thought of another story my father had told me about a lazy man in North Carolina.

North Carolina was full of lazy men: Oh, in those early days you could let the pigs and cows roam and get fat. You didn't need to manure the land: you could just move on and build another cabin. The bees were on the hillside making sourwood honey from the gum-tree for you. But anyway there was a man who was powerful lazy—I reckin thar wasn't a man in the hull state of Nawth Cahlina was as lazy as he was.

He was so lazy they had to feed him as if he were a child to keep him from starving to death. Yes; and they had to feed his wife and childern too, because apparently, he wasn't too lazy to git himself a lot of childern—and his wife was a good woman, but she couldn't be expected to feed the whole family.

Anyway, it got to be a sin and a shame the way that man wouldn't do a thing for himself. So the men folks in that neck of the woods had a meetin' and decided that, if he didn't mend his ways, they'd have to bury him alive. For he was practically dead anyway.

Well, he didn't mend, so they made him a coffin. He did gather enough energy to say: Make it good and roomy and easy, boys! They said they would, because they appreciated comfort themselves—being just *normally* lazy fellows—and never had anything *personal* agin the lazy man. It was just his mortal burden. Well, they dug the grave and hefted him into the coffin and nailed down the lid and started the wagon toward the buryin' ground.

They were all walking along beside the wagon. The wife and childern were walking along too, but nobody was saying a word—and everybody was looking mighty melancholy. They all just hated to bury Ole Watt. After all he was the *laziest* man in North Carolina. And they were kinder daggone sneakin' proud of him fur that. They were almost to the buryin' ground when one of them spoke up and says: I'm willin' to give Watt a bushel a corn, pervidin' you all ain't agin hit. We-uns ain't agin' hit. Did you hyear him, Watt? I hyeard him boys, Watt says through the coffin. Air ye willin' to reform an' rustle around fur yer childern? I'm willin', Watt says. Well then, we'll let Ty give you that bushel a corn. Hold on, Watt says, mortal weary, through the coffin. Air it shelled? Naw, Ty says. It hain't shelled. Drive on boys, Watt says, like he fell asleep in the coffin.

I looked at the old mill, Lee thought, and the wild waste of the country—and I began to understand the story. I began to see how heartbreaking the story had been—and not funny at all. I began to see the melancholy of the country and to think, for the first time in my life, of my father as a North Carolina boy, born after those four years when his father had been marching on other men's business. I began to feel the defeat in the air before I got to Uncle Pink's house.

I knew you were a Harrington minute I set eyes on you, Uncle Pink said. I knew you were Robert's boy. Both of you look like Jud when he was a young man. Pinckney Harrington shook my hand with a small hardsurfaced cracked paw as he looked at me shrewdly with watery blue eyes. He was a small man in a pair of blue jeans suspended by one gallus over his left shoulder.

Behind his left ear, in a veiny pouch of skin, there hung down some eggshaped tumescent mass. The pouchskin, blue with the veins and stretched tightly by the bulk of this tumefaction, looked faintly damp.

Uncle Pink seemed to be talking to me in a way I did not yet understand at all. From a great store he was showing me samples: an aspect of my father, a glimpse of my grandfather or his brother, a memory or two of them both before the background of those hills, those unpainted ruststreaked houses and those long-gone years of the Civil War which had added a glut of memories to this country in some forty months.

My female cousin, a teacher who had gone to Le Gallienne College for Women, said Uncle Pink got himself involved in Shotgun Wedding Decadence. He's a bad egg. I've got no use for him. Pinckney Harrington? my uncle, her father, said. Shif'less, no'count. Lives in the hills. Plays a fiddle. Got a lot of childern in ten counties. War? Hell no! The war never done nothin' to him. He was just low

down and ornery fore the war was even thought of. But Pinckney's a smart feller. Trouble with him he buried his talent under a
bushel. He lives up thar in the hills and lets on he don't give a
damn.

They said Uncle Pinckney was caught behind a laurel thicket with
the woman he married—a mountain woman, she was supposed to be
and much younger than he. Uncle Pinckney must have been around
seventy-five; and the shotgun wedding to the hill girl must have
happened at least twenty years ago—but there were five or six young
children standing around the door beside a graying woman with a
lean face and descending belly and breasts.

She was wearing a blue printed calico dress, drawn tight to the
waist and blousing over, which gave her a loose strawstuffed appearance. She looked at me steadily with sharpfocussed brown eyes. Lee,
Uncle Pinckney said, this is yore Aunt Sally. Sally, this is our nephew,
Lee Harrington. Well, howdy? Aunt Sally said. He's the spit an'
image of Jud, ain'ty? And these are your cousins, Uncle Pinckney went
on: Anna and Elizabeth, Zebulon, Jeremiah, Judson—for your grandfather, and Moses—we hardly expected him at all, Uncle Pink said.
'Twas almost as if we had found him in the bulrushes.

Anna, who was perhaps sixteen, wore shoes and stockings from a
mailorderhouse. But she looked at me with a level unselfconscious look
of her brown eyes and smiled. Hello, Cousin Lee. She put out her
hand with the grace of an outdoor beast, her small waist swaying a
little. All the rest of them shook hands shyly.

Anna had fine features, freckles around her nose, long straight
legs and firm round breasts. Uncle Pink looked at her with a reminis-
cent and prideful look. That girl, Uncle Pink said, reminds me of her
mother when we were sparkin'. Ain't she purty? Papa! Anna said,
not in a bashful giggly tone such as you might have expected from any
young girl whose Papa's her own true sweetheart, but in a slightly
sharp reproachful tone. As she said it her neck grew a little red; and
her mother smiled.

Yes, Aunt Sally said, he's the spit of Jud, all right, if you can
judge by the pitcher. That's right, Sally, Uncle Pink said, he is—and
that's judgin' from life, when Jud was younger than when that picture
was taken. He's a Harrington, I can tell, Aunt Sally said. Mother always said Judson was a Cawdor, Uncle Pink said. She said: Look at
that boy—there's not a drop of Harrington blood in him. He's no

kin to you folks. Pinckney grinned, baring his yellow and brown tobacco teeth. He's a Harrington, all right, Aunt Sally said, but he
favors Jud and Sion more'n he does you.

Well, Lee, come in, Uncle Pink said. The victuals are purt near
ready, ain't they, Sally? You must be right hongry, boy. I'll bet you
ain't et since sunup—it's a good piece from Caldwell here. He spoke
the hill dialect with a little overtone of irony and not consistently—
and a phantom smile curled up the corners of a reddish mouth under
his shapeless gray brownstained moustache. Sally shore kin cook good
he said.

Oh, she could cook, Lee remembered. I don't think Pinckney Harrington had over ten acres of hill land—and he didn't work it much.
But I sat down to that trestle with no tablecloth to biscuits four inches
in diameter and light as a feather, a half dozen combs of sourwood
honey, tender roasting ears, goldenbrown fried chicken, tender yellow
wax beans, greens cooked with sidemeat, fine yellow cornbread, sweet
potatoes, new potatoes, homesmoked ham, so tender you hardly had to
bite at all, buttermilk, fine homechurned butter, white and brown
sugar, hot rolls lighter than the biscuits, deepdish hotapple pie, cherry
cobbler with thickcream—and fine strong coffee out of a five gallon
enameled pot. All this was one meal and eaten off tin pie plates with
steel knives and forks and drunk from tincups. Uncle Pink unbuttoned
the two top buttons of his fly and fell to—so did the children. They
were all good big eaters and there was a great plenty of everything.
And there was plenty left when Aunt Sally and Anna began to clear
it away. I'm sure too, that these were no company victuals, for they
hadn't expected me; and they all sat down to it as if it were nothing
but the commonest of routine meals. After the meal proper, there
were apples and cherries and grapes on the table just to munch at or
top off on or to fill your belly good and tight and pull your hide good
and taut so that you would feel warm and fed and satisfied.

Boy, Uncle Pink said, I've gone good an' hongry in my day, an'
I don't study to go hongry eveh again.

We went out on the porch; and he took out a homemade leather
tobacco pouch, filled a corncob pipe and lighted it with the thick
satisfaction which comes from the anticipation of tobacco smoke over
a full belly. So, he said, drawing a smooth long drag of the fragrant
homecured smoke, my dear little niece, Clarissa, sent you up to see
your wicked old uncle.

She told you, I've no doubt, that I knew a lot about the Civil war and your grandfather—but that I was not really decent folks. She filled you up with dark innuendoes about shotgun weddings and ruint hillbilly gals. No, Uncle Pink, she didn't say— Now, don't spare my feelen's, boy, Uncle Pink said. I'm an old reprobate, not fit to tie the shoes, let alone look upon our Pure Southern Womanhood. The Methodist kinfolks down in Caldwell don't like me. I'm an old pariah—I'm the prodigal son who never came home, nor made a dime.

You know, boy, there are folks born and raised right here in this county who've never been out of it—and your Aunt Sally in there's one of 'em. Why, she planted a cedar tree years ago and named it fur Jim Collis who ruint her sister, so that soon as it was tall enough to cast a shadow across a grave, Jim'd die.

Well, the damn' thing grew up just tall enough to do just that; and not long after, Jim died, all right, and made a widow out of her sister. For he'd been persuaded—Uncle Pink hoisted a pair of quotes around the word with his voice—to make her his bride. And not only that, Sally's brother, Bedford, went to the arms of Jesus in the melee.

They found Jim and him, stripped to the waist with their left arms tied together with a stout rope, and a pair of Bowie knives in their good right hands. Near the place where they bled to death there was a couple of jugs with a splash of corn in 'em. Sally hasn't planted a single damn' cedar tree since.

Bedford was a wild, lanky hillbilly, who'd just got a call to preach Christ while he was still between the plowhannels—an' he set out to reform Jim. They were both lickered to the gills.

But that's not to the point, Uncle Pink said. You want to hear about your grandfather and the Eighty-sixth North Carolina regiment. You'd love to hear that yore ole granpappy was a chivalrous young Southron with a sword of justice in one hand and a mint julep in the other, but such things were not so.

Jud was a nice boy. I was ever right fond of Jud—mebbe I was fonder of Jud than the rest of us: Let's see—there was Sion and Joshua and Saul and Martha and Cornelia and Daniel and Jud and me. There was Paul and Timothy too, but they died as childern— almost babies—and I never knew them except as headstones in the family burial ground and in my mother's desultory references to them through the years of my childhood: Those were made as if she were referring to a burnt papyrus which had been in the library at Alexandria. So, for me, Paul and Timothy were always secret and remote. Perhaps Paul would have been a tall man like my brother, Daniel. Timothy was marked with a little cross over his heart. It rained the day they buried Timothy and the preacher dropped his grandfather's bible, which had come all the way from Edinburgh, in the mud. I thought Paul had had the yaws. And I thought the yaws were birds, Uncle Pink said. And I always saw Paul—and do still—walking around the fields in a set of long baby skirts followed by a solemn procession of strange black birds, not like crows—but bigger. They had golden beaks and the same purply black feathers as crows when the sun fell right on 'em and red roses growing out of the tops of their heads—and their eyes were red and shining as rubies. They follered Paul around solemnly, saying: Yaw-yaw, yaw-yaw, yaw-yaw, slow and careful of the way they pronounced it in deep niggerpreacher voices.

I would see Father come into the house and hear him say to mother: Where are those yaws? And Mother would answer: Paul has the yaws, Ezekiel. Ah, Father would answer, that boy has taken to the yaws and the yaws have taken to him. He has had the Call.

To this day I can still see Brother Paul, who died before I was born, walking through the fields with the yaws following him. Timothy, I never saw so clearly, but when I did see him, he was always hanging on a cross like Jesus—and over his heart, was nailed another little cross. He always had a crown of mountain laurel on his head and a sweet, innocent expression on his face—no suffering at all.

I have never before told these fancies of childhood to a living soul —and I tell them to you only that you may form some idea of what a boy's imagination might have been like in the North Carolina Piedmont before the war. Once when I was older—say ten or so—I asked my mother if it was true that Paul had the yaws. Pinckney Harrington, you must never use that word again. What are the yaws? I asked Mother. Pinckney, use that word again and I shall ask your father to punish you. I found out later what the yaws were, in truth, but I shall always think of them first as those goldbeaked roseheaded, preachervoiced birds following Paul through the fields and being careful of their pronunciation.

Now, Uncle Pink said, you must not think of the war as being long ago or out of date, or of this country in that day as being anything but here and now for your grandfather and me and your Uncle

Sion, who was in the Eighty-sixth North Carolina regiment too. It's true that we lived in a backward provincial country, and that we didn't get much news of what we may call the Outside World for convenience. But it is also true that we awoke in the mornings of the Eighteen fifties and sixties as boys who lived in the Modern World. You can be sure that we had heard of the big Cunard steamships which were crossing the Atlantic ocean; and when we talked of the telegraph a great excitement possessed us.

I remember how Sion and me used to talk of trains long before we had ever seen one—and later Jud used to ask us about them.

We did not have much: Father had set out from Virginia as a young man and drifted from the Tidewater section of North Carolina to the Piedmont, where he bought some land and negroes and built himself a fine frame plantation house. He reset some boxwood hedge around the front porch and in the back yard and went to work industriously to make it a fine productive plantation.

But it seems that, back in Virginia, one of his brothers, a man who could not see a fly buzzing around two molasses jugs without backing the fly to light on one or the other, had gambled himself out of the University of Virginia, duelled himself into a fugitive—and saddled their father with his debts. My father felt obliged to help his father with this burden. That was how my father's family began to lose ground. I believe only Timothy was born in that old house. I learned long since, and from no member of the family, that my father was forced to sell it because of this brother, of whom, besides the charge that he was a gambler and a duellist, the only other bit of hearsay says that he knew Edgar Poe at the University and recognized Poe's genius to the extent of laying a bet on it.

But the story says that Father removed to a smaller farm in this neck of the woods. That's where your grandfather and the rest of us were born. No, Uncle Pink said, we were never *exactly* poor white trash, for it was always right hard to fall into that category in this section of North Carolina, but it was a near thing after the war, I can tell you.

Jud and I were at Chapel Hill for a couple of terms after the war, for even then, Father wanted to do what he called make something of us. We'd been born in a fairly large cabinlike house, which was not a half mile from here. And Father still owned a fairsized chunk of land, three buck niggers, who must have been prime field hands in their day and a cook who was married to one of the bucks—or said she was.

Nevertheless Mother had a good bit to do. She spun and wove the wool and cotton and made our clothes until we were big boys—and even after that. And Father worked good and hard with his farming to get something ahead to educate us. I remember one winter we ate so many grits, I began to hate the sight of 'em. Even today, I seldom eat 'em—though after the war there were times when I was glad to get 'em.

Your grandfather, Judson, was maybe fifteen when he and I went down to Caldwell to join Zebulon Vance's old regiment. We signed up at the courthouse—there was a whole company from Gadkin county. Well, to be scrupulously correct about it, there was maybe four companies' strength all told through the war. For the Eighty-sixth was entirely killed about twice in the course of the war.

I reckon Jud and me thought that war was somethin' like a big picnic with firecrackers where all the soldiers wore bright buttons and pretty uniforms with gold braid—and after the battle got themselves waited on and petted by the ladies.

Sion had already got himself shot at Seven Pines. And we had it from somebody's letter that he had saved old Elisha Wagg's—the captain of the Gadkin county company—life at Malvern Hill. Well, Jud and me, like most boys of the time wanted to jine Jeb Stuart's cavalry, but we didn't have any hawses. It was a bitter thing I can tell you not to be able to get into the First North Carolina Cavalry, for they wore plumes on their hats and rode hell-for-leather all over and around the Yankees. And what was worse, all the girls all over the South had heard about 'em. So that every female's dearest dream was a young planter-aristocrat in jackboots, sabre and a black ostrich-plume. There was a passel of talk about beauty and chivalry. Somehow every man who got up on a hawss and rode around with the cavalry corps of the Army of Northern Virginia was a True Knight.

Women and hawses! Uncle Pink said. They bet on the hawses and fought oveh the women. The hawses were the most useful; they would carry them where they wanted to go. Mebbe the women did manage the plantation house and swoon at the right times—mebbe they did make bandages and attend the wounded. But I never saw any of 'em. And they were spoken of only as Paragons of Purity and Beauty and Womanhood. Almost any gal whose father had a few nigrahs and a farm that grew a few bales of cotton or a hogshead or two of tobacco thought of herself as a baroness at least. The daughters of the big plantations thought themselves equal to royal duchesses. They

kept sayin' the words Honor and Chivalry and Pure Sweet Womanhood over and over to themselves until they believed that they were
the only real lords and ladies holding their lands en feoff from God,
Who had favored them. They kept thinking that they were some noble
mystical thing the nature of which had never been rightly plumbed.
Oh, there were some beautiful highspirited women among them—and
most of the planters were howlin' brave. Some of 'em were right smart
scholars too. But all of 'em tried to act as if the Southern Aristocracy
was privy to some divine secret that nobody else knew, when it was
nothing more than a matter of acres and niggers.

There never was a lot of high-falutin' aristocrats in North Carolina.
Zeb Vance came down from the hills of Buncombe county and went
to Chapel Hill. I think he lived in Old South where your grandfather
and I stayed. We were never so tony as Virginia and South Carolina.
We knew that we were thought of as lowborn beside Virginians and
South Carolinians and that touched us in the quick. And we knew too
that we were just as innately aristocratic as any uppity South Carolinians or Virginians—even the ones of us whose daddies owned the
least niggers knew that. Still the boys from the big plantations got
the pretty pampered gals and rode the blooded hawses and wore the
fine clothes. And the war was fought to save the hawses and gals and
clothes for those same boys.

But did Jud and Sion and me know that? Not on your life! We
joined the old Eighty-sixth North Carolina Infantry with the idea that
we were a couple of fine knights like you read about in Sir Walter
Scott's books.

CHAPTER XXI

I HAD been ordained a priest of the Protestant Episcopal church,
Wagnal said, when I brought Katherine back to Knoxville, Iowa in
the fall of 1865. Since it was sometime, then, after Appomattox, his
family had given Rome up for dead.

It was at sunset, I think, for I heard Myra, your grandmother, tell
of it many times: The Hanks house was on a little hill. Myra was sitting
on the porch to get the cool of the evening and some of the younger
children were playing in the yard. He came, walking slowly and un-

steadily, up over the hill—and Myra saw his skinny silhouette, black against the red sky.

One of the children said: Look! Look at the old scarecrow-man! Ain't he funny! Shh! Shh! Myra said. Never, never make fun of anybody! You don't know ever what'll happen to you. And then she saw it. She got a view of some angle or movement which had been well-known to her since she could remember this world. Oh! Myra said. Oh! Oh! My Goodness! It's Papa, Ma! Ma! she screamed. Ma! It's Pa. He's come home! Oh! Pa! Papa!

She was out of the white picket gate, running toward the poor tottery shadow which was coming up over the hill. Papa! Papa! She almost knocked Rome down when she put her arms around him. Now, Myra, honey, Rome said, Now, now, don't you touch me any more—I'm none too clean. But he was clean—there was a little train dust on him, that was all. It was then she noticed how bad and thin he looked—and his hands. They looked black—and it seemed to Myra a little finger was gone.

Run in and tell your mother to get some water hot, Rome said. And get me Dr. Wagnal, if he's home. He ain't a doctor any more, Papa—he's a preacher. A preacher? Episcopal, Myra said. She took her father's arm and led him to the porch. He sat down panting on the porchedge as Mrs. Hanks came out. Romulus! Romulus! she said. Where have you been? Where? She started to kiss him. No, Lorna. Not now. They said it was not catching in Baltimore, but do not touch me yet a while. I am a loathsome thing. Where were you, Romulus? In Andersonville prison, Rome said. I did not die! I did not die!

Mrs. Hanks and Myra looked at each other in wonder. Papa had spoken in a high screechy way and laughed and when he opened his mouth his gums looked black with blood in the dusk. I did not die, Myra! Rome said screeching out a cracked laugh. I said I would come home to Ioway, and I came. Where's Thomas? Thomas! Thomas! He means Doctor—Reverend Wagnal, Myra said. Go get him! Mrs. Hanks said. Get him! And tell him to bring his medicine—that your Papa's home sick.

He fainted before I got there. He fainted and squittered in his trousers, before they could get them off—but Mrs. Hanks had him washed and in bed when I got there. He was asleep. He lay there on the bed muttering in his once fine live beard—now like so much dirty hay. The outline of every bone in his skull was easy to see; and his breath made the air fetid all around the bed; his legs were covered with dark purple scorbutic ulcers, with elevated fungoid surfaces. Two of his toes were gone; and there were maggots in one of the stubs. I stayed a couple of hours before he opened his eyes. Thomas, he said, I'm glad you've come. Where did they take you? Atlanta? Bates is not here, but Toothless is. Oh, Thomas, there's a drummer boy here like Drumbutt—wears a red cap. He's got a sailor who keeps the rest of 'em off him. The sailor was in the British Navy before he went with Porter. Sodom. But they took us in boxcars—and Toothless saved me. But my side hurts yet. I'm glad you're here, Thomas. Maybe you can help me sleep. I can't sleep for the pain and the itch. Ah, no, Thomas, I am not glad, for Dante's hell was nothing to this. Sodom, Thomas. I should like to know the truth about it. Perhaps there's a history. My side, Thomas—get the maggots out. I can't sleep. Last night they took everything I had—even the letters from Myra. He said he didn't get no letters from home here, and he could read good too.

I turned him over on his left side, Wagnal said, and the wound was closed but still red. On the right it was the same way but a little lower. He was hot as a blast furnace. Mrs. Hanks put her hand to his forehead. It's only fever, I said. I gave him an opiate. For two months I gave him opiates. And Mrs. Hanks fed him as much as she could. Myra and she sat beside the bed, holding his hand at night and stroking his forehead when he began to gabble.

This coal oil lamp sitting here now, Wagnal said, seems only to deepen the gloom around us. It is a long time now since any light but the sun at high noon does anything but plummet me down into the depths of darkness. I never venture into the streets here at night, because the electric lights, falling on the lawns and parkings in the summertime through the almost substantial heat—the heat curtain, the membranous heat, the gauzy heat of the night, the cobweb tent of heat over all,—because the electric lights falling on the lawns and parkings, the jimson weed and ragweed and milkweed on vacant lots, the elmtrunks and mapletrunks and the sheathing and the stone of the houses plunges me down into the nethermost region of the hell of the *old* night. For now I am old. And each memory is a shock that racks this big, clumsy arthritic frame. No, Wagnal said, with soft-sibilant-old-man-whistling in his words like a breeze playing around the corners of a long-moved-out-of-not-played-in house. No; I cannot stand the dim light shining through the heatgauze over the sounds of children laughing and screaming and screendoor slamming and the escaping steam and the slow bells of the locomotives—and the long blast of the engines whistling the crossings on the prairie. I cannot stand the light over these things, for when I see it over them, I know again that I was young and that I am old now and that I walked in a street in Keokuk thinking of Katherine Theron as Harold Bates walked past me with a girl with a primpedup red mouth on a silly ovalface. I cannot stand the light falling over the little spots of night, for I know it is falling in New Haven and Edinburgh and Iowa and Georgia and Mississippi and Tennessee—and up on the hill outside of town on Katherine's grave.

That summer in Knoxville when Rome first came home I did not know how light falls upon the earth. For Katherine was with me—and even the yellow wickflame beside Rome's bedhead, which threw shadows around his sunken eyes and in all the crevasses and creases of his face, which had not been eroded so deep at Atlanta—did not frighten me. But perhaps, even then, I knew that light was there—with gloom and shadows poured over the sounds of summer, as if black, thick suffocating oil were forced down your throat thickly with a piston.

Why, boy, I saw Atlanta burning in the night, the ammunition trains blowing fire into the dark of August. I saw the firelight of a hundred plantations licking the Southern night. I saw it bouncing on the barrels of bronze Napoleons from the North as they moved down the road toward the sea. But I did not know anything about light then.

I can see the bones in Rome's cheeks now—I can see all the shadows from the oil lamp as I did not see them then. For Katherine was at home two blocks away or sitting across Rome's bed from me, holding his hand down tight to the quilt so that he would not thrash the cover off until the fever was broken. I see Katherine and Myra and Mrs. Hanks wiping his sweatshining forehead and the Star-of-Bethlehem pattern of the quilt rising and falling in convulsive jerks as he breathed.

Thomas, Katherine said, you must not let Mr. Hanks die, for I love him. He smiled at me last night with his black gums and his pale lips and called me, Myra, honey. Now, I love him Thomas—even the sores on him. So you must never let him die. He did not die then. For a good many years I thought that it was because I did everything

I knew how as a doctor—and because after I got home from each visit, I went into my study and knelt down on the floor and prayed hard that the Father, Son and Holy Ghost would save Rome. For I loved him too—and before God, sir, Wagnal said, when Katherine said she loved Mr. Hanks, it made him twice as dear to me. Shuball York and Don Trott and old John Simpson used to come in to see him while Katherine and I were there. Then they would come home with us. Katherine would always ask Myra to come, but she never would until Rome was out of bed.

We used to walk the two quiet blocks to our house on a stone sidewalk beside an iron fence. On one corner there was a big square brick house with a chimney in the middle of the roof and keystones above all the windows. Don Trott used to start off singing:

> *There was an old man, and he had two sons—*
> *And these two sons were brothers.*
> *Josephus was the name of one,*
> *Bohunkus of the other.*

We all joined in—even old John Simpson, dour as he was. At our house Katherine gave them elderberry wine and popped popcorn in a skillet—and Don Trott ran home five blocks and back with his mandolin. We sang until good and late, Shuball beating time on the floor with his wooden leg. Little Brown Jug and Lorena and The Girl I Left Behind Me. All of them worshipped Katherine. And then I was happy. Well, perhaps I was happy, Wagnal said.

Katherine and I had a fifteen-room white frame house. It had a wide porch all the way around three sides of it with jigsaw scroll-work everywhere there was a place to nail it to—a tower with round windows in it and a cast iron railing of maple leaves around the top. We had a deep lawn with a long white picketfence around it; and before the front gate there was a white steppingstone on either side of which was the iron figure of a small negro boy in a brightpainted yellow sailor hat and a green coat—each was holding out his right hand, a ring to tie your horse to. But you know how they looked. There was a pair of them here on Hamilton street in front of the old White place. Katherine and I used to walk past them on summer nights just to see and remember how those in Knoxville looked—but their coats were yellow, and the lawn wasn't as deep, and the porch was shallow and high and only covered the front of the house—and the trees hadn't the girth of those in Knoxville.

But perhaps they *had*. For I was happier in Knoxville and Katherine was happier there for a while—though people did not like it when she rode old Percy. He was six then. He and the Cellini ewer were the only things that she brought from Mississippi with her. Her Father had forbidden her to marry me, and, though he did not allow himself the melodramatic gesture of cutting her off without a cent, he made it so unpleasant for her that she took nothing but the horse and the ewer, gifts from her grandfather.

Oh, we knew that Una and Clint were married. It was in the Burlington papers: Brevet Major-General Clinton Belton, formerly colonel commanding the Hundred and Seventeenth Iowa Veteran Volunteer Infantry, one of Burlington's most promising young attorneys-at-law and Republican National Committeeman for this district and Miss Una Theron, daughter of Mr. Fulke Theron, II, Theron Plantation, Messenger's Ferry, Mississippi, a direct descendant of the First Earl of Theron and William the Conqueror, were united in marriage at the First Protestant Episcopal Church of Burlington, something 1865, Wagnal said. The bride wore a wedding gown by the famous dressmaker, Worth, of Paris, France: white satin embroidered with seed pearls. The veil twenty yards of the sheerest tulle was caught to her hair by a bandeau of pearls—

They had taken a house in the most fashionable section of Burlington; and Una had set out to astonish and confound the natives. She gave them oysters on the halfshell, consommé, sweetbreads, chicken cutlets, pheasant, ices, charlottes, candy, tea, coffee and four kinds of wine for luncheon. The Burlington women must have begun to hate her before she got Clint away from there and to Washington. Oh, I believe there can be no doubt that she was thoroughly hated and feared in Burlington—as she was later in Washington. But she was never hated by the right people, the people who could advance hers or Clint's position—until they had lifted her as far as they were able.

After marrying Una, Clint must have found himself losing some of his popularity with the political brigadiers and colonels whom he had cultivated, with Havanas and Bourbon, during the war, for, as I remember it, there were a good many of those old boys who had no grammar, twanged outlandishly through their noses and pretended that they were of good common stock—as common as dirt and friends of the people—perhaps on the ground that the people preferred to be cheated by men who appeared to resemble themselves in ignorance, uncleanliness and a certain vulpine cunning, which would meet with such appreciative phrases as: 'I God, ole so-an'-so's purty Goddamn' cute, ain'ty? Shore can't git ahead a-him. He's too Goddamn' smart fer 'em.

From the beginning, however, in the camps of the Army of Tennessee, when the Crimean and Drumbutt had served the whiskey, they had been a leetle suspicious. An English batman pouring good honest American licker to good honest American politicians serving their country in a great cause! (Oh, they thought of themselves in those terms, for they were delicate thinkers, all right. They could take a premise and think it all around Robin Hood's barn—until they had so exhausted it that it would weakly yield them up any conclusion they wished.) And, when they came to think about it, Clint Belton had always been a little too well-groomed for a volunteer officer. Take Sherman, take all those doggy West Pointers, even take that fellah Stuart—well, naow they hadda right to spruce up. They was use to it. It was a part of a reg'lar soldier's discipline—but there reely wasn't any call for an Ioway volunteer to strut around like a featherassed bird. They had always thought that Belton was jist a leetle too slick fer his own good—too Goddamn' much of a purty rooster. They had come to believe that somehow demagoguery and political graft were guiltless, if they were clothed in roughandready plainasanoldshoe garments.

Little Clint cared about these fellows now—or, if he had cared, it would have availed him nothing. For Una was, more and more, making the decisions and planning the strategy. General Grant was their house guest when he stopped in Burlington on that tour he took with President Johnson and Admiral Farragut and General Custer. While he was there Una allowed nobody to meet him and petted and flattered Grant until, I've no doubt, he thought her one of the most beautiful, charming and tenderhearted young women in the world.

I can hear her, Katherine used to say: Dear General Grant, why don't they let you alone—after those horrible four years you so willingly gave to your country? General Belton and I have often said to ourselves that such tiring trips as this should not be commanded by that person—that tailor—in the White House, haven't we Clinton? And Katherine would tell me how Una would sit there at table, with all her cold regal airs concealed, making poor, old, shy Grant wonder how so beautiful a woman as this could be so reasonable and so understanding—and making him remember how Rawlins had brought him those fine Havanas (which he couldn't tell from the cheap weeds he used to buy in the stores at Galena and Cairo and Springfield when he couldn't raise enough money to buy a uniform and his volunteers made fun of him). Oh, yes, Grant was charmed that he didn't have to have this beautiful woman tied to a post, gagged and her rations stopped for a day, as he had had to do to the regimental badman in Springfield, to have her salute him. From the beginning, Una must have had him in the palm of her hand. And Clint was learning from Una. Oh, I've no doubt that he fancied himself as the dashing young lawyer-general, a Harvard man who had gone pioneering and commanded a regiment from Iowa, later to become a brigadier and finally to be brevetted Major-General—but this woman from Theron House near the Big Black River had taught him humility and, more than that, a good many things about getting on in the world.

There was, however, an alarming circumstance which attended the upward march of Una and Clint. It had cost money to astonish and humble the wives of the political brigadiers and the society ladies of Burlington. You did not get bluepoints on the halfshell from New England in the sixties without paying for them; you did not get Worth to tell his rosary over your gowns for nothing; and you did not serve four kinds of wine at an envy lunch for nothing. Clint's practice in Burlington was ample for a life of simple plenty—but not for what Una thought was her due. Money came in in great quantities from Mississippi, until the beginning of the year Eighteen hundred and sixtynine. That year gave the Black Republican newspapers almost as fine a story as the time Butler waved the bloody shirt: Mr. Fulke Theron, II, and Rasselas, his negro servant, who had served him at Balliol College, Oxford, were found dead and naked in the middle of the drive before Theron House—they were bound together lip-to-lip. The negro was horribly mutilated.

Nobody saw the fire: A negro admitted to the judge that he seed a reddinin' up in de sky las' night oveh tode Gen'l Theron's place, but he calcalated de Gen'l was buhnin' some mo' cotton fo' feah de Yankees gonna take it. That was in 1869 when cotton was seldom burnt to save it from the Yankees—and everybody had known for a good long time that even during the war no cotton had ever been burnt on the Theron place. The negro reckoned that the white folks wouldn't have to buhn no mo' cotton soon as Gen'l Pemmuhton and Gen'l Lee whupped the Yankees. A scallawag prosecutor told the negro that the war was over. Yes, suh, maybe it oveh—I ain' sayin it ain' oveh. He was trembling. I cain' tell mahse'f—Warner county too big. Did you see any Ku Kluxers? You mean ghos' of Cunfedit sol-juhs? Naw, suh. Ain' seed any sence I fetch drink a watah to soljah kilt at Shiloh las' yeah. He ain' had drink sence de battle an' he drink down de whole bucket. I ain' eveh seed no mo'.

Did you know Rasselas, the Theron negro? I knew him some. He talk white. He talk funneh—not like niggah.

The next day the carpetbag judge found this negro lying trussed up on the steps of the Jackson courthouse. The judge *thought* it was the same one anyway. He was naked and all the hair was singed off him and his eyes had been poked out and a court subpoena was stuffed into his mouth. He had been shot and stabbed about a dozen times— and the fire that singed his hair off had just begun to roast him. Of course he had been castrated. The distinguishing feature of the killing, however, was discovered when the judge pulled the subpoena out of his mouth; there was no tongue.

Katherine and I arrived at Messenger's Ferry after Mr. Theron and Rasselas had been buried. The mounds of the graves were still fresh and high when we drove into the park. I had never been there in the winter. The moss dripped with a week's drizzle and the trees—some with no leaves and whitish bark—sweated. The roads were a hopeless mass of loblolly.

Cady Ocamb—Colonel Cady Ocamb—had sent the wire to Iowa. He drove us out from Jackson in a surrey. I can see his prizebull face now, grave and heavy as he guided the one old livery horse into the gap where the iron gate with the griffons, lions and crocodiles had been. I am still of the opinion, Mrs. Wagnal, Ocamb said, that you should not undergo this ordeal. Thank you, Colonel Ocamb, Katherine said. I wish to see what's left of the house.

We could smell the damp ashes as the old horse's hooves and the wheels scrunched on the gravel. I noticed in the lighter dark of winter in the park that there were spots where there was no gravel now—

and it seemed to me that several trees were gone, though I could see no stumps in the high grass and weeds.

Colonel Ocamb, Katherine said, who are these fools in flannelette nightgowns who killed my father? I cain't say ma'am, Ocamb said. Are you a Klucker, Mr. Ocamb? I am not, ma'am, Ocamb said stiffly. Who did that to my father and Rass? Well, ma'am, I ain't alone in mah belief that it was an outrage pupputrated by the freed nigrahs. This tuhble deed, ma'am, was no doubt the deed of the Loyal League nigrahs—black hahted rascals that they ah. They wished to possess Mr. Theron's land—and they did not like his faithful nigrah servant. Such outrages, ma'am, ah bound to transpiah while the govahmint is in the hands of the scallywags and cahputbaggahs.

It was not they, Katherine said, because was not my father considered little better than a niggerlover himself? I had not huhd of that ma'am, Ocamb said, his great face falling into a bullsly look. Was it not that my father made dangerous remarks in Jackson and Vicksburg? Was it not that he said that he failed to see the difference between the negro race and the white, except for the pigments? No, ma'am, Ocamb said, still looking straight ahead of him at the spots empty of gravel in the road.

Well, Mr. Ocamb, Katherine said, I do not believe you. I think that you and your shirttail paraders killed my father. And the only reason I rode out here with you was to watch you as you answered the questions I have just asked you. You are not a good liar, Mr. Ocamb. Thank you, ma'am, Ocamb said. Puhaps, suh, you wish to offah some suppoht to youah wife's statements. Yes, Colonel Ocamb, I said, I am at your service.

Cady Ocamb, Katherine said, and you, Thomas, listen carefully to me. It was my father who was killed. There will be no more shooting for honor. You will not risk it, Mr. Ocamb. You're brave, I'll grant you—but you do not want to get all your friends into trouble and have a regiment of Yankees camping on your wife's doorstep. Please apologize to my husband. Katherine's eyes were slits and her dimples were up in her face—she was smiling with rage.

I beg youah pahdon, suh. I apologize. He was looking at the gravel on the drive in front of the houseless columns. Now, Thomas, to make it even, apologize to Colonel Ocamb. Thus honor will be satisfied, Katherine said. I apologized.

I still think you a liar, Colonel Ocamb, Katherine said. Thank you, ma'am, he said humbly, looking at Katherine with a sluggish bovine yearning look. And I know you to be as brave as a Spanish bull.

The columns stood soot-blackened with long rivermarks where the rainstreams had trickled down them showing pinkly through the black. And on the drive there lay bits of charcoal—woodghosts of the house. The pediment was gone, nothing of wood remained except a shutter blackened on the front wall. There was a wind from the othah way, Ocamb said, or it would have been the pahk. The whitewashed walls were smoked in splotches; and where they weren't the thick layers of whitewash came off in little checks when you put your hand on them.

I picked up a fragment of one of the porcelain waterclosets; and Katherine found a key of the harpsichord and a bit of the frame which had been around the quadroon. But we found nothing else.

The little Venus in the park had been beaten to pieces as with a hammer; and the Greek temple had lost a column. Come, Katherine said, let us look at the graves. Katherine walked around the two box sarcophagi and stood looking at the new gravemounds for a moment. Let us go now, Thomas, she said. Let us go back home and never come back here again. It is too damp and sad here.

I saw Ocamb looking at a corner of flannel caught under the lid of old Fulke's tomb. I do not think Katherine saw it.

CHAPTER XXII

YOUR great grandmother, Uncle Pink said, got hold of some fine gray broadcloth from Richmond and some firegilt buttons from Wilmington that had come over on a blockader, and made Jud and me some uniforms. She must have had an idea about how we felt about knighthood, for she made the jackets neat as anything. I think Father knew too, for he bought us some fine boots and a pair of leatherbound diaries—I never wrote in mine, and Jud burnt his.

We joined the regiment in Virginia in the winter of sixty-two—and that night we went out into the woods and rolled around in the dirt, because hardly anyone in the regiment had a uniform. Most of 'em just had a pair of homespun jeans and a jacket and a hickory shirt—and right much of the time the jeans and jacket were cotton.

But we were luckier'n fools. Ole Wagg, the captain of the Gadkin county company, was an ignorant kindhearted ole critter, if ever I saw one. He had a voice and a neck like a prize bull. He didn't have any uniform, but he wore a rusty black cutaway coat with a sword and pistol strapped into the meat of his belly. It was the biggest pistol ever I saw—we had a lot of funny names for it. Maybe he himself had sewed the captain's shoulder straps on his coat. He was half hillbilly and always 'lowed his Pa had fit at King's Mountain. He said the War was a war fur God—and he could coat scripter to show hit was. He never allowed anybody to say anything in his presence about our new uniforms—and he took care of the Gadkin county company as if they were his own childern. Anything he could share with us he shared—anything but hardship. He tried to take all that on himself. Many's the time on the march I've seen him throw a boy on his back and tote him a mile or two. And nobody ever dared plague the boy who got toted. If he hain't built fur it, he cain't holp it! Wagg used to say glaring.

We had a long tall feller, another half hillbilly, Harrison Lacey by name, who was as mean as they make 'em. He came from way up in the Toe river valley. They used to say he had killed a half dozen men before the war and liked to kill 'em with knives, 'cause they bled so good thataway—same as he liked to hunt bar with knives. He was proud and independent an' as damn' ignorant and superstitious as ever I knew a hillbilly to be. He wouldn't take orders from no man livin', he said. Wagg told him to go fotch some firewood to cook the grub one night—and Lacey reckoned he didn't study to do no woman's work. He jined fur fightin'.

Wagg told him twice. The second time Lacey pulled out a knife and went fur Ole Wagg. Some of the other boys stepped up to hold Lacey. Git back! Wagg says in that bulltone. I'll hannel him. Well, Lacey come up like a big cat, fast an' easy an' cautious, the knife ready fur Wagg's ribs. Wagg lumbered around a little an' stood still. Soon as Lacey got in close an' swung down with the knife, Wagg grabbed his wrist in that big meaty paw of hisn and put the other arm around Lacey's waist. That move of Wagg's didn't look fast, but it was. I thought Lacey ain't never met him no bar like this'n. After Wagg got that holt, it was just a matter of time. You could see the meat standing out in ridges under their clothes—and finally you began to see Lacey bendin' over backwards. Then his hand opened and the knife fell out on the ground, but Wagg still kept a-bendin' him over backwards. He did it so slow you couldn't tell how much power he was usin'—but I remember listenin' for Lacey's backbone to crack. He put him on the ground and held him there for a minute.

Well, Lacey says, you got me. Git the killin' done. I hain't aimin' to kill you, Lacey. You better, by God, Lacey says, er I'll kill you when I git up. Don't be a Goddamn' fool, Lacey, Wagg says. We got other killin' to do. I'll make you a proposition. I'll fight you any way you pick after the war's oveh. Meantime whilst I'm captain here, you obey my odehs. Ain't neveh been at no man's beck, Lacey says. This yere's wah, Wagg said. You hain't at my beck—you at the beck of the Kunfedrit Gov'mint. I ain't holdin' myself up as a better man than you, but I'm captain and represent the Gov'mint—and you at the Gov'mint's beck. After the wah, I'll fit you with fists, knives, pistols er cannon. Is it a bargain? Lacey allowed that it was all right and tuck orders from Wagg from then on—but I saw him finger his knife and look at Wagg several times after that.

Gettysburg, Uncle Pinckney said,—what they call Pickett's Charge. The Highwater Mark of the Confederacy! Why they call it a high-water mark, I never could tell. Mebbe a highblood mark. That would be better. And *Pickett's* Charge! It would be just as correct to say Pettigrew's Charge. The Virginians got all the credit for that assault.

You know we might have got 'em that day. Yes, sir, we might have got 'em—if something hadn't happened. They said it was old Long-street's fault. I read a lot of pieces in the *Century* Magazine, one where Longstreet himself said it wasn't his fault—but that was after he turned scallawag. But whose-ever's fault it was—it was a killin' for the Yankees.

After a good many years, Lee, you git to thinkin'—and you think how could I have been such a tarnal fool? That wasn't my fight, or Jud's, or pore Sion's. It may have been Robert E. Lee's and Wade Hampton's and Jeb Stuart's—but it wasn't even ole Tom Jackson's. let alone Zeb Vance's.

There were, as you know, three days of the battle of Gettysburg. When we marched into Pennsylvania, I thought it was the purtiest green fenced-in, tidied-up country ever I saw. They ain't shif'less up there like we are down here. I liked it fine—looked as if there was a-plenty of everything for everybody. It didn't look so damn' tired and shabby as this country looks even in the spring.

Michigan and Minnesota, what they like? Jud said. Where are they, Pink? Don't you remember yore jogaphy? I said. Father taught you himself—with his finger on the map. I wasn't much hand with jogaphy, Jud said.

There's cartridges there, I said. You'd better git some. There ain't many in the wagons, and we got orders to git 'em. The young Yankee's blood was thick and clotted on the grass beside his neck where the minnie ball had tore a big hole. Flies and bugs and ants were crawlin' all over his face. The ants were diggin' into his wideopen blue eyes. He had Michigan on his belt buckle and collar—Michigan and a number. Mebbe twenty-four.

There was right many of 'em around Jud and me in that field— some of 'em marked Michigan and some of 'em marked Minnesota. Mebbe *I* shot him, Pink, Jud said. Mebbe you did, Jud, I said. What of it? That's what we jined fur—to shoot Yankees. I wonder what Michigan's like? he said. Ain't there a lake up there? Shore is, I said. Mebbe he went swimmin' in it, like we used to do in the Gadkin. It's too big, I said—like the ocean. They go swimmin' in the ocean— Look at that! Jud hollered.

Not more'n fifteen feet away Lacey was sticking a Yankee in the belly with his bayonet. The Yankee had thrown down his musket and had a holt of the sharp blade (Lacey kept it honed good) trying to twist it out of his belly. You've seen a constipated man settin' on a privy with his face screwed up? Well, that was the way the Yankee looked. He'd run backwards and shove and twist forwards. Lacey follered him with a grin on his face, shoving hard on the bayonet till it came out the Yank's back. The Yank keeled over with his hand still holding the bayonet—they were all bloody and cut to the bone. The constipated look came off his face, and he looked surprised. Lacey howled a wolfhowl, put a bare foot on the Yank's belly and jerked the bayonet out through the cut hands. Lacey loved knives: he kept his bayonet whetted to a gnat's heel. I saw him many's the time workin' at it at night with a whetstone and his shoesole—when he had one— for a strop. He'd git a glitter in his eye, like a poet or a fiddler, and he'd test it with his fingernail. Purty, hain't it? he'd say.

The bluebelly's legs drew up a little, and his head let loose of life and lolled over to one side. Lacey stood there with the bayonet, wipin' it on a little rag. I needed them shoes, he said. I honed fur 'em.

A little chunk of sour cornpone out of Jud's vomit stuck on the nose of the Yank at our feet. Lacey was taking off his Yankee's shoes. He was a-pullin' like hell, for the man's feet were still hot, summer infantry feet, swollen up like a hoptoad. He got 'em off and the socks too and swung 'em over his shoulder. Then he gave the Yankee a good goin' over, but he didn't find anything more he wanted, so he walked over toward us.

What's the matteh, son, yore stummack weak? Gahddamn' if he didn' puke in that bluebellie's face. Now, ah wouldn' stand theah like a bump on a log. Ah'd git me some ca'tridges. Hisn'll fit yore muskit. Gen'l Hill was a-sayin' to me to'thah day—jist like Cunnel Zeb Vance usteh say: Gahddammit, Harrison, have I got to keep hackin' at you men tuh git ca'tridges. Ah cain't keep troublin' Gen'l Lee about ca'tridges, when he's got ole Joe Hookah an' all the Yanks tuh whup.

Lacey looked down and saw the shoes on our Yankee. By Gahd, he said, I'm gonna stock up on shoes. Kep' tellin' me we was gonna git some store shoes in Gettysbuhg yestiddy—ah allow we had tuh git us some Yankees fust.

You stay away from that man's shoes, Jud said. Ho! ho! Lacey said. Hain't you the purty rooster! Jud pulled his musket up and aimed it pint blank at Lacey's belly. Lacey, he said, you git away from him or I'll spill your guts out. My gun's loaded and primed. Jud's hands were trembling. Well, I'll be a son of a bitch, Lacey said.

Old Wagg came up from the branch in the little clearing where the water was red. He saw and heard. Lacey, Wagg said, you git! Git oveh thar and wait till we form, er I'll kill you now, so help me Gahd, ah will!

Lacey walked off with a mean look in his eye. He'd got only a little way when Jud fell over backwards. Sun's hot. You take keer of yor brotheh, Pinckney. Th'ow some watah in his face and tote him in undah yon shade tree.

Michigan, Jud said when he opened his eyes. I'm goin' to Michigan. What'd he do, Pink? What'd that son of a bitch of a hillbilly do to me? He didn't do anything, Jud. Old Wagg just walked up and offered to kill him again. You got sun touched and Wagg told me to throw water in your face. Sun? Jud said. I was scared, Pink—scared as hell. I was so scared when they stood there shootin' at us this mornin', I stopped and remembered thinkin': I'm froze like a rabbit now. They can't get me now. I'm scared of that Lacey.

I didn't blame him, Uncle Pink said. Lacey wasn't hardly human;

he looked like a good big chicken-hawk, or a turkey buzzard, or a
Goddamn' big carrion crow—or mebbe a mean starved timberwolf.
He had a matted beard full of mites—and I never saw a man had a
wickeder look in his eye. You couldn't, in truth, call Lacey human. I
don't believe there was anybody in the regiment, except Ole Wagg,
who wasn't afraid of him—and neither Ole Wagg, nor Lacey was
afraid of anything. But Lacey was cruel and Wagg didn't have a mean
bone in his body. I reckon he'd a killed Lacey if he'd had to—but only
if he'd a had to.

That first day at Gettysburg was the first real war for Jud and me.
You and I can sit here under the honeysuckle vine and talk about war;
and I can tell you how there were Yanks across the branch with loaded
rifles in a field and how we had loaded rifles too. I can tell you how we
went towards each other and started firing at each other—and how I
saw boys and men bleeding at the mouth, the head, the breast; with
ankles shattered; with legs blown off. There was one Yankee lad—I lay
down near him, and he died while I was there without saying a word
—with blood rolling out of his neck onto a fine white linen shirt. He
made a gurglesound a little like my pipe.

When I first lay down, his face was still pink and white, and with
his black hair, it made him look like Mary Ivy Dula, the girl that Jud
wanted to spark back in Gadkin county. The blood kept dribbling
down onto his kepi, which lay beside him, and coloring the white
clovershaped corps badge on it. And I can tell you that I lay there
thinkin': Damn' if that boy don't look like Mary Ivy Dula, while he
got white and the shirt and cap got redder and he stopped gurgling.

But there is something metaphysical, mebbe, about battle—something in the ether between the two armies. It is not a smell, or a look,
or a taste, or a noise, or an emotion—it is something that you remember
(not all of it—not all complete, however) for years. Maybe you remember the smell and the look and the feel and the taste and the noise, but
they were thrown into you then and mixed up and jogged around as
if they were in a mortar being pounded around by a pestle with something else, some X, being added—and you yourself and thousands of
others being pounded into this mixture. No; Uncle Pink said. It ain't
hate, fear, anger nor pride. It's something else, Lee. It's something
curious and cruel—it's something like that hillbilly brother-in-law of
mine felt when he got a call while he was walkin' along between the
plowhannels. All of a damn sudden a man feels powerful strange. He

looks around him and says: This is the earth I walk on every day; these are the trees that shade me; there is the sun again—but where am I? And, what in God's name, am I?

The call comes to them walking between the plowhannels: It comes to them as it did to my brother, Joshua, who, in his licker, wrote a long poetic tract in Eighteen eighty-five on the Second Coming in Eighteen eighty-nine and printed it in Eighteen eighty-seven by mortgaging his farm.

I know how it was with them: they must have felt the way I did at Gettysburg on the first of July Eighteen sixty-three, or the way I have felt at sunset sometimes on this porch with the honeysuckle close to me and Grandfather Mountain far off over there. They had to—they just had to call it somethin', so they said it was God or The Call.

Why, Lee, I reckon you don't know yore Great Uncle Joshua had a conference with the Archangel Gabriel right in these very hills? I didn't figure you'd know. The tract on the Second Coming ain't déclassé, but that conference with old Gabriel up on Sourwood mountain sounded just a mite too much like a hillbilly preacher's didoes for yore precious cousins. It was gittin' too much like talkin' in The Tongues—or the jerks. And yore cousins don't go after God in such a lowborn way. They belong to the genteelest particle of the Methodist Church South.

I heard one of 'em say Joshua's tract on the Second Coming was very scholarly, but he made an understandable slip in chronological calculations—'cordin' to their figgers it was due in Nineteen eighty-nine. But you can bet they never mentioned that Gabriel business.

CHAPTER XXIII

WE HAD roast pig to eat before Pickett's Charge, Uncle Pink said. Wagg himself and Wheary, the sergeant-major, came in with three good sized shoats. Wagg carried two, one over each shoulder—a couple of hundred pounds at least—and Wheary had one on his back. Wagg sent some of the other men for the rest.

You, Lacey, Wagg said, you and Dance Sudderth fotch me some fiahwood. We gonna have pohk. The tobacco juice trickled down into his fanshaped beard as he threw the pigs on the ground and took out his knife. He schlooped the tobacco juice up and hollered for water as he began to butcher the pigs. You thar, Jud, an' you Pink! Fotch me some watah, if yore studyin' to set yore teeth in a juicy piece of pohk. Sion, you cut me some forkéd sticks. He cleaned about a dozen pigs and put 'em on ramrods himself and seasoned 'em up and told Lacey and Sion how to keep the fires. He didn't let anybody tell him how to barbecue a pig. He cooked all that pigmeat himself and passed it out to the regiment. He had the whole passel of us under his wing, for Colonel Burleson and Lieutenant Colonel Lane, a pair of politicians from Yancey county, had been killed July first and Major Dula had to he'p with the brigade. I think Pettigrew had the division.

There was a Virginia battery near us—I remember now how the sun slanted through the trees on the Napoleon guns. The cannoneers were lying round the cannon on the burnt grass, looking toward the smell of the pork. One of 'em got up and sniffed and grinned and barked like a bitchfox. We all laughed—and Wagg said: This yere's fur my boys yere, but any man can bahk that way gits a smell at least. Ah'll send you a foot! Everybody hollered and even ole Lacey let out a screech like a buzzard. Wagg waddled around his spits catching the grease in fryingpans, smacking his lips as he tore off a little hunk of golden cracklin now and again and ate it down, or shoved it into the mouth of one of the men around him. He made Lacey mix up corn meal and pig grease and cook the pone, because Lacey was good at that.

We were all standin' around droolin' at the mouth when a tall feller with dusty jackboots walked up to Wagg and saluted. He was slim with big bulging shoulders and one of the purtiest golden beards ever I saw—and like a little girl's hair, all full of ringlets. He had on a brown cavalry hat with a black ostrich plume—the hat brim pinned back over the feathers with a gold Palmetto star.

Ah'll be dawg if it ain't Jeb himse'f! Dance Sudderth said. Lacey laughed in his screechy buzzardvoice. Wagg turned around that velvet-muscled bullneck. Well, suh? Wagg said.

Cap'n? the man said in a voice soft as rich fur. Yes, suh, Wagg said, looking up at the boyface under the Jeb hat. Wagg returned the man's salute and spat, dribbling a little stream of homecured juice down a graystreak in his beard. Cap'n, ah lost mah hawss. Lacey screeched out another mean buzzard laugh.

Lacey, Wagg said, close that trap a yourn. His bullvelvet neck moved his head back to the cavalryman with a nice ripple. You lost yore hawss, suh? Wagg said. And mah rigiment too. Ah figgahed you might let me he'p with youah batt'ry heah. Ah use' to he'p Majah Pelham— Well, suh, Wagg said, schlooping his tobacker juice in, yore laborin' under a misapprehension. That batt'ry hain't ourn. We ain' hawss ahtillery er hawss cavalreh—we git around on shank's mar'. We fit on foot for three years. Suah you didn' smell ouah pohk meat? Some of the men laughed soft, but Wagg didn't turn around that time. Well, Cap'n, ah cain't say ah *didn't* smell it. But ah said to mahse'f, those men look like they could lick the hell outa one of Gen'l Wade Hampton's beahs, so ah come ovah to inquiah if you needed any he'p. Ah thought you was ahtillereh by the cannon theah.

Them thar's Virginny cannon, Wagg said. What's yore outfit, young man? Wagg fumbled his tobacker farther back in his jowl. Jeff Davis Legion, Cap'n. Mah hawss was shot out from undah me at Fleetwood. Cap'n McGehee said to go find me anothah an' ketch up with the rigiment. Ah found one, but he broke a leg last night runnin' away from the Yankees. Ah had to shoot him. Ah cain't find hide naw hair of mah command—an' ah suhmised you might be willin' to take on some extra he'p. Well, son, we ain' hightone hawss cavalreh heah, but the ole Eighty-sixth Nawth Cahlina's as good foot cavalreh as Ole Jack eveh marched blue in the face. You from Virginny? No, suh, Missi'ppi. Well, Wagg said, I reckin I kin holp. We was eight hunderd 'fore we hit Pennsylvany—I don't reckin we got more'n three hunderd now. Wagg looked at Jud and me, then back to the cavalryman. What's yore name an' rank, young man? Reese Eliot, suh. Private. Wagg grinned.

You, Jud, and you, Pink! Carreh this cavalrehman oveh to yon wagins and git him a Yankee muskit and some U. S. ca'tridges. Let me make you acquainted with Private Jud Harrington and Private Pink Harrington. It's an honah, Reese said. Jud and me looked at him and then at each other.

He wasn't much older than either of us, Uncle Pink said, but he looked it. He was the kind of a boy that had been called Ole Reese since he was ten mebbe—the kind of a boy that looked strong and quiet and gentle and seemed to be right even in his wildest moments. One of the main things about Reese, Uncle Pink said—the thing that made Jud take to him like he did—was that he never said anything about Our Glorious Cause, and he never acted as if he knew anything *you* didn't. But he never seemed at loss as to what *he* was gonna do.

Jud and I got him between us and he walked along with us half like he was under our command and half like we were his hosts. He kicked along careless-like through the grass—and Jud and I noticed he had a pair of silver spurs jingling on his jackboots. We saw the sabre he wore was gold-hilted with a United States eagle on it and fine gold-wove tassels hanging from the hilt—and a sabretache dangled against his left jackboot. He had a big Colt's revolver hung in a U. S. holster too. His uniform had been finer broadcloth than Jud's and mine, but it was weathered and dirty and torn.

Say, Jud said, you got a hat like Jeb Stuart's. Reese smiled—he had the whitest teeth ever I saw. Suah have, he said. Gal gave it tuh me—lil ol' gal in Chahlottesville. Prettiest gal eveh I saw. Onleh trouble—she cain't make up huh mind between me and Gen'l Stuaht. That's a Yank sword too, I said. Did you capture it? It's mah fathah's Mexican wah sword. He made me a presun' of it. Was he in the cavalry too? Jud said. No, Reese said. He was a majah in Cunnel Jeff Davis's rigiment. Cunnel Jeff Davis made him a presun' of it.

I thought you said you were from Missi'ppi, Jud said. Ain't Charlottesville in Virginia? Suah is, Reese said. I was studyin' at the Univuhsity of Vuhginia when the wah broke out. Oh, Jud said, there was a boy from Caldwell there, Willie Fitchett. He's in the First North Carolina cavalry too. Do you know him? Fitchett—Willie Fitchett? Reese said. Seems like I huhd the name. I swear, Uncle Pink said, Jud looked relieved. That Willie Fitchett came home to Gadkin county in the winter of Eighteen sixty-two after hawses and courted Mary Ivy Dula—all the time wearin' around a hat with one of his ma's old hat plumes in it.

Those plumes in the hats of Stuart's cavalry weren't so much; a good many of 'em were nothin' but tailfeathers out of a turkey or a Spanish rooster. Best one ever I saw was the one Reese was wearing. He did look the nearest thing to a knight ever I saw, Uncle Pinckney said.

He had a light shelljacket, which looked as if it couldn't be buttoned over the bulges of his shoulders and neck—but there wasn't anything bullish about him like there was about Wagg. I can see him still, kickin' along with that sabretache slappin' against his jackboot. I can see him reach up and sweep that Jeb Stuart hat off his head—and the plumes stirring in that July air in Pennsylvania. Suah is hot! he said.

It's gonna be hottah foah the Yankees today though. Ah heah we gonna hit 'em this aftahnoon with the whole ahmy!

We ain't heard it, I said. How do you know, Reese? Jud said. Well, Reese said, ah been lookin' foah the Jeff Davis Legion all mawnin', an all the men in Longstreet's corps said they huhd Gen'l Lee was fixin' to hit 'em with evehthing we got this aftahnoon. Ahtillereh was gettin' readeh. Eveh gun was movin'! Now, if ah can just git me a good rifle, we can git in among 'em and whip the hell out of the Yankees, cain't we? Shore can! Jud said.

Why, that boy, yore grandfather, was plumb fascinated with Reese Eliot from the time he set eyes on him. Here was Old Reese, right out of the cavalry that Jud had longed to join, a University of Virginia man—and a man that hadn't an offensive air about him. And when Reese spoke of whipping the hell out of the Yankees, you could be sure that he didn't hold any personal malice.

Uncle Pink's tumefactive mass waggled in the blueveined skinsac behind his ear as if it were an egg about to hatch. Jud kept askin' Reese questions: Where'd you git that Yank pistol? Reese pulled out the heavy Colt's and handed it to Jud. Captured it, Reese said, at Fleetwood. Captured a cahbine too—a Shahp's cahbine—but ah lost it when mah hawss was shot out from undah me. Yes suh! Yankee rode right up tuh me shootin' that pistol—so close he almost buhnt mah whiskahs. Reese chuckled sorter reminiscently, Uncle Pink said. Ah said, Mah Gahd, man! Suah is sorreh shootin'! He put the pistol away an' stahted hackin' at me with his sabah. Suah made it sing around mah head. Well, ah knocked him off his hawss with the flat of mah swohd and captured him—pistol, cahbine, swohd, hawss an' all. Ohdnance officah said: Look heah, Reese, you take this pistol an' cahbine. You ain't got any—an' Gen'l Hampton told me to see you wuh all ahmed, if we had to disahm the whole Yankee ahmy to do it. So ah got me a new pistol an' cahbine. Cahbine was a new breech-loadah too. Suah hated like hell to lose it. Mah hawss too. Pretty a bay as eveh you saw. Ah had him at Chahlottesville.

That boy, Reese, Uncle Pink said—I don't know as I *eveh* heard a voice like that again. I don't know as *eveh* I saw as fine a boy. And yore grandfather—I don't think he ever found a man in his life who could come up to Reese. And he kept at him. He had outa Reese how he had been on the ride around McClellan and how he saw the women buryin' Captain Latané—and how the women in Richmond took on oveh Gen'l Stuart. Why Reese even told him how he and Major von Borcke used to go out and shoot squirrel. Majah von Borcke suah likes his lickah too, Reese said. An' you oughta see the swohd he totes—fo foot long! He suttinly *hannels* it too. Ah saw him git in among some Yankees—an', be Gahddamned if he didn't cut two of theah heads off. No! Jud said. Ah sweah to Gahd! Reese said. Those Prussians suah ah wile men!

All the time Jud was pumpin' Reese, Uncle Pink said, we'd been walkin' along a ridge back through the woods. Pretty soon we came out into the sunlight of a wheatfield where the wagons were—two of 'em marked Eighty-sixth N. C. over the U. S. Near the wagons there was a Yankee field forge that had been captured somewhere—mebbe Fredericksburg. And there was one of those slim-barreled Whitworth guns standin' gee-haw beside it with a broken axle.   ,

The blacksmith was sittin' cross-legged on the mashed-down wheat, cookin' a wad of cornpone on a piece of iron over a rock. The field was cut up with wagontracks. Jud and me got Reese a .58 calibre Springfield musket with U. S. arsenal marks and a hundred and fifty rounds of paper minié cartridges. Reese hefted the musket and laid a hand on Jud's shoulder: Suah fixed us up for the Yanks, he said. Yes suh! Yes suh! Jud said, as near like Reese as he could make himself sound.

I cain't git that Whitworth gun outa my head, Uncle Pink said. It was a breech-loader—first one eveh I saw. Reese walked oveh to it and said: First one of these eveh I saw. Ain' wuth a good Gahddamn'! the blacksmith said. He said it like he didn't care. He was the drawlyest feller eveh I heard talk. Spits out fiah behin' and busts huh axle mighty neah eveh time she rars back. Give me a muzzle-loadah any day! She does? Reese said. He patted the swung-back britch-block as if it was a dawg. Yes suh, he said to Jud. They run 'em through the blockade from England. Ah read about 'em in the Richmond *Examinah*. Shoot fast and fah. Cannoneahs don't like 'em, the blacksmith said. Hain't reliarable. Ah patched this one up twice a'ready since we come to Pennsylvany. No suh, that piece ain' wuth its hide'n tallah, the blacksmith said as Reese swung the block shut and twirled the closing screw. No suh, the blacksmith said like a preacher. Give me one of them brass Napoleon guns any day. You cain't shell anything good under a mile away with this yere son of a bitch.

He pointed to three Napoleons standing a little way from the Whitworth. Take them guns thar—tuck 'em from the Yanks at the fust battle a Manassas, an' been a-farin' 'em eveh since an' sahshayin' 'em all oveh hell an Vuhginny—an' by Gahd, ther purt near as good as when they come outa the U. S. arsenal.

Well, Reese said, ah ain't so much of a gunnah mahse'f. He snapped the new musket to carry and turned to Jud: Well, Cap'n, he said, shall we git back an' tend to the Yankees. Yes suh, we'll git back to the rigiment and whip the hell out of us a few bluebellies.

The waggling of Uncle Pinckney's encysted earegg stopped for a minute, Lee remembered, and he stared beyond the honeysuckle as if he were trying to see Reese and my grandfather again—as if he were trying to see the fields and trees in Pennsylvania where he had been in the summer of Eighteen sixty-three—and where he had never been since. I would have dearly loved to see that country again. Why, even now, I could go to Gettysburg and walk to where that Whitworth stood, and I could find the rock that the blacksmith was cookin' his pone oveh.

I can remember the walk back to the regiment too: It was on the way back that we run onto the buryin' detail. They had a long shallow trench dug and were gatherin' Southerner and Yankee alike. Some of 'em were stiff with their arms up in the air—they were fairly fresh kilt—and others were limp with their bellies swollen up with the deathgas in 'em—they were gittin' black in the face. None of 'em had any shoes on. No sir! We never buried a pair of shoes after Eighteen sixty-two that I can remember—and not many clothes. A couple of boys on the buryin' detail picked up a dead Yankee with a belly full of gas—and he let out a big ughhh! They dropped him. An old sergeant laughed like a rooster. Gahd A'mighty, he said, that thar's a *dead* Yank!

They lay in the shallow trench like you could stand 'em up and have a company front ready for action. Here and there was a board stuck up behind some openeyed boy—a name and regiment written in pencil, or burnt in the wood. I saw 'em begin to throw dirt in the eyes of those dead boys. I saw Orren Brabble dead with his eyes open and Drury Bugg and Old Jeems Marsh—all from Gadkin county. And they'd all been alive on the second of July. Further on there was a trench filled in, but at one end, a forearm with a hickory shirt sleeve on was stickin' up pointin' at the hot sun. Why, Goddamn' it! I remember now. Orren Brabble got a cake from his mother and give

a little piece of it to every one of us in the company—a mere sliver—
and took the smallest sliver for himself.

You could hear 'em yellin: Baaattery! Fooorward! in the heat from
behind the ridgetop—and you could hear the sound of the batteries
moving like a lot of springless wagons on a hot lazy summertime street.
And as Jud and me and Reese walked back to the regiment, there
were flies and bees and birds in the air. Through the timber on the
ridgetop we could see dozens of cannon limbered and moving—
and get the rattle and jingle of 'em as if we were listening to
an approaching circus parade on a hot day when we were little
boys.

I remembered how Jud and me had seen Captain Ivy's North
Carolina battery swing down the main street in Caldwell, jingling and
smart, with Ivy at the head on a fine black horse and a lot of men
we knew in gray uniforms sitting up on the caissons and riding the
horses—appearing to us half 'as strange romantic soldiers and half as
boys we knew on the roadside or in spring wagons or loafing at the
store—boys who had no right to turn into soldiers riding beside the
limbered, shiny, brazen guns, who had no right to go out and do the
things which were done in books and in our own heads as we lay
belly down in the grass. Jud and me were the *only* soldiers. *I* was
the only captain—major, colonel, general, prince, king. And now here
were these—many of them the worthless, shif'less critters that our
father had told us they were—dubbed knights under our noses! Old
Clay Morris, settin' up on a caisson, peart as a jaybird. Wasn't he
hardly *any* better than the most lowdown, no'count white trash in
Gadkin county? Did he ever own even *one* nigger?

We could see the cannon coming into battery, the sun glaring on
the barrels, the cannoneers digging in, the horses being picketed. Look
theah! Reese said. Theah's anothah Whitworth breech-loadah. Suah
gittin' ready to shell the hell out of 'em. He pulled a twist of tobacker
out of his shelljacket. Have a chew, he said to Jud. I knew that the
only time Jud had eveh tried to chew he got sick as a cat, but he bit
off a piece of the homecured. Yes suh, Reese said, weah suah gonna
throw some iron on 'em. He laughed, pleased as Punch. Weah suah
gonna shell the hell out of 'em. Oh, I had a chew too, Uncle Pink
said. But I knew how. Anyway, Judson and me felt as if we and
Reese were blood brothers—and the whole Army of Northern Virginia
to boot.

I watched the oscillation of Pinckney Harrington's tumefactive earegg: Like some captive Humpty Dumpty, it seemed to sit, wagging slyly and whispering all the time, behind my uncle's ear: No great falls for us any more, Pinckney! We're purty sly fellers, Pink. I sot hyear with you a right smart time, Pink, and you and me knows we ain't a-gittin' up nowheres jist to fall off an' bust our head.

Uncle Pink stuck his hand behind his ear and gently drove a spring fly from the damp skinshell of his tumescent companion. The ground, Uncle Pink said, the look of the ground comes back to me now: The still unburied swollen dead, men and hawses, lay all over the fields below the ridge; and underneath our feet were throwndown muskets, swords, cartridge boxes, books, jackets, bayonets and all of that which is always called the debris of the armies. Ourn wasn't much account I'm here to tell you: by Eighteen sixty-three even the officers didn't have many pair of handmade boots and silvermounted pistols—and damn' few of the soldiers had anything but camp-made rawhide moccasins.

When Jud and me got back to camp with the recruit, Wagg and Abner Snead, who was one of the handiest butchers in Gadkin county, were cutting up the meat. Wheary was he'ppin': Here ye air, boys, Wagg kept sayin'. Go right tuh it. The men had pigmeat skewered on bayonets, bowie knives and jack knives. Harrison Lacey and Jim Poe were fryin' the pone oveh the fire—and somebody had gethered in all the coffee everybody had. The muskets were stacked in a kind of a square around the men to keep off raids on the grub. The flag leant against one of the musketstacks: it was blood red with a blue St. Andrew's cross and stars—and full of holes. But it was silk. The red field had the battles sewed on in strips: Seven Pines, Gaines's Mill, Malvern Hill, Oak Grove—Eighty-Sixth North Carolina Infantry. Colonel Burleson's wife made it.

Brother Sion was settin' cross-legged on the ground beside the flag, in a walnut-dyed Yankee zouave jacket and a pair of butternut homespun britches, eatin' pigmeat—but not very hearty. I remember hearin' Lige Boggs honin' fur collard greens and molasses. He had eyes like a couple of hackberries and a gray goatbeard.

Hyear you, Pink and Jud, Wagg said, fotch thet hawss solger oveh hyear. We livin' high! Cain't whup the Yankees on an empty belly, can ye, Cap'n Albright? Albright was captain of the Yancey county company. He was big and bar'lchested as Wagg and red in the face. He had a short black beard and looked like he'd been weaned on cawn licker. The sweat was runnin' down his face in cricks, but he was nibbling almost like a bird at the pigmeat. Shore cain't, he said gently. Shore nough cain't.

Well, Uncle Pink said, Jud and me got Reese between us—he wouldn't go ahead—and led him up to Captain Wagg's barbecue. Go tuh it, boys! Wagg gave us three extry large and choice hunks of pig. Cain't hev you a-goin' back to Jeb Stuaht a'sayin' the Nawth Cahlina foot cavalreh cain't tek keer of its guests, Wagg said. Thank you, Captain Wagg, Reese said touching his plumes.

Ah cain't see thar's any call to feed the cavalreh hyear, Lacey said. Lacey, Wagg said, that'll do! Mistah Eliot ouah guest—and we don't study eveh to let a guest of the ole Eighty-six go hongry—do we men? Everybody said yore Gahddamn' right we didn't. And Wagg said: Lacey, I'm right down ashamed of you. I 'clah, I am. Lige Boggs grinned a little and Dance Sudderth sniggered. Then Ole Wagg straightened up and looked all around him severely and pompously. His eyes stopped on Lacey. All of us looked at Lacey. And, Wagg said, Colonel Buhleson not cole in his grave—mebbe not even buhied. Wagg schlooped and dribbled a trickle of yaller tobacker juice into the gray streak on his beard. He spluttered some with his mouth when he got angreh. Lacey, wheah's yore mannahs? Lacey shore looked like a sulky buzzard. He parted them whiskers a hisn and said: I didn't aim to be ornery, Cap'n.

You could see Reese was flustered. Jud blushed, but Reese got a-holt of himse'f. Thank you, Cap'n Wagg, he said. Ah'm suttinly honohed to be a guest of the Eighty-sixth Nawth Cahlina—ah'm honahed to be able to he'p. We too are honahed, suh, Wagg said. He'd been a mountain schoolteacher once—and he had a mighty queer set of company manners.

But nobody felt like laughing. Abner Snead broke into a little cheer—and then all of us let go with a Rebel yell except Lacey—and Sion. Sion just sat oveh there by the flag starin' at the ground.

We were still eating when all that ahtillery Jud and Reese and me had seen going into battery cut loose. A young staff officah on a hawss rode up and hollered: Who's in command heah? I am, suh! Wagg hollered back. Have some bahbecued pohk? You couldn't hear very well, but you could see everybody was laughing. Wagg waddled up to the officer with some ribs on the end of his sword. Compliments of the Eighty-sixth Nawth Cahlina, Wagg yelled—Pennsylvany hawg-meat.

Took it? Uncle Pink said. I hope to tell you he took it! When Wagg held it up to him on the end of that sword, he just changed from a man into a watery mouth. He took it and tore off a hunk and yelled with his mouth full. This is Gen'l Pettigrew's brigade, ain't it? It was a few minutes ago, Wagg said. It was Cunnel Buhleson's regiment day before yesterday, but it's mine now. Well, Cunnel, the officer yelled with another mouthful of pohk. Cap'n, Wagg hollered. Cap'n Elisha Wagg, Twenty-sixth Nawth Cahlina Troops! The man on the hawss hollered: I got to find Gen'l Pettigrew. Have your regiment ready to move at a moment's notice. Yes, suh, Wagg answered. Gen'l Pettigrew'll be that way. The courier rode off chewing Wagg's pork.

Wagg went over to what was left of the last pig, picked up a spare bone and began to chew at it—but there wasn't anything to speak of on it. Must've been forty men rushed up to him with their pork held out for him to take. Wagg stood there bewildered. Git, Wagg said, I et a whole pig while it was cookin'. Well, Uncle Pink said, his voice trembling a little, he hadn't done a thing of the kind—a cracklin or two was all he had. But do you think he'd touch a morsel? He wouldn't! But he damn' near had teahs in his eyes, boy. He stood theah with that bullneck up in the air, his eyes a-waterin'. He kept chewin' the pig bone he had and sayin': By Gahd, boys, we ain't gonna fohm till we finished ouah pig.

Jud and me took Reese oveh to Sion and introduced him. We were sorter proud of Sion, for he was color sergeant and had been at Seven Pines—and Old Wagg said Sion'd saved his life at Malvern Hill.

Wagg got the regiment formed in two lines an' said: Set down whur you are, men. Soon as we git the order we can git up. Jud and me and Reese were beside each other. I saw Old Wagg take a Bible out of his pocket and walk over under a tree, moving his lips as he read to himself. Captain Albright walked off to one side with his hands clasped behind his back. Jud was watching an ant struggling with a little piece of pork in the grass.

The owl foah all his feathuhs was a-cold, Reese said. I didn't know it was Keats then, Uncle Pink said. Ah had me a pet owl once, Reese said. Suah had feathuhs. He had foh layahs of feathuhs! Did he? Jud said.

We were all gittin' nervous. For a while I couldn't figure out what it was. Then I looked over at the battery of Virginia Napoleons. They weren't firing. The quiet. That was what was gittin' us. It was hot and quiet and there wasn't even a breath of air. It was so still you could sit there and study the ground or your musketlock or the man's coat who was next to you down to the smallest detail as if you were at home in the afternoon lying on the ground under a shade tree, or out with some scientific expedition that had all the time in the world— only here you were afraid.

I remember looking at a dead Pennsylvania bee in the grass and wishing for some sourwood honey. There wasn't even a musketshot.

I won't ever forget Sion walkin' across to us with the flag in the leather socket on his belly. The flag was hanging down slack on the pole; and he walked slow as if he was walking in his sleep. He came up to Jud's feet. Heah, Jud, he said, handing Jud a package made of an old Charlotte newspaper, you keep this; it gits in the way of my flagbelt. He didn't give Jud a chance to say nothin'. Just marched off with the flag, and as he walked away, a little breeze caught the silk and spread it out holes and all against the summer sky. I could see Malvern Hill and N.C. on it.

Mebbe it was because yore Uncle Sion was totin' the flag—mebbe it was because I was young, but I looked at that flag and felt my throat git full. I saw Harrison Lacey git kinder blue in the face. Reese looked at it and smiled. He had a little book of Keats's poems in his hand. Squirrel's got a whole crib full of nuts, he said. Gonna have lots of good juiceh nuts foah wintah. Sit around the fiah and crack himse'f all the nuts he can eat. He laughed softly. Just eat the hell out of 'em. Suah would like a good cig-gah. He sighed.

CHAPTER XXIV

Now Lee, Uncle Pinckney said to me, flipping his blueveined earegg with two fingers, mark what I tell you, boy! I heard the two guns of the Washington Artillery that started the greatest cannonade the world had ever known up to the twentieth century—the signal guns. They went off almost at once. Then they began that long scudding roll; and the ridges and the hills roared and shook. I could see the Virginia battery laying the weeds flat in front of their muzzles. Over on the opposite hill where the Yanks were, puffs of white smoke began to show in the sky. My ears began to ring; the gullies and draws echoed.

Reese leant over between Jud and me: Wish you and Pink and me had that britch-loadin' Whitworth we saw this mornin'. We could suah pick us off a Yank or two! He looked over toward Cemetery Ridge. I'll bet you we hit 'em with the whole Gahddamn' ahmy!

A thunderstorm? Uncle Pink said. Well, you could *call* it that. You don't feel the ground shake under yore feet—and the thunder doesn't keep up all the time—and the hot air doesn't smell like burnt gunpowder. When it quit finally, it wasn't as if something big had happened and was over and done with. No. Everybody knew that the cannonade was nothin' but part of what was goin' to happen.

Wagg came out from undah the tree with the Testament in his hand and waddled out in front of us: And the Lawd said unto Jeremiah, Wagg said: *Out of the* NAWTH *an evil shall brek fo'th on the land. For, lo, ah will call all the families of the Kingdoms of the* Nawth, *saith the Lawd; and they shall cyme, and they shall set every one his throne at the entering of the gates of Jerusalem, and against all the walls thereof roundabout, and against all the cities of Judah. Thou, therefore gird up thy loins, and arise, and speak to them all that command thee: be not dismayed at theah faces, lest ah confound thee befo' them. And they shall fight against thee, but* THEY SHALL NOT *prevail against thee; fo' ah am with thee, saith the Lawd, to delivah thee.*

See that ridge oveh there! Wagg hollered. The gates of Jerusalem! *Gird up thy loins!* I can see Wagg standin' yonder, Uncle Pink said, with the sun on that ole black hat and blackgreen frockcoat with the swordbelt pinchin' into the bullmeat on his belly so's it hung oveh in a roll. He unfastened the old Confederate web holster with the end cut out of it where he kept the biggest and heaviest pistol in the Army of Northern Virginia. We use' to call it Ole Wagg's field piece, or Ole Wagg's twelve pounder, or Ole Wagg's Bull Pistol. Let the pig settle good, Wagg said. We got ordahs to dress on Gen'l Archah, an' he ain't up yet. Let the pig dygest—and remembah what the Lawd said unto Jeremiah. Majah Dula is goin' to ride with the regiment—but

I'm not goin' to ride. I'm gonna walk right along with you and holp you whup the Yankees. *Gird up thy loins!*

Everybody let out a Rebel yip—till Wagg stopped 'em. And Jud and Reese and me could see Sion movin' our flag through the air to the end of our line. Behind us there were hoofbeats: I suppose the staff officers and couriers were gettin' everything ready. It seemed like a long time since the cannonade. I heard somebody say—might've been Lige Boggs: Weah guidin' fo' that clump of timbah near Seminarry Ridge oveh thar. Somebody else answered. Hell's far, this yere's Seminarry Ridge—that thar's Cemitarry Ridge oveh thar. Then Lige, if 'twuz him, answered: It don't make a damn—it'll be Cemitarry Ridge fo' the Yankees whureveh we ketch 'em.

You could see the line of skirmishers go out. They didn't look much, Uncle Pink said, just little gray brown spots movin' across the open field on a hot day. Even when the musketfire started, it wasn't much after that cannonade—and there was a good deal of smoke and dust in the air, so's you couldn't see anything plain. I was thirsty fore we eveh stahted.

I could look oveh and see the Yanks and a few cannon on their ridge. Reese was standing there with that Jeb Stuart plume stirring in a hot wind. What'd I tell you? he said. Old Man's suah gonna hit 'em! Ain't gonna be a Yank in Pennsylvania tonight. Next to Jud in line Lacey was standin', quiverin' like a mad dawg. That mean buzzard eye of hisn was meaner than ever I saw it—he was lookin' up at that honed-up bayonet. I remember thinkin' his ole hat looked as if it had laid on the ground all through the spring rains and then had the dirt dried into it by the sun. You wanta hold onto that pigmeat you et today, he said to Judson. I could see Jud's face was white as yore shirt, Uncle Pink said,—but I reckon mine was too.

Some more cannon had opened: and Jud would blink now and again and close his eyes tight for a second or two. Up the line back of us I could hear a hawss galloping. Then I saw Pickett's men begin to move out onto the fields below. Pickett's Charge. Whenever you hear about it you think of a big army, maybe on horseback, rushing across a big open space and waving their swords and firing their muskets and hollering like hell—all happening in the clear air, so that you can see 'em cutting down the enemy and the enemy shell breaking in among 'em. Well, it wasn't like that: you couldn't see much: A good number of men walkin' in a fairly straight line across a smoky dusty field—a red flag now and again and the line gittin' crookeder all the time. Somebody said the regimental bands played—but I never heard anything but guns.

I saw a battery galloping forward across the field once that day—bouncing and kicking up the dust—but even that when you're far from it doesn't look like much. It ain't fast! But that didn't matter. We felt something big was fixin' to happen.

We got the order over the hot air. Forwaahd! It seemed lazy and fur away—even when Wagg hauled out his sword and stood out in front of us and bellowed: Fohwahd—Maahch! and we started to walk towards Cemetery Ridge.

I looked up the line and saw Sion's flag: once I read Seven Pines on it and Malvern Hill. Heah we go! Reese said. Heah we go, Jud! Heah we go, Pink! Gonna lick the hell outa the whole damn' Yankee ahmy!

We marched along easy except for the dead men and hawses and our own guns we had to march through—those cannoneers shore looked tired and dirty. Lot of 'em were sittin' on the guntrails panting like they had just finished a hard race. But they hollered out at us as we went past—some of 'em even waved their hats. There was one bunch of dead hawses we went past: they looked like wooden hawses the way their legs stuck out.

Keep closed up, Wagg hollered. An' remembah what the Lawd Gahd said to Jeremiah! After a little way you could look around, Uncle Pink said, because it was such a long walk in the hot sun to the Yankee lines—you could look around and wish for a drink of water and wondah what was goin' to happen. You could look up and down the line and wondah if that part oveh there had hit the Yankees yet. For a while I thought the bayonets looked like a tall steel picketfence in the sun. You could walk along and figgah: I got me a Yank in front of me comin' at me with his bayonet. I can't shoot him, because I just fired. Shall I jump outa his way and come in and stick him from the side, or shall I knock his bayonet to one side and stick him from the front, or shall I mash in his head with a club-musket? Supposin' he gits me fust? Supposin' I tuhn and run—and he sticks me in the back? And I kept thinkin', if it wasn't so damn' hot and I had a drink, I wouldn't really mind gittin' kilt.

Look theah, Reese hollered. By Gahd! theah's an officah wearin' an *ovehcoat!* A Yankee ovehcoat at that! I saw him, Uncle Pink said, but I couldn't think at the time what Reese was laughin' at. Fur as I was concerned a whole battalion of overcoats in July wouldn't have surprised me then.

It was General Dick Garnett. He was just out of an ambulance and still sick, but he rode in with the men in his old Union army overcoat. I don't think I had eveh seen him before and I never saw him after. He was killed that day. I waited until Eighteen eighty-seven to find that out in a piece in the *Century Magazine*. The man was sick, buttoned up in a blue Yankee overcoat, on July third—a hot July third —riding into what *he* knew was almost certain death. My Gahd! Uncle Pink said. Who remembers Gen'l Dick Garnett now? Who remembers anybody but Lee and Jackson and Grant and Sherman?

We kept on walkin', Uncle Pink said, in a long line. I could hear a rumbling in the ground, but for a while I couldn't make out what it was. Then it dawned on me. Why, by Gahd, I said to myself, it must be our feet. We're pickin' 'em up and settin' down. Ten thousand pair of feet, thinks I—that'd be twenty thousand feet. Be a good many won't make any noise after today. Some men hollered, but I couldn't make out what they said.

I quit listenin' to the feet and I heard maybe a battery limbered— it had a lumbery sound like a springless wagon, but it jingled like a battery. The dust got thicker, but nothin' seemed to happen except we was goin' for a walk. Just a damn' fool walk in the sun when we could've been lyin' under a tree asleep. I looked up toward the opposite ridge and saw smoke break loose.

It must have hit the line about ten, fifteen foot to the right of me, for there was a gap there—and Jud and Reese were still there beside me. Down at the end of the line I caught a glimpse of Sion with the flag— opened out and rippling slow on the hot air. I could see the holes and still all the names of the battles.

Now that they had us out in the middle of the field, the Yankees opened right up with their cannon. Another solidshot or a shell that didn't explode hit Abner Snead in the right leg and tore it off. The blood spattered on Jud and Reese. Behind Abner a diagonal line of men went down—maybe six. Lige Boggs—Lacey said later—got that solidshot or unbursted shell in his belly. It went clear through him and rolled and skipped away on the field as Lige lay bloody and flopping with his guts spillin' out—but already dead, like a chicken with its head cut off. I saw Abner jump up from the ground and hop up and

down on the leg he had left. He hollered once, then he fell oveh with
the blood spurting from his thigh stump—and then he toppled oveh.

Ole Wagg was still out in front. Close up! he hollered. Remembah
Jeremiah! He walked along backwards. You know what I can remember about him? Uncle Pink's eyes looked away back on Dixie
that time, Lee said. I can remember how his belly was cut into with
that belt and how it joggled up and down every backwards step he
took. He put his hand up to his mouth and hollered loud: Come out
hyear, Sion! Come out hyear with the cullahs! I saw Sion run out
with the flag jerkin' and pullin' the hot air above him.

Goes youah brothah with the cullahs! Reese said.

I looked at Cemetery Ridge one minute and saw the Yankees and
guns, and I looked the next minute and nothin' but smoke with red
far flashes comin' out of it. All of 'em seemed to be pointed at us.
The dust from our own feet got thicker and thicker, but I could see
the lines gap open—and see the men begin to cough from dust and
smoke. They warn't usin' any solidshot now—canister and grape was
breakin' all around us. It got so thick I couldn't tell how close we
were gittin' to the ridge—but my legs felt as if they were climbing. I
could get glimpses of Wagg walkin' backwards out in front: I could
see him twistin' that bullneck of hisn to look oveh his shoulder. And
I could see Sion's flag beside him and, now and then, Sion walkin'
along as straight as he could oveh the holes that the Yanks had kicked
up in the field. Reese and Judson were still near—and I caught Lacey's
buzzardface out of the corner of my eye.

I saw the railfence then, Uncle Pink said. It was 'longside a road.
There was a few of our boys behind it shootin' at the Yankees. I saw
one man plain, lyin' on his back bitin' a cartridge—I saw him git his
musket between his knees and ram it home. Ole Wagg and Sion were
almost at the railfence when I saw hit happen.

I saw Brothuh Sion's head neah the flagstaff one second—and then
the next I saw the flagstaff and flag and all the names of the battles
marchin' along beside Wagg with no head near it. I saw Sion walkin'
along beside Wagg—at attention—without any head, totin' the flag.
It's in the smoke, thinks I. I'll see all of him in a minute. I even shut
my eyes and opened 'em quick to clear away the cobwebs—but there
was Sion, still walkin' along a little ahead of Wagg, who was still
waddlin' along backwards. I even recognized Sion's shoulders. I saw
his hands still on the flagstaff. He's lookin' down, thinks I. He'll throw

back his head in a minute. But he didn't. He must have marched six steps, before Wagg caught the flag and waved it.

I saw Jud and Reese running forward. I don't remember running myse'f. One minute I thought I heard Captain Albright holler: Close up! Next I was with Jud and Reese lookin' down at Sion. The blood was spurting out of his neck and I could see the gray of his windpipe —and his adam's apple workin'. I kept thinking': That's Sion, all right. I know those shoulders and back like a book—like I know the road from Caldwell to Blowin' Rock. But there wasn't any head at all.

Jud looked like a froze rabbit then all right. He didn't even move until Reese put a hand on his arm. Come on Jud, boy, Reese said. Let's you and me git us some Yanks. He looked peart, all right, Uncle Pinckney said. He held that heavy musket as if it was a light stick of kin'lin' wood.

Jud started on with him. Harrison Lacey had taken the flag from Wagg. Wagg was hollering: *Out of the* NAWTH *an evil shall break fo'th upon all the inhabitants of the Land!* Oveh the fence, boys! Git the Gahddamn' niggerlovin' bluebellies. They got little Sion! Remembah Zeb Vance and ole *Nawth Cahlina*—but hol' yore fiah till we git oveh!

That was whar the heaviest Yankee musketfire started. The minnie balls began to whistle and the railfence shed splinters like a sawmill. Wagg and Lacey were running toward the fence screaming. Reese and Jud were right after 'em. I think I saw Dance Sudderth and James Poe and Wheary. Wagg had put up his sword—he had a musket.

I must have run after 'em. I got across the fencerails—or they were knocked down. Reese and Dance Sudderth and Jud and me were firing into a Union battery behind a low stone wall. When we began to load, I saw Reese slump down behind the wall and thought they'd got him for a minute—but then I saw him jerk Jud down to the ground. I lay down to load too after that. But Dance Sudderth didn't need to lie down; he fell over easy with the blood shooting out of the left side of his neck. Over to the left outside the stone wall, I saw a thick line of Yanks with muskets. Oh, I wasn't afraid now. I'd begun to git used to it. Nothin' seemed to matter. I saw Jud and Reese roll over on their backs to finish loading—Jud was bitin' cartridge as calm as if it was target practice. Reese got up crouching. Wagg was still on his back ramming home a cartridge. Lacey had the flagstaff in one hand and was shooting a pistol into a Yankee near a cannon.

There were a good many Confederates comin' up behind us when the Yankees burnt into us with a round of canister. I got blood in my face and heard Reese yell: Canistah! By Gahd, canistah! Save that bullet in youah rifle. Let's git oveh the wall and in among 'em.

Wagg was right near us: Eighty-six Nawth Cahlina! Eighty-six! *Out of the* NAWTH *an evil shall break fo'th!* Rally hyear! He pointed to Lacey and the flag. Git the Gahddamn' bluebellied bastuds. Little Jud! You, Pink! An' the cavalreh! Oveh the wall, boys! Give 'em the cole steel!

I can see Ole Wagg trot up to that wall and climb it like a bar on a rock. He stood up on the wall and aimed at and shot a man who was about to pull the lanyard of a Napoleon. Then he jumped down on the other side like a ton of brick. I remember his bullmeat shivered with the shock. Lacey was beside him with the flag.

Looked to me like all the Yanks' faces ever I saw that day didn't have no more expression than a turnip or a stick of kin'lin' wood. My hands were skinned and bleeding—I must've skinned them on the stone wall, but I never knew how it happened. James Poe and Wheary were comin' over the wall and Reese and Jud were oveh. I saw a couple of Yankee ahtillerymen ramming what looked like a double charge of grape into a Napoleon gun. Reese killed one with his musket and Wagg beat the other over the head with his clubbed-musket. I heard it hit—like whalin' a sack of meal with a piss-ellum club.

Just about that time I saw a Yankee ahtillery officah walkin' up to Jud. The Yank had a little squashed cap on with a white shamrock on it. He had a wooden Injun look on his face and a heavy Colt's in his hand. He was fixin' to shoot Jud. I pulled up my musket and started to fire, but Jud got his up and jerked the trigger with one motion. The Yank was powerful close. His pistol went off in the air as he went over backwards. Looked as if he jumped up—mebbe he was blowed up—off the ground. There was a big hole in his blue ahtillery jacket. The edges of the hole were burnin'—and his bare hide looked like a sidewalk where a firecracker has gone off, with blood in the middle of the explosion. I saw all that, Uncle Pink said, before the Yankee went oveh backwahds and hit the ground.

The Yankee infantry kept comin' in from the left and rolled us up. Lacey had stuck the flag of the Eighty-sixth in the ground, and he and Wagg were trying to turn the Napoleon, which the two Yanks had been loading. The rammer was still in the muzzle. Split—mebbe by a minnie ball—it looked forked, like a snake's tongue. Wagg's back arched like a plowhawss and the gun swung around on the Yanks. Reese ran around to the lanyard. Wagg and Lacey stepped aside, and Wagg yelled: Fiah! Reese jerked the lanyard. It went into 'em canister, rammer and all—it was a Gahd's wonder the bar'l didn't break. Wagg picked up another rammer and Jud and me got canister. Wagg and Lacey rammed in another charge just as the Yankees closed up and came on. Reese had out his Yankee pistol firing into 'em as he pulled the lanyard again. They were right up on the gun. That charge blew at least two Yankees in two—and the legs and heads off a couple. I saw something light on the ground mebbe ten yards away. I think it was an arm.

But they kept closing in: Wagg was beating 'em off with the rammer; and Lacey was slashing around with that sharp bayonet. Gahd! Uncle Pink said. I saw him rip the mouth out of one Yankee boy—and he had a grin on his face while he did it. But that kind of thing couldn't last long. There were too many comin' up. I saw Jud poke with his bayonet, pull back and put his foot against a Yankee and pull again. The Yankee grabbed the bayonet with his hand, like that one had done with Lacey. Lacey was tearing the flag off the pole.

Then, suddenly, I saw Reese: He had his father's Mexican war sword swung high oveh and back of his head. His shoulders looked likely to bust his jacket any minute—and they swelled up when he brought the sword down and threw it back again, time after time. Two Yankees went down under it with their heads and shoulders bleeding. He stood there restin' for a little spell, his jacket crept up and tight across those shoulders, the buttons open careless and his plumed hat jammed down oveh his ears. Then he hollered at Jud: Come on, Jud! Let's git back!

Now, Union batteries were galloping along the crest of the ridge near the cemetery. I could see a few bewildered-lookin' Confederates climbin' back oveh the wall. We started to run, Reese and Jud and Lacey. I stumbled oveh a dead hawse's legs, and Reese picked me up. The hawses were in heaps—dead and wounded—and so were the men.

Time we got to the wall there were right many climbin' oveh. We got oveh and to somewhere 'longside that railfence that hadn't been

knocked oveh. Git down! Reese said. Snake undah it! We threw ourselves down and wriggled through on our bellies. Then we crouched
and ran a piece. We almost fell down and lay flat, panting.

We could hear ourselves panting. There wasn't much musketry or
cannonading now. A lot of legs passed by us just walkin' slow. Jud
still had a grip on his musket and he was coughin'. I had mine too
and, for the first time, I noticed the bayonetblade was bloody. Reese's
father's swordblade was right under my nose. It was hot and bright
in the sun where the dirt wasn't stuck in the blood on it. Sticking
out of Lacey's coat was the Malvern Hill on the flag. In his right hand
he had Ole Wagg's Bull Pistol and in his left a stone. He'd lost his
sharp bayonet.

We saw somethin' movin' near us. I grabbed onto my musket
harder, until I saw what it was: It was a man settin' up. He pushed
himself up with his hands. He still had an old brown slouch hat on
the back of his head. He had tears in his eyes.

Before Gahd, boy, Uncle Pink said, I neveh hope to see anything
worse. Below the man's nose there wasn't any face. His lower jaw
was gone and you could see his open throat—there wasn't even any
tongue. But the palate was there twitchin' around in a great blood-
oozy hole with powdersmut on the white skin around it. From the
hair and the look of what face there was left, it was a boy of about
sixteen—worst thing about it his eyes looked familiar.

The eyes looked at me study; and the tears run down into the
bloody hole. He pointed to my musket and then back to himself. I
couldn't move.

Reese saw him and began to load the Yankee Colt. He capped a
nipple, cocked the hammer, took the pistol by the barrel and got up.
Come on, he said. Le's git back and find the regiment. We went on
ahead—and he came up with us. We just walked back; we couldn't
run. Well, we suah hit 'em anyway, Reese said.

It was a strange part of Seminary Ridge—not where we started
from—Uncle Pink said. Men were comin' back just like we were.
They all looked bewildered.

There were some officahs on hawses—one with a redjacket and a
queer hat. One of 'em in a plain shabby gray uniform rode out to
us. He had a Vandyke beard like yore grandfather use' to wear. I
knew him in a minute, even if I'd never seen him before. It was
Lee. Nobody could mistake him. By Gahd! You could feel him. It

was all my fault, he said. We must all stand together now, to save the rest.

I didn't say anything, but Lacey came p hollering: Look Gen'l Lee! he hollered, and ripped the flag out of his jacket. I saved the Ole Eighty-six flag.

Lacey began to cry—and the Old Man took off his hat.

That was what they called Pickett's Charge, Uncle Pink said.

CHAPTER XXV

ROME went to Kansas first in the early spring of sixtynine, I think, Wagnal said. Then he came back home to Knoxville and sold off everything; the house, the land and the livery stable and paid the note or the loan or whatever it was. I never had any doubt that Clint got the ten thousand dollars.

Una had about ten thousand left of the Mississippi money. They must have borrowed five from the bank of a political brigadier friend in Keokuk, for Una gave a party for the man and his wife just before she and Clint left for Washington.

Hmm! Katherine said. It's money Una wants there. Catch Una wining and dining a Burlington banker after she knows Clinton is General Grant's new Secretary of War! That made the total about twenty-five thousand, cash in hand—and, of course, there was always credit in Washington for a new Mr. Secretary.

I believe Clint and Una were still in Burlington when Rome took his family to Kansas. How Mrs. Hanks, first, and Myra, next, found out about Rome's loan or endorsement, I never knew. But they found out: Myra told Katherine:

Mamma's health ain't too good, Myra said. And Papa and General Clint made a bad investment. I guess General Clint lost a lot of money too. Oh God, Katherine said, Una! She'll spend it for clothes from Paris. Isn't there anything you can do, Thomas?

Maybe she spent it for clothes, but it was not enough for Una.

And poor Rawlins had T.B., Wagnal said. Maybe, if he had lived, Old Grant—as empty and childlike a son of chance as he was —maybe, if Rawlins (one political brigadier who believed the solemn speeches he made) had lived, Grant wouldn't have become the comic

pawn that he became as President of the United States. But I heard
that they were estranged, before Grant, remembering the old days in
the tents of the Army of Tennessee and feeling the warmth of heart
that always comes too late, perhaps never comes except in retrospect—
made him Secretary of War.

Solemn, portentous, sententious old Rawlins. He was a fair grape
of wrath all right and ought to have delivered the Sermon on the
Mount or saved souls under a tent. It was said that he used to stick
his hand in his coat Napoleonwise and walk sentry-like before his
tent after Shiloh, repeating A Man's a Man for A' That. That was
what Unconditional Surrender Grant's brains did for relaxation. But
he died.

Clint sent Grant a short telegram of condolence, signing himself
Brevet Major-General Clinton Belton, Army of Tennessee. (Una
composed it.) Grant was touched: those cigars and maybe those *sub
rosa* nips of brandy or Bourbon that Clint had got down Grant's gullet
without Rawlins finding out—and Una's mothering in Burlington.
What was more natural than to appoint Clinton Belton Secretary of
War—to gather another one of the old comrades of the bivouacs of the
Army of Tennessee to him. He did not know that he was appointing
Una.

Clint went to Washington, but Una, feeling, I suppose, that she had
been marooned so long among the uncivilized yokels of Burlington
that she needed to replenish her arsenal, sailed for Paris. The Burlington papers copied the New York *World* when she returned four
months later. The society reporter said that Worth, himself, had re-
tired to a cave and fasted for seven days before he created Mrs. Belton's new wardrobe: Gold wheat-ears embroidered on green satin—
forty pairs of shoes. Mrs. Sprague, the reigning belle of Washington,
was dethroned

Ah, Katherine would say, Una's enjoying herself at last. From now
on she'll make 'em squirm. She'll be in the White House before she
leaves Washington, if someone she's trodden on doesn't kill her. Her
pretty neck would snap like an icicle. We were both born with cauls,
Kitty said—but it was still as death and clammy the night Una was
born. When I was born it thundered and the dogs howled and Mammy
said her husband saw three tall men, ten feet tall, in long coats and
stovepipe hats lying dead across the turnpike. But the night Una was
born, Mammy said she saw something in the sky over the house—but

she would never tell what it was. And whenever anyone mentioned it her eyes rolled up in her head as if she were a dead woman. She said the dogs lay down and trembled without howling and a pet chicken died on her cabin steps. Grandfather never liked Una: he never abused her as he did me. He never made her drink tea instead of coffee because he liked tea himself; he never made her read lewd books, as he did me, to instruct me in the ways of designing and destructive doxies. He was always polite and ceremonious with her.

Once, in his cups, he said to me: There's your sister, my fine little wench, as coldhearted a whore as you'd find in a week's journey through the international brothels of Paris, a barren beauty, an intriguer, a passion in reverse. There's no heat in it. That old fool of a negro bitch and her signs and cauls and trembling dogs. I've no doubt that what she saw in the sky was a great ice-floe breaking over Christendom. Una's a true Theron, all right. The first Earl betrayed a good many heads to the block to get his belt. Oh, he was a bloody old bastard. He saw his best friend hanging in an iron cage without even so much as the flick of an eyelash. As for us, you and me, we are not thorough-breds. We have some disgusting *canaille* in us somewhere—some warm-hearted ancestors. There was one, I know, who disappeared completely after he refused to sleep with Elizabeth. Some said that they hardly realized he was disappearing, he did it so gradually, a part at a time—until there was nothing left of him but a wellcut doublet seen bowing around the court on the old hag's Portingale surgeon.

Oh, Grandfather had his cold side—perhaps not cold, only calculating: he calculated how to get every wench he wanted for his lechery. He had a boundless lechery. He shot—and stuck, for that matter—a good many men over women. He said that if men chose to brawl over drabs, they ought to make sure that there were no better brawlers.

If, he said, I could find a worthy receptacle deep enough for my love, I should marry her, except you, Katherine—incest has been too long out of the fashion for an old beau like me to revive it. Someday there'll be a lucky young ruffler—but God help the fool who gets Una.

Strange, Wagnal said, that Una, who cared so little about her father that she did not even think about going to Mississippi when he was found dead—that, indeed, she made a decision not to go, for there was a lawyer down there to handle what was left of the estate, and her going would have tied her name more tightly to a nasty scandal which was not that her father met a dark and violent end, but that he had

been killed because he was thought to be a niggerlover, a stigma which
she judged highly unfashionable—strange that she, whose motives were
as cold and clear as the light from a polar star, should have made the
mistake which ruined the ladder of her ambition, breaking all the rungs
at once and landing her in a worse position than had been hers when
she was a girl living on a miasmal and obscure Mississippi plantation
with nothing but mirrors and the provincial fire-eaters to curry her
prodigious vanity. But perhaps I am wrong. Perhaps Una had a passion
for beauty; and it was this alien warmth in the vastness of her arctic
soul that undid her. Perhaps those dresses from Worth, the bandeaux
of turquoises and pearls for her hair, the forty pairs of shoes, the
feel and shimmer and sound of the silk, the lovely coralshadow look of
her own breasts as she saw them framed in Worth's subtlest pink threw
her into a very passion of love for beauty itself and not a mere thing to
further the ends of ambition. Mind you, I do not say that, even for an
instant, she forgot or altered her ends, as most of us do as we dawdle
along on the fool's errand we have had thrust upon us. Oh no, Una
was no pamphlet distributor, who tosses his papers under a culvert,
knowing he will get his twenty-five cents anyway. She had her own
papers to deliver: She was waiting to inform Woman that Mrs. Clinton
Belton—better, Una Theron—was the queen of them all who would
stand for no damned trifling from any of their feline breed. She knew
their smell. And she *was* the Queen of them all when it happened.
Why, God Almighty, Wagnal said, how in the name of all that's holy,
could any of them have expected to hold out against her.

Perhaps Kate Chase Sprague, who was urbane and cunning and
beautiful did so for a while—and hoped. But the Washington ladies
must have known immediately they saw her that here was God's punishment for all their sins—for all the adulteries they had projected
upon their pillows before idly falling asleep at nights. They knew then
that all the partners of all these adulteries—at least those who had real
bodies—were lost. But they could see also, that, though Una's eyes
might seem to give hope to man, there was nothing behind them but
the movement of a great glacial ambition ready to pass over everything before it. That men could seldom see—even the most cynical
Latin ministers and attachés.

It was the carpetbag lawyer who settled the Theron estate in Mississippi—Burrus, I think his name was—a jackleg shyster, who knew
little enough about Coke and Blackstone, but had enough sharp prac-

tice to cheat the eyeteeth out of the unwary. He came along to Washington with fifteen thousand dollars, perhaps, the amount he said he had salvaged from the Theron estate—but there must have been more. He came when Una needed money to shine.

Kate Chase Sprague, the brilliant girl who had them all round her little finger until Una came—the girl who used to sit parasol in hand before the tents of the Army of the Potomac and leave escorted by a different set of fatuous staffofficers every time she visited, with never anything less than a Major-General driving her back to Washington—was still to be conquered. Lincoln himself had listened to Kate's advice —he kissed her a shade too enthusiastically at her wedding. Pale pink silk, diamond tiaras, the accounts of Mrs. Sprague's brilliance in the New York papers, her damask covered pavilion—these were all a great weight for Una to lift and cast aside, but she was equal to it. With the help of Burrus, she pulled it off.

Katherine used to say that she could see Una's every move with the man. He is a little man, Katherine said, the seat of his trousers is too near the ground and he has got a black untidy beard and what he thinks is a fine gimlet eye. Didn't he get out of Mississippi before the Kluckers killed him—and didn't he turn a pretty penny down there outa them niggers. I think that Una must have let him into the house in Lafayette Square herself. She heard the howd'ye do, ma'am, and saw the black string tie and the illcut silkfaced lapels and the not too clean cuffs and the funny way he held himself because of his back. She saw the little gimlet eyes estimating the prices of the Parisian furniture and bric-a-brac, the price of the gown and jewels she was wearing—greedily but with sly uneasiness. How do you do, Mr. Burrus? How kind of you to come so soon—how very kind of you to make such a splendid settlement of the estate.

Nothin' at all, ma'am. Jist routine. The fee was five hundred dollars. Katherine said it must have been a thousand to begin with, but it couldn't have stayed at that figure long with Burrus's little eyes resting on the curve between Una's breasts, for Katherine knew he came in the evening. She knew that Una would have received him in something décolletté. Oh, maybe it came down to four or even three hundred— Una had all the manoeuvres of the dishonest whore down pat. She let him look all right—she let the little smoky gimleteyes rest on her finewove hide, but she said presently: Oh dear, Mr. Burrus, the General has so many social obligations, now that he is at the side of dear General Grant, his wartime friend, I am afraid I shall have to cut short our pleasant interview. Oh yes, Burrus said. Official life. Well, I was in the war myself. Indeed? What regiment? Indiany, Burrus said. (It was discovered later that he had been a sutler.) We was at Shiloh and all down through there. Many's the time I seen Gen'l Grant and yore husban' tawkin' over the campaign over a seegar and a cuppa cawfee.

Ah yes, Una said. Yes, ma'am, Burrus said, them were the days of companionship around the ole camp far. Many's the time I wisht I was back in the ole Army a Tennessee. They was vycissytoods and tribulations, but the comradeship with big-hearted pat-ree-ottic men made up for that. Ah yes, Una said. Well, Mr.—ah—ah—Burrus—I can't thank you enough for your splendid and competent settlement of the estate. Now, ma'am, Burrus said, screening the gimleteyes with the curious, slightly swollen big-surfaced eyelids which reminded Una of the downcast eyes of a saint or a madonna painted on canvas. She could see the sideways downlook of the dark pupils, not boring now, but seeking the place to drive their bits in. Now, ma'am, Burrus said, softening down his hardcrass yankeevoice, that's just the way I feel about you and the General.

He began almost to whisper his words—a sort of softwhine it was. Maybe he was remembering how six of them came up to his hotel room in Jackson. Mr. Burrus, it has come to our ears that you plan to remain in Warner county. Tonight we have come to warn you that for your own good you had better be gone by tomorrow. If you are not, we shall return to give you a taste of the hickory.

The room was silent. They were standing around him as he sat on the bed's edge, one boot on, the other off. The man was in a long red flannel robe with the belt of a Confederate web holster gathering it in at his middle. The faceless face was made of red calico with the eye and mouth holes bound in white and a red cloth tongue lolling out. Burrus could see the muddy boots and the gray homespun trousers where the red flannel stopped. And they were just like any boots and trousers that a man might see in thousands of streets wearing out warp and woof and shoeleather in the way it had been worn out since the first sheep had been sheared and the first cow skinned. The man in red spoke, but there were others in black behind him and one had a tough elastic hickory stick—Burrus could hear it quirting through the air like a bullet ricocheting—and one had a blacksnake whip caught looped and shiny and strong in his hand. They looked a little like him and Sis had looked in the lookin' glass when Ma made them those witches suits and they put candles in the punkins to go and scare the neighbors back in Terry Hut.

I ain't a-going to go, Burrus said. I ain't a-going. The man in the red robe took a whistle and, pushing the red cloth tongue aside blew a short, shrill, gurgling blast. I'm a-going to stay, Burrus said. And I'm a-going to find out who done that to Mr. Theron and his nigger.

Two of the black ones had him by the arms then; and then they were marching him down the hotel steps through the empty lobby into the dusty street. He hollered once, but he couldn't after that, for one of them tied a snotty handkerchief over his mouth—it tasted green and salty on his tongue.

They put him on a horse, facing toward the rump, and tied a rag around his eyes. He began to tingle at the base of his spine, and he thought maybe he was going to dirty his pants, but he didn't. He heard the shrill gurgling whistle several times and the leather creaking as they got down off the horses. There wasn't a word said until his coat and shirt was off and he felt a tickly wind on his back and chest as he stood on tiptoe reaching his wristcords. Then he felt the big, firm hand on his back—an almost caressing touch—measuring the stroke to come. He heard the quirt of the blacksnake through the old, miasmal air of Mississippi, and he thought: Why, God, this is awful to do a man thisaway—to take him out and strip him down and beat him with a whip like he ain't got a right even to be spit on—to take him like they was God himself and hurt him hard and beat all his dignity outen him. It ain't right—an' I got my rights. I'm a human, ain't I?

The blacksnake cut and cracked around his back, winding its snake-tail over the tendermeat under his arms and on his breast and across his hardenedup man's nipples. Then he got the sharp canine, tiger-taloned slash of the little end and the sharp goosefleshed pain running back from it—and felt the wind squish out of his belly from the force of the blow. He heard it and felt it for eight strokes. Then there was water on his face, and he began to feel the raw sting of his back and breast, as if he were a giant with a huge tender hide.

Now Mr. Burrus, the one in red's voice said, now that we have brushed you a little to remind you that we cannot brook disobedience, we will remind you again that you will either leave Warner county by tomorrow night or we will kill you. I hope I ain't hollered, Burrus thought. I hope to Christ I ain't. Oh, God, let me see the day I can git 'em.

He paid his bill to the hotelkeeper at noon and got on his horse, riding towards Vicksburg, his shirt sticking to the drying raw meat and blood on his back.

Yes, ma'am, that's jist the way I feel about you and the General. Now that the General's Mr. Secertarry of War, ma'am, he's gonna need a good bit of help—a good few public servants to do his bidding. He raised his eyegimlets to Una's face and sought to drive them into the quartz surface of her blue eyes, but he dropped them again. Yes, Una said and waited. Well, Burrus said, now that the General's— Yes? Una said. What is it you wish, Burrus? Burrus looked up angrily. Well, *Mr.* Burrus?

Well, Burrus said, there are places with tradin' posts—say, like Fort Sofa. Good men is needed for traders—not ongrateful men that'll be liable to bite the hand that's feeding 'em. Oh, Una said. At which post Mr. Burrus do you think you could serve your country and the General best? Well, ma'am, Burrus said, still looking down, for there was no need now to look at Una's hard naked eye, Fort Sofa's in the Territory and needs a good manager. Ah, Una said. I've heard that a good trader earns twenty-five thousand a year. Well, ma'am, I don't— Mr. Burrus the moment I saw you I knew you to be a man of benevolence and charity, Una said. Now, I have a private charity for which I could use, say, ten thousand dollars a year.

Ten thousand! Burrus said. I have heard, Una said, that a good many post-traders are generous men. I heard recently of one who had charities of twelve thousand dollars a year to his credit. Living as he does among the poor Indians, who have been corrupted by our horrible firewater, touched his sensibilities to the extent that he gives the money to one of the ladies here in Washington to be used for unfortunate people. Well, ma'am, Burrus said, there's a good bit in what you say—a good bit. Shall you be here in Washington, say, in two or three days? Una said. Then come again at the same time, say Thursday.

It is a matter of record, Wagnal said—and even the little two-by-four paper in Knoxville—people began to stare at Katherine and me. More than once we heard Mrs. Belton's sister and other hushed scraps of sentences. The gossips began to whisper that I'd married a Rebel and a fallen woman. Her Pa was killed by the Kluckers because he slep with a nigger. Well, I ain't for human slavery, but I always been dee-cent an' I don't want to have any truck with any ole niggerlover. I always say there's a place for the black and a place for the white—an' it up to them to keep their place.

One day, God forgive me, Wagnal said, I hit a man. He was coming out of the saloon or the hotel bar—and I heard him behind the swinging doors shooting off his mouth. That holy old son of a bitch, Wagnal— him and his niggerlovin' wife. He wasn't a very big man—Worsham Jones was his name—the hostler who had once worked in your grandfather's livery stable. He didn't have any front teeth—people said he had pulled 'em out to keep from going to war as the toothless boy did at Shiloh. He was a little, stringy, scraggy, blear-eyed fellow who always smelt of horsedung and urine and his own foul sweat. He came out of the swinging doors with Katherine's name on his lips, and I forgot myself—I forgot how big I was and hit him in the face. His head snapped back and I thought I heard his spine crack as if it were a piece of stovewood splitting. He fell backwards, and his nose began to bleed down into the wide gap left by his cartridge biters—and the blood ran down his shabby, stubbly yellow gray quarter inch long whiskers. People backed away from me in fear. I must have looked crazy mad. But I got over it soon.

I picked up Worsham Jones and helped him down the street to the sheriff's office—Don Trott's father was sheriff. Mr. Trott, I said, I wish to plead guilty to striking this man. I have comported myself in a most un-Christian manner. I happened to hear him passing a remark about my wife—in a public place—and I could not control my temper. Well, sir, Mr. Trott said, well, sir, Reverend Wagnal, I can see how you felt. And it's not my business to do anything unless the other party wants to complain. Worsham, you goin' to swear out a complaint? He didn't hear me right, Worsham said, I never said a Goddamn' thing like he said I said. He had a gang with pick hannels— Worsham, the sheriff said, Captain Hanks missed a good bit a money from the till of his livery barn not so many years ago—and Mrs. Hanks could never account for them two mares that you said died. I lived here twenty-five years now, man an' boy, Worsham said, an' I ain't never had nothin' but bad luck. By Gahd, they're allus a-pickin' at me a-tryin' to make out I ain't an honest man. Him and his gang jumped onta me, but I ain't sayin' nothing, fer the reason I couldn't make it stand up in a court a law. I wouldn't never go to a-lawin' 'cause I'm a pore man and wouldn't stand a chanct.

Worsh, the sheriff said, why don't you git? Git? Worsham said. Yeh, the sheriff said, looks like the town's gittin' too damn' little to hold you. Then he turned around to me and said: There ain't any complaint agin' you under the law here, Reverend Wagnal. Are they any complaint agin' the other party here—slander mebbe? There is no complaint, Sheriff, I said. Well, he said, you can git, Worsh. Now, Doc, Mr. Trott said, don't you let any trash like that git you down. Missus Trott and me knows how you taken care a Don durin' the war—and they ain't a decent man er woman in this town's gonna stand by an' see you an' Missus Wagnal abused. They can put that in their pipe and smoke it.

But it wasn't the same. Perhaps it was because Rome and his family had gone to Kansas, or because Shuball York went away too and John Simpson died and we didn't meet at Rome's and walk home to our house and sing songs of an evening any more. Maybe that was it in part—but there was no doubt that all of them knew the story about Una's selling post-traderships and getting caught. Getting caught was the sin. Don't ever mislead yourself on that score, young man.

Why, before it happened every Goddamned woman who could get hold of a paper (and who hadn't been snubbed too obviously by Una in Burlington social life—though even those were prone to follow her fashions and boast of their former intimacy with her) and read what Una did or what she wore in Washington Society was bound to copy her to the limit of her husband's purse—or try to copy her in bumpkin's fashion. Inwardly all of them cursed Una's reputation and envied her—and when she was caught each breathed her secret deepdrawn sigh of relief that God had removed such a formidable foe from the feminine lists. Now they had only that frumpy Mrs. Trott to show up in the matter of bonnets, or that forward and perky and too beautiful Wagnal woman who was now shamed by her sister's thievery, or that silly Mrs. Abel who *said* her brother was a big banker back East, or that Mrs. Dunn who wore such *extreme* clothes, that if the truth was known they'd bet there was a touch of the tarbrush somewhere and what was more they wouldn't be a teeny-weeny bit surprised if she didn't turn out to be from a *bad* house maybe down in New Orleans.

Could Katherine have been otherwise but bored and annoyed in such a village and such a situation? And though she loved our old deep-porched, deep-lawned house and the little iron negroes holding out their iron rings for the horses, she did not want to stay. Thomas, she said, we must leave. I cannot stand this place any longer—I cannot abide it. It is a bore, an evil humdrum bore. I shall die if I live here any longer. We could go to New York state, I said. There are two churches there. No, she said, there is one in Fork City, Kansas. I think it's a little wood church, square as a box—with vines on it. General Jeb Stuart helped to collect the money to build it when he was just out of West Point. I saw him in Richmond once on a sleek black stallion when I was just fourteen. He had a black plume on his hat and a great fan beard. He was only a colonel then, but he was the talk of the town. Let us go to Kansas, Thomas.

That is how I came here, Wagnal said. And Stuart, Goddamn his foppish soul to hell, Goddamn his sanctity and his success and his plumes and his horses and his banjoman, Sweeney, and his Prussian dragoon, von Borcke and all his fire-eating heroics—even his death-wound at Yellow Tavern—Goddamn them all to hell, Wagnal said quietly, his old voice whistling on the sibilants. He was dead and rotting away, but I'll venture to say that a million women still prayed for him—still prayed his ghost into their beds before they fell asleep to dream of those plumes, that beard, and that black stallion-charger of his and his comicopera escort—all jackboots and horsepistols and sabres and beards and firegilt buttons going along the turnpike to the tune of *Lorena* on a minstrelshow banjo. And Stuart with his Goddamned knee crossed over the saddle, singing.

Why for fifteen years I had the holy, erotic body of Major-General James Ewell Brown Stuart in bed with me and my wife—between us like a rusty Confederate sabre. But I didn't know it then. I did not know that the bones of the Brian de Bois-Guilbert, the Galahad of the Confederacy, the Light Cavalryman of the Nation, had sepulchred themselves in my bed. Or perhaps I had known it a long time. Maybe the very instant that Katherine articulated the words which had been screamed shouted and cooed and prayed out all over the Confederacy—which had been breathed moistly through young sweetmoist lips to the fine linen pillowcases of a thousand silly ovalfaced primplipped girls—maybe that first time she said them softly in Knoxville, Iowa, I knew. But in those days we weren't great hands to admit that anything but two and two made four.

I think that one Sunday after Katherine was dead, I was in the church up there and the service was going on or just over and I fell into a reverie, thinking of the new bronze plaque the parish had put up to the memory of Stuart, the *preux chevalier sans peur et sans reproche*. It struck me that this Galahad had cuckolded me and continued to cuckold me for years. And he had slipped away again as he did when he rode around McClellan. And good God Almighty, what could I do, loving Katherine as I did—and both of them dead and maybe right then in each other's arms in heaven.

CHAPTER XXVI

PAPA was at the store in Elgin when they stopped in the yard by the pecan tree to water their horses. Myra looked out of the window, because she always looked out of the window when anyone came by the house. Most days there was little enough to see. And she got so tired of the dust and the snow and the mud and the grasshoppers—and with Mamma loading up the saddlebags with quinine and elderberry bark salve and foxglove and cherry pies and riding off on Old Caesar to help the neighbors and Papa staying at the store all hours and acting as judge and Sister Hettie so cross and Brother Ream off in the fields all day and Sister Ellen so funny and quiet, she was just lonely and that was all there was to it.

After Knoxville, Ioway, Elgin, Kansas, wasn't much, she could tell you. Indians and settlers and a mover or two. Sometimes she thought Ma might just as well stay home and let the whole push starve or die of malaria or cholera or just plain laziness. Why, some of them didn't have anything to eat half the time, and they had every bit as good places as Papa had. They still had one room cabins and shacks and some of them still lived in those old soddies full of bedbugs and fleas and ants —and the women too shiftless to keep a good house. Why, a lot of them couldn't talk good English. Why, when Papa brought them here last year, she just sat in the wagon and looked at the one-room shack he had built and burst into tears. And he said: There, now, Myra, honey. There now. We'll have to have a little time, honey. Well, it hadn't been long until they had a nice big house—not so big as the one in Knoxville but better than any around there—and a barn and a corn crib. Papa had some pride!

Still it wasn't near so nice as living in a town. But Papa would sign that old General Belton's note—and for ten thousand dollars! And lose his livery-stable and have to move away from Knoxville. And they stole him blind while he was away during the war—especially that old Worsham Jones, a poor white trash fellah that come from Kentucky and pulled out his front teeth so he couldn't chew cartridges and wouldn't have to go to war. Papa went off the first thing—and he was from Kentucky too and owned niggers once. But he was only elected a lieutenant and him an officer in the Mexican war too. But anyway there was a lot of the men and just young boys back in Knoxville that just said they wouldn't volunteer at all if Papa wasn't made colonel of the regiment.

But it was just like Papa when he took the Knoxville boys to one side on the drill ground at Keokuk and said: Gentlemen, we will go to this war and we will not bother about who is colonel and who is not. You will remember that Mr. Hanks will be with you and will do what he can for you no matter what kind of straps he wears on his shoulders. And even that big lunk of a fellow, Sleepy Bates, who didn't look like he had right good sense came around to the house and told Ma what a good man he thought Papa was. And young Rufus Lamb, that grocery boy, cried when he told Ma about Papa talking to them. Papa told her that Sleepy Bates was killed in the battle of Atlanta and that he was shot in the knee at a place called Corinth—and through his side at Atlanta too, before they took him to that awful Andersonville prison. And besides Papa couldn't hear good on one side because the cannon at Shiloh went off too close to his ear.

Mamma read her Papa's letters while they were scraping linen rags and every kind of white cloth for lint for the Sanitary Commission. And it seemed that there had always been so many dead or hurt that she knew: Sleepy Bates and Frederick Ware and Mr. Shuball York and that boy without the teeth and so many boys. And all the time Papa was in danger too—and he almost starved to death himownself in that old prison. My, how she hated those old Rebels. Once she wrote to Papa and told him so, not remembering that Papa's brothers were Rebels until after she mailed the letter. When she got Papa's answer from Vicksburg, Mississippi—written on the Big Black River that he said wasn't black—he didn't say anything about her saying that at all. And there was a greenback in the letter that Papa said was for some ribbons for a new bonnet. She thought she loved Papa better than anybody in the whole wide world and wrote to him apologizing about saying those things about the Rebels.

Now she could see the men in the yard better. There were three of them. One of them got down off his horse and led two of the horses up to the wooden trough near the pecan tree. The other one whose feet weren't in the stirrups sat on his horse kind of funny. She had to go away from the window to see her biscuits in the oven. She had just finished looking at them and trying them with a broomstraw when the men knocked at the back door.

That Wood Sipperly with his old dirty beard and that dirty old soldier coat was standing there with a pistol strapped on him holding his horse and Milt Gaby in a pair of homespun breeches and a buckskin jacket was sitting in his saddle with a rifle in a sheath sticking up beside him. In the middle between Sipperly's and Gaby's horses there was a young man—really not much more than a boy—sitting wearily in the saddle of a claybank mare that looked like Mr. Ed White's horse. The boy looked at Myra sullenly. His eyes were swollen and there was a dried dribble of blood on one of his pink, downy cheeks and a dark drop or two on his bright yellow neckcloth. Gaby had the claybank's bridle in his hand. Myra saw now that the boy's legs were tied under the mare and that his hands were tied behind him.

Mornin', Miss Hanks, Sipperly said with a silly grin. Air the Judge to home?

No, Myra said, not smiling. Mr. Hanks hasn't come home to dinner yet. Sipperly shifted from one foot to the other and petted his beard under Myra's cold, suspicious gaze. Is there anything *I* can do for you, Mr. Sipperly. He was such a dirty old fellah and always smelt like whiskey and stables and everybody knew about him and that squaw he had out at that old soddy he had on what he called his place.

We was wonderin', Sipperly said, sniffing the biscuit smell. We been a-riding all night and ain't et—we was wonderin'—

Myra fixed them some bacon and eggs and gave them some of her biscuits on the kitchen table.

Shore is good, ma'am, Gaby said, chewing one egg and one biscuit.

Myra silently buttered and honeyed a halfdozen biscuits, poured some coffee, sweetened it and put in some good thick cream. Then, taking a half dozen strips of bacon from the skillet, she went out to where the claybank was tied to the hitching post under the pecan tree. She untied the reins and led the mare to the back stoop where a fly or two droned over the honey and bacon. Nervously, she brushed them aside—and tied the reins to the doorknob.

Hungry? Myra said, her face pink and her blue eyes averted from the boy's face.

Yes'm, the boy said sullenly.

Like biscuits and honey? Myra said.

Yes'm, the boy said—and then choked out: Thank you, ma'am.

Lean over, Myra said.

The boy leant over, and Myra fed him her biscuits with honey and bacon and coffee. He ate loudly and greedily. Thank you, ma'am, he said again, after Myra had wiped his mouth and washed his face. He was better-looking without the blood on his cheek. That wasn't their notion, he said nodding toward the kitchen and moving one of his Texas cowboy boots which Myra noticed had a little triangular hole in it that showed his bare toe.

No; it wasn't. Is this your horse?

No. 'Tain't theirs neither. They took it and put me on it to save their own hide.

That there's his story, Miss Hanks, Sipperly said. He was standing on the steps with several new yellow strings of egg yolk on his beard. That there's his story. I calcalate the Judge's down to the store, ain't he?

I don't know. Mr. Hanks may be on his way home to dinner.

Papa was just driving into the yard. There was somebody sitting on the seat of the spring wagon with him—a man with a silky beard in a broad old soldier hat.

Papa and the man got down off the wagon, and Papa tied the horses.

How d'ye do, Judge? Sipperly said.

How d'ye do, Mr. Sipperly, Papa said.

We got a man here—Sipperly began.

Myra, Papa said, looking toward the house.

She went inside. She always tried to be obedient to Papa. But she watched them from the kitchen window: Papa talked with them a while and Sipperly and Gaby and the boy rode away and Papa and the man with the beard and the old soldier hat came in. Of course Papa had a beard too, but you expected a man as old and dignified as Papa and you expected that old Sipperly fellah to have a ratty one with egg in it—but somehow you didn't expect the young man with Papa to have one, especially as big and black a one as he had, though maybe he wasn't really as young as he might be. He held himself straight and limped just a little with his left leg as he came into the kitchen with Papa.

Myra, Papa said, this is Mr. Beckham. He came into town today, and he's going to help at the store. Mr. Beckham, this is my daughter, Myra Hanks.

How d'ye do, sir, Myra said primly, thinking how straight he held his shoulders and how nice and crisp his black hair looked.

How d'ye do, ma'am, he said in a big hearty voice, though he wasn't such a big man. I said to the Captain it was just bully of him to ask me to dinner.

Papa, Myra said, you shouldn't bring company in our old kitchen. You take Mister—you take the company in the parlor. Dinner'll be ready soon. I had Brother Ream kill a chicken and I've got biscuits.

She took Papa and the stranger in the parlor and sat them down—but before she sat them down she asked Papa in a whisper: Papa, what are them old dirty men going to do to that boy?

Now, Myra, honey, nothing, Papa said. I told them to put him in the store woodshed until we could get the marshal.

I don't like that old Sipperly, Papa. There won't be any rope?

No, honey. No.

Myra went to the dining-room and began to set the table, putting on the best silver. She thought Papa said his name was Beck or something. He'd been in the war because he'd called Papa Captain that way —and most everybody called Papa Judge, here.

Ma didn't get back for dinner, so Hettie sat at the foot of the table and Papa served, but Ellen wouldn't come out of her bedroom because she was bashful and pouty.

Mr. Beckham was from Philadelphia and was an old soldier of the Army of the Potomac. He was shot in the battle of Gaines's Mill in the Seven Days' Battles around Richmond, and was taken prisoner and sent to Bell's Island in 1862—two years before they took Papa to that awful old Andersonville. He'd come west because a newspaper fellah said you could grow up with the country—and he thought it was a boss idea.

Why, in 1862, Myra said, we lived in Knoxville, Ioway; and Papa was in the battle of Shiloh—and we were all scared to death. But Papa only had his knee hurt—but my, oh my! how we missed him!

Mr. Beckham was looking at her, holding up his chin proudly and smoothing his beard that was so black and silky against one of Ma's best white linen napkins. Mr. Beckham was all the way from Philadelphia.

The next morning after Mr. Beckham was there when she had finished doing the breakfast dishes and dusted, she didn't know what to do. She could have sewn, but she just couldn't sit still. She kept thinking of the boy tied on the horse and old Wood Sipperly and then Papa bringing Mr. Beckham home to dinner—and Mr. Beckham being in the Civil War too and being shot and taken prisoner like Papa.

She went in Papa's Room off the parlor and looked in his bookcase for a book; but she had read *Ivanhoe* and *Ormond*—and there were a lot of old things in Latin like *Livy's Works* and *The Lives of the Caesars* by Suetonius and then a book called *The Origin of Species* that had caused so much talk about apes being our ancestors and *The Advancement of Learning* by Sir Francis Bacon and *Childe Harold* by Lord Byron, which reminded her of Sleepy Bates whose name was Harold and *Shakespeare's Works* and *Napoleon and His Marshals* by J. T. Headley and a lot of other things that were all too deep for her. Papa was a great reader and smart as a whip; and he had taught school in Indiana; and Mamma married him there. But none of his books was interesting enough. So she told Mamma she'd saddle up and go down to the store at Elgin and see if Papa had any new Butterick patterns from New York.

Mamma helped her saddle up Old Caesar—and Sister Hettie said: Humph! She's goin' to see her new beau. But Ellen smiled sympathetically. She rode out of the yard with Ring, the puppy yipping at Old Caesar's heels. He was a black Shepherd puppy with a little white ring around his throat and just a darling. And Old Caesar didn't mind him —and it was such a fine morning—and wheat was coming up out of the black dirt in such crisp green shoots!

Mr. Beckham came out of the store and helped her down from Old Caesar and hitched him to the post and said:

Good morning, Miss Hanks! Ain't it a tiptop morning?

She got down in the sunlight feeling so fine that she didn't even look at the painted Osage on the pony with the stick candy braided in his mane—nor really notice the funny sad stare the Indian gave her.

Good morning, Mr. Beckham, she said. Where's Pa—Mr. Hanks?

Why, let me see, he said. He took the wagon and went off about an hour ago. I don't recollect where he said he was a-going.

Oh, Myra said. I thought maybe he had some new patterns in the store.

Well, Mr. Beckham said, you just come right in and look. I don't know that I know where they are. Ain't it a just bully morning?

She said she couldn't find any new patterns; and Mr. Beckham was a-telling her about Philadelphia, when she saw Papa and the marshal, Mr. Ernie Stewart, drive up in the spring wagon. Papa and the marshal got down and stood there squinting in the sun. Mr. Stewart had a rifle; and they looked pretty serious, so she walked out and spoke to them.

Mr. Stewart took off his hat and said Myra got prettier every day —and Papa smiled a little. And Mr. Stewart looked up toward the wagon awkwardly. But Myra saw the end of the rope and the Texas cowboy boots sticking out from under the blanket and the little piece of barefoot through the triangular hole before Mr. Stewart could drive away. The poor boy hadn't even had any socks.

Papa! Papa! she said. That boy! I don't believe he did it. No siree, I don't.

Now, Myra, Papa said. Now, honey.

You let them, Papa! You let them! She began crying.

Myra! Papa said.

Oh, oh, I'm sorry, Papa—I know you didn't. But he was such a boy —and old Wood Sipperly!

I know, honey. They told the marshal he got out of the woodshed. Mr. Stewart and I found him. He's going to question Sipperly now—

Questions!

Myra, child, please forgive me. I should have known.

Oh, Papa, excuse *me*. I know you couldn't help it!

She got on Old Caesar and rode home, tears blinding her all the way.

Rome unlatched the kitchen door and held up the candle against a dark, muttering March night, but Rome discerned the matted black-brown beard and the eyes looking out from under the brim of the wide felt hat.

Well, sir? Rome said.

Rome? the voice came muted and deep from under the beard. Brother Rome.

Loosh! Brother Lucius, Rome said softly. Come in.

Loosh looked over his shoulder toward the road. I cain't stay, Rome. I thought mebbe I could bait mah hawss and git a bite to eat—

Why, sure, Loosh, Rome said. The candle sent the shadows shivering upward on their faces.

Rome put his boots on and his trousers over his nightshirt and lit a lantern. As they walked to the barn with Loosh's horse, a wind blew over the grass, thunder muttered again and then bloomed over the hill like shaken tin.

There's going to be some weather, Loosh, Rome said. You'd better stay the night.

I cain't, Loosh said. I got to ride a fur piece befoh mawnin'. It thundered again hard. Puts me in the mind of Shiloh, Loosh said.

Shiloh? Rome said. Were you at Shiloh, Loosh?

I was, Rome, Loosh said tenderly. Sho was. I recollect seein' a feller with a six shooter farin' at our flagtoter—farin' cool an' slow, with his sword put up and drawin' a bead down eveh time he squoze the triggeh. An' look like eveh time he fared he got himself anotheh flagtoter. I was settin' in the crotch of a tree, an', thinks I, that shootin's too damn' peart. So I draws down a bead on the feller right between the eyes. Mah fingeh just started to mash down on the triggeh—she's a fine hair triggeh too—when somethin' henders me. I takes me anotheh good look at that feller, and by Gahd, thinks I, he shoots like Rome. Of course they was all them whiskehs and the smoke, but I set thar and watched that feller till he put up his six shooter and began farin' a musket and then I knowed it was Rome. An' I had me a bead! I didn't far anotheh shot all day. That was you, wasn't it, Brotheh Rome?

That just about fits it, Rome said.

I knowed it was. By Gahd, when I seen that shootin', you couldn't fool me. Reminded me a the day you killed them Shawnees that got Pa. I had a bead on you with that rifle Pa give you just before the Shawnees got him—yore own gun. I threw it in Owl Crick that night and lit out—an' neveh went near the damn' wah since. I ain't any too Gahddamn' finicky, seein' it's a hard row to hoe gittin' along in the world, but I reckoned Gen'l Albert Sidney Johnston wouldn't miss me too much. An' I neveh studied to shed mah own brotheh's blood. I

don't believe they eveh missed me—anyway Gen'l Johnston was killed.
I reckon they just wrote me off as kilt at Shiloh.

Rome put his hand on Loosh's shoulder and held it there for a
moment. Come in, Loosh, and have some supper, Rome said.

I cain't stay long, Rome. I'm on my way to mebbe Mexico. I was
up in Abilene a month ago and they was askin' me about a bill of sale
fo me and my pardner's hawsses. I just didn't like the idy a them
askin' me with a six shooter—me havin' been in the battle of Shiloh
and seein' so many dead men they was common as dirt—

Are they after you, Loosh? Rome said.

I don't know, Rome. I neveh inquiahed. But I got seperated from
mah pardner. He said he knowed a fellah out in this neck a the woods
called Wood Sipperly. He wasn't much more'n a boy—kinda purty boy
with light hair and down on his face—allus dawgged out in Texas
boots and a yeller neck cloth. He said Sipperly'd hide us out, an' I
was to look fur him at Sipperly's place.

Loosh, Rome said, you won't find that boy there. You'd better go
on without him.

Well, Rome, Loosh said, I reckon I'd be obliged to hunt him up—
him bein' mah pardner an'—

Loosh, Rome said, his voice on a deadcalm level, my advice is to
go on.

Oh, Loosh said. You know this yeah Sipperly?

Yes, Loosh.

Oh, Loosh said. He was remembering what Ma had said to him and
Granny and Little Ream: You boys always heed your Brother Romulus; he's wise. That was a good many years ago.

Little Ream was eveh a one to follow you around, Brother Rome.
Whateveh come a that boy?

I buried him at Shiloh, Rome said.

Well, Loosh said, he was eveh as bright as a cricket and allus a
great hand to coat his Brother Rome and read a passel of books. What
side was he on, Rome?

He was a lieutenant in a Union regiment from Kentucky, Rome
said.

He knew *you* was a Yank, Rome, Loosh said. But take Granny, he
said, after leaving a little time silent for the low thunder. Granny was
a far-eatin' states' rights man. Him and Little Ream quarreled right

bitter. Somebody in Abilene—I don't recollect who 'twuz—he knowed
a Granville Hanks that got killed in Ohio with Morgan. An' anotheh
man said Granville Hanks was with Morgan all right and holped the
Old Man break out of that Indiana pen and then went oveh to Vir-
ginnie and joined up with Mosby—but afteh he let his hair grow out
whur they cut it off in the pen. That sounds more like Granny—always
nervous and skittish and sassy.

Yes, Rome said, and Granny could ride. He paused. You know,
Loosh, I saw that prison. Gold must have helped.

Sheetlightning outlined the low hills to the east and the sullen
thunderpeals seemed to roll over and under the ground.

When they got to the kitchendoor, Rome said: You know, Brother
Lucius, that it is not like me to deny shelter to my own, but I think it
would be better if you waited in the barn. I'll fetch you some things
for your saddlebags. Here's the lantern. Saddle up again and be ready.
I had wished for you to know my family, but—

Don't you worry yore head, Rome. I kin see what your gittin' at.

Now, Loosh, let's not put it that way.

Put it any way. The both of us knows thar's a-plenty a rope an' a
damn' sight too many stout limbs in this country. He took the lantern
from Rome and walked back toward the barn. He hardly needed the
lantern now, for the lightning was flashing fast.

When Rome came to the kitchen, Myra and her mother were waiting in flannel wrappers.

What's the trouble, Mr. Hanks? Lorna Browne said.

No trouble, Lorna, I'm just helping a traveller.

Myra, Lorna said, turning her sharp hawkface to her daughter, go
in and turn down the bed in the spare room.

No, Rome said, he can't stay. His business is urgent. What have we
to eat that'll do for his saddlebags?

I'll get it, Lorna said.

But, Papa, there's going to be a storm. Why won't he come in?

Myra, honey, where's my oilskin coat?

She knew it was no use to ask Papa anything more, so she went to
find the oilskin. Rome went to his desk in the room off the parlor and
took a hundred dollars in greenbacks from a pigeonhole.

When the two women saw him out the door, it had begun to rain
a few big scattered drops. He carried cold chicken, bread, cold biscuits,
a glass jar full of hot coffee and the better part of a side of bacon under

the oilskin. He paused once in the lightning to put the greenbacks in the package of biscuits.

Loosh was sitting on a box in the lanternlight, shoving a cartridge into a singleaction Colt's.

Well, Rome, I was right glad to see you.

This oilskin will keep out a little of the weather—and be careful when you open the grub not to lose any of it. I was right glad to see you, Brother Loosh. It reminds me of the old days in Kentucky. Oh, Loosh, where did you boys bury Ma?

Right beside Pa. Little Ream had stones cut with their dates.

Loosh swung over into the saddle. Rome stood holding the lantern.

Goodbye, Rome.

Goodbye, Brother Lucius.

Just as the lightning showed Brother Lucius' bearded outline black beside the pecan tree the rain began to come down hard. Rome heard Ring howl a little in the house. He was wet to the skin when he set the lantern on the kitchen table.

Myra made him drink a cup of hot coffee and he lay awake all the rest of the night, thinking of the rain at Shiloh and Wagnal and Clint Belton and General Grant and Little Ream and the Shawnees and California and the Mexican war and Kentucky when he was a boy.

CHAPTER XXVII

THERE were about eighty of us after Pickett's Charge, Uncle Pink said. Oh, a few more came in afterward when we got back into Virginia, but I don't reckon we was more'n a hunderd and fifty when all was totaled up—and we had eight hunderd when we marched into Pennsylvania. Ole Wagg and Dance Sudderth and James Poe and Sergeant Wheary and Lige Boggs and Brothuh all kilt. Lacey said Wagg was dead shore enough—died hollerin' scriptur. Evil comin' outen the Nawth, Lacey said. Tuck it in the belly and the haid at the same time—went down like a stuck hawg. Lacey just had time to pick up the Bull Pistol. He sat around mopin' about Wagg fur a long time— said thar wasn't nobody eveh fit as good.

Gahd, Uncle Pink said, I remember we shore felt turrible the next night. We was plumb wore out marchin' along the roads in the rain—slipped back'ards and forrards and sideways eveh step we took. Cole and hot at the same time we was: Afteh all that heat and then the storm, we didn't care much where we was goin'. I kept slippin' along in the mud with Jud beside me and Lacey in front. Seems like I'd go to sleep walkin' along with the rain in my face. I'd wake myself up cryin' like a baby. Mebbe I was cryin' for Sion who was lyin' back there in the rain by the fence—and his head Gahd knows where in that big field we charged across. Mebbe I was cryin' for Old Wagg or Dance Sudderth or Lige Boggs. But I think I was cryin' because of what they did to us. They got no right! They got no right! I kept sayin' to myse'f. How I figured that, I cain't tell, Uncle Pink said. They had as much right to shoot at us as we did them. But they beat us back and ground us down and sent us home. I use' to say it wasn't a fair fight. But there ain't any fair fightin' in the world. It's just that way.

There was a boy next to me in the column that night said: If we'd had Ole Jack, it'd been a differ'nt story. What rigiment? Lacey says. Nineteen Vuhginia, the boy says. Vuhginny? Lacey says. Well, you git on back to 'em. This yere's a Nawth Cahlina rigiment—and we don't want none of you hyear. Leave him alone, Lacey, Jud said. I will, if he keeps his trap shet about Ole Jack. If we'd a had Zeb Vance today we'da licked 'em alone. Everybody kept hollerin' about how the Virginia division was cut up. Cap'n Albright must've got sick of it.

Next day—mebbe it was the next, I don't remember, he got a-holt of me. Pink, he said, you write a good hand, don't you? Well, I did write a *fair* hand. My fingers is bad, he said. I want you to set down and write me a letter to Guv'ner Vance. Well, we clumb up in a wagon; and he found a piece of wrappin' paper and a pencil—and we wrote the letter.

My dear Governor: I will trespass upon your indulgence to communicate the sad fate that has befallen the old Eighty-sixth. We went on about the heaviest conflict of the war having taken place in the vicinity of Gettysburg, Pennsylvania. We told Vance that Colonel Burleson was killed; we listed all the dead and wounded we could remember down to Orren Brabble and Lige Boggs and Dance Sudderth and your Great Uncle Sion. We have only about eighty left for duty, we said. We told about Wagg's gallantry and mentioned Sion being kilt with the flag. And Albright made me put in Jud and Lacey and me. We even told how Reese fought with us and how he he'ped turn the gun. Thar, Albright said, that's in the records now. Ain't nobody gonna say the ole Eighty-sixth wasn't in the worst of it.

Well, Uncle Pink said, it never made any difference. It was always Pickett's Charge—named for the Virginia division. People who don't know what it was always say Pickett's Charge. Oh, Zeb Vance got the letter all right—it got printed in the Official Records—and he hollered for years about how Nawth Cahlina didn't git the proper credit. Even when Longstreet wrote those pieces for the *Century Magazine,* he had to stick in a sentence about how well the men from the Old Nawth State did their duty because he was a Republican and a scallawag and had to justify himself someway. But I don't care any more, Uncle Pink said. As I see it now, I wouldn't care if I'd ever got back across that stone wall. I even wish sometimes I'd died with the yaws like Brothah Paul.

After that fight at Gettysburg yore grandfather got white and thin for a long time. I don't know whether it was what he found out about war, or whether it was because Reese Eliot found his rigiment and left us—and Jud couldn't be a hawss soldier like he wanted to be. Anyway, it got so Jud didn't talk to me so much any more.

I was right fond of Jud. He was never a big boy, nor very strong—and judging from the way I felt myself, he must've been scared to death until we got to that wall and oveh it. I don't know how anybody who got oveh it could have been scared any more that day. It wasn't bravery. No, suh! You just didn't give a tinker's dam what happened, if you got that fur. But it must've cost Jud a peart effort to git thar—I know it did me. We weren't men like Wagg, or Lacey, or Reese. They were just nacherly born insensible to feah. But not us. I know all right. When we were boys Jud and me use' to walk along a place on the Chimney Rock Road at night—a place whur they said hit was haunted. I remember, even it was bright moonlight, we use' to take a-holt of each other's hand. Yes, Uncle Pink's earegg lifted up and down, how we got through Pickett's Charge without runnin' away, I'm not sure. Mebbe I'd've run, if Sion hadn't got shot. Mebbe Jud would've run if Reese hadn't been with us.

When we got back home after Appomattox, Jud kept at Father to send us to the University of Vuhginia. Father, send Pink and me to the University of Vuhginia. Well, Father had no objection to education, but he remembered how much his brother's Vuhginia education had cost him. Jud was set on Vuhginia mebbe because Reese was there—and he even got Mother to he'p him devil Father. But it didn't do any good. Best Jud could do was Chapel Hill. I didn't care.

Spring before we went Jud got a new suit—purty one that a man in Caldwell made. And Mother altered it till it fit him fine. It was Confederate gray—almost Confederate gray. Nobody had many clothes or very good ones in those days. It just happened to fit Jud as good as it did after Mother got through—and he looked good in that beard he'd grown in the army. Mary Ivy Dula had married Willie Fitchett, so Jud began to give himself airs and go sparkin' around. Somebody said he was a reg'lar beau—the best dressed man in Gadkin county.

I've traveled some, Uncle Pink said, both out and in of books. Took me a good long time to see that being the Best Dressed Man in Gadkin County was a little like runnin' a race against yourself. Jud didn't see it like that then. Mebbe he never did, but he did have flashes of revelation, I think. The fact remains, however, Uncle Pink said, the blueveined humpty dumpty behind his ear waggling again on his perpetual brink, that Jud was the Best Dressed Man in Gadkin County.

He knew it too. Nobody eveh introduced him as Judson Harring-ton, the Best Dressed Man in Gadkin County. But mebbe Mary Ivy Dula Fitchett, standing beside her frontgate one day when Jud was ridin' by, said: Jud Harrington! You just git down off that hawss and come oveh heah and talk to me. Ain't you even gona wish me happi-ness? Why you've hahdly spoken to me since you came back from the wah. Mebbe she even said, since you've been the Best Dressed Man in Gadkin County.

A flighty gal, Mary Ivy Dula, Uncle Pink said, a damp lecherous look appearing in his watery blue eyes,—but a fine form. Kinda purty in the face too, for all the Gahd's face that she had a sly milky look and fluttering eyelids. She hadn't been married to Willie Fitchett a month, I reckon, before she was hollerin' out at Jud across the front gate.

Jud hadn't been in Jeb Stuart's cavalreh, but the Eighty-sixth had begun to git talked about. It was Zeb Vance's ole rigiment—and that letter Cap'n Albright and me sent from Gettysburg got printed in the Charlotte *Observer*. It had Jud's name in it. And then there was that new reputation of Jud's as the Best Dressed Man in Gadkin County. On top of that Mary Ivy had been used to gittin' just about everything Mary Ivy wanted. Her father owned half of Caldwell and everybody called him General Dula, though he was never more than a Majah. He gave Mary Ivy and Willie the house whur she hung on the gate. Picketfence it had around it, painted green, and a stone block in front of the gate with a ring in it to tie up yore hawss.

Well, as I said, Mary Ivy got about evehthing her little scatterbrain could think of—but in order to think of anything, it had to slap her in the eye. Jud's new gray suit and him on a black mar' of Father's ridin' along the street. She all purtied up standin' by the gate. Judson Wade Harrington you're not going to pass me by without even so much as a howdy! and you in Poppa's regiment, too. There was that face of hern above the gate in front of the vines on that front porch.

No denying it was a purty face in a way: a slim purty face with a slim nose that quivered like a rabbit's—and a purty white skin. Had a nice ripe mouth too that was always quiverin' fur this or that. Seemed to me she looked as if she was always in heat—a breeder. No; a man cain't hold it against Mary Ivy that she was like she was. A woman could—but I don't see how you could have changed her. Now, I wouldn't a call her a deep, hard breeder, but she *was* a breeder.

Well, she hung onto the gate and said: Why, Judson Harrington, you know I've just been achin' to see you! You, one of the heroes of the battle of Gettysburg. You just oughta hear the purty things people keep sayin' about you. I reckon Jud got down off the mar' and walked up to the gate. How *ah* you, Judson Wade? I'll bet that's what she said. Fine, thank you, Mary Ivy, Jud answered. You just come in and see my new house, Judson Wade. Willie ain't heah. He and Fathah's gone to Pine Spruce on business—but you can't get out of it.

Jud was a fine rooster when he was away from the hens, but you can bet he blushed and stuttered. Oh, he went in. He had to. If Mary Ivy started that kind of thing on a boy, it was just like you were about to fall asleep on a feathuhbed: you couldn't fight agin it. Jud must've settled back with a sigh. Now, I'm not sayin' that Mary Ivy lay down with him that first time. But it wasn't long after that she did. I could tell by Jud's actions. He got to swaggerin' around and sparkin' around all oveh the county. He got a passel of poontang around Gadkin county, before he and I left for Chapel Hill. Got to

lickerin' right smart too—you couldn't do anything else and be the
Best Dressed Man in Gadkin County. As I see it now, Father must
have suspected him of hell-raisin' and lickerin': He caught me totin
Jud in at night a couple of times—but he made out like he hadn't
seen anything. He didn't even say anything about the mulatto gal
that lived in a cabin down in a holler near home. Jud used to git
a jug of molasses in Caldwell on credit and tote it out to the mulatto
gal fur a change of luck.

Her ole pappy lived with her. He was a free nigrah before the
wah, but he neveh had his stepdaughter to support him until after
the wah. When the nigrahs were freed she run away from Captain
Frisbie's place—she was the captain's daughter. But she was prime. I
kept tryin' her out right much mahse'f—and I don't reckon I eveh had
so much fun. Huh pappy use' to set outside so that nobody'd be
disturbed.

I neveh could figgah out about Mary Ivy, until long afthewards.
She must've talked Willie and her daddy out of goin' after Jud. Why,
Willie Fitchett, don't you be so childish. Jud's just a boy and a
very deah friend of mine. How could you suspect me, the woman you
married, of such horrible things anyway. She might have gone so far
as to tell Willie that it was an insult to Pure Southern Womanhood—
and Chivalry, for that matter.

That might explain how I run onto Willie Fitchett begging Jud's
pardon for misjudgin' him one night in a Caldwell saloon. They were
both lickered, but still it sounded sincere. I always held the opinion
that one of Mary Ivy's children, Isabel Ivy, was the spit of Jud, but
I never heard anybody else mention it. Ole General Dula horsewhipped
a man—a poorwhite named Jones—for sayin' he beat him out of his
property. The General did beat him out of it—that was the trouble.
Dula met him on the square with a blacksnake whip and beat the
hell out of him. Right smart of whippin' in those days—and Dula was
a Klan leader, so nobody was gonna pass any remarks about who his
granddaughter looked like.

You know, Lee, I don't eveh understand how my fathah permitted
Jud and me to go to Chapel Hill. Jud's new suit had started to wear
out a little before we went to the university, but Mother got him a
new one—and me one too. She made us some linen shirts out of
boughten cloth—and Fathah allowed us to take hawses. And hawses

was valuable then. Jud took the black mar' and Fathah got me a hawss off a man named Maior Cawdor, who lived on the Hickory road.

I reckon he was a majah in the Fifty-seventh Nawth Cahlina—and three or four of the Cawdor boys were in the rigiment. We allus knew them—but Ole Man Cawdor was a clannish critter, a Seven Day Adventist and cracked as hell on the subject. His fathah had been a Scotch Presbyterian who liked his whiskey too well. Mebbe that accounted for Ole Cawdor takin' up that quare flavor of religion. Anyway, he was a solemn old bird. People would say: Ole Man Cawdor never fit in the wah on Saturdays—or mebbe it was Mondays—because it was agin the Seven Day Adventist way of thinkin'.

The men in the Fifty-seventh said you had to be a Seven Day Adventist to git mentioned in his reports. His boys was in the rigiment and fit good too—but the Ole Man would never let 'em be officers, though one was elected a lieutenant and one a captain, and even the youngest could've been a sergeant. But not him—he wouldn't let 'em—said it would look bad for their fathah.

I guess they never liked the Ole Man very well—and they hated the Seven Day Adventist religion. The one that was kilt at Chickamauga was fixin' to die of a bad belly wound, when somebody says: I'll go fotch yore Paw, Jed—name was Jedediah. No you won't, Jed says. You fotch the Ole Man an' I'll kill him too—hain't no use increasin' the casualties. I hain't a-goin' to spend my last minutes listenin' to no Gahddamn' preachin'! What you kin fotch me is a good snort of cawn.

That was the way the story went. I cain't vouch for how true it was. People said the other two boys weren't dead, but they never came back from the wah. Some said they went to Mexico.

Old Cawdor and his wife and daughter and a bound boy ran his place. Might've had more at one time, but people said they died off because he made them fast so much. More'n likely they died of the cholera, because I never thought he was as bad as he was painted.

His house was sufferin' for paint just as much as any house you can find around here these days—but, by Gahd, Uncle Pink said, it was shore neat. It made you sick to think of all the work that must've been wasted in that yard and inside the house. Dawgs wasn't even allowed near the house; stables was clean; and the buggy was in the shed, for it was greased and shined within an inch of your life. And Gahd he'p me, boy, if eveh I saw cawn fields and punkin' patches like hisn—with neveh so much as one weed in 'em.

You must've figgered out by now that this yere Cawdor was yore great grandfather, Gahd's Chosen Cawdor—Daniel Cawdor.

He use' to breed a few hawses, so Jud and me rode out thar on the mar', me up behind, to git me a hawss to go to college on. Jud had a jug of cawn, and we lickered a little on the way out from Caldwell.

This ole feller talks in the tongues, don't he? Jud said. No, Uncle Pink said, rubbing the tumefactive egg, the secret encystation of years of defeat and corruption, Jud always spoke better English than I. Even I spoke better than I do now. You may have noticed how I catch myself now. Why, I was considered a good scholar in Gadkin county in my time. Maybe Jud said: Old Cawdor's a fanatic, isn't he, Pink? He's what they call a Seventh Day Adventist, I said. Let's slow down and have a drink, Jud said.

The upshot of it was that we got there with licker on our breaths, and late by a quarter of an hour. Young men, Old Gahd's Chosen said, you git no hawss from me—strong drink is a mockah. He had a fiery fanatical eye on us. I saw his old woman look out of the window and shake her head.

He just stood there on the porch staring us down. We decided we'd better git and started to mount the mar', when Anne Cawdor came out on the porch.

Father, she said, these young men came to get the horse you *promised* them. The old man had never been known to break his word—considered it his duty to Gahd. Besides, Father, there is cholera in Gadkin county; and spirits are the only thing that keep it out of the system.

Cholery! Old Gahd's Chosen screamed. Cholery! Jedediah, fotch me my swohd! Now, Father, the girl said as gentle as eveh I heard a body speak. Father sometimes doesn't remember, she said to us. Jedediah was killed at Chickamauga—and I had two brothers and three sisters die of the cholera. It gets him wild sometimes—the very word.

She was only about sixteen. She had on a white shirtwaist and a dark homespun skirt. At her throat was that big cameo pin. I don't doubt you've see your grandmother wear it. She was a slim girl with the nicest hazelcolored eyes eveh I saw. I always dearly loved your grandmother.

Cholery, Old Gahd's Chosen said. Gahd has taken more of my children with cholery than with the swohd. Sit down, young men, I'll fotch the hawss. There were a couple of splitbottomed chairs on the porch. We sat down; and Anne brought us some coffee and biscuit and honeh. It's not sourwood, she said. Lightning struck our tree. You must please excuse Father, Mother says. He was badly hit in the head at the battle of Chickamauga—and lay all night in the rain before they found him. Sometimes he has spells—once he had the falling sickness. But I shan't talk to you about the war. You were at Gettysburg, weren't you, Mr. Jud?

By Gahd, Uncle Pink said, Jud was hers then. *Mistah* Jud. I could see him swell up like a hoptoad. We were both there (he didn't call her *anything*), Pinckney and I—and our brother, Sion. I'm sorry, Mr. Pinckney; I had heard, but I had forgotten.

If she hadn't been so purty and gentle, she would've sounded prim. She had been a schoolteacher—and I'd heard she'd even taught nigrahs. Jud was looking at her with a soft foolish look in his eye, when the Ole Man came up with the bay gelding.

Heah, young man, he said harshly, heah's yore hawss. That was twenty dollars, Father told me, Judson said. There is nothing due, your great grandfather said.

He would take nothing for the gelding. And Anne, standing behind him, looked at us and shook her head. She was right: Old Man Cawdor was not a man to be argued with. Once on the streets of Caldwell, a year or so after that, I saw some nigrahs crowd a woman off the sidewalk—three drunk buck niggers. Old Cawdor saw it as he came out of Avery's Feed Store.

He walked oveh to 'em and looked at 'em with that wild fiery eye of his: Sons of Ham, he said, not loud at all, git out into the road. Now git down on yore knees and ask Gahd to forgive you—and then beg Miss Jane's pardon. The three nigrahs, Loyal Leaguers, they were, got down on their knees in the mud. They had on secondhand broadcloth suits with brass buttons and goldbraid that they had bought somewhere from carpetbaggers at a fancy price, and they didn't hanker to git 'em dirty—and more than that, they had loaded pistols that the white Loyal Leaguers had given them. But they were skeered. Please fo'give us Gahd! Please excuse us, Missy! Now stay thar till I tell you you kin git up! Old Gahd's Chosen said.

Miss Jane Wade, who was by the way kinfolks of ours, said: Thank you, Major Cawdor. Madam, Gahd's Chosen said, it is the duty of every servant of the All Highest to keep the lowest offspring of the black sinners in his appointed place. Miss Jane was about as skeered as the niggers when yore great grandfather looked at her.

He went back into Avery's to finish his trading. She was oncomfortable about those niggers kneeling in the street, so she said: You can go now boys. No, ma'am, they said. We ain' goin' till Mahse Cawdah give de wohd. He go' put de debbil on us, if we don' do lak he say.

Well, Miss Jane Wade went on home, and evehbody in town came down to see the three niggers kneelin' in the mud in their gold braid. Let me see—I think they were originally Old General Dula's Sam and Ellum and Joe. Evehbody came down to see 'em. They were right in the square where the Confederate monument is now. Even the white Loyal Leaguer's Leader came down and stood on the sidewalk—he had on a new pair of boots and wouldn't go out in the mud.

Look yere, boys, he said. They ain't anybody can make you do a thing like that thar. Yawl's free. Git up offen yore knees. Yawl's got the vote. We sons of Ham, Ellum said. Yes, suh, Joe said. We waitin' fuh Mahse Cawdah—he gonna gi' us de wohd.

About an hour later Old Gahd's Chosen came out of Avery's store.

He looked at those three nigrahs a minute and said: Well, sinnahs, mebbe you can git off yore knees now, but eveh time you see Miss Jane, you git out in the road and get down on 'em till she passes—and thank Gahd you ain't struck dead. And they did it too. I saw Ellum do it years later when he was an old man—and Sam and Joe and Miss Jane were dead—to Miss Jane's niece who looked like her. Then Gahd's Chosen turned and looked at the white Loyal Leaguer.

It was Old Chicken Cruppy. Nobody believed he ever went to wah. But after the wah, under Guv'nor Holden, people use' to say he stole a chicken and got elected to the state legislature—and that he had his eye on a turkey gobblah so that he could git elected to Congress. Chicken looked at Old Gahd's Chosen, but not in the eye—and started to git. But yore great grandfather was too fast fur him. He took Chicken by the shoulders and shook him till his teeth rattled.

Your great granddaddy was satisfied with that so he turned loose of Chicken and slapped him hard on the left cheek. Chicken just stood there. Now, said Majah Cawdor, tuhn that othah cheek around!

There were people who said that Chicken wasn't right bright—anyway, he turned the right cheek. And yore great grandfather slapped him hard on that cheek. Mebbe that'll teach you the principles of Christianity, although I doubt it, yore great grandfather said. Now go and sin no more. And if I eveh ketch you misleading the sons of Ham again, I'll introduce you to the proper Wrath of God.

Chicken walked away with his tail between his spindly legs. He waᵣ a little pore feller, sorter gray in the face and weaseleyed. I didn't feel sorry fur him then, Uncle Pink said, but I wish I had. I never took no heed of how he must've felt. He'd been whupped down fur so long. Then he got a chance to tell the niggers what to do—but even the niggers wouldn't listen to him. And they'd listen to Old Gahd's Chosen Cawdor.

At the beginning of the wah, I remember seein' Cruppy in Caldwell. He was jawin' with some white trash about Gen'l Stuart ridin' around McClellan. By jing! he says, thar's a gen'l fur you. Cain't whup Ole Jeb! I'm gonna jine his comp'ny. I wuz born in Vurginny anyways. These yere Lubbers 'round hyear makes me sick!

Then they began to plague him: Well, Cunnel Cruppy, when you gonna jine Ole Jeb's cavalreh? Soon's I kin git me a good hawss, he says.

Finally, nobody saw him for a long time. He showed up after the wah with an ole bar'l hoop swohd hangin' from his middle by a piece of curtain cord.

Whur you been, Cunnel Cruppy—with Ole Jeb?

Shore have, Chicken says. (He didn't git the name Chicken till after the wah, when he went to the nigger legislature.) Fit the Yanks to a standstill—onleh trouble they don't know when they whupped.

What battles you been in, Cunnel Cruppy? Whar's yore hawss?

Shiloh, Fo't Donelson, Atlanta and Vicksbuhg, Chicken says. Shore fit heaveh! Hawss was kilt out frum undeh me in Pickett's Chahge!

Shiloh and Donelson and Atlanta and Vicksburg were all in the west; and Jeb was with the Army of Northern Virginia in the east—besides Shiloh and Donelson were fit and lost 'fore Chicken eveh left Caldwell.

Shore got quare swohds in Jeb's cavalreh, Cunnel Cruppy, people said.

Thet thar swohd's drunk Yankee blood, Chicken said. Hit's bit deep in Yankeemeat.

People laughed in his face until the Loyal League came. You could see how he would hate 'em. Barns commenced burnin' all oveh Gadkin county. Eveh man that eveh pestered Chicken had a burnt barn.

CHAPTER XXVIII

THAT boy, the silly stupid lad, had been pumping the organ badly— and I went back there to tell him about it. He looked at me with that empty face of his, and I picked up the breadknife. I could have killed him with relish, Wagnal said. So help me Christ.

Maybe Katherine was riding Percy and Stuart riding that black stallion she had seen him on in Richmond when she was fourteen— two years before I knew her and she had had him in her heart all the time—and everything was clean and new, not too new, for Katherine's riding habit would be blown by the wind and falling in careless folds over the horse and the horse furniture and all the leather would be seasoned and live and dark and rich with polishing and use. Stuart's uniform would be new with fine firegilt buttons and light blue facings on his Confederate Major-General's coat and the leaves and stars on his collar shining out in confounding brilliance from underneath his great auburn Zeusbeard and his black plume waving under the gold Palmetto star on his caughtup softfelt hat.

They were riding at the head of a long troop of men and women all in brilliant colors, red and gold, blue and silver, emerald and yellow, all on sleek horses from dappled gray to purple black. And all the people were young as grapes just ripe and tightskinned on the vine or cherries on the tree are young—all firm in tightstuffed, finecolored hides —all with firm springy haunches. All eagle-eyed and vivacious, all rid- ing through the great grassed meadows of heaven to the jingling of the spurs and creaking of the leather and the little chains and metals of the harness. All talking softly and pleasantly or daringly and dashingly or singing or smiling and laughing. The women's eyes were bright and deep with the light of invitation and the men's eyes were warm and eager—all happy and easy and wild and free, with no consequences. Never any fatigue lying in wait—never any nausea—never any recriminations.

I saw Katherine riding through the great meadows and paddocks of heaven and I saw Stuart riding there beside her as plainly as I now see that cheap print of The Night Watch and that dingy oil lamp. By God, it was not right that I, who had worshipped and protected and loved the girl since sixtythree in Mississippi, should see her riding through the Elysian Fields, happy with Stuart, and I caught in this miserable, bleak, cramped little town in a stale smelling little stone temple mediating with God for a people who did not care for God, or Heaven, or Christ —a people who cared only that the Protestant Episcopal Church had the reputation of being the most stylish church in the town.

There was the silly stupid face of the organ-pumping boy, whose duty it was to send wind through the empty bellows so that a none too agile organist who believed that the Poet and Peasant overture was the *ne plus ultra* of musical composition, could wheeze out a genteel noise from the musty pipes for the faceless, rustic, little, socialclimbing fools who stood croaking in the pewspaces. No. I did not consider offering this stupid windpushing boy to God as a sacrifice. I said to myself: I shall just get rid of this ugly personification of stupidity. I shall transmute it back to earth again and let the real wind blow over it—let the birdfartings be blown from the belfry. I saw the communion bread. I should have killed him if it had not been for that. But I said, Look here, boy, you pump that organ properly or I'll slit that throat of yours —and it won't be a neat incision.

Wagnal chuckled sourly: The boy scuttled out of there—and bloody fast I can tell you. And next Sunday they sent the town marshal to pump the organ. The old fool had that pearl-mounted pistol strapped to his belly and he puffed like a locomotive.

But after the boy had gone that day, I knelt down and prayed God that he would take me to Katherine then and there—and that he would take Stuart away from her. Then I got up and drove the knife at the Major-General J. E. B. Stuart, C.S.A. on the bronze—you can still see the scratches.

Everything was quiet—I knelt down again and must have been three hours on my knees thinking and praying. I could feel the empty church around me and the cool stone walls and the empty bright insect-quick dandelionfilled Sunday afternoon outside around the church and over the unmown backlawn of the church. Everything was motionless and quiet and sunfrozen and all my days were rigid pictures in my head flipping over like the peepshows in a penny arcade—but with no illusion of motion. Katherine on the stairs in Mississippi looking down on Clint Belton and me; I on the stairs looking down on Katherine who looked like a flower opening; Sleepy Bates in the tent as he looked when he said, I don't mind bein' shot at but not thataway; the Crimean telling about blowing the Sepoy from a gun. But God did not speak to me or give me a sign.

From that day onward I began to think: There is no God, or, if there is a God, it is something on which I had not reckoned—it is something which is blind and cruel, running in a set of cosmic grooves like a Leviathanic shute-the-shutes. Something with no humor but unconscious humor, something whose finest irony is mere accident wedded to chance. They—my congregation and the villagers—who had never reached a cognizance of one small atom of the earth around them, began to say I was mad.

Why, by the body of Christ, boy, how could they judge? Had they even a splatter of the gray matter, the wherewithal with which to become mad? You cannot conjure madness out of a cabbage. You cannot craze a block of wood with an axe. You cannot blow the brains from a squash. You cannot sell such a fine fierce commodity as madness and pass it over a grocer's counter. All you can buy here is cabbage cunning from the village lawyer, that wooden product, commonsense, you can have by the cord, for the hauling. But madness! Ho, boy! How many Hamlets are there here? It makes not a damn which way the wind blows, they all know a hawk from a handsaw every day in the week and Sunday too. You can't fool them. You can bet your bottom dollar on that. Ah, yes, they are full of sanity and commonsense and homely wisdom. None was born on April First. They all know their ass from a hole in the ground. They're nobody's fool. And why—for what have they stored up all this sanity and commonsense? Why? Why? Why?

Wagnal's voice quieted and he went on softly sibilant, again almost whispering, with his eyes faraway.

Burrus, the jackleg lawyer, whose dignity was beaten out of him by those red and black nightshirts down in Mississippi—they may have been ghosts of the Confederate dead from Shiloh or Chickamauga or only frustrated men who had never had any niggers or money or fine women or any pretense to dignity to lose, who thought then, after the war: The war done it. I woulda been a big man, if it want fur the war, if it want fur the Yankees—Burrus had a wife. She was the one who cheated Una out of her kingdom—rather, she was the instrument.

Tall, rawboned, with a lightblue evil eye, which gave you the feeling that she had once taken a deep wound in her soul or that she thought she had been bilked of her just deserts in life, she was not altogether homely. But she was a nymphomaniac shrew. Her tongue was a claque for herself, and she whined and whimpered all the time at Burrus, who was not as tall as she and harried with the duties of the trading-post, in which she would not help (she would never turn a hand to keep his house well either), and the purpose of revenge which he had begun to plan against those dealers of nocturnal justice, those men who had judged him and beaten him into a cringing bleeding-backed animal down in Mississippi. Burrus was trying to save money. Perhaps the idea was to hire enough Pinkerton spies to go down there and find out the names underneath that red and black flannel and calico, whose boots those were that looked just like any other shoeleather wearing out—and, oh, with loving tenderness he thought of this—whose hand and arm and shoulder muscles had curled that blacksnake around his back in such a spirit of an avenging God. Who, in Christ's name, he muttered, are they to judge me? To brush me a little—to touch me up! Because I did not own a lot of niggers and talk with a mouthful of mush, because I did not sweat my dollars out of a nigger's hide, because I did not have a change of luck in the quarters behind the big house, I ain't a gentleman—I ain't fitten to set at the table and talk to them Goddamn' ladies a theirn. All I'm fit for is for a dozen-onta-one to take out and beat like I was the dirt under their feet. And maybe I can reely do somethin' fur the Indians like Mr. Lincoln done fur the niggers.

When the Pinkerton spies had found them, maybe Burrus didn't know what he would do. Maybe he had guns loaded or blacksnake whips stashed away and a gang of paid cronies to help him. But he had begun his search when the scandal came. The Pinkertons had already sniffed at the dragon's trail—whether or not they were right is another matter. They were General McClellan's secret service in that campaign which ended up in the Seven Days around Richmond—and they kept telling him that there were a hundred thousand Rebels on hand to blast him off the map, with the result that Richmond was saved by half that number.

But it was the letters which came from the Pinkerton operative from Washington, where he thought he had run one of Burrus's chastisers to earth in the Senate—it was the letters: Burrus always took them, read them secretly and hid them from his wife. But one day she saw a postmark. She thought Una was writing to her husband. From that day on she grew silent. She thought and lay awake at night brooding and listening to the coyotes howling as she planned out what to do. That took a while.

Meantime, Burrus, who had grown used to her shrewishness, nagging and whining, looked up from the tall, slanting desk where he was keeping the accounts, and lidding down his madonna eyes and slanting them off to the floor, said aloud to himself: What's wrong with her now? What have I done now?

Oh, Burrus would have done it all right, if he thought he could. But he could never really conceive himself as Una's lover. Maybe that first night when she beat down his fee to less than half of what he had decided to ask, maybe, leaving the house in Lafayette Square, he had tried to imagine himself with enough money, enough cleverness, enough good looks to go into the bedroom of a woman like that and get into bed with her and put his arms around her and kiss her. But he couldn't even turn the knob of the bedroom door—and when he thought of her with her clothes off his inward eye dazzled and he could see nothing. It was that she was so damned beautiful and remote that little Burrus couldn't believe she did the business in bed in the regular way like all women did it. He almost concluded that she would have some goddess-like way of contactless fornication. He must have known that while he was looking at her breasts in that evening gown—that look which cost him five hundred dollars—he must have known that he was gulled even as he began to look.

So when his wife began to look at him in silence, how could he imagine that she had flattered him the way she had? Una's lover! Good God, Burrus, a draggletailed, usurious little army sutler, a petty carpet-bagger, a hardscheming, fruitless little conycatcher. When he did find out, even after he was ruined and his dearest plans to run the night-shirts who had humiliated him to earth and make them eat their own medicine had gone by the board, even then he felt a coldhot chill of pride up and down his spine. And perhaps, for a moment, then, he could have been Una's lover.

But how could he know what that woman of his was thinking? Cora—Cory, he called her—was strange enough to him. She could nag and howl and scream at him all day and then climb, naked and hot and speaking tenderly, into bed with him.

She decided. She wrote Una an anonymous letter, cancelled the stamp with the postmark of the trading-post herself and saw it off with her own hand. Stay away from other pepul's husbands you dirty disrepable huzy you are worse than those Women of Babylon kep in luxry and jewels My Husban is a good Man and loves Me but he has been Tempt. A Wronged Lady, it was signed.

How she expected to conceal who she was that way, nobody ever knew. There are many who must be coy in everything—it has not been given them to make anything but a twisted move, perhaps because they have been born twisted and then so twisted by life. Cora began watching the incoming mails with the silent fury of a foxbitch.

Do not believe that Una ignored the anonymous letter. Oh no. She was in no position to follow the advice of the etiquette books. She smelt trouble. Though she had married a shrewd enough lawyer, and had come of a cold shrewd family which had always followed the main chance even in its vices, she was bearing the awesome burden now of reducing the queen of the capital to the undeniable position of lady-in-waiting—she wanted it definitely known that Mrs. Sprague was second fiddle. She wished passionately to have it set down as an irrefutable fact. As, in the penal code, it is required that the physician stand, his ears plugged with the black buttons of the stethoscope, his hand guiding the microphonic diaphragm over the thorax of the thing that hangs blackhooded at the end of inertia, until there is no further roar or flutter in his ears, in the same way Una required that she be recognized as the Toast of Washington. But she was not satisfied with the social stethoscope held once or twice in the ears of two or three society reporters. She wished the rival pronounced dead and buried in the quicklime of social oblivion. Something definite must happen: the cartridge must be fired, extracted from the chamber and the case held up that she might say: See, it is empty. Because she was working thus towards her coronation, she had little time to consider curiously the letter from Fort

Sofa. And, of course, she did not show it to Clint, for she had never told him of her dealings with Burrus. Clint was prone to be too cautious and would not have approved so dangerous a deal. Thus it was that she *did* write Burrus the first time she had ever written him, telling him of the anonymous letter and warning him to be careful that nothing came to light.

Cora, the shrew with the evil, unpigmented eye, was there alone that morning when the halfbreed brought in the mailbag. She had caught Burrus out by some shrew's trick or other that day. The halfbreed laid the bag on the counter and she quickly gave him a bottle of Hostetter's Bitters and said, git! sharply. Even while she was still staring at the worn leather ends of the binding, she knew with a kind of furious foxlike joy that inside this canvas and leather, in which there were a few mailorder catalogs, some bills, a Butterick pattern or two, there was one letter that would feed her jealous wrath. She could feel it there. She had it out of the bag, the padlock relocked and the seal diddled into a semblance of unbroken-ness—anyway the seals had often been broken in transit; Burrus suspected the halfbreed—and was in the bedroom with a chairback under the doorknob, leaving the store and post office empty, before Burrus got back.

It was just the kind of a letter that would feed her jealousy. She derived a good deal of satisfaction from it because it was vague: Dear Mr. Burrus:—I have received an anonymous letter postmarked, Fort Sofa, in which you and I figure in a ridiculous affair of the heart. As my attorney, I wish you would look into this discreetly—and also do what you are able to safeguard my pecuniary interests. I trust our advantageous connection will continue. Una Belton. It was written on paper with the Theron griffon, lion and crocodile on it—finer paper than Cora had ever seen. *Mr.* Burrus! she said to herself. *Mr.* Burrus, indeed! She may as wella said Dear Honeybunch. And her pee-cunn-arry interests! Cora had never seen the word before and, instead of connecting it with money she connected it with lechery. And as far as askenserned, she muttered at the Theron stationery, I bet she ain't true to him. Them Washington wimmin lifts their skirts to anyone that takes their fancies. Her eyes began to burn with passion as she said the words to the walnut commode. She stuck the letter behind the round picture of the horses' heads and went into the store where Burrus was opening the mail sack. When'd this come, Cory? Oh, the mail sack? she said. Little bit ago. Joe brought it. That halfbreed! Burrus said fingering the seal. I give him some of that medicine, Cora said. Ummm, Burrus said. He lidded down his eyes and slanted a look at the gray pine floor. Looking up for a minute, he saw the hot, wild look in her eyes and something else. Then he knew she had got something out of the mailbag.

It must, he thought, have been one of the reports from Pinkerton's. And he did not wish to tell her, now, at least, perhaps not ever, what he was planning. She did not know about the nightshirts and the black-snake—he had said the stripes on his back were where a livery nag had dragged him under a harrow. He wanted to remain secret and obscure as possible about his humiliation in Mississippi until he had brought that red nightshirt to its knees and inflicted upon it some intense bitterness that would sour its soul for the rest of its days. After that maybe he could find some way to make the nightshirt's bitterness public. A nigger in that Washington hotel saw his bloody shirt. Gahd A'mighty, Cap'n, you ain't been Kloo Kluxed, has you? Burrus had kicked him out of the room.

The night of the day she stole the letter Cora took him to bed fiercely and held him hard against her biting him and whispering steamily in his ears. He had no time or energy left to figure out how he was going to get the Pinkerton letter away from her—or what he was going to tell her about the semi-code it was written in. He was worn out the next day—and that night she acted the same way. He was trying to go to sleep when she said:

Burrus, this woman in Warshington, D. C.—she ain't purty as I am, is she? What woman? Burrus said—although he knew that even if he had only looked at Una to the tune of five hundred dollars, there was only one woman for him in Washington. She ain't as good to be in bed with as me, is she? Cora said. What woman? Burrus said. His vanity began to feed a little even then. Don't you try to tell your Cory there ain't any woman. Don't you play possum with me. Cory, Burrus said, I don't know any woman in Washington but Mrs. Belton that I done business for about her ess-tate. Ah, Cora said, you done business for her all right—monkey business. You done the business in bed with her. In bed? Burrus said. I only been in her house twice: once when I settled her ess-tate an' once when she got me—us this tradership. God! Cora said. She takes care a her men like all gitout, don't she? She sure keeps 'em in fine style—makes her ole man give 'em post-traderships. Burrus, I wouldn't ever a-thought you'd a let a woman keep you. No woman's keepin' me! Burrus yelled. Why, Goddamnit, Cora, no woman's ever kep me. I pay out good hard-earned dollars for this place. Oh, she said, you do? Well, it's the first I heard of it. Who gits 'em? I thought we kep it all. I thought we was a-saving to reetire in our old age. Burrus, where's that money? What bank's it in? If you don't tell me, I'll tell you what I'll do—I'll write to President Grant himownself and tell him that woman's been a-usin' gover'ment fun's to keep her men like the Whore of Babylon she is. Cory, for God's sake! Burrus said. He took a long sigh.

After a while, during which all he could hear was her fast wheezy breath, he said: All the money we got that's ours is in the bank. I kep tellin' you in the beginning there's arrangements you got to make to git a tradership—an' they cost money. So, Cora said, there's arrangements, is they? Well, Burrus, the only arrangement I ever heard about was a female arrangement back in Warshington. So you're a-keepin' *her,* eh? So you're a-helpin' to keep her while she's in bed all the time with another man—or God knows how many men. You ain't a-gitting much out of it, are you?

Cory, Burrus said, slowly with pauses between the words, it's nothin' but business, I tell you. To git one of these posts you got to give back half the profit. It's business—pure business! It's business, all right, Cora said. You can call it pure if you want to, but I got another name for it. I seen that kinda business done in redlight houses when I was ten years old, but it only cost them men two dollars and sometimes only a dollar—and them wimmin' was gittin' good money fer it, takin' into consideration who they was. But you, her voice came in a tight hardhiss, you! You gotta go to Warshington, Dee Cee, and git yourself a hightone hussy that does you out of half the profit when you got a good wife to home who works herself grayheaded for you and takes care of you good—a purty wife, if I do say it myself as shouldn't.

Maybe it took her two or three days and nights to tell him about the anonymous letter she had written to Una—and about the letter from Una. Give them to him? Oh no! Not her. Not Cora. If he was to leave her for that whore of Babylon in Washington, she'd have something to hold over him. Those days and nights must have been a hell for Burrus: Every time Cora got to talking about Una being a Whore of Babylon, she would whip herself into the frenzy of a bitch

in heat and go for him so wildly that he could not refuse—until the
night he was worn out.

He shoved her away from him and got out of the bed, leaving her
stringy, hot, imperative passion to claw the sheets. She got up after
a while and walked into the parlor where he was lying awake on the
floor. She looked at him with cold hate. He felt it, though his eyes
were shut. Maybe it was that night she wrote the letter to the Senate:

Ther is a skarlet Woman seling tradding posts in Warshington to
keep her and her men in sin I know becaus my husband bout one
He is her lover too Cora Burrus. She sent it the next day—and that
night she crawled into bed naked and pulled Burrus's nightshirt off
him again.

As I said, Clint didn't know that Una had sold the post to Burrus.
He thought it was some sort of a reward—a chunk of the spoils for
settling the estate in Mississippi. There was a point in cunning at which
Clint's mind stopped—a point where, for all the clear planning he had
done, he grew fatuous and inexplicable in an inhuman way. It was as
if the scheming-machine, the clever, foreseeing groundear, the photo-
electric cell was made to a certain gauge and would work only within
that gauge's limits. A personal caution was one of those limits. Thus,
when a friend—a henchman, let us say—on the Senate committee came
to him with the news that it would be moved to impeach him the next
day, because Mrs. Belton stood accused of selling a post-tradership to
a man named Burrus, a carpetbagger and a jackleg lawyer who had
been flogged out of Mississippi by the Ku Klux (the committeeman a
Democrat knew this), the Eye of Mars that was used to threaten and
command, grew momentarily like the eye of an ox bumped on the
head by a stockyards hammer.

It was in the morning and Una was not up. Even under this stress,
however, he knocked on her door. Who is it? Una said coldly through
the door. Murphy—this was her maid—have I not told you never to
disturb me before eleven on any account! Now go. Una! Clint said.
Una! Oh, she said. Well? I must see you. It's important! Well, she
said slowly, unlocking the door, come in.

She sat up in bed, the pink silk coverlet all around her. There was
a little sleep-puffiness about her face—and Clint thought it lent the
illusion of warmth her coolness needed. Well, Clinton? she said. Una,
my darling, Clint said. You had some dealings with a fellow named

Burrus. Did you—did you get any—ah—consideration for that trader-ship at Fort Sofa? Una stared at him as if he were the lowest sort of fool. Really, Clint, you didn't suppose the little carpetbagger got it free, did you? Don't you know that such things are part of our legitimate income? Hadn't you thought of that? How is a woman in my position to keep up her obligations? But Una, dear, Clint said, they found out. Mrs. Burrus wrote the Senate a letter and a Democrat got hold of it. They'll move to impeach me today. God, Una said, that bloody woman. She thought I wanted her little jackleg lawyer.

The question is, what will I do? Clint said. She pointed at the gilt escritoire: There's pen and ink there. Write out your resignation quickly, take it to Grant and make him accept it before they can take action. You've still got time to do that. That will check them, stalemate them, take their breath away. Act maligned to Grant. Swear to God it's not true. Tell him it's a Democratic plot. Ask him if he thinks me capable of such a base act. Remind him of the good old days in the Army of Tennessee and ask him if he thinks such a good soldier as yourself who had such nice Havanas and liquor could possibly be mixed up in such a scandal as selling post-traderships. Over Una's perfectly modulated voice there fell a thin membrane of sneering.

Clint heard it all right, but he was busy writing the short resigna-tion. There was no time to adopt an attitude toward the voice of the woman he had married. In ten minutes he was driving to the White House as fast as his fine team could run.

CHAPTER XXIX

THE DAY General Grant was inaugurated Mr. Beckham came to supper with Papa, and he said it was just bully now they had a man like General Grant to run the country. The Hero of Appomattox would show these politicians what a soldier could do. As for himself, Mr. Beckham had been out of the war when General Grant took command of the Army of the Potomac, but the boys from his regiment, the Fighting Ninety-seventh Pennsylvania Zouaves, said General Grant was hunky dory. Myra liked to listen to him when he talked with his head thrown back like that and his beard so black and silky.

Papa said that, yes, General Grant would probably make a good president and that he had known General Grant both in the Mexican war and the Civil war and that he was a very unassuming man. Papa seemed to be thinking a good deal about it but not saying much. But then Papa never said much. One day Myra had heard him say to Brother Ream: Remus, always reserve judgment about any man. I will not quote the Bible to you, son, for I know young men do not like Biblical advice, but remember that man is a tentative image of a god. Myra did not quite understand what Papa meant, but my, oh, my! how she admired him and loved him. Why, she didn't believe she had ever heard Papa speak a cross word to anyone in her whole life—and the Lord knows he had had provocation often enough. And how Ring and the horses and even the silly sheep loved Papa. And it was plain to see that Mr. Beckham worshipped the ground that Papa walked on.

While they were eating supper something happened that was embarrassing in a way and made her feel kind of proud in another. That old Osage—well, he wasn't really old and not a bad-looking fella for an Indian—came up to the house with his painted up pony with the bright colored rags and stick-candy braided in his mane, and Papa had to go out to see what he wanted so he would go away. When Papa came back to his supper, he was smiling. And he smiled first at Ma and then at Myra.

Well, Lorna, he said, you almost lost a daughter, but I was too sharp a horse-trader for the chief.

Well, Mr. Hanks? Ma said, her dark eyes shining like berries.

The chief brought his best pony to trade for Myra—and when I refused that he offered me six more and a couple of squaws to boot. He said, hair like blackbird wing.

Myra blushed and said, Oh, Papa! And Mr. Beckham said, loudly, You just bet your bottom dollar the chief knew what he was doing all right! After he had said that Mr. Beckham's face got a little red, but Papa said something about General Grant's home in Galena, Illinois or somewhere and building a side walk and a house for the General that saved the situation. During the rest of the meal Myra could feel Mr. Beckham looking at her when she didn't see him.

He told about his brother who was in the Pennsylvania Cavalry during the war and said now that they'd put General Grant in the Capital maybe the old soldiers would get their rightful pensions. But Myra could see that he was thinking about her all the time. Afterwards

Brother Ream said: Well, Myry, you could just land a beau in the middle of the Sahara desert. And Myra could see that Hetty was a little jealous, but she said Mr. Beckham seemed to be a fine upright young man. And Ellen looked at her kind of sad and yearning like in her eyes.

The very next morning as Papa was getting ready to go to the store the Osage came again. This time he was a-riding his painted up pony and had a whole herd of ponies—about thirty—following him. Myra saw him ride up to Papa and hold out his hand and then get off the pony under the pecan tree and talk and motion with Papa for a long time—about a half an hour. He was all in feathers and buckskin breeches and a bright blanket and he was taller than Papa and Mr. Beckham and so straight. Finally he got back on his painted up pony in a kind of stiff strained way; and Papa stood there beside the wagon in the yard looking out toward the Lombardy poplars and the silverleaf maples where the ponies were raising the dust as they followed the Indian, nickering and blowing, down the road. Papa turned and walked toward the house when the parade got a piece down the road.

He walked into the house smiling. Myra, he said, Myra, you must know how much your Papa thinks of you now. Myra laughed, feeling a funny glow all over her and kissed Papa on the whiskers that weren't as nice now as they were before he came back from that awful old Andersonville prison, but were still nicer than anybody's because they were her Papa's. Oh, no, she said. Not all them horses, Papa! Not all those ponies! That old Indian! Yes, honey, and a half dozen squaws too. I've little doubt it was everything the poor Indian owned. Papa went out and got up on the wagon smiling to himself.

And even if she *did* say that *old* Indian, she kept thinking of his dark sharp eyes and the way he looked at her—and she thought it was kind of sad, even if he was only an Indian and just a savage.

Tom Beckham was standing in the door of the store looking out over the flat country to the east, thinking about Brother Joe and him swimming behind Pap's barge in Canal street back in Manayunk before the war and Molly and the girl in Richmond that night after Savage's Station—and Myra Hanks. He was just standing there thinking and chewing tobacco when that fellow Sipperly drove up in front of an old log house across the street—if you could call it a street.

Sipperly had a good-looking team of horses hitched to a spring wagon and there were several good sized kegs in the wagon. Sipperly waved enthusiastically to Tom. Tom waved back with restraint. A half-breed Osage came out of the log house and began helping Sipperly unload the kegs. Several Osages hung around and watched the process with dark and avid eyes.

Tom wondered what in the Jesus that Sipperly customer was up to now. Not that Tom minded a drink of liquor—no, many's the time he'd gone pub-crawling with the boys in Philadeffy, but with a bunch of Indians around—

Captain Hanks drove up and got down from his spring wagon.

Good morning, Tom, Captain Hanks said.

Good morning, Captain Hanks. Every time Tom looked at Captain Hanks he thought what a grand man he was. Why, by Jesus Christ, there was a man who had been in two wars and in Andersonville prison and all over the country—and what was more a well-read man too, a scholar—and he didn't crack himself up to be any better than any other man. Captain Hanks was smiling to himself when he walked up to Tom.

Tom, he said, I turned down a chance to become one of the biggest horse-traders in the territory this morning.

How's that, Captain? Tom said, in his most important voice.

Well, sir, that Osage came back this morning with his whole herd of ponies and wanted to trade them for my daughter, Myra,—and what is more, he offered to throw in a half dozen squaws to boot. When I turned him down, he went away heartbroken.

An' by God! he'd a got the best of the bargain, Captain! Tom said, hotly, speaking before he thought and turning a real red under his beard.

The captain smiled at him and said: That's what I thought, too, Tom. But it wouldn't do to tell Myra.

Mawnin', Judge Hanks! Sipperly was standing in the sunlight with his eyes squinted up. One of the Indians was helping the halfbreed unload the kegs while Sipperly watched.

Captain Hanks bowed and said gravely, Good morning, Mr. Sipperly. He didn't say anything to Tom, and the two of them went into the store out of the sun.

Just who is that Sipperly party, Captain Hanks? Tom said.

Well, Tom, Captain Hanks said, I don't know much about Mr.

Sipperly except that he says he was in the Army of the Potomac. He talks of fighting at Gettysburg, and he says he fought Indians after the war in the regular army. In any case, he still wears the army blue.

I wouldn't be a Goddamn' bit supprized if he was a skedaddler, Captain Hanks! Tom blurted.

Well, Tom, I don't know—I don't know.

The captain looked worried and walked away from Tom toward the packing box desk at the back of the store.

At noon he told Tom that he would be riding to Independence early tomorrow morning.

Because he lived and bached in the back of that old store, Myra brought some dinner down to Mr. Beckham. For with Papa away in Independence, Mr. Beckham wouldn't really be able to get his own dinner and tend to the store at the same time. So she rode Old Caesar down with a package of dinner for him.

Well, that's just boss, Miss Hanks—just boss! Mr. Beckham said in his bluff way. And she went back to the stove in the back of the store and heated her biscuits and made some tea for him because he couldn't drink coffee since the war, him being on Bell's Island like Papa was in Andersonville. Mr. Beckham said that her biscuits were just ay number one firstrate bully and he'd heard that that Osage had tried to trade the captain out of her—and that maybe the only good Indian was a dead Indian. But you could just bet your bottom dollar that was one time an Indian knew what he was a-doing. Myra got a little pink; she could feel it. So she said right quick: What were them old Indians doing over there in that old shack that Milt Gaby had built. She saw three of them going in as she rode up to the store. She did, did she? Mr. Beckham said.

Well, that Slipperly fellow—Sipperly, Myra said; Sipperly, Mr. Beckham repeated—it looked as if he had a few kegs of firewater over there. Oh my, Myra said, that ain't safe! Well, by Jesus, Mr. Beckham said, getting excited, I didn't like that Slippery's—Sipperly, Myra said —Sipperly's looks the first time I saw him with that boy tied on the horse up to you Papa's place. Looked like a Goddamn'—excuse me, Miss Hanks—skedaddler or a bounty-jumper to me. Well, my, oh my! Myra said, I must get back home. You'd better let me close the store and ride with you, Mr. Beckham said. No, Mr. Beckham, thank you,

Myra said. There's no horse here. Well, I could take you up on the pummel, Mr. Beckham said.

But she said she would go alone, and just as she was going out that halfbreed that hung around with Old Sipperly came in and wanted some tobacco and Mr. Beckham had to wait on him. And though she heard Mr. Beckham say if she'd wait a minute, he'd help her on her horse, she went out and was about to get on Old Caesar when the Osage came up.

His dark eyes were burning with a kind of worshipful look in them and he didn't say a word, but just walked up to her, his moccasins making not a sound, and took hold of one of the braids of her black purply hair and felt of it and then he took the other in his other hand and felt of it. At first Myra wasn't really afraid, for he didn't do anything at all but just stand there and look at her as if he was a little bit of a boy looking at a cookie or a piece of stick candy.

She was just so fascinated that she didn't do anything either—didn't even back away from him until she smelled the liquor on his breath. Then she backed away and called: Mr. Beckham! loud.

The Osage let go of her hair and looked at her so sad and then all the expression went out of his eyes and he staggered across the street where Sipperly was. Just as she said: Mr. Beckham! again and louder another Osage galloped his pony in front of the store and let out a couple of screams.

Mr. Beckham ran out of the store with no hat on and his beard blowing back.

Oh, Mr. Beckham, Myra said. Them old Indians are drunk. That old Sipperly got them drunk. That old Osage came right up to me and took a-hold of my hair braids. He smelt just like a whiskey bottle!

He did, did he? Mr. Beckham said, his eyes getting wild. Well, by Jesus H. Christ, where is he?

He went in that shack, Myra said.

You go in the store, Myra, honey! Mr. Beckham said fast, his eyes flashing. And lock the door inside.

But, Mr. Beckham! Myra said, and Mr. Beckham took her by the arm and almost dragged her into the store. She locked the door from the inside, and watched Mr. Beckham stalk across to the shack through the window. He was limping a little with his left leg, but his shoulders were thrown back and his beard was blowing a little in the wind. He walked right in the shack, not even bothering to close the door. It couldn't have been more than a minute until Sipperly shot out of the open door in the dust—and Mr. Beckham came out after him with his fists doubled up. Mr. Beckham came out all bent forward with his eyes wide open and starey. He leant over Old Sipperly—and he was talking loud: By Jesus, no one can call me a name like that! You let me catch you selling any more liquor to the Indians, by God Almighty! and I'll take a musket to you!

Then she saw Mr. Beckham grab him by the arm just as the smoke and flash came out of his sleeve and she heard the bang. And as Mr. Beckham beat him on the wrist something shiny flew out into the center of the road. Mr. Beckham shoved him down in the dust, not even looking backward at the two Osages who had come to the open door, and walked to the center of the road and picked up the little pistol. Then he turned around and said:

And I'm a-going to give you till tomorrow to close up—and then I'm a-going to fetch the United States Marshal!

He put the little pistol in his pants pocket and came over to the store door. Myra unlocked it and let him in.

My, oh my! Mr. Beckham, she said, that's just awful. You mighta been killed a-fooling around with that old Sipperly. My, oh my! her voice was almost hysterical. Where is that old gun? Where is that pistol?

Mr. Beckham locked up the store and put her on the pommel of the saddle and rode old Caesar back to the farm. She made him give her the pistol, which was a double-barrel Derringer pistol with silver trimmings made in Nashville, Tennessee. And Mr. Beckham said Sipperly was probably a Copperhead or a Rebel. But anyway she and Mamma hid the Derringer pistol and Papa's Colt's pistol and Papa's rifle and shotgun, because they were afraid—Mr. Beckham was so excited! He was just in a condition to go out and shoot somebody.

After they'd hid the guns, she saw Mr. Beckham's poor wrist was all blue gray and spotted. It turned out to be powder burns; and she and Mamma did it up in lard. And Myra said: My, oh my, Mamma! I just didn't realize how near Mr. Beckham was to being killed. Mr. Beckham, don't you darest to do any sich a thing ever again on my account!

Late that night Papa came in with Mr. Ernie Stewart. While they were having some supper in the kitchen, Myra told Papa what had happened.

Well, Myra, Papa said, Mr. Stewart has arrested Sipperly. I went to fetch Mr. Stewart this morning, just as soon as I could after I found out Sipperly was selling liquor to the Indians.

Where did you put that old Sipperly? Myra asked.

Now, Myra, honey, Papa said. Don't you worry. Mr. Stewart and I secured him well.

Just then Mr. Beckham came into the kitchen—he hadn't even undressed to lie down, Myra could see—and began to tell Papa now that he was home, that he, Mr. Beckham, would have to start for the marshal. Then Papa introduced him to Mr. Stewart and told him about them having secured Sipperly. And though Mr. Beckham looked a little disappointed, he said that was bully! Captain Hanks was always a jump ahead of everybody in everything.

Myra told him to take off his clothes when he went back to bed so he could sleep comfortably. And she went back to bed and couldn't sleep for a long time for thinking of the Indian holding onto her braids and Mr. Beckham calling her, Myra, honey, and the shot and the whole exciting day. And she wondered if it was son of a bitch that Sipperly had called Mr. Beckham.

CHAPTER XXX

GRANT had already heard. Una was right: Grant could not believe what they were saying of Mrs. Belton. Poor Rawlins, dead a long time now, yet it seemed but yesterday that he had stood in front of the tentflap saying in a breathless intense preacher-like voice: You know your weakness, Grant. You know also, Grant, that you can let liquor alone. Yes; it was that day the man made the photograph of him, Major-General Ulysses S. Grant, leaning against the tree with one hand. He looked, that day, the most like Old Zack in Mexico and he was proud of it. Well, I have done it. I am greater than Old Zack now: It was a bigger war, and I am President of the United States too—and there are more states.

The times are buried now when I was a cashiered drunk who

couldn't pay his bills. But Rawlins is dead and Reynolds at Shiloh and all those boys I knew at the academy. And so many at Cold Harbor—so many farmer boys like me when Ma used to call me Lys back in Ohio. They used to sew their names on their jackets at Cold Harbor so their mothers could find them.

But Rawlins was not there, Wagnal said, and if he had been, I doubt that he would have told Grant to act differently. He would have remembered Clint's civil manner and the cigars—and what man of them could have suspected that Una was what she was. Grant remembered the tents in Tennessee and the home in Burlington. He accepted Clint's resignation. If he had believed that Una had sold a post-tradership, her selling it would have lent sanctity to the act. For Grant was a worshipper at the Temple of Venus as were all men who saw Una except myself (who had married Katherine) and the Crimean and Drumbutt and even the Crimean admired her, for there was something complete about Una which commanded a certain admiration.

Grant wrote the letter of acceptance, gave it to Clint and walked out of the White House, forgetting that his fine pair of horses was waiting for him. He walked along the riverbank all that afternoon, thinking how he had first met Rawlins in Galena: The soft-tanned calfskin he had tacked to Rawlins's desk, the years of dusty sweaty summer afternoons and general stores, the years when not even the veriest loafer had given him a second thought, the years when he had given up and a sodden weariness had weighed him down. The day Sumter fell and Rawlins spoke in Galena. And then the years of the war when the simplest statements he made were put in the papers: the note to Buckner demanding unconditional surrender.

He saw again the tents—not in the winter or the rain—but always in moments of spring or early summer, the flaps rolled up, the officers sitting around posed in canvas camp chairs, some leaning theatrically on trees or tentpoles because the photographer had asked them to act natural. Only last night he had looked at the pictures of himself again. He remembered the haircuts, the uniforms, the hands-in-the-pockets attitudes, but he could not remember what he was thinking then. What had I in my mind then? Was it Rawlins's talk the night before? That cornfield at Shiloh where you couldn't step on the ground for the dead? That man, Rome Hanks, that night at the Landing—after the first day? He asked me who was in command. Luck maybe. God?

How did I get through those years? Why am I not dead now of that bullet that struck my scabbard at Shiloh?

But it was better with the army than it is now. Why did I ever let them put me here? And he thought of the days before Vicksburg on the march and the green around the tents and the smell of horses and leather and black powder and the high sweetsick smell of the fields he fought after the cannon were silent and the muskets cleaned and the boy-blue ranks closed up. And he thought how, all over America now, there were men of thirty-five who were the boys of his Army of Tennessee—and how those who then had said: hit Rawlins in the head to knock out Grant's brains, must have voted for him, saying, I was with Grant from Donelson to Vicksburg. I was with Grant at Shiloh! I saw Grant talking to Pemberton at Vicksburg—and they carried off that Goddamn' tree a piece at a time.

But Grant's acceptance of Clint's resignation didn't stop the motion for impeachment, Wagnal said. It fell to a Harvard roommate of Clint's to propose the impeachment. The man's voice broke for his dear old classmate. There was a fight in the house over whether or not a man whose resignation had been accepted could be impeached. Sympathy for Una ran high. Oh, she played it out with proper strategy and tactics, all right. Everybody began to say that Clint was hiding behind her petticoats.

Those women in Knoxville began to say now that poor Mrs. Belton, who had such good taste in clothes and was such a leader of fashion and gave all those nice parties for the President and the senators— and would certainly be a better and more representative woman to have in the White House than the general's wife—that poor Mrs. Belton was a much maligned lady. Yes siree, bob. That husband of hers—humph! If the truth was known he wouldn'ta got anywhere at all if it hadn't been for her. The women began to call on Katherine with sweet, mellow, sympathetic faces: These must be trying times for you Mrs. Wagnal—but just remember that we all understand. Katherine gave them tea and looked at them, from the eyeslits with the little imprints of voiceless sardonic laughter in her dimples. They were puzzled: they expected her arms around them and the outpouring of grief and sobs and tears; they expected to give back thickfat tears of smug sympathy. But they got nothing but Katherine's silent, wildly amused face before them over the teacups.

They got not even any acknowledgment that Katherine knew what they were talking about. Ah yes, Katherine would say. It will be a trial to leave Knoxville: this beautiful old house here, this *lovely* deep lawn, those dear little iron negroes holding one's horses—and you dear, understanding ladies. It will be a severe trial.

All the while they were hearing these words—words almost like the words they were used to hearing in similar circumstances, yet with some nuance of mystery, for the house was quite an ordinary old house in their estimation; and who, of them, gave a tuppenny damn for the little iron niggers,—they saw Katherine's Age of Innocence face teetering on the edge of wild laughter which they knew would come at their expense—and some way or other, to their disgrace. Who and what was this woman who made them all look so tacky and feel all thumbs?

But they would not retreat. Their feline intuition may have been strong enough to tell them of their coming humiliation, but they were country cats. They would not be warned. A dozen of them came one afternoon not long before we left. They brought quilts and handkerchiefs and fancy work bedspreads as farewell gifts to Katherine. They were a church society of some sort.

Katherine sat them down and gave them tea, listening to their chatter and smiling that smile that every moment threatened to be laughter. Oh, they finally brought up the subject of poor Una again—as if it had been clumsily plotted to seem natural when they made up the farewell party: Such an awful time moving and all. Sich terrible things happen to everybody—good honest people too—these days. People jist don't know where misfortune will strike next. More tea? Katherine would say. Oh yes, it will be a tiresome trip. But Fork City has such a charming little church—stone with little Gothic windows and a wooden vestry.

They couldn't stand it any longer. It happened, Katherine said, as if by pre-arranged signal. Now, Mrs. Wagnal, the soothing feline voice said, we don't want you to think we're prying, but we do so want firsthand news. All our sympathy is *for* your dear, dainty, beautiful sister. We are sure that she is being persecuted. We don't believe this horrible thing about her.

Katherine's silent expression broke into a light, derisive laugh. Dear ladies, she said, dear, dear ladies I must warn you not to waste your sympathies on my poor, beautiful, dainty sister. I got my information about my sister's persecution from the newspapers. I know as little of the details as you do—but you may be sure that my poor, dear, beautiful sister is as guilty as all of you would be, if you had been equipped with looks and spirit enough to attain her position. Dear ladies, my sister, Una, is a haughty calculating woman, who would not even turn her head to speak a harsh word to one of you. She would sell as many post-traderships as any of you, if you were sure you would not be caught. Now that your idle and boorish curiosity has been satisfied, do take your trumpery and go. There is no fee for this news. It is quite free. Katherine was still smiling. She did not even stand up.

Why, Mrs. Wagnal! You ain't serious! Why, myohmy! They fluttered and flounced out of the house. Katherine sent the needlework gifts back to them.

When I came home, Katherine was sitting on the porch with a glass of brandy in her hand, still laughing. She stood up on her chair and put her arms around my neck—and her hair danced around her eyes. And I saw all her brilliant beautiful coloring in the afternoon sun.

Burrus said: Good God, woman! Good God! Wagnal said. Take the bread out of our mouth and get me put in jail! You slep with her, Cora said, though this must have been only self-flattery. It was cool, but there was a slick film of ecstatic sweat on her forehead and among the hairs on her upper lip and the three hairs in the mole on her chin. You knew her carnerally. You fornercated with her. You paid her for it with more money'n I ever seen. You kep her—a strumpet in silks and jewlry. Defraud ye not one the other, except it be by consent for a season. But I didn't, I tell ye, Cory, Burrus said. I hope to die if I did. He that committeth fornercation sinneth against his own body! The Lord, He showeth me the way to save thy soul, Burrus. And the Lord saith write unto Warshington, Dee Cee, which is like unto Babylon and Sodom and Gormorrah—and lead them unto the truth.

She had nothing on but a dressing-sacque and she threw it off her and stood naked in the store. This is *your* neckidness, she said. A wife's neckidness is a husband's neckidness. An' every brave an' halfbreed crittur in the Territory will know *your* neckidness, Burrus.

Burrus got the dressing-sacque back on her and tied her up. He got a doctor to come and give him a certificate that she was ill and couldn't be taken to Washington. He left her locked in a room in the house of a quarterbreed midwife and started, alone, for the capital.

Clint was never impeached, but he was arrested. Oh, yes. They arrested him, all right, but they didn't put the dashing secretary in jail. Not General Belton! They put a policeman in front of the house in Lafayette Square and one behind. Clint had it all planned out for him and Una to skip the country. They were to get out on a boat down the Potomac, hit for New Orleans and sail from there to Europe on a forged passport. Una would not hear of it. Oh, she was courageous. Look here, Clinton, she said, we're staying in Washington. Nothing will come of this. They may say they're trying to impeach you, but it's me they're after. And I never saw a five-for-a-cent senator yet who could bring himself to do anything against me. Keep calm. Nothing will hurt you, though you may never be president now.

It was sleeting. And Una could see the policeman shivering under a tree in front of the house. Go out now, she said, and fetch that man inside. Say, Mrs. Belton and I cannot see you so uncomfortable. Bring him in and give him some whiskey, coffee, dinner—anything he wants. We need him on our side.

One thing can be said for Clint; he always recognized and adopted superior wisdom or cunning. He went out, fetched the policeman in and gave him a drink and a good dinner. No, sir, the policeman hadn't ever believed any of this business about selling post-traderships. Hadn't he been in the Army of Tennessee—and wasn't it many's the time he'd seen the General in camp and on the march. Why, by God, he seen the General take that Rebel kernel by the nape of the neck and the seat of the britches—never hoped to see a purtier sight, if he lived to be a hundred. And Missus Belton—why the gall of some people! A beautiful lady like her soilin' her hands a-sellin' post-trader-ships. Una put on her most innocent smile.

The next day, as the police guard changed around the house, a reporter accosted the policeman. Had the Beltons tried to escape? Escape? the policeman said, fingering the haft of his hickory billy. And why would they want to escape? They was innocent. They asked him in out of the sleet. They fed him. By God, he couldn't do anything to them senators, but he could pound the head off anybody what said a wonderful lady like Missus General Belton—or the General who he knew well durin' the war in the Army a Tennessee—coulda done anything like that. Even the jailer of the former Secretary of War and Mrs. Belton believes them innocent. It was a fine story. Una's fame and popularity were still rising.

Poor Burrus arrived at length. He had been thinking on the way. He was not such a fool, really. When he got into Washington, he knew what Una would say to the committee, if she were called before them. Mrs. Belton *has* loaned me money. Yes, sir, I had the honor a bein' her lawyer. I settled her ess-tate down to Messenger's Ferry, Mississippi. She loaned me money to git started at the post. He told them that and showed them the certificate of Mrs. Burrus's illness, pointing sadly to his forehead. Ah! the committee said, Ah! Ah, yes! Of course, under the circumstances, Mr. Burrus could no longer serve as post trader at Fort Sofa. Burrus's Madonna lids dropped, and he looked slantwise and downward.

Oh, it got into the house and senate, all right. They had a fine debate for a couple of months. The few fire-eaters from below the Mason-Dixon line yelled at poor Burrus, calling him a carpetbagger and a skunk. They reminded each other that Belton had married a Southern lady, whose father had been a blockader and false to the cause that had nourished him. The Tacitus, or the Thucydides, or the Macaulay who writes the annals of our epoch will engrave them with an inexorable pen. Why, now, gentlemen, when a high cabinet officer bolts from office in advance of the charges of corruption, shall the historian add that the Senate used the demand of the people as a farce, and deserted its high functions before the sophistries and jeers of the criminal lawyer?

Clint's lawyer had jeers and sophistries, all right. Why, Gentlemen of the Senate, are not all the accusers Democrats—men who cannot forget those glorious fields where *they* lost *by mere misfortune* to General Belton's *blind Union luck?* Disgruntled former slaveholders who cannot forget the days when they battened on the bloody sweat of their dark brothers held in durance vile—the days before General Belton and thousands of his stout-hearted kind marched, at the call of our Great Martyred Liberator, against and vanquished their invidious so-called democracy. I tell you it is a matter of politics. My client was a general in *Sherman's* army. Nay, in Grant's army.

It was a matter of politics, in truth, Wagnal said. Clint got a vote for acquittal which followed exactly the Radical Republican majority. For a while, Una was still Queen of Washington—and Clint became one of the highest paid lobby lawyers in the capital. Perhaps the setback on the road to the White House reached some deeply encysted spirit in Una. Perhaps it was only disease brought on by her courtesan's vanity. In any event, she wore a décolleté gown one bitter night and within a week was dead.

Pneumococci are great levelers of vanity and ambition, Wagnal said. They are batteners upon beauty or hideousness. For these shy retiring microscopic fellows fairfirm beautyflesh is as good as ugly anilemeat or dry white senile tissue—meat is meat to them. Ah! they say hungrily. Human meat is going to a cold party tonight without its coat. Oh! they say gluttonously. Those shoes! Hah! ah! Hah! There's holes in 'em—and the streets are wet. Do they say: What tender lobes! What fine breasts—only a little cramped from tight-lacing?—if we could only suckle at those rosy paps? Do they say: We'll larrup him one in the wind? No. All they do is burrow in rudely and gorge. They have not even the providence of the Ethiop, who lops one steak from the live bullock. They thrust their hungry gullets down into the live meat and spoil a million meals—for they are sure of a million more than they can ever eat.

But in Una's fair lights, they did one thing nothing else had ever done: they raised her heat. With the dry, crepitating râle, there came the warmth she had never felt. She died in hot rigors.

The cabinetmembers carried her into St. John's and out again. A lovesick little bureaucrat-clerk fell into an epilepsy of baroque sorrow on the icy walk. Even Grant looked at her breasts swelling under the satin with the eye of a necrophile. All the ladies of Washington turned out for the funeral weeping as joy burst in their hearts to the tune of: I still live and She is dead. There were personal telegrams from three kings and all the great dukes. And Clint, his Eye of Mars wetting for his lost glory and ambition, dwindled suddenly to half the man he had been as the earth hit the coffintop.

CHAPTER XXXI

BUT, Uncle Pink said, pausing and the motion of his tumefactive egg pausing with him, you want to hear about your grandfather and my brother, Jud Harrington.

I can scarcely believe it, but Judson and I were at the University of North Carolina for a year—well not quite a year, but part of a college year. But I cain't tell you much about college in those days. To tell you the truth, Jud and me did little or no studyin' at the university. But it was shore a purty place—built around a well and a

poplar tree. Seems to me the founders rode up on the hill on hawses
and says: We'll found us a university hyear—but first we got to have
a drink. So they tied their hawses to the poplar tree and went oveh
to the well to git a chaser for the cawn. Mebbe that ain't right—
mebbe the well was dug later. Fur who eveh hyeard of a scholah and
a judge of good licker needin' a chaser.

I didn't care much where I was long as I could git a good drink
of licker now and again and there was a purty gal or two close—but
Jud was right down onhappy because we wasn't at the University of
Vuhginia. We were restless too: after all hadn't we been heroes in
Pickett's Charge—and wasn't Greek pretty tame after the High Water
Mark of the Confederacy? And maybe we didn't amount to so much
just comin' to Chapel Hill.

Oh, we'd been to the wah, but there was plenty among the other
scholahs who'd been there too. I remember one man from Buncombe
county had had his right arm shot off at Antietam. And Old Bull
Pettibone, who tried to teach us Greek, had eight minnie balls in him
that he got as a lieutenant colonel in Jeb Stuart's cavalreh.

He wasn't really old; he just looked that way. I reckon he had
a right to. One of those minnie balls was in his throat—or mebbe just
the hole from one—but it made him so he couldn't talk plain. I didn't
listen to him much, so I cain't construe a single word of Greek now
But I wish I had. By Gahd, I neveh saw a man who loved anything
like Ole Bull Pettibone loved the Greek language.

But the onleh thing in Gahd's world I remember about my Greek
studies is Old Bull standing behind the desk in his shabby silkfaced
frockcoat on a hot day with the sweat shiny on his face sayin':

As a wule onwy whimmive werbs have hecon aorwes.

And I can repeat the first four letters of the Greek alphabet.

Ole Bull had a joke about copulative conjunctions he used to tell
too, but how it went, I cain't recall.

Ole Bull Pettibone. Evehbody made out like Ole Bull spoke plain
as day even when he wasn't around. For he was a great hero. They
used to tell how he charged into a rigiment of Yanks at Fleetwood,
hollerin' a battlecry in Greek, killed six and took ten prisoner. And
as I said, he wasn't old either. He was in his thirties—but he looked
old.

He had a black, grayshot beard, dead-lookin'; and his hair was
gray at the temples. He looked tired in the eyes—and there were times

he was grouchy as hell. His face had a passel of lines in it. But what really makes me remember Ole Bull was Jud's trouble with him.

Bull was a Vuhginian and had gone to the University of Vuhginia and then to Heidelberg, I think. Lucius Battle used to sweah he had sabah cuts on his forehead. Lucius used to say: You wait, Pink, until he gits his sideface to the winder and you can see 'em stickin' out. But I looked and looked and neveh could quite see 'em.

He had the reputation of bein' one of the best swohdsmen in Lee's army. They say he licked the West Point champion easy, before the wah.

It was before the wah too that he married with a Chahlottesville gal whose father was an ambassador or suchlike. Bull taught Greek a year at Vuhginia—and they would have given him his job back there. But—though we never saw it—the fact that he couldn't talk plain got him down. That was the reason he came to North Carolina. He hadn't been known there like he *was*—and anyway all Vuhginians thought it was a little bitty ole backwoods school. Mebbe it was.

Anyway, the story went around that Bull had offered to release his wife—make her free to git a divorce or somethin', but that she had refused to listen to such a proposition. So she came to Chapel Hill with him. She was part of Judson's trouble.

She was a belle of about twenty-three. Went to school in Paris. Raised in Europe. You kin see how she'd commence to git boahed in a Nawth Cahlina college aftah the wah. Most of the professahs were oldah men; and their wives were purty plain beside Miz Bull Pettibone. She may have been the reason Ole Bull started askin' his students to tea and suppah.

Anyway Jud and me went. I saw Jud look at her that first time. Jesus Gahd, Uncle Pink said, rubbing his earegg, remember arclights —how the fiah use' to jump between little black sticks? Well, that was the way it jumped out of Jud's eyes and lit on Nancy Pettibone. I neveh realized till years later. And you couldn't exactly say all the fiah was from Jud either.

Histah Hudson Heahinon of Halwell, Bull was sayin' to his wife.

She had her head about her, that gal, Uncle Pink said with old admiration in his eyes.

How do you do, Mistah Judson Harrington—anothah of my husband's fledgling Greeks, I take it?

He might've written our names out 'forehand, but I doubt it. I think she just figgahed 'em out from what he called us. Gahd! She looked crisp as an apple in the mawnin' dew—but delicate and tender. Jud kept the arclight eyes on her too much—even that first time. And nell, I couldn't blame him.

She had dark blue eyes and white purty skin and hair black as the yaws that followed Brother Paul in my dream. She gave us ham and homemade wine and some kind of cookies. Said it was hahdtack wah fare, but not to mind—one day we'd be havin' champagne and pheasant. Well, Uncle Pink said, I've yet to have 'em.

Ole Bull talked very little. He let his wife do the honahs. You could see how he would with that impediment—and besides, I think being stuck away at a college that was hardly open at all sorter got him. And all of us sat around like the young yahoos we were gapin' at his wife and listening to that Vuhginian and European talk of hers. Good thing there weren't many of us—only about six in the class—or we'da driven Bull crazy.

Nobody actually mentioned the wah, though there were three or four others besides Jud and Ole Bull and myse'f who'd been in it; but some way another we got on the subject of Vuhginians and Gen'l Stuart. Jud mentioned Reese Eliot.

Why Mistah Harrington, Miz Pettibone said, do you know Reese? He fought with my rigiment at Gettysburg, Jud said before he thought.

Ole Bull frowned, but Jud didn't see *him* at all.

But he's from Mississippi, Miz Pettibone said. I know him well, don't you, Joseph?

Es, Ole Bull said, Hoctor Eliot's son. I haught him hum Hreek. I hid'nt ho oo wuh acwhainted with he hung man.

CHAPTER XXXII

MEBBE Jud was a great ladies' man, Uncle Pinckney said. 'Twas always a great puzzle to me. I don't reckon he was though—it was just his luck. He was a purty good-lookin' young feller—and Pettibone's wife had heard him tell of Reese Eliot at Gettysburg. It was Reese who got Jud into that trouble—really.

And Bull Pettibone's wife: She might've been a daughter of one of the First Families of Virginia, but being raised in Europe and having her husband all shot to pieces in the war I reckon, was the reason she acted the way she did. What I refer to was that there must have been something between her and Jud. I wouldn't go so fur as to say positively there was—but I smelled somethin'.

He used to go to Bull's house in the afternoons when Bull was not there. One day in March—a raw day—Jud said to me: Pink, I'm not goin' to Greek today. You better, Jud, I said. Bull don't like his students to stay away. And I'm goin' back to Caldwell tomorrow, Jud said. I'm through with the university. What's the trouble, Jud? I said, but I already smelled it.

We'll take a ride, he said. We left Old South about noon and rode out to a patch of timber and set down behind some trees and wrapped up together in a blanket. Jud gave me a pull at the jug and said: It's Bull Pettibone. He called me out. What? I said.

A duel, he said. When? I said. It's oveh—done with, he said. Early this morning. Oveh Miz P? I said. I reckon, Jud said. I coulda killed him. He was so angreh his pistol went off before he aimed it. He stood theah waitin' for my shot. Well, Harrington, he said, hiah! And I shot into the ground. He told me he wouldn't have deigned to meet me if I hadn't been a membah of the Army of Northern Virginia—and that if the hairtrigger on his pistol hadn't played him false, I'd be as dead as I deserved. I *reckon* that's what he said—that's as near as I could make it out. He said that if I didn't go away, he'd kill me like a dawg.

Who was the seconds? I said. We didn't have any, Jud said. He said we'd have to trust each otheh. The one who could was to clean one pistol and put it back in the case and take it to his house—the other pistol was to be found beside the man who accidentally shot himself. He had the choice—and I reckon he thought he was too good with a swohd.

Then you're goin' home, Jud? I cain't stay here, Pink. I cain't see her any more, and I cain't go to my Greek class—and I neveh did like it here anyway. I wanted to go to Vurginia. Zeb Vance was here, I said.

She gave Reese that plume and palmetto star on his hat, Jud said.

Now, Lee, Uncle Pink said, taking the tumefactive cystskin between his thumb and forefinger, that was all your grandfather told me about it. Bull Pettibone died the next year; and Nancy Pettibone married a Yankee senator and went to live in Baltimore. I think they closed Chapel Hill down shortly after that—about the same time Chicken Cruppy tried to git a hawss doctah in as Latin professor.

Jud and me left Chapel Hill the next morning. We got back to Gadkin county with one of Jud's gray suits still in purty faih shape and found that Fathah was porer than we eveh thought he could be. Jud sparked around a little while, but he stayed away from Mary Ivy Dula Fitchett and all the married women. He kept goin' down in the holler to see Cap'n Frisbie's mulatto daughter, until one day he and I were ridin' past Ole Gahd's Chosen Cawdor's place.

Young gentlemen! Gahd's Chosen yelled.

We turned in and got down from our hawses. Come in and make yourselves at home, Cawdor said. We sat down on the porch and Anne brought us coffee and biscuit—and sourwood honey this time.

A social club, Ole Cawdor said, is a fine thing for young men, providing it has the correct ideals, don't you think so, gentlemen?

We were a little flabbergasted—at least I was. Jud had a wise look on his face. My young men, Ole Gahd's Chosen said, have fohmed a club of young men foah puhposes of edification and jollification.

Fathah has a Church, Anne said. He preaches every Sunday.

Jud sat lookin' at Anne Cawdor, who had on what may have been the same crisp white shirtwaist and the same homespun skirt she had on the day we got the bay gelding. Ole Gahd's Chosen went on talkin' about the debates and good times his club of young men had. And they ah, he said, all veterans of ouah cause and wish to preserve the traditions of ouah fathahs. We ah goin' to meet Thursday evenin' in Pine Spruce schoolhouse. Will you gentlemen honah us by being ouah guests?

Jud took his eyes off Anne long enough to say he'd be delighted. We'll come, won't we, Pink?

The onleh reason I said I'd go was because I wanted to see what kind of a club Ole Gahd's Chosen could git up. I didn't ketch on till Jud and me was on the road fur home. Jud told me: It's Night Riders or Invisible Empire—something like that, Pink. Its the Ku Klux Klan, he said. Remember what Ole Cawdor did to Gen'ral Dula's niggers and Cruppy?

Jud was right: it was the Klan, although we called it The Invisible Empire so we could deny it was the Klan in cote. I wouldn't've jined, Uncle Pink said, if a squad of buck niggers with muskets hadn't pushed me off the sidewalk once in Caldwell. As 'twas, I didn't like it any too well—I don't think Jud did either.

We use' to ride from noon till dahk into the next county and whup a nigrah fur burnin' a barn—maybe hang a nigger. One or twice we whupped a white man. And once we shot a carpetbagger. To start with it was fun in a way to dress up in the calico robes—we had red and white ones. But I neveh held with it much. I reckon it was because the niggers and carpetbaggers we hanneled were all from othah counties. We neveh did avenge ouah own wrongs—the membahs from othah counties did ouah jobs and we did theahs so as to avoid the law.

Fathah's barn got burnt by the Loyal Leaguers, and that did make me feel like I was right—but not for long. Anyway, I stayed with 'em till they disbanded. I think Jud jined just because he thought he could see Anne Cawdor more often, though he seemed to hate the carpetbaggers right much—and he had thought the world of Brothuh Sion.

Jud married Anne Cawdor that same year; and your father was born in Eighteen sixty-nine. He was born oveh a store in Long Leaf. Gahd's Chosen and our fathah had set Jud up in business. It was hard scratchin' though—and Jud neveh was much of a hand in business. Evehbody got into him. He didn't see cash money from one season to the next; and he got a shed full of homecured tobacker in trade that he couldn't sell fur love ner money.

That gray suit of his wore out; and Anne made him homespun britches and jackets. He took it purty hard, Jud did. Why, if they hadn't had a little cawnpatch and a few turnips beside the store and a cow and pig or two, they'd've starved to death. Would have anyway, if it hadn't been fur Anne, your Grandmother Harrington. She took care of the cawn and the critters and fed Jud and the children.

Your father was a fairly strong feller, but there were two, Reese and Pettigrew, who died. Reese died at two and Pettigrew at five years. Rickets they had. They neveh et right.

Licker took a-holt of Jud fur a while—and sometimes he left Anne and went down to see the mulatto wench. And I don't rightly know, but I think he went to see Mary Ivy Dula Fitchett once more, but she wouldn't have nothin' to do with him.

He couldn't afford to keep a hawse, but he kept one to ride around the country to Klan meetin's. I think he got mixed up with the law. Anyway, he was in a passel of trouble. He lost the store and he and Anne and the children went to live on our farm with Fathah—Mother had died the year before. The old Harrington place's not fur from here—place whur your grandfather and I were born—and your Aunt Cornelia and your Uncle Hampton.

Jud kept a'gettin' more and more melancholy. Anne tended the farm mostly, and he tried his hand carpenterin'. I lived with 'em a little, but I was too busy lickerin' to stay with 'em much. I used to he'p Anne with the cawn and the critters a little while Jud was off carpenterin'. Once he had a long job on a gristmill and made a hundred dollars. Anne needed clothes and so did the childern, but he came home—clean from Charlotte—with a new gray suit and a new hawss—and half lickered up. Now don't git the idy your grandfather was mean. He was carryin' a turrible load of trouble. He'd allus wanted to amount tc somethin'. He'd allus thought he was a great hand with the women—and he had been The Best Dressed Man in Gadkin County. Remember that.

He neveh had a chance. Why he might've been a poet. And if he'd got into Jeb Stuart's cavalreh, he might have come out of the wah a hero and been governor of the state. I neveh had right much gumption myse'f. I didn't care much whether school kept or not, as long as I had three good meals a day and licker and tobacker and a gal or two. But Jud—you could tell there was something in him. He got sadder and sadder. He borrowed money on the farm. He bound your father out to old John Swinton as a carpenter's apprentice for three years. Finally there wasn't hardly enough left to eat on the farm.

Seems to me, Uncle Pink said, that John Swinton went to Kansas first. Your father wanted to git away from Nawth Cahlina—and Kansas was still purty much the Wild West in those days. I swear, I think I was there the night Robert broached the subject. Fathah, he says to Jud, John Swinton's in Kansas. We could go there. No, Jud said. Not that Free State.

But Jud liked the idy. He was allus ready to try somethin' new. It must've been around Eighteen eighty-two when Jud and Robert lit out fur Kansas. They worked their way along and got to Abilene in about three months with about thirty cents between 'em—and no baggage. They built houses and barns. And John Swinton got Jud a job makin' coffins in Abilene.

In Eighteen eighty-three or thereabouts they sent fare for Anne, Cornelia and Hampton. The farm was sold, but it didn't bring but about five dollars apiece to them above the mortgage. I gave my share to your grandmother. God bless you, Pinckney, she said. I always knew you were a good man.

Well, I reckon time the family got to Kansas, Jud and Robert had a house built in Fork City. And Robert had seen his first camera. I remember he sent me a picture of Jud and Anne in front of the house—painted up and neat it was. Come to think of it I never saw Brother Judson, except in a picture, after Eighteen Eighty-two. Your daddy, though, came back the year before you were born; and he and I drove out to the ole place.

We were drivin' along in the red mud when along come a bar-footed young feller walkin' along in the rain with a sack oveh his shoulder.

What you got in that sack, boy? yore fathah asks him.

Groundhawg, the boy says.

Whur you takin' him? Robert says.

Fotchin' him to town to sell him, the boy says.

Open up the sack, and let's see him, Robert says.

Well, the boy fotched him oveh to the wagon and opened up the bag and thar was as skinny a little groundhawg as eveh I see.

How much you aim to git fur him? Robert says.

'Bout a quatah, I reckon, the boy says.

Hyear, Robert says. It's five miles to Caldwell and rainin'. Take this quatah and go home—you ain't even got any shoes on.

The boy took the quahtah, but I'll bet he neveh went home. I'll bet he went on into Caldwell and sold himself that groundhawg.

Your fathah didn't say anything for a long time—and then he says:

I remembah the first pair of shoes eveh I had, Uncle Pink.

Shucks, I said, Bob! Boys neveh used to need shoes. Why, I neveh had shoes to speak of even when I was in the ahmy.

He didn' answer. I could see he was thinkin' of Nawth Cahlina when he was a bound boy to old John Swinton.

Your Aunt Cornelia was always a great hand for ancestors, Uncle Pinckney said the next morning after a breakfast of ham and eggs, potatoes, grits, biscuits and sourwood honey. Used to draw family trees. Used to moon around right much about her daddy bein' The Best Dressed Man in Gadkin County. She wrote me I don't know how many letters about the family—and when I told her the truth once too often, she stopped writin' to me and began on yore Aunt Clarissa. I reckon Clarissa must've made up purtier things about the family than eveh I could think of.

I git a feelen, Uncle Pink said, rubbing the blueveined eggskin, that mebbe the family wasn't altogether to blame fur bein' what it was. Fathah told me long ago that when he was a boy in Vuhginia, it was in the nature of a sore disgrace to run away to Nawth Cahlina. Used to be that under the King of England nobody came hyear except people who were afraid of bein' thrown into prison for debt, coast pirates and criminals, witches, runaway slaves, escaped indentured servants and critters who were too sickly or too Gahddamn' lazy to make a livin' in Vuhginia or South Cahlina. Fathah said that though these were only the beliefs of his grandfather, he still felt guilty when he came here. Even when he came—it must have been in the early Eighteen hundreds—there was a lot of people here couldn't tell you the name of the county they lived in. And many of the roads could hardly be seen with the naked eye. And what or who the Cawdors were before your grandfather came along, I don't know— but you can be sure there was madness in the Cawdor family some- where. Ole Gahd's Chosen was evidence enough of that.

It's a great blessing your grandmother wasn't as religious as her fathah. There was somethin' creepy about Ole Gahd's Chosen: he had a clammy eye. Those three nigrahs of Gen'ral Dula's kneelin' in the street in their new lodge uniforms. An ordinary man couldn't do that sorter thing—to do it a man's got to be tetched. And if they're tetched they're generally sick.

There's a passel of sick people in this state—and look at how they used to die as babies. Paul and Timothy. Paul with the Yaws. Reese and Pettigrew. We all git some affliction. Look at that behind my ear. Doctor down in Caldwell says t'other day: Pink, we ought to take a knife to that 'fore it git any wuss. People'll think yore allus hongry goin' around with an egg behind yore ear! But I said no. I said: Doc, this yere surgery's all right, but not fur Pinckney Harrington. If you started to cut that off, you'd find you had to go deeper and deeper— and purty soon you wouldn't leave me any head. Besides that's one of the reasons my wife married me. Mistah Pink, she says to me, that's a right purty onlaid egg you got behind that ear a yourn. Now, if I'd a-been Jud, I'd a had it took off long ago—but the main thing, Lee, is to feel as good as you kin and let looks go to the devil.

We had been walking uphill along a redclay path among volunteer corn, a few rhododendrons and a heavy patch of weeds, when we came to the top of a little hillock. The gravestones were sticking up through the weeds and corn, damp and thin and rusty.

Here it is, Uncle Pink said. It's the Harrington burial ground. I bought it. It's just on the edge of the old place. Paul and Timothy's both up here; and here's where the preacher dropped the Edinburgh bible in the mud. Reese and Pettigrew's here too. I don't know why I bought it, except that I always dearly loved to think of Paul and the yaws. *Paul Ezekiel, Born July 4, 1835, Died August 17, 1836. Beloved Infant son of Ezekiel and Clarissa Harrington. Timothy Wayne, Born January 5, 1825, Died June 3, 1835, Beloved son of Ezekiel and Clarissa Harrington*. And all the other graves: of Reese and Pettigrew and my great grandparents and Saul and Joshua and some slaves—Daniel's wasn't there, nor my grandfather's which was back in Kansas. There were two plain stones off to one side. Niggers, I think, Uncle Pink said,—old nigrahs father brought from Vuhginia with him, Charles, mebbe and Caesar. I don't remember 'em.

For all I know, Uncle Pink said, there may be nobody hyear on this hill. People I bought it from used to work this land—they may have moved the stones around.

Daniel and me buried Fathah. Daniel said the prayers. He was right quare too, Daniel. Went off somewhere a long time and never came back—until he came back a preacher. Tall rawboned feller who never looked as if he understood a thing that was said to him. Had a sad look in his eye. He was a chaplain in the Fifty-eighth Nawth Cahlina. They say he killed more Yanks than anybody in the battle of Chickamauga—and spent all night prayin' in the rain fur 'em.

But Daniel and I were never right friendly. He used to come up to me and say: Brothuh, don't you feel the sperrit movin'? and whale me on the back hard when I was a little boy—so I was allus skeered of him. He used to go preachin' to camp meetin's. And they tell me that Dan had a passel of brats all through the hills hyear. Him and some sister would git to talkin' in The Tongues and 'fore they knew it, they'd gone and done the business. Seems he was allus able to convince 'em it was Gahd's will. He'd kneel down with 'em and say that they were married in the sight of Gahd. He'd tell their fathahs he felt the sperrit of Solomon in him.

Oh, he believed it. You never saw a feller thought he was more sanctified than Daniel. He was bit by a cottonmouth once, and he knelt down and prayed—and his leg neveh even swelled up. But I never liked him. You just couldn't git to know Daniel. He was too close to Gahd.

We didn't say anything as we walked down off the hillock burial ground. And the next morning I got into the wagon and drove back to Caldwell past the grayboards of the old mill which my father had photographed with the little old Poco Camera in Nineteen and three.

And I thought of the boy with the groundhog in the sack, but I didn't see a soul on the muddy road.

CHAPTER XXXIII

PAPA gave them one of the spring wagons and one of the horses; and Ma put two chairs in the wagon for them to sit on. Beckham had a pony he had traded from the Osage who had tried to buy her from Papa. Mamma and Hetty had made her a new black silk travelling dress as a surprise and got her a new chip hat in Independence and trimmed it up. It sat down almost over one eye and beat the New York and Paris millinery all hollow. She herself helped Ma and Hetty cook the chickens and cake for the lunch and remembered to put in four wings for Beckham.

Beckham stayed that night at the house; and they got up early the next morning—before the sun. And everybody had breakfast with them. Papa gave Beckham a hundred dollars for *them* and slipped her twenty-five dollars for herself and shook hands with Beckham and kissed her. Hetty and Ellen cried and Ma told her to mind her responsibility. And Ream said: Well, My, maybe that Osage will quit hangin' around the farm now.

Ring barked and frisked around the horses and made them nervous as Beckham drove them out of the yard past the pecan tree—and you could tell he was just real sorry to see her go. When they passed the Lombardy poplars and the silverleaf maples and the quince bushes she almost burst out into tears. And she looked back at the house and the kitchen that used to be all there was of the house when Papa had first brought them to Kansas—and, my, oh my! She just couldn't believe it was the same place. Why, it was larger now than it was when Mr. Beckham came—only four years ago. And there were the young orchard trees that Papa had set out that would be bearing soon. And Ring was a grown up dog and not a puppy any more—and would soon be an old dog.

General Grant had made Papa postmaster of Elgin and wrote him a letter and mentioned their friendship of two wars. And Papa had given them one hundred and twenty-five dollars all for themownselves. She wasn't just sure she ought to have taken her twenty-five, because Papa didn't have any too much—grasshoppers and drought and everything. And the postmastership didn't pay anything to speak of. And even if he was still judge, he almost lost money on that. All them old settlers came to Papa to be married, because he never charged them a red cent to do it, if they didn't offer him something. A lot of them were just old trash and not decent—like that old fellah and that woman who'd been living together for years and decided to be married on account of taxes or pensions or something. And then there was that fellah who told Papa he'd send him a load of potatoes if the marriage turned out all right and if he had any potatoes. Papa just smiled. Papa was *too* good—just too good. And Mamma always taking things to eat around to those old trash that *still* lived in soddies and one-room shacks and some of them were here before *they* came from Ioway.

Beckham sat up straight in the chair—and they drove along in the gray morning light, the chairs jolting in the wagon. They stopped at noon under a maple tree. The sun was out then and they ate their lunch and Beckham said, smiling at the chicken wings: Myra, honey, you just bet you know the bossest piece of chicken. And she said: Don't get it on your whiskers, Beckham.

It was late in the afternoon when they got to Independence, but Judge Roamer married them and asked Myra about Judge Hanks. And Marshal Ernie Stewart and his wife were their witnesses and stood up with them. And Beckham said: By Jesus Christ, Mr. Stewart,.

I haven't seen you since that fellow Slipperly— Sipperly, Myra said. Sipperly, Beckham said, got out of Captain Hanks's woodshed. You can just bet that fellow was a Copperhead, or a Rebel, or maybe, by God, a bounty-jumping skedaddler!

Mr. Stewart said maybe it was a good thing he got away because somebody might have strung him up. And a good thing—a God-damned good thing if they had, Beckham said.

Now, now, Beckham! Myra said. Don't you swear!

Excuse me, Myra, honey, Beckham said.

Mr. and Mrs. Stewart tied an old shoe to the wagon and threw some rice on them. They had the rest of their lunch, that Ma and Myra had put up, sitting in the wagon. Then they went to the Ross House—and when Beckham registered, he almost wrote her down, Miss Hanks.

They undressed for bed in the dark and Myra could see the moon over the prairie outside and she got to thinking of Papa and Knoxville, Ioway, and the money he had sent her from the war in Mississippi to buy a ribbon for her bonnet and Mrs. Washburn's Seminary in Knoxville and how Pa said Mrs. Washburn's son pulled his front teeth out before the battle of Shiloh with a mandolin string but he wasn't a bad boy and about that poor Harold Bates that they all called Sleepy and the tears began to roll down her cheeks. And she thought of the Indian looking at her hairbraids and Beckham hitting that old Sipperly. And then of Papa again and how good he was to give them one hundred and twenty-five dollars when he had had to pay sich things as that old ten thousand dollar note of General Clint Belton's he had signed. And even when General Grant made General Belton Secretary of War he hadn't paid Papa a cent. But Papa hadn't said a thing except: Well, I see General Grant's made Clint Belton Secretary of War. And Papa was getting older too; his beard was all shot with gray all through it. She sobbed out loud and put her nose into the pillow.

Why, Myra, honey, Beckham said, what's the matter?

She didn't say anything—and when Beckham put his hand on her shoulder, she drew away a little. He didn't move, and finally she broke into sobs again and said: Oh, Beckham, I was thinking about Papa. Then she put her face in Beckham's beard; and her tears ran down into it.

There, there, honey, Beckham said. You'll be seeing the Captain a whole lot—you just bet you will. Why, he's a grand man! Sedan ain't so far from Elgin.

After a while Beckham's silky whiskers against her cheek made her feel better, but she couldn't really put Papa out of her mind.

CHAPTER XXXIV

ROME saddled up Lavinia, patting her and not talking to her, but thinking that he was now twice a grandfather. He felt in his inside coat pocket to see if the twenty-five dollars for the granddaughter, Nora, was there. Of late he had discovered sad changes in himself: He could no longer concentrate when he read Suetonius and Livy and the new book by Mr. Darwin—with an English imprint—which he had got because he had enjoyed *The Origin of Species* and believed that every man ought to read what Mr. Darwin wrote. His mind would go back to Kentucky, and he would puzzle about what Pa did when he was a young man in Virginia—and what he was that year at William and Mary College.

More and more Rome was looking backward and inward: Why had Pa called him Romulus Lycurgus? It was not Ma's doing: she hadn't had the names in her family, nor the learning in her head. It must have been out of Livy. He still had Pa's old Livy, and he knew the legend of the founding of Rome well enough: The twin boys by Mars out of Rhea Silvia, Numitor's daughter, thrown with their mother into the overflowing Tiber, washed up in their cradle at the foot of the Palatine Hill. Their mother dead, they were suckled by a she-wolf.

The saddleleather squeaked as Rome pulled himself laboriously up. The she-wolf. Well, he said to his mind: I have never been weaned from the she-wolf's milk, and I have never found a Palatine Hill, nor built a Rome, nor had a twin brother. But little Ream died like a Roman at Shiloh. My twin, born five years late and died in my arms (when I was turning the furrow for the wall) at Shiloh. And Beauregard retreated to Corinth just as Celer rushed to Etruria. Yet where is my city? Not even a ruin, for it was never built. Two wars gone and wanderings longer than Æneas'. A creak in my bones, Ma and Pa and little Ream dead in Kentucky and Tennessee, Lucius hunted like a beast, and Granville dead because he is lost. He rode down the lane past the Lombardy poplars, the quince bushes and the silver-leaf maples. They looked dry and hot already in the early prairie morning. Barking, Ring had followed him a little piece past the pecan tree—and Lorna had waved from the door. Rome waved back and felt again in his inside pocket for the money. It was there; then he remembered he had felt before.

If it hadn't been for Clint Belton, he would have enough to provide properly for his children and grandchildren. General Clinton Belton—Mr. Secretary of War now and never a word from him. The years in Knoxville and the years in the South with the regiment ran through Rome's head without order: Clint coming into the office of the stable in Iowa: Rome, I need your name for a month or two, I'm pressed. Of course, Clint. How much is it for? Only ten thousand, Rome.

Ten thousand took the stable and all the horses and what was in the bank. Clint had never said a word or written a line.

At Pittsburg Landing he had told Clint how to talk to Grant. And all the reports Rome had written for the regiment—though it was not his duty—and never once had Clint added any mention of him. Rome knew he had done his duty well—and that he might have been colonel of the Hundred and Seventeenth Iowa, if he had stooped to the methods of a wardheeler. Of course, Clint; how much? Only ten thousand, Rome.

And those Shawnees lying dead beside Pa: He remembered that morning well, a deep, green morning with the sap stirring and every sprig of green moist with life. Pa lusty for work with his axe and Little Ream chirruping and Loosh and Granny taking things in their long stride and laughing with their blood running free in their veins. The Kansas morning was not like the Kentucky morning. Kentucky was deep in the South and closer to the warmth of the world, yet it was not so burning and violent as Kansas—nor ever so cold and bleak. And California—oh, there was everything there, all right: mountains, sea, deserts, orchards, vineyards and warmth every day at midday and no stifling heat at night. Yet it was empty—blank as the blue sky over it on a fair day.

As blank as I, who am marked and tagged now as a recessive variety—a hybrid or a sport perhaps too, even a survival. Only ten thousand, Rome. Fifty-four. My stomach worse—bad since the winter of sixtytwo. My bowels—no bowels since Andersonville. One finger, two toes—scurvy. Deaf on the left. My joints stiffer since last winter. What's that tree down the road, a cottonwood? Don't remember it. And I could see the buttons on those Rebel uniforms across the Big Black River that fourth of July in 1863.

A little lizard ran up on a rock by the roadside, and, for an instant, as the little reptile sat frozen in the sun, Rome thought of Mexico and Grant near him in the chaparral and the gray green lizards and the copper sun. Grant gave me the Postmastership of Elgin that night at Pittsburg Landing in the cabin door. He had been drinking; he was on crutches. And I said: Who, in God's name, was in command? God was in command, and Grant was God's man. The negroes said, bress God and Gen'l Grant.

At Shiloh he didn't do anything and Beauregard went back to Corinth. He almost went home when Halleck came. I heard many of the men say that if you'd hit Rawlins on the head you'd knock Grant's brains out. But it was not so. You'd have had to hit God on the head to knock Grant's brains out. Grant was just there in the landscape with the army and he would say yes or no and it would go down in a trickle to a man who would say forward or load, to a company which had never seen Grant and didn't much like what they had heard of him. And so Grant rode on with a cigar in his mouth and the look of old Zach Taylor on him, not even realizing what was going on—never knowing what that great hunk of humanlife in shoddy blue around him meant. He was almost nothing but a little stoopshouldered bystander with the protective coloring of blue and stars and an ignorance so bottomlessly deep that God chose him to survive—chose him to survive, because he did not know what he was doing and does not know now what he is doing.

All those years after Mexico: Cashiered from the army for drink, a dirt farmer in Missouri, a house agent downattheheels and then the Hero of Appomattox over the planter-gentleman-general, whose ignorance wasn't bottomless enough for God's favor—who, most regrettably for himself, had an inkling of what he was doing and had so little protective coloring that he became a ghost before he died.

On the road and the pastureland ahead, Rome saw the water—mirage of the July sun—and the few cooplike buildings of Sedan. A little crossroads named for a Prussian victory. He urged Vinny into a trot.

Good morning, Captain Hanks! Tom Beckham said, his beard stirring in the hot breeze. You just go right in and see Myra and the baby. The baby's been a-watching for Grandpa Hanks since early morning. You just bet she has—and Harry, why, by Jesus! he can say Grandpa Hanks, and don't you ever forget it!

How's Myra? Rome asked.

Just boss, just boss! She'll be up and around in no time at all. You go on in, Captain. I'll take care of Vinny.

Myra and the baby were in bed. The baby lay, in long, hot skirts, close to her mother. Rome could see her hair was going to be light— like his mother's. The baby looked up at him and chirped like Little Ream and grinned delightedly.

Well, *Papa!* Myra said. She knows *you* already!

Rome picked up the child, Nora, and held her in his arms. She chirped and cooed and seemed to laugh; she took hold of his beard with both small hands.

She's a little like my mother down in Kentucky, Rome said, his eyes far away. And she's like Little Ream. You never knew your grandmother, did you, Myra?

No, Papa.

Rome was silent. You never knew your grandmother, did you, Myra! He had heard himself say it with amazement. Of course she hadn't known her grandmother. He was getting old. He was nearing his dotage. A very Polonius. Only fifty-four and his mind closing the past up like a telescope—scrambling it up like an egg.

Myra, he said quickly, pulling the envelope from the inside pocket of his dusty, broadcloth Prince Albert coat, here's something for my granddaughter. It's not as much as Harry had, but it's the best I can do now.

Oh, Papa! Myra said. Thank you, Papa! You're so good, Papa.

The baby pulled at Rome's beard again.

CHAPTER XXXV

MAYBE Burrus was back in the Territory trying to settle up his accounts at the Fort Sofa trading-post, Wagnal said. Maybe Clint thought the West would heal him. Summer, Eighteen Seventy-six!

Why he took that trip out there in the middle of the summer, I don't know. Why a man of Clint's age, whose eye of Mars was not so threatening or commanding now, would get aboard one of those chattering, dustchoked, bumpy little cars in a heavy broadcloth frockcoat and a top hat—a car in which the railroadmen still halfsardonically, half-in-earnest left up the signs saying: Please Do Not Shoot Buffalo from the Windows—why he started for those sucked-dry, grasshopper-stripped, dust-whipped, burnt-brown steppes where every whitleather-tanned, crease-necked old party who owned a section or two was trying to sell it and get the hell back to the greenfields of Somewhere where there was water and life and un-dry women and licker and no God-damned flats and hillsides full of dry buffalo grass to catch fire and burn him out nor any gullywashing thunderstorms to wash through the soddy roof and dirty all his traps—why Clint started for the Great West, I don't know.

He wasn't hankering to be a pioneer any more. He'd had enough of that nonsense in Ioway and the army. But he did get on that train. Oh yes; I know he did. He even had the Crimean with him—his faithful batman. The general had become more accustomed to traveling in that way during his extensive campaigns in the Western Theatre of the War of the Rebellion.

He got on the train: There were engines with those funnelshaped stacks on them—all named: the General Thisorthat, the General Soandso. And there were screenwire fireguards at the top of the stacks to keep the sparks from setting the prairie on fire, for they were all like Roman candles—and cowcatchers. And—oh, Jesus, boy, as forlorn little brown and yellow stations—with the Great World dripping slowly into them through the mechanical drip-drop, drop-drip of the lonely telegraphic keys—as you ever saw.

And at some stations along the way—maybe at two or three—where the General Thisorthat chuffed petulantly up to the watertank, the telegrapher would walk out on the gravel—or maybe it was still just pulverized dirt—with his eyeshade still on and his arms black with sleeve protectors to his elbows, and say: Excuse me, sir, but ain't you General Belton. I got the advantage of you, I bet! Well, sir, I was in the Hundred and Seventeenth Ioway or I was in General Crocker's brigade, but I seen you many's the time. I said to myself, if that ain't General Belton, I'll eat my hat—an' I jist made free to come out and ask to shake your hand. Damn' few of us got to shake the hand of the Hero of Atlanta and the Sekertarry a War.

And Clint, remembering that this was the way that votes were got—not remembering, or not having resigned himself to the proposition that he could not use any more votes—would say, putting out his Washington, Dee Cee, hand to the G.A.R. yokel: You haven't got the advantage of me at all, sir! Maybe I can't call your name, but I'd remember that face a thousand years. We soldiers—and you ought to know it—don't forget.

Later the yokel would say: An' by God, Gen'ral Belton come up to me on the platform, an' I said: I got the advantage of you, I bet, Gen'ral! Advantage, hell! says the Gen'ral. Do you know my name? You're Gen'ral Belton of the *Ioway* brigade, ain't you? I says. Why Goddamn' it Doesmith, he says, afore I was *Gen'ral* Belton, I was major of the Hundred and Seventeenth *Ioway* Volunteers Infantry when you was a private in the rear rank a Company K standin' next to Doakjones! *You* got the advantage! An' then he slapped me on the back an' says: How's the wife an' kids? Fine'n dandy, I says. Well, Gen'ral, the joke's on me—it's shore on me! An' then I ask him about them pensions, an' he says: I'll make a note of it, Doesmith, an' see to it personally that yourn's mentioned in the *right quarter*.

Some of those yokels saw Crime too: and some of them remembered the tall wooden horses and the ropes around their wrists and ankles in the Georgia sun—and some of them said, remembering only with the great heart and dewy eye: Ho, Crime! How in the hell's the wooden cavalry? How's the Goddamn' Crimean Horse? Where's Drumbutt?

Thus, his drawers sticking sweatily at the crotch, his collar wilting under the damp broadcloth, his eyelids gritty over the fading eye of Mars, every black Stetson old soldier hat seen from the dirty coach windows reminding him of the days of his dead glory, Clint thundered across the North American continent toward the frontier at the breathless speed of thirty miles an hour.

He may have had it in his mind to ask the jackleg lawyer-trader, Burrus, the quick-and-easy-money man, the Indiana sutler, who will no doubt be, maybe is a sutler in heaven, flapping about on scrofulous, secondhand wings, trying to sell goldfilled wingtips, brummagem harpstrings and slightly used fine dress swords of only one-third spent greekfire to the heavenly host—perhaps he wanted to ask Burrus if there had been any records of that cotton he confiscated for Theron's blockaders to Liverpool. Perhaps he went with the purpose to do what he tried to do fixed in his mind.

His journey was over a week old when he took the stage to Sedan. Perhaps he got there at midday on a day when the Kansas sirocco was still and the thick gray dust lay powdered and printed in the streets—there were two or three about a block long—with horse-shoe and bootheel, square American toes and the long beaded scars of tobacco juice with grains of dust on top of the turnedover bubbles. The two or three streets—the whole town, for that was all there was of it—was naked to the hot, blinding furnace of the sun which looked like the open door of a steelfurnace.

The settlers had set out rows of sapling elms and maples, and built little wooden enclosures a foot square around their skinny trunks to keep the wagon hubs from scarring them and the horses from gnawing away the bark—indeed, to protect them from the jack-knives of lonely men and little boys and the backs of stray and itching buffalo. The biggest of these trees then were only a little above the groundfloor windows of the houses. And so there was no shade, no bosky dell, no relief from the thick drysoup of heat that glittered upwards toward the sun, making mirages of dry water on the deserts of dust.

There was a sparse litter of limestone rocks on the main street—not macadam, not any attempt at paving—just what the plow and spade and drag had turned up. Behind the thin fringes of rickety saplings sat the painted frame-siding houses and stores, not a green branch topping their wooden horizon—nothing but the twisted iron lightning-rods, bulged with porcelain balls in the middle, overreaching the brick chimneys.

Oh yes. Sedan would burgeon into a metropolis of the plains: the rails would come; the trees would grow; and elegant new houses would soon be a-building. Now, there were a place called The Farmer's Home and Restaurant, outside of which on the wooden sidewalk stood an empty wooden chickencoop made of saplings and a light spring wagon for produce; a livery-stable, white-fronted with gaping doors for the two or three carriages and, above these, a door for hay, open, with creaking pulley tackle above it at rest, so that the three-foot high T and A in stable were concealed; an implement house, where plows, harrows and even those new-fangled reapers of old man McCormick's could be ordered, or, luck being with you, bought from the floors; a dry goods house with yards of turkey red and figured calico, flannel and little silk, a tacky hat or two, some Butterick patterns and a Singer sewing machine; a store with whiskey in kegs, tobacco and flour, acetic acid vinegar and bacon; a photograph gallery.

And there was the Beckham House, Wagnal said, your grandfather's hotel. It had about a dozen rooms, two chimneys, and two or three saplings on the corner side of it. Built in the simplest logcabin style of American houses, it did have a good wide porch on the front with six fairly fancy posts holding up the flat roof. There were four windows in the front—two on either side of the door which opened onto the top of the porch—and above the windows, arching upward toward the apex of the roofpitch, was BECKHAM HOUSE, painted in great, red block letters.

I can hear my grandfather now, Lee thought: I don't want any God-damn' *fine* print, so's a man'll have to strain his eyes to see it's a hotel and whose hotel it is. I want the sons of bitches slapped on there five foot high—or more—and Goddamn' good and red. And because, in the logcabin-child's-conception-of-a-house style of building, the front is smaller than the sides, my grandfather said to the painter: Now over there's four windows too, but we got some room over here—you make 'em six foot high over here. Sandwich 'em in between the windows and leave off the HOUSE. Jist BECKHAM. I calcalate that'll be a-plenty. But make 'em in *red*.

As one of the city fathers, he hung the corner street-lamp to the corner post of the front porch. When the letters were on the hotel, he walked through the thick dust of the street to the Farmer's Home, limping slightly from the minnie ball he got at Gaines's Mill, about faced and looked at the hostelry: By the gods, they could see that all right—even at night, if there was moon enough to help out that streetlamp.

The Beckham House in Sedan, Kansas. Summer, Eighteen Seventy-six. Why, boy, Wagnal said to me, you cannot imagine how dry my very bones feel now as I think of that time and place. Oh, there were rag rugs on the floor and clean sheets and quilts on the beds—your grandmother would always see to that, even if she were dying. There weren't any bedbugs and the meals were fine, from lush cherry and apple pie, back to the rich potroast or fried chicken. Oh, I've no doubt that it was the cleanest, most comfortable, most sumptuous hotel on the frontier. But down near there the soil begins to redden and all man-meat becomes jerked alive in the summer time and frozen for the winter. In those days it was a bleak land of hopeful saplings—a land waiting industriously for shade and moisture.

Why, down the street from your grandfather's hotel, two or three doors in the only block, there was a photographer, one Keland. He had a set of stereoscopic views of New York City and Washington, D. C. and Paris. People used to drop in and sit near the cool, damp door of his darkroom and look at his iron headclamp and those stereoscopic views under the little north skylight. By God, they would say, they sure got streets back there. They sure got some buildings, ain't they? God, look at them paintings in that Loover! Well, it ain't agonna be long till we have a firstrate city *here*. Why, by God, we already got a photograph gallery. You can git your picture took here. The west sure draws men to it.

But they never believed that the saplings would grow (though some of them did), that the town would ever be anything but a place to pause over night, a place to buy a barrel of flour or a sewing machine—a place to grow lonelier than you were in the farmhouse where your land lay all around you. A place to look at a hunk of limestone in the street at noon and think of the tall trees in Ohio, the dark green of Pennsylvania and the Great World outside this sea of dryland where you were marooned in the brazen sun.

Well, Wagnal said, Clint and Crime put up at the Beckham House and wrote their names on the register. Tom stood in the mirage on the dust and took one of the grips from the stage. Whew! Clint said. Reminds me of hay foot! straw foot! in the army. Is there such a thing as a bath, sir? You just bet, Tom said. Clint signed the register, maybe with John Clinton and Crime's name—Mibble or Gribble or whatever it was. Tom brought him a tub and three buckets of hot water into one of the downstairs rooms, where Myra's lace curtains hung down straight before the open window and you smelled the hot dust and a faint sharp horsedung and urine smell from the stable down the street, though there was no wind. There you are, Tom said. Not too hot, not too cold.

Thank you, sir, Clint said. A man called R. L. Hanks—he lives around hereabouts? Captain Hanks? Tom said. Why, he's my wife's father. He lives down near Elgin—about thirteen miles from here. Do you know Captain Hanks? Ah yes, Clint said. I knew him in the Army of Tennessee during the war—a friend of mine. Well, sir, by God, Tom said, putting out his hand, how d'ye do, sir? Any friend of Captain Hanks's is a friend of mine. My name's Tom Beckham. How do you do, Mr. Beckham, Clint said, shaking the vote-giving hand.

Yes, sir, Tom said. You won't find a finer man in the whole world than Captain Hanks—not if you was to be hung fer it. Yes, Clint said, I know. He is a fine man. Don't you fergit it, Tom said. He ought to a-been a Gen'ral. (Tom still pronounced been bean as his father had.) Him in the Mexican war too—but he didn't get his just dues. He was in an Ioway rigiment—I don't recollect what one. Why, Tom said, there was a whole Goddamn' kit and boodle of young puppies permoted over his head. That Belting fellah—that Secretarry a War. Ah yes, Clint said, there was a good deal of injustice done. What outfit were you with, Mr. Beckham? Why, Tom said, I was with the Ninety-Seventh Pennsylvania Volunteers, Lincoln's first hundred thousand—Zouayves they was. Corp'al, F Company. I would of been a first lieutenant—I was promised a commission in another rigiment, but the son of a bitch went back on his word! Ah, Clint said. Army of the Potomac, eh? Yes siree, Tom said. Wounded at Gaines's Mill and sent to Bell's Island.

Myra gave Clint and Crime some dinner. Mamma, Tom said, I want to make you acquainted with Mr. Clinton. He knew your Papa in the war. How d'ye do, Mr. Clinton, Myra said. It seems to me your face is familiar. Was you ever in Knoxville, Ioway? No, ma'am, Clint said. It must be these whiskers of mine—all of us men look more or less like beavers. Oh, now! Myra said. Beckham tells me you're a-going to see Pa—Mr. Hanks. Yes, Clint said, I'm driving over this afternoon. My! My! Myra said, you just better wait until later—you'll get sunstroke. I told Beck—Mr. Beckham jist this morning I never seen sich a summer in all my born days!

Now, Mamma, Tom said, Mr. Clinton knows what he's a-doing. He's an old soldier. Well, I don't care, it's jist *awful* hot. Was you in Pa—Mr. Hanks's regiment? Clint said: I was in the same brigade part of the time. Well, Myra said, he'll be tickled to death to see you. We don't get to see many old friends out here in Kansas. Myra looked sharply at Clint and the Eye of Mars neither threatened nor commanded—it looked away. Old Rome Hanks's daughter, eh? Well, she was still a pretty enough woman, though she looked tired. She had black hair almost as beautiful as Una's. And married to this Beckham—and living in this Godforsaken desert, running this hotel. Hotel indeed! One jump from a logcabin.

Maybe Tom walked over to the livery-stable and asked Mr. Cassel to give Clint and Crime good horses. Maybe he actually stood and pointed the way over the little rise: Take that road and you'll come to a row of Lombardy poplars and some silverleaf maples. You can't miss it. And tell the captain, hello, for me! Tom wouldn't even take anything for the room and meals: From a friend of Captain Hanks—hell no!

Oh, they found it all right, even though it was dark and the lantern was feeble. Crime drew the horses to the side of the road near the quince bushes. They stomped a little in the hot dust and switched their tails and tried to chew at the branches. A bit of water for the animals, sir? Crime said. No, Clint said. Not now. Just wait here until I come out. We'll hunt a stream then. Yes, sir.

Clint could see the yellow windowlight on the rise and he walked toward it trying to keep to the path, but straying into the prairie grass. He walked up on the porch and saw the light and shadow move on the walls of the hallway and the shine of the dark walnut newel post on the end of the baluster. He smelled the coal-oil and milk smell of the farmhouse and saw the little bugs on the screendoor and heard the bootsqueak coming behind the highheld, flickering lamp.

CHAPTER XXXVI

MOTHS sat on the screen outside; the little bugs got through. They circled and wheeled around the smoky lampchimney, which Lorna had polished that morning, and fell, dying, or maimed, on the open pages in the yellow light under Rome's eyes. A cicada or two burred dozily in the orchard and a stifling August sirocco, which had risen before nightfall, dried the earth, fetched the dust through the screens and dried the sweat in Rome's graying beard. At times the wind, sluggish and slight tonight, was still: and the window frames did not rattle: then a black veil of nightheat enveloped the orchard and the well, the whole flat and gently hilly landscape which would have been within the field of Rome's vision had it been moonlight or daylight.

Darkness and quiet, Rome thought. Dark as Andersonville, but quieter. The groans and the raiders: memory. The lamplight falling on the pages of the book, the small pool of light around him in the room off the parlor, the tick of the small graygreen insects hitting the lamp-chimney or the pages of the book, the tiny wingwhirrs, the cicadas, the creak of the sideboards of the house, the soft warm swish of the few leaves that the grasshoppers had left on the trees only thickened the dark and quiet, so that Rome saw all the earth as lying simultaneously in darkness and silence, from the icelocked polar seas to the thick orchidaceous and sinister tropical jungles, places which he had never seen except on the lantern slides of his brain, but which he still wished to see, not with the fire of a young and lusty man who sits upon a dock and smells the sea and the rope and the tar and thinks of how the ship would come to Liverpool or Shanghai or Lisbon at nightfall, but with the desire of one who knows the decks and rope and bows are not for him—and his only ship is this four walled cage—this house, this home earth around him.

Say I had been to Africa, Asia, the Americas and Europe and all the major archipelagos and lived with all the peoples of the earth—reached out with the antennae of my senses and made notes on this "knowing" of mine. It is not exactly the vain desire to leave a monu-ment, but say I had written a book and taken it, strongly bound, well-printed on good paper, with my name—my ghost—on the title page, in my hand, I could have felt the heft of the good, tightpressed pages of the folio, the quarto, the octavo—even duodecimo—volume and said: Well, herein is what I have concluded, though the observation may be faulty and fuddled, though my meaning is, at times, obscure, because I had no words—there are no words—with which to transfer it to other minds. Now I no longer have anything more to say, except simple statements predicated by the verb to be and modified by simple adjec-tives symbolizing such as color or density.

Rome, turning his head from the dark window, looked down at the page on which lay the small body of one of the graygreen insects, one of its wings wrenched out of its folding-place under the shield which protected their transparent film. Dishevelled, laid low, the bug stared at the sub-head on the page: "The Term Struggle for Existence, Used in a Large Sense."

"I should premise," Rome read and Mr. Darwin had written—Rome knew—before the battle of Shiloh, "that I use this term in a large and metaphorical sense, including dependence of one being on another, and including (which is more important) not only the life of the individual, but success in leaving progeny. Two canine animals, in time of dearth, may be truly said to struggle with each other which shall get food and live. But a plant on the edge of a desert is said to struggle for life against the drought, though more properly it should be said to be dependent on the moisture. A plant which annually produces a thousand seeds, of which only one of an average comes to maturity, may be more truly said to struggle with the plants of the same kind and other kinds which already clothe the ground. The mistletoe is dependent on the apple and a few other trees, but can only in a far-fetched sense be said to struggle with these trees, for, if too many of these parasites grow on the same tree it languishes and dies. But several seedling mistletoes, growing close together on the same branch, may more truly be said to struggle with each other. As the mistletoe is disseminated by birds, its existence depends on them; and it may metaphorically be said to struggle with other fruit-bearing plants, in tempting the birds to devour and thus disseminate its seeds. In these several senses, which pass into each other, I use for convenience' sake the general—"

Flipping the dying insect from the page, Rome turned to the end of the book: "It is interesting to contemplate," wrote Mr. Darwin perhaps beside a warm fire in a clean well-lighted room, "a tangled bank, clothed with many plants of many kinds, with birds singing on the bushes, with various insects flitting about, and with worms crawling through the damp earth, and to reflect that these elaborately constructed forms, so different from each other, and dependent upon each other in so complex a manner, have all been produced by the laws acting around us. These laws, taken in the largest sense, being Growth with reproduction; inheritance which is almost implied by reproduction; Variability from the indirect and direct action of the conditions of life, and from use and disuse: a Ratio of Increase so high as to lead to a Struggle for Life, and as a consequence to Natural Selection, entailing Divergence of Character and the Extinction of less improved forms. Thus, from the war of nature, from famine and death, the most exalted object which we are capable of conceiving, namely, the production of the higher animals, directly follows. There is grandeur in this view of life with its several powers, having been originally breathed by the Creator into a few forms or into one; and that while this planet has gone circling on according to the fixed law of gravity, from so simple a beginning endless forms most beautiful and wonderful have been evolved."

Perhaps, Rome thought, the implications—moral, philosophical and religious, to say nothing of the uncatalogued biological, zoological, anthropological, and other scientific details—may have awed Mr. Darwin as he wrote beside the fire. Perhaps he was appalled by the fathomlessness of what lay beneath his own words on the one hand and invited and charmed on the other by the same quality, which would draw him into more rapt examinations of the wings, gills, vertebrae, vestigial parts of the elaborately constructed forms of the earth and hold always before him the imperative and enchanting *ignis fatuus* which a man must pursue through the swamps of ignorance, if his life is to be anything more than a sluggish nightmare with never a waking moment. What a storehouse of varicolored wings, what a waving company front of fronded antennae and palpi, what neat rings in that arachnid!

Rome wished that instead of tramping from one part of the great North American Continent to another, instead of having followed a vague desire for something, of the name of which, of the shape and color of which he knew positively nothing at all, he had been able to direct his faculties, as Mr. Darwin had done, toward scratching the surface, toward some work of penetration or discovery which would remain to astonish himself with wonder to the end of his days—and perhaps survive many years after his death to fill the eyes of all who could interpret its symbols with a light of wonder and lead them on toward the secret of life and the truth about all things. But Mr. Darwin's pen moved in tranquility and content: he had never viewed such a segment of the process of Natural Selection (indirect, it is true, Rome footnoted his thought) as occurred on the banks of the Tennessee River, April sixth and seventh, Eighteen Hundred and Sixty-two, among the higher animals.

Shiloh: The Civil War, which was to Rome ribbons of muddy river and a long, hot, muddy, dry, devastated strip of the South, filled with whiskers and malaria-tinted eyes in ranks, ending in scurvy behind a wooden stockade in a Georgia bog, was also Pittsburg Landing on the Tennessee river, the morning, day and night of April 6, 1862: a day of individual men seeking to survive in a concentrated destruction. But he could not long keep his mind on this quasi-scientific view

he had been led to take of Shiloh, for Shiloh had brought up the inward sight of Little Ream dying in his arms, of all the bloody men
lying pierced, broken and buffeted in the mud, of the horses he killed,
of the man in the Tennessee regiment who was told by his colonel to
get the battery of Napoleons, and all the violence which had brought
no benefit to anybody concerned (and many not concerned)—except
the doubtful benefits of obliteration to tired spirits, the problematical
partial re-fertilization of a few Tennessee cornfields and the salubrious
results of open air exercise upon the bodies of those soldiers who came
through the battle whole, the last perhaps being, in most cases, cancelled by the effects that so savage and heartless a metaphorical struggle
for existence as Shiloh must have had upon minds mostly young and
of very small compass at the time and without much experience of the
methods and instruments of the higher animals recorded upon them,
effects which must have been several, including: the planting of fear,
suspicion, disgust, bravado, cruelty, cunning and thousands of varia-
tions of these adjuncts to existence.

For Rome's own part, he had come to Shiloh—still one of the
bloodiest battles of the bloodsoaked earth—with what he believed to
be a mature opinion of war and its necessities. But Mexico had not
prepared him for the affair at Pittsburg Landing. True, he had seen
the Captain's jaw knocked off by the roundshot and the homeless
tongue wagging in the air; and he remembered the men, with their
coats open in the manner of scurvy Old Zack, shooting down Mexicans
who were unarmed and not even soldiers—and that without even so
much as taking the cheap seegars from their mouths. It had been a
cruel and dirty war, but all of it had nothing in it like the impact
with which the battle of Shiloh struck him. Now, in the August night,
his little pool of light around him, with the graygreen insects ticking
against the lampchimney and the open pages of his Darwin, he could
see the wildwhirl of the Army of Tennessee (perhaps because Grant
had inherited a fondness for liquor) on that damp April morning:
Frightened men running everywhere, camps, sibley tents, wagons,
mules (the dead one that was not freshly dead lying flycovered and
stinking near a card-scattered wooden pavilion, against which leaned
the dead infantryman with the bewildered look on his face), sutlers,
wagons, twisted men, tinware strewn in company streets, flags rippling
out torpidly in the breeze.

But now, fourteen years after, the dense details of this battlefield had melted into and become tightly entangled with the subsequent skirmishes, actions, movements and battles in which he had been engaged: Corinth, the investment of Vicksburg, an unnamed skirmish (with the aid of the Tenth Ohio Battery) at Messenger's Ferry on the Big Black river, the battle of Atlanta. Thirty-nine when he arrived at Pittsburg Landing, his mind was no longer a fresh tablet, for the recording of the images, pressures, tastes, sounds, smells that it had been when he had known Grant in Mexico. Yet even then, because of the early violence which he had known, such as the killing of his father by the Shawnees, the killing of Bull Tone and unnumbered fights with men, the elements and nature incarnated in such as rattlesnakes, buffalo, Canidae of various kinds, etc., his memory's accurate retention of the details had begun to be impaired. That is, he could not, for instance, be sure that the sequence of his mental images represented the sequence in which he had taken their impressors to him.

Now, by a sort of mental trickery, he could be almost sure that the muddy smokebound street, a minelike passage of sooty warehouse buildings through which he had marched with his regiment on a chill dark day, was near the flinty cobblestone levee in St. Louis in place and before the battle of Shiloh in time, inasmuch as he could recall no other city through which he had marched with his regiment while it was still, so to speak, a virgin regiment with no penetration of its ranks by minié balls, shot or shell. He could not remember any other day in his military life which had so depressed him with the damp chill weather, the mixture of soft coal smoke and fog in the stagnant air, the total indifference, the almost-contempt of the St. Louisans whom the regiment passed (on the way to the levee where the steamboat *Die Vernon* waited) and who waved not one handkerchief, gave voice to not one weak cheer, nor, indeed, even turned their heads (with the exception of a few heavy, perhaps German-brewer faces, seen for a moment through streaked windowpanes) aside to see the Iowa soldiers march to the river to embark on the steamboat voyage which was to take them to General U.S. (Unconditional Surrender) Grant's Army of Tennessee, which was to take them—and this, many years after, filled Rome with queer and obscure wonder about the ways in which men go toward their dooms and the relations of chance and doom— and almost literally set them down in one of the most terrible battles of the earth.

Besides these fixed points of memory, labeled: March 28, 1862, embarked St. Louis; April 6, 1862, arrived Pittsburg Landing, Rome could embellish memory with fading ocular, auditory, olfactory, tactual and lingual impressions. He could elaborate the trip on the Mississippi and Tennessee rivers with the taste of raw sowbelly, soggy hardtack and muddy insipid riverwater, and the sweatsmell of a thousand none-too-clean men—the smell of a mob or a beast.

Aside from these few mental records which he was able to place in a proper, if loose, sequence along with some of their trappings, he was unable to arrange the notes which his mind had taken except in a way which he considered unreliable. Sitting in the pool of light, the graygreen bugs catching in his graying beard, assailing his ears with their small foreboding and annoying whirr, his eyes glazed with the effort of remembering, and his thoughts fugitive and fast—a circumstance which worried him—turned to the act of remembering itself:

He considered how a muddybooted foot brought up and placed on a gray, cracked wagontongue, or a grease-ringed wheelhub could call up the vision of his brother Lucius stopping a wagon on a Kentucky road to pass the time of day with the driver. He could see Loosh, easy and graceful, as he set the stock of his rifle on the ground and brought up the foot; he could hear him say: Well, Eph, or Newt, or Jim, how air you? and hear the man answer: Tol'ble, or peart, or that he had the misery in his back or an ague. He considered how the sight of his brighteyed grandchild, Nora, lying in her crib and her chirpings as she lay there could bring up the walking, moving pictures of Little Ream—not as he had seen him alive for the last time at Shiloh in the loghouse hospital on the landing, nor as he had seen him cold and stiff with a crust of dried blood around his lips the next day, before he and Wagnal laid him in the too-shallow and now totally unmarked and forever lost grave—but as he had been in Kentucky as a boy, hopping along beside Rome asking questions and taking the answers as infallible just because they came from the lips of the brother he worshipped. The dead Remus Hanks, the sixfoot piece of stiff meat and bone with the eyes open in an idiotic stare, the sacred brother-corpse, which Mr. Simpson, chaplain-surgeon of the Hundred and Seventeenth Iowa Volunteers, had saved for him, Romulus Lycurgus Hanks, the grieving brother, he sometimes remembered when he saw a wet shallow hole in the ground, or a bayonet above a mantelpiece or in a lumber-room, or a tincup—for he and Thomas Wagnal had dug his brother's

grave with a bayonet and tincup; or, again, he remembered that dead
Ream of Shiloh when he encountered the sweetsick smell of unburied
dead flesh: some settler, leaving his claim near Elgin, had killed a
broken-legged horse and left it lying in a field; or a suspected horsethief
had been hanged and left to hang in the sun; or fresh bodies had been
placed in the trees of the Indian burial places. Then Rome's olfactory
nerve would send the overpowering sweetodor message to his brain
and again he would be in the muddy camp, days after the battle, when
the spring sun and air had begun the decomposition of the shallow-
buried and unburied dead, wondering if the rain had washed the soil
away from his brother (which, even then, a few days after the burial,
he was beginning to think of as the childbody which had trotted beside
him), as it had from the bodies of many soldiers—for Rome had seen
arms protruding from the earth, arms protruding from puddles like
travesties on the legend of arm which took the sword of Arthur, whole
bodies with gas-inflated bellies sighing as the gas broke away as if the
men were in some strange extra throe of death. And then he saw himself over and over again squatting under an oak jabbing the ground
with a bayonet, throwing the earth aside with a tincup—working fast,
for, though he was not sentimental about the useless inanimate body,
he could not bear the thought of what was once Little Ream being
trampled by a mob of wild campers-out with guns—in 1862, still very
little more than a mob of heedless boys on a lark, led by ambitious,
snide, cunning, cruel, drunken, brave, obsessed, arrogant, opportunist
men. To be trampled by such a mob would, somehow, he believed,
have robbed little Ream of his youth in Kentucky, of the dignity he had
had as a child—and, indeed, oh indeed, Rome said to himself, he was
my brother.

For that matter Lucius and Granville were his brothers too, but
between them and him there had been nothing but the common feeling
between men who know the look of the hide, the superficial habits,
opinions and methods of each other and hence know, within certain
limits, how each will react to certain stimuli. Between him and Ream
the understanding and sympathy had been deeper: While each was
unique, not as every man is unique, at least in the whorls of his fingertips—a poor distinction which is the only one that penology gives joy-
fully to those wretches who come within its corrective clutch—but as
men who do not go about the petty businesses of life only to keep, if
possible, their pulses beating tranquilly and their little affairs going on

from day to day in the groove that is within their ken, and, therefore, as undisturbing as a blank blue sky—as men who consider too curiously for the Horatio in all their kind. So he had had in Little Ream one who was twice a brother, one born of the same mother and infected with the same wish to look beyond the blank blue sky for something which would dazzle and confound those who were nothing more than pulsebeats in quickmeat.

Yet Rome wished that Ream had not conceived such a worship for him that it had led the boy to Shiloh and his death. The thought of Ream joining a Union regiment in Kentucky, because he had heard that his brother, his god and his mentor, was a Union man, warmed Rome's heart, but it also reminded him that he had led little Ream into folly and brought him to a fruitless death in a dingy loghouse on the banks of the Tennessee river where whole men were being subtracted into cripples because they had heard a band play or a judge or a senator shouting about a glorious cause from a rostrum or a platform under a bright flag—words which could never materialize, words which had never meant anything at all to men like Ream and him, Rome, but that they had been duped again by the ambitious who had stood to gain by rattling the sword but never girding it on. I killed my brother.

There in the corner by his bookcase he saw, as his eyes lost their remembering-glaze and fixed on the objects in his own time and space, his sword, scabbarded in scratched and tarnished brass, its pommel surmounted with an eagle, its hilt covered with sharkskin, its blade signed, P. D. Moll, Solingen. He had carried it in two wars: In 1846 he had cut a Mexican in the neck with it—at Shiloh he had beat the frightened driver away from the horse. Outside of these actions, it had come out of its scabbard only for drills, parades, and to cut the air. Now it would come out no more at all. He laid down the Darwin on the table beside the smoky, bugstained lamp, reached over and picked up the weapon. He pulled hard, the blade gritted and came, as if reluctantly from the scabbard. On the "Moll" there was a dark, rusty stain, which his son, Ream, when very young, had insisted eagerly was blood. Rome had said that it could not be. And when the boy looked disappointed and disillusioned, he was sorry both because of the boy's disappointment and because of the eagerness of youth to revel in and enact in imagination all bloody strife. Why, Rome thought, are strife and bloodshed things which man is born to love? Why? Could there not

have been some other way to puff and strut? Maybe if women were
not watching—

A somewhere-known footstep was coming toward the house. Rome
picked up the bugstained lamp and walked toward the door, the sword
still in his hand, forgotten.

CHAPTER XXXVII

CLINT saw the face, Wagnal said, and the beard—the eyes straining
from the sockethollows into the dark behind the mill scrollwork of the
screendoor. The little bugs were jumping around the lampchimney.
God, Clint thought, he's been a long way since Georgia. Good evening,
sir, Rome's voice said slowly. Come in. Then maybe he saw the door
was hooked and absentmindedly lifted the hook out of the screweye
with the sword. Clint looked curiously at the sword and stepped inside
the lightcircle in the hall. He's ready all right—he knew I was coming.
The beard's irongray and dead, the shoulders are down—and he's thin
as a racer.

Good evening, Clint said. Good evening, Rome. Why, Rome said,
it's Clint—Clint Belton. I was reading. Come in and sit down—I must
have picked up this old toadsticker— Rome shook his head to ward off
the little bugs from the thickhot nightair around his beard and ears.
Good evening, Clint said again. I was out this way on a trip—and I
thought I'd drop in on you. Yes, Clint, Rome said. I'm glad to see you.
The little stifling sirocco swished and a cicada burred outside in the
browngrass. Sit down, Clint, Rome said. I was just thinking of the day
we marched through St. Louis to the levee—the day we started for
Pittsburg Landing. Ah, yes, Clint said. The Landing. He looked
down. It hasn't been so long, Rome said. Fourteen years, but it seems
like a century. I was thinking of Wagnal—and—Shuball York and that
Bates boy. Ah, Clint said. And that boy who pulled his teeth.

Well, Clint said, I've come to stop your thinking too hard, Hanks.
You think you're going to hold that one minute over me the rest of
your life as you've done for the last fourteen years. He had the revolver
out—maybe it was still the same one he had shot the Louisiana Grays'
lieutenant and Bates with—and cocked. What one minute? Rome said.
You know, under the bluff. I lost my nerve for a minute—any man's

liable to do it. You have yourself—but you weren't caught at it. You knew that, Hanks, and held it over me all down the years. If it hadn't been for you, I would have been a brigadier before Atlanta. If you hadn't written those letters to Stanton, I'd have been a major-general —maybe a lieutenant general before the war ended. Maybe, I'd have been president.

What letters to Stanton? Rome said. I never wrote any letters to Stanton. You're mistaken, Clint. Look here, Hanks, Belton said, I was a lenient officer during the war—and I expected some intrigue in the army, especially as it was a volunteer army. For a long time I didn't believe it of you—I believed you were one of my loyal company officers. But not long ago, I began to see. You and Wagnal and Bates were as thick as thieves—and you and that toothless simpleton deserted at Atlanta. Now, Clint, Rome said, we were captured— That was your version of it—the boy hasn't shown up yet. He died in the prison pen at Andersonville. You *say* he did, Belton said. I say he *couldn't* die. Why, I shot at him at point blank range at fifteen feet and he didn't die. Your hand trembled, Rome said. I saw it. Oh, you did, eh? Belton said. Then why did you trust a murderer with ten thousand dollars? Well, Rome said, I was not sure until now that you were shooting at the boy. I was not ready to believe it of you—perhaps I was not ready to believe such a thing of man. Maybe you were shooting at him because you thought he was giving ground. Oh, hell, Hanks, you talk like Old Simpson or a woman from the Sanitary Commission. Perhaps, Rome said, I *did* believe it then, but I did not want to believe it. You began shooting at Bates before Corinth. You hit him twice: once on picket duty and once in the works at Atlanta. I know that now. Wagnal and I would not believe him then—and after Corinth he changed his mind. He would not believe that as brave a man as you—he saw you riding up and down the line drawing fire—would kill his own soldiers.

Well, Clint said, he found out what I'd do. Maybe, Rome said. He couldn't see behind him. Don't accuse me of cowardice, Hanks! I wasn't, Rome said. I said only that he couldn't see behind him. And you trusted me with ten thousand dollars—I always thought you were a hayseed and a fool, Hanks! What's wrong with you—had a call to preach Christ in the woods? You believe this business of turning the other cheek? Well, you won't be able to turn either cheek when I get through with you. Telling me I'm a coward! Why, I got a Congressional Medal—and a brevet major-generalship! I never called you a coward, Clint. I think you are a cruel and suspicious man who was ambitious once—and shrewd. Now, I think you are not well. I think you do not know what you are doing—you have lost your touch. I'll show you who's lost his touch. I should have shot you first and not bickered with you. I don't care to hear you praise your own virtue.

You are not shrewd any more, Clint, or you could have seen that I was far from praising my own virtue. I have not even learned how to deal with your suspicion—let alone your ambition and cruelty. I have not even learned to deal with what I find in my own mind. I do not know what virtue is. Well, Clint said, you'll find out damned soon what it's reward is. Waiting for me with a sword! How did you know I was coming? You're a great sneak, Hanks.

No, Rome said, if you mean in the Other World, I will not. You won't shoot me, Clint. You are still too selfish. Why should you? The bluff, young Bates's death at Atlanta—it's fourteen years now, and who would believe it? You might be elected president on the strength of the persecution. What would I gain? And the debt—you know I couldn't make you pay up. Why should you shoot me? It's not frugal.

You think I'm a coward, don't you? Clint said. I don't know what the word means, Rome said. Maybe it means bad bowels, or ignorance, or great learning. Why should I think you a coward when a thought can make me quail for days? Why should I think you a coward when I am so cowed by the vision of loneliness and boredom that I quiver all over my carcase when I lie beside my wife at night? What if she should die? What if all my children should go away? What could I do? Where would I live and how? Or what if I had had my head blown open and lived for hours like that Rebel boy at Shiloh? What, indeed, would I have done, if it had been my back and not my brother Remus's that was broken in 1862? What, above all, would I do if I did not wake from the dreams I have of lying again in the stockade at Andersonville? No, Clint, I do not know what cowardice is.

Why did I go with the regiment to Shiloh and Atlanta? Why did I follow you at the risk of my life? Was it because I believed that I must preserve the Union and free the black slaves? Was it because I was a brave man who believed in the Right? No, I had my eye on the main chance—oh, not so much as you—but I wanted the distinction and the spoils which come to a conquering hero just as you did. No, I was not humanity's hero—and you know how little we did for the blacks. I am afraid to think of what has happened since the Hero of Appomat-

:ox got into the White House. If this constitutes cowardice, then I am a coward. When I read Mr. Darwin's book, I thought we were getting better than the beast of prey—that everything was somehow arranged.

Maybe Clint went out while Rome was talking, Wagnal said, with the gun still in his hand hanging down loose at the side of his frock-coat. He walked through the meatbaking heat with the hotbreeze drying the coldsweat on his forehead trying to think what to do, where to go, who to shoot, why he had come to Kansas, why he had ever been born and gone to Harvard and come out to Ioway. He was trying to understand what Rome had said to him and to think why he hadn't shot Rome. He was thinking over everything from Shiloh to Atlanta: each shot he had fired, each scratch he had got, each awed look he had collected from the yokels who had seen him, say at Atlanta, pulling Colonel Lumpkin over the breastworks. He thought it all through and came to the telegraphers who came out of the stations to shake his hand. Well, he said to himself, they still think I'm all right—they still know me.

Crime was waiting, holding up the lantern, and for a moment, Clint saw him as he had been at Corinth that night: Not quite young, bucktoothed and stringy and servile—and slick as you please. Been doin' a bit of fowlin', sir? Bit dark, ain't it, sir? By the by, sir, you wished me to charge the men a certain amount for transporting their cabinets, sir? And, I think, sir, you said something about a slight remuneration for mine and the boy's services, sir? And thank you for the brandy, sir. Oh, I think we understand each other, sir. Clint halfraised the pistol and then put it in his pocket.

Oh Crime saw, all right, Wagnal said. But he didn't say anything —he just laughed softly. They got in the buggy and Clint felt tears rolling down his cheeks—but they weren't human tears. Go ahead Sergeant Fell, Clint said. That was his name, Fell—Herbert Gribble Fell.

> Up the close and doun the stair,
> But and ben with Burke and Hare.
> Burke's the butcher, Hare's the thief,
> Knox the boy that buys the beef.

That's it, Wagnal said. It was an old song.

CHAPTER XXXVIII

Rome would awaken again feeling the spent ball numb his knee at Corinth, or feeling the Raiders' clubs on him in the prison pen at Andersonville. Lorna would stir in her sleep, a coyote on the prairie would howl and Rome would turn over thinking—in the bleak Kansas night—of Clint Belton, wearing new buck gauntlets, riding up and down the line of battle on the cavalry hack in Mississippi, shouting at the men and drawing the fire of the crazy Texans.

Again and again now he would remember a time at Haines's Bluff or Atlanta when Clint had said: You, Hanks, form your company here! Rome knew now. You, Hanks. No Captain, no Mister, no Rome —and spoken in the voice a planter might have used to a Negro. And in the presence of the Iowa boys who had respected Rome for years. You, Hanks. Then Clint had smiled through his beard and lent his eyes an arrogant commanding look; and the light had caught the bright new colonel's birds perched on his shoulders.

Shuball York had looked at Rome for a moment with wide blue eyes. What'd he say, Mr. Hanks? What'd Colonel Belton say? Nothing, Shuball. Nothing of a personal nature—just a military command.

Just a military command. Yes, yes. Discipline well-maintained helps toward promotion. But, you, Hanks! was not a military command. And from Clint Belton: If I had not fed him in my house—if I had not watched him dandle Myra on his knee. If it had only been, you, Rome.

Those words were spoken in sixtythree or four, but Rome remembered them as clearly as he remembered Loosh's boot-toe on a cracked gray wagontongue, and Loosh saying: Californy, eh, Rome? As clearly as he remembered a thousands scraps of talk and scenes. You, Hanks.

He had been reassured the night Clint came into his tent and offered him and Wagnal the brandy bottle: I tell you, Rome, I get lonesome for our days in Iowa. How long have we been down in this Godforsaken miasmal country? Well, Rome, and you Thomas (to Wagnal) we'll build a metropolis in the west. And I've written to Washington about that majority of yours—and yours, Thomas.

He got to be Brigadier-General Clinton Belton at Atlanta. The Rebel colonel died of shame. And now Rome knew that it was not a slip of the tongue. It was, you, Hanks, that he meant. Hanks spoken cold and hard was the only way that Clinton Belton had ever thought of him. I've come to stop your thinking too hard, Hanks.

Shuball York had been sending him the Burlington papers for a long time—and now and again he got the New York *World* himself. Clint Belton was hardly ever in them now, but Rome remembered when he had married the elder Theron girl—it was before Thomas Wagnal had married the young one. The Burlington papers then were full of stories about Mrs. Clinton Belton's fifty pairs of shoes (or was it forty?), her Parisian ball gowns and negligees, her jewels and her coral parasol-handles. Worth, the Paris dressmaker, said the New York *World,* had fasted for seven days over her trousseau.

When the one with the piece about Clint's wife selling post-trader-ships came, Rome was sorry for Clint. Clint had set such store by show. And the Southern Belle: Rome knew what Una Theron (was it Una?) would be like: pretty, arrogant and heedless, incapable of affection for anything but power to bring her pomp and pride. Indeed, Rome thought, not as good as a Roman courtesan. *Only ten thousand, Rome.*

He had hidden the papers from Lorna and the children—on a ledge in the corncrib. (He wondered why he had ever saved them at all.) No use to hear them speak bitterly about the note that had turned their home into a prairie: That old General Clint Belton! If it wasn't for him we'da never had to leave Ioway! If I have my way, Beckham, you'll never go on anybody's old note. Now, Myra, honey—he's from Phila-deffy.

Rome had heard enough. He coughed; and his daughter looked up. Oh, Papa! Myra said with an ashamed look on her face. There, there, Myra, he said.

When Shuball York had come stumping along on the wooden leg he had bought cheap in St. Louis, Rome was sitting in the office of the livery stable reading Volney's *Ruins*, feeling as if it were just before supper and too early to eat and too late to do anything else. He had felt that way ever since, after Andersonville, he had got up from his sick bed and gone back to work—morning, noon and evening.

Well, Shuball? Rome said.

Mr. Hanks! Shuball said. Then he blurted irrelevantly: Shire New-ton finally got it. Four years—and then a strayshot at Bentonville. He shifted his wooden leg apologetically, hoping Mr. Hanks would say nothing about it.

Poor Shire, Rome said. I remember him at Pittsburg Landing with the flag. He was a fine boy.

Mr. Hanks—Shuball paused nervously.

Yes, Shuball.

You know, if it hadn't been for your company bein' infantry, I'd a been in the calvary. You know I'm good with hosses—

Yes, Shuball, Rome said. And I've lost a hostler—Worsham Jones left me. We old soldiers should stick together.

Rome put out his hand. Shuball took it. He couldn't say anything at all—and tears began to come. Rome smiled kindly.

I'll expect you tomorrow, Shuball.

But Shuball had not worked for him long—and yesterday Rome had got word from Ioway that he was dead. Now Rome had begun more and more to see the wide continent of North America spread out before his mind's eye in one great nocturnal panorama. It was empty of towns, except for a few such as the little ones of Knoxville, Iowa and Corinth, Mississippi. He saw it at night on the trail to California when the wagontrain had been corralled. He saw himself in a buckskin shirt, lying under a single blanket in a great waste place, feeling the wide band of his moneybelt on his belly underneath his clothes. He saw the continent all around him—and the wagontrain on the night that the loutish boy from Missouri had crept toward him with the English steel handaxe he had taken from the Indian he killed and scalped. Rome remembered how the Indian's axe had crunched into Davis's skull before the boy, Bull Tone, killed the Indian. Bull Tone had not even raised the axe over him, but Rome knew he was about to raise it, and he picked up the Walker six which lay cocked beside him and fired as the axe began to twitch. The flash was a pretty orange flame in the night—and for an instant, Rome saw the sandy soil and a bloody splash on Bull's face. Joe Chiles was standing over them with his musket and a lantern.

Joe saw the axe lying beside Bull's hand—and what was left of Bull's head. Calcallated to blame it on the injuns, heh? Joe said. Well, Hanks, I reckin it's fer the best. Bull had a natcherly acquisitive disposition.

Yes, sir, said a voice in the dark. And he was gittin' too God-damn' handy with that Hudson Bay Tommyhawk. Rome Hanks done right—nothin' more'n shootin' a rattler.

Bull was the first man he had killed since the Shawnees who got Pa. He remembered getting up from the ground and going to lie under another wagon while the others buried Bull some distance from the corral. He lay awake for a long time thinking about life and death and justice, and he was sorry he had shot Tone—sorry that he had not given him the moneybelt, sorry even that he had not lain still and taken the axe in his skull. For, he thought, not that it was a terrible thing to have taken a human life, but that by killing even such dangerous and destructive fellows as Bull Tone, he had helped set a money value on life. And the setting had been maybe a lowering. There had been a hundred and fifty dollars in gold in the belt. God knows, life was cheap enough. Rome felt insignificant and cold and unloved and hunted when he thought that his life was worth no more than a hundred and fifty dollars. He was tasting the milk of his foster-mother, the she-wolf, from whose dugs he was never weaned.

When he first read *The Origin of Species* in Knoxville, the year before the war, he began to think again of the man he had killed—and of how he had survived the Shawnees and Bull Tone's axe and Santa Anna's cannon.

One early spring night with the wind whistling and howling around the house, when he lay thinking of these things and of the bullets at Shiloh and Little Ream and Brother Loosh drawing a bead on him with his own gun, he knew that he had tempted death too long. He would die soon, not even having survived to the end of his life—with no one even to bother to set down his parting words. He thought of General Lee and Stonewall Jackson dying, both crying for Hill to come up,—though Lee had died in his bed long after the Army of Northern Virginia was scattered over the world. In a moment he was homesick for the Armies of Mexico and Tennessee, for the foolish *heart* remembers or forgets best. And Rome, in his house at the edge of the Kansas prairie, with his family around him, was as a man marooned in an icy waste of solitude.

Pa, said Ream's voice from the dark doorway. Them lambs in the pasture in this snow—

Yes, Ream, Rome said. I'm coming. You go along out to the barn and saddle up. I'll be right out.

Those lambs of course. Two days old. He swung his legs painfully to the floor, thinking of all his bivouacs on the earth—and how, now, even the warm bed did not rest him. He dressed feeling the rheum gather in his eyes.

In the kitchen he lighted the lantern; he saw the powdery flakes whirl and eddy in the edge of the dark. He saw Ream's light in the barn and a faint powder of snow already piling up on the branches of the pecan tree. Ring yipped a little.

The fold was not far. Two lambs were dead, but they brought four to the kitchen across their saddle pommels. Lorna and Hettie made beds for the half-frozen beasts beside the stove and gave them warm milk in a baby's bottle. When Rome got back to bed his teeth were chattering.

The next morning he had a fever. Lorna gave him brandy and quinine and put a mustard plaster on his breast. But he asked her to take it off.

Please let me be comfortable, Lorna, he said.

But Mr. Hanks—

I'll be all right, Mamma, he said.

Lorna did not like his tone. She called Ream into the kitchen: Saddle up and ride to Independence and bring Dr. Vögel back tonight—tonight, Ream. Do you hear me? Tell him your mother is worried about Mr. Hanks. Tell him that he knows I'd never bring him on a wild goose chase. Now hurry!

Why, Ma, Ream said, he ain't that bad, is he? A doctor?

Now, never you mind, Ream, she said. Just do as I tell you.

At one o'clock the next morning, Lorna saw the doctor's buggy lamps coming up the road by the snow weighted silverleaf maples and Lombardy poplars. She set the coffee on the stove and put more wood in the fire. He came in with heavy powdery snow on his shoulders and beard and eyebrows.

Vell, Mrs. Henks, Ream says dere iss someding amiss vit die Judge?

He went out last night in the snow after these lambs. He's got a fever now and he hasn't spoken right for several hours.

Such liddle fellows, the doctor said, looking at the lambs. Bitte, led us look at the Judge.

CHAPTER XXXIX

You AWAKE, Lee thought, in the vast night of all the years. You awake somewhere in the vast night: Everything is around you, all time forwards and backwards and all space. At night, in your bed, you see everything that has been or will be. And you awake at some place where you have never been, nor ever will be: You awake at Gaines's Mill, lying in the hot, blood-reddened swampweeds with Tom Beckham, or you awake with Robert Lee Harrington, carpenter's bound boy, as he leaves Gadkin county, North Carolina, on his way to make coffins in Abilene, or you awake with Romulus Lycurgus Hanks and General Ulysses S. Grant as they stand in the rain on the night of April 6, 1862 at Pittsburg Landing, Tennessee. Or you awake lying on your own deathbed in a body you do not know. And you cry out: How could I have known? I tell you, I didn't know! All right! All right, Goddamn it! I'll go back and look again and heed and look again and heed—

You awake at the corner on Mississippi street in Lawrence where you took your mother's slap to your bull's head, or with Sister Thérèse when your mother was dying as a little child, or standing in the street with Dee Given and Breezy Gortz and the three-speed bicycle, or out in Riverside, California, with Grandma Hanks in the underground passage in the Glenwood Mission Inn in 1910. You wake less loved and more bewildered.

An ambulance and a police car sirened in the great sandy dark perhaps going toward the beach; and Lee snapped on the bedlamp blinking as if he were batting his eyes a time or two. He lit a cigarette and lay frowning, speaking aloud in the cold damp air:

What demon drove me here? I might have stayed at home and pushed the Century camera around the pinefloor under the good north skylight; and photographed cavalrymen on *papier maché* chairs and babies and middleclass oldwives and farmers' family groups and gooching wedding parties—and golden wedding aniversaries. The celluloid collars, the necks like stovewood, the inflexible poker backs and the great brown hands—the leathernecked soilstupid women staring into the big Woolensak Optical Company portrait lens. Bat yer eyes a timer two. Now you folks just look natural. Watch the little birdie. But I would go where I have gone again, for there was no place for me there. Now I know there is no place for me anywhere.

And he thought tenderly of his tin sword rusted away in the ordure of the privy; and Grandpa Beckham coming home with *Hairbreadth Harry* under his arm in the snow; and Anne's furframed Desdemona face haloed around with incredible snowflakes; and Mamma combing her hair for a long time; and the twists of tobacco they were going to take with them on the trip; and the taste of the waffle Uncle Joe bought for him in the dusk of the Manayunk evening when he made the man blow his trumpet—and how Papa must have bent his poor shoulders over the coffins in Abilene; and of the girl who used to come to his rooms from Iffley village—and she came once when the Isis was frozen over for the first time in thirty years and God, how young and warm she was in bed with him. Her father was a major in the Indian army; and she wore fur mittens on a string around her neck like a child. And of how Papa never went to college but had had much to bear—and of how not all the scalding tears in the world were enough to shed for the homesickness which comes in the night, and for which there is no cure—no train, nor ship, nor any place to go.

Bat yer eyes a timertwo a-purpose, he heard his father saying back in the year of Nineteen and twelve perhaps—back under the good north skylight, standing on the plain pine floor of the operating room where the rubbertired rollers of the fine varnished welljoined Century camera stand ran. The camera which had a big lens marked Woolensak Optical Company with a black metal funnel on it for a shade. He could see the little smooth rolling wheels on the stand with its elevating gears and tilting devices in brass and the piece of heavy sawtoothed cardboard that Papa had made for a vignetting apron stuck in the frame which came with the camerastand.

He could see Papa coming out of the darkroom with his slightly bent-forward walk—a little harried, his Sunny Jim wisp of hair on his baldhead standing upright where the blackfelt focussing-cloth, which was attached to the Century camera with a curtain rod, had pulled it up. And he could see him put the wooden plateholder in the camera and slide down the amazing and seemingly intricate little polished wood slide which was made like the slide of a rolltop desk, only much better joined and slicker.

He could even hear the good sound of the wood parts of the camera as Papa—after turning off the little light at the little red cambric-blinded darkroom window—slid the newly loaded plateholder into the camera and rolled back the slide, revealing the yellow sensitive film of emulsion on the 5x7 Cramer Dry Plate, inside the dark compartment of the bellows, to wait for the impression of the Actinic rays of light on the face in front of it. Bat yer eyes a timertwo a-purpose, he heard Papa say again with the big openended rubber bulb in the hand with brownstained fingernails. Now, study! Papa would say. Don't look at the camery. Look just about over yonder—and think about somethin' nice. Click! he heard the shutter come open as Papa's strong hand, with the thumb over the hole in the end of the bulb, squeezed and held. Click! he heard the shutter inside the big brass-barreled Woolensak lens close as Papa took his thumb off the hole in the bulb and let his hand come loose. Now just sit still, Papa would say to his sitter. Just relax, and we'll git another negative to make sure.

Then, after Papa had said: You can see the proofs on Saturday, he would take up the plateholders impassively—if the sitter had not annoyed him by moving, or setting his teeth, or looking unhuman and not natural—and, turning on the light before the red window, would dive into the cool dark smell of the developer and acids. Or, if the sitter had annoyed him, he would shake his head slightly to one side and say: Daggone! Ten to one I'll have to make a resitting, and dive into the darkroom with an air of disgust for all mammals who moved or looked unhuman while being photographed. They saw some pictureshow actor looking that way, he would say.

As Lee lay squinting in the night, this series of pictures of Papa—almost as if he, Lee, were a Cramer Dry Plate multi-exposed—passed in his mind quickly, not flat as on a screen, but deeper and sharper than life, as are the braces of photographs mounted on a card and looked at parallactically through a stereoscope. Now, in the midnight moment of a Los Angeles room, his heart strained to go back to the operating room of Nineteen and Twelve in Fork City. He wished to be as he was then, a boy hiding behind a painted background, watching his father make a picture of Mrs. Hickenlooper, the musicteacher, in a high lace collar with the diamond prize medal from Vienna at her throat, or General Joffray with goldbraid under his gold epaulettes and a long trailing cavalry moustache. He wished to be as he was then, forgetting the wretchedness of the bloody lung, the dull ogre of school, the faces of the boys he hated, and the terror of the words that Mamma could say, and the places on the street and in the house which it was a torture of fear for him to pass—and how you would go blind if you played with yourself.

If he could go back now and know that all the rat's litter of things which had happened would happen, would he be here in a shabby Los Angeles room, with the grime of Experience rubbed into him so that he felt dull and dirty? The packrat, Experience, he said aloud. It drags in putrefactive corpse-fragments. The camera of experience bats its lens a timertwo.

CHAPTER XL

DR. VÖGEL, Ma's homeopathy doctor from Independence, called it pneumonia, but Myra never believed that he ever knew what it was. The little German wagged his head and clicked his heels and said it was pneumonia, but he didn't fool Myra at all. He didn't know what Papa had.

She sat by Papa's bed for twelve whole hours without ever closing her eyes once—and Papa never knew her. His eyes were open a good deal too; but he looked at her and didn't seem to know her or recognize her.

He kept saying things like: Ma, they got Pa—those Shawnees! and Hand me that rifle, Ream! and Of course, Clint, as much as you want, and Steady there, boys, hold your fire! and I'm sorry, Clint, you didn't deserve such a woman! and Sodom and Gomorrah! and Back! That's the deadline! and Buggery they call it in England! and Are they after you, Loosh? Where's Granny? Granny could ride, and Stay in front of me, Ream!

She listened to Papa saying those things, knowing that they were about the Civil war and the battle of Shiloh and General Clint Belton and Papa's brothers and something she didn't understand about that awful old Rebel prison at Andersonville, Georgia. She was seized by an almost unendurable tenderness for Papa and Papa's harsh hard life he had lived. She remembered how she had cried when she first saw the one-room house Papa had built here in Kansas, and she cried again for shame that she had caused Papa so much pain by her tears. And that letter she had written to Papa about the Rebels when he was down in Mississippi—she was so ashamed of that. Why, his two brothers, Loosh and Granny were Rebels—and he'd just seen his brother, Little Remus, die.

She remembered how Harold Bates had talked about Papa back in Knoxville—and how everybody had thought Papa ought to have been elected Colonel of the Regiment. But that Old Man Shaw had been made colonel—and even that old Clint Belton had been made major and got to be colonel over Papa's head. Why, he was just no better than a thief!

There was a queer green light on the snow outside; and new flakes were swirling around in the wind. Papa was mumbling around in his delirium and saying: What was the matter today, Lieutenant Grant? Who in God's name was in command? And Dr. Vögel, who hadn't gone home at all, came in and said: Vell, Miss Hanks, you go ged some resd, yess?

But she wouldn't go away. When Papa died that night Beckham held her tight in his arms, and if he had let loose of her she would have broken open she cried so hard. For she guessed she had loved Papa better than any of them. And Ring cried in the barn. And it was awful because Papa hadn't even wakened up and recognized her before he died.

Mamma took it very quietly and asked Beckham to go to Independence to see Mr. Parkerson about the coffin. So Beckham cut off a stick to Papa's length and rode to Independence that night. She and Mamma and Hettie laid Papa out and closed his eyes and put flatirons on his feet so his legs wouldn't draw up out of shape. When he was washed and combed and everything he looked so nice—just like he was asleep and like he was a long time ago back in Knoxville before the war when he hadn't been in that old Andersonville prison. Not tired and worried. But while they were washing his face and combing his hair, Hettie said: I'm a-going to have Papa's Bible and his books and his war sword.

Why, Hettie Hanks! Myra said. How can you begin to talk that way about having Papa's things even before he's in his grave. And anyway, I'm going to have Papa's books and his sword. He always said I could.

Well, I never heard him say you could—I never heard him say anything about it at all! Hettie said.

Well, anyway, he did—himownself! Myra said. And besides Ream ought to have Papa's sword. He's Papa's own son; and a son has a right to his father's sword that he carried in two wars and at the battle of Shiloh and that Reverend Wagnal kep', all through when he was in Andersonville prison!

If she couldn't have the sword herself, Myra did not want Hettie to have it. Now that Papa was dead she was even jealous of his things.

Now, Hettie! Myra! Ma said. Stop it! Now, of all times! What if your Papa could hear you? And who knows but what he can! Be ashamed!

Ring howled and cried all night that night in the barn. Beckham and Mr. Parkerson and Reverend Reynal came in the morning with the coffin. Reverend Reynal prayed and preached and told about Papa being in the Mexican war and at the battle of Shiloh, where he acquitted himself with great valor, and the siege of Vicksburg, and in the cruel Rebel prison of Andersonville, Georgia—and fighting for our country's Glorious Cause against human slavery.

They took Papa's coffin to the little cemetery where there were a few settlers buried and some of John Brown's men and that big boy in the yellow scarf that Myra had fed that day. They took it in a spring wagon; and Mr. Parkerson drove. She went with Beckham and Mamma and Hettie in the buggy—and Ream rode Old Caesar.

When they let the coffin down with the ropes, it began to snow again; and Beckham and Reverend Reynal and Ream helped fill the grave. Ring got out of the barn and followed them, and Beckham had to carry him away from the grave and back home and tie him up. She and Beckham had to hold him in the buggy all the way back— and he bit Beckham.

By Jesus, Beckham said, I never hope to know a better man than Captain Hanks.

When they got home it was snowing hard; and they had to take Ring in the house, because Beckham was afraid he'd go back to Papa's grave and stay there and freeze to death. That was why they had to tie him up.

Those lambs in the kitchen started bleating so hard they finally had to shut Ring up in the cellar, though he was a shepherd dog.

Myra went out into the kitchen and looked at their silly wooly faces. Those nasty old lambs! she said. I wish I could just take the poker and beat them to death!

Beckham came into the kitchen and tried to put his arms around her, but she drew away.

CHAPTER XLI

BECKHAM doted on the child. From the first, when he said: She's her Papa's girl, you just bet your bottom dollar, she is! Myra could see that he would love Nora best. Somehow she thought maybe it was like it was with Papa and her. Papa had named Ream for the little brother he had loved so much back in Kentucky when he was a boy and who was killed in the battle of Shiloh—but he had loved Myra best just the same. She *knew* that.

Well, Nora was a lively little thing, just chirping like a cricket and grinning in her cradle and clucking at Beckham all the time—and from the very beginning happy to be anywhere and do anything with him. Not that she wasn't always a lively little bit of a thing, but she was just more than lively with Beckham. He used to swing her up on the pommel of the saddle and ride over to see Grandma Hanks with her. And he'd put her down on the ground and she'd try to wool old Ring around and get all dirty.

No wonder when she got sick Beckham went around with a wild look in his eyes and his beard not combed and flying. No wonder he didn't eat to do any good at all.

Beckham, she said, you've just got to eat your supper. You won't help that child any by starving yourself to death!

How's that? Beckham said, as if he hadn't heard a word she said. I said, you've got to eat, Beckham. Now, Myra, honey, don't you worry about me. I'll eat a-plenty.

Nora lay unconscious in the crib in the next room. Beckham got up and went in to look at her. He stood there beside her looking so helpless with his beard sticking out—looking as if he wanted to tear the sickness out of her and take it into him.

The child whimpered as if its heart would break while Beckham was standing there looking down at her. Myra saw him turn suddenly and tramp away from the side of the crib, his shoulders thrown back, his eyes as wild as the day he had knocked that old Sipperly into the middle of the street.

By God A'mighty, he said, not so awful loud, but as if he meant it a-plenty, I believe that Goddamned Dutchman would stand by and let the little thing die. By Jesus H. Christ, I've no use for a son of a bitch like that who calls himself a doctor!

Now Beckham, Myra said, don't excite yourself. You know that old swearing's not going to help the child a single bit.

By God, Myra, Beckham said more loudly, I'm not a-going to endure it any longer. I'm a-going to saddle up and fetch another doctor. Why, by Jesus H. Christ, I don't think that Dutchman could tell what was the matter with Captain Hanks, if he was to be hung fer it! Beckham's beard was sticking out, he was wagging a finger at Myra—and now he was shouting.

Beckham! Don't use sich language, Myra said. That ain't going to help the child any. And besides, Dr. Vögel's all right! Ma and Papa both swore by him themownselves! Myra said, forgetting that she didn't think Vögel ever knew what was wrong with Papa when he died.

Beckham stalked out of the room, his eyes burning wilder and wilder. Myra sobbed.

My, oh my! My, oh my! she said over and over to herself. It was the first time Beckham had talked to her that way. But he was excited about that child. And then, of course, when she really thought of what happened to Papa, she couldn't blame Beckham. He did love that child so. He loved Harry too. But when Nora was born, he said she was just boss in that bluff way of his and she's her Papa's girl and by the Gods, isn't she pretty? Beckham was so like a child himself at times, she couldn't even be jealous of him.

He got the saddle on one of the horses—the little one, Little Mac, because it was the first one he saw—and rode up to the door:

Myra, just you get me that derringer pistol! he said.

Now, Beckham! I'll do no sich a thing! Myra said. I know better than to let you have a gun the temper you're in.

Now, Myra, I want that pistol! Beckham said, the wildness set stubbornly in his eyes.

Well, I won't give it to you! I won't have you takin' a gun to any doctor—I just won't hear of it, Beckham!

Beckham had ridden off down the road swearing and mouthing. She could hear him above the sound of Little Mac's hooves.

She did not go to bed that night; and early in the morning when the pink light fell on Nora's crib, lighting up the flushed little face, the buggy wheels and hooves sounded on the dirtroad. She went to the door: Beckham was still riding Little Mac, who was drooping and lathered. And Dr. Vögel and another man were in the buggy and their horses were lathered too. Beckham's face was white and drawn, but calmer now—though his eyes still looked wild enough.

Oh, Beckham, Myra said in relief that he was home again—and that the doctor was all right.

The two doctors got down from the buggy and Beckham dismounted stiffly and led them into the house.

How is the child, Myra? Beckham said.

Well, Beckham, Myra began, but he paid no attention to her. The little German stroked his goatee and followed Beckham. The other, who carried a stovepipe hat in one hand and a black satchel in the other, followed Dr. Vögel.

It vill be bedder, Dr. Vögel said, if ve look at the child alone.

I'm a-going with you, Beckham said loudly.

They went in. And Myra could hear them talking in low tones and then Beckham's voice raised, saying:

By God A'mighty, by the gods, and by Jesus, my daughter won't die for want of anything I can get her if I have to get it at the point of a musket!

Then Myra heard the other doctor saying: Now, Mr. Beckham, I'm inclined to agree with Dr. Vögel's diagnosis in every respect. And he has prescribed all that he can for her. Why, sir, everything in the world that can be done—everything that medicine can do—is being done for your daughter. And you may rest—

But she'll live, won't she, Doc? Beckham said in a hoarse quiet voice.

With the care she is evidently getting, she'll have a good chance. But peritonitis is a very serious thing. You must be very careful, sir,—very careful. And keep her in bed and *quiet* for a long time.

Yess, Mr. Beckham, Vögel said, a long time. Doktor Templeton iss ride.

Myra, standing in the door, heard death in the sententious bedside tones of the doctors, saw Beckham's head drop forward a little and heard his voice break:

Ain't there anything we can do for her? Beckham said.

Just keep her quiet, Dr. Templeton said. She looks to be a good strong child.

Myra saw tears rolling down Beckham's cheeks.

Oh, Beckham, she said. Beckham!

Little Mac, the old pony, died that night.

In the spring God suddenly reminds you one day what summer is like in Kansas: You begin to feel the great hot suction of the sun pulling the water from the land and you think that here there are only two seasons, violent and sluggish. And then you think that there is only one, summer—and that all the earth is cracked, all the leaves dusty and curling, and all the grass graybrown. Flies sit sluggishly on warm stones in the sunshine, waves of heat come up from the ground at your face and you walk nervously but aimlessly believing that the next moment you will find a place that is cool—that the next instant you can just step out from under this tent of heat. But even in the shade there is nothing but an airless curtain of heat, a screen between the eye and reality. Every motion on the earth is not a motion but a sunwashed paralysis, a still life in baredry bones, like a wellcured skull, white on the desert. And then, in reality, summer comes.

Beckham rode over to Grandma Hanks's every day and brought back a gunnysack full of ice out of the icehouse on the pommel of his saddle. Myra cracked it and put it in a hot water bottle to lay on Nora's stomach. That and the pain pills was all that they could do for her.

Harry stayed at his grandmother's; and Myra and Beckham took turns watching beside Nora's crib through the hot nights. Beckham got thinner and thinner. Everytime Nora would whimper or smack her lips or stir a little in the night, he would lean over and put his hand on her forehead and say: There, honey, don't you fret. Your Papa's right here beside you. Then he would fill the waterbottle with fresh ice and tenderly put it back on her stomach.

Even on the nights that Myra watched, he got little sleep. For he would hear Nora whimper and would get up and come into the room as if he were a man hypnotized.

What's the matter, Mamma?

Nothing, Beckham. Nothing. The little thing just cried in her sleep like she does. You go back to bed—go back to bed, Papa.

Tom Beckham could not go back to bed. He paced about the house thinking now of the girl in Richmond after Gaines's Mill and now of Ramrod Jones with no eyes in the tobacco warehouse and the maggots in the eyesockets on Bell's Island and the maggots in his own thigh and now of how he and Brother Joe used to swim behind Pa's barge in Canal street. Why, by God! that little girl of his couldn't die. She just couldn't. Even if Captain Hanks, who'd lived through two wars, *was* cut off in his prime. By God, I've come a long way to get a wife and little daughter like Nora—and I'm not a-going to lose her.

Twice in a month, when Nora had whimpered more than usual, he went to Independence for Doctor Vögel, who looked at the swollen little belly and the thin arms and legs and muttered: Amasing! Amasing! Then turning to Beckham, he said: She iss doing vell, Herr—Mr. Beckham. She hass a goot chance.

Grandma Hanks rode over on Old Caesar several times a week with pies and preserves and broth; and Mrs. Stacy, the wife of the man Beckham kept store for, brought Myra everything she could think of. And Mr. Stacy tried to make Beckham stay away from the store altogether—when he saw how thin Beckham was getting.

One evening at suppertime, when Grandma Hanks was putting the victuals on the table and Tom and Myra were sitting in the hot dining-room trying to eat their suppers, two nuns came in to see the parents of the little girl who was so ill.

May we see her? Sister Magdalena said.

Yes, let us see her, Mrs. Beckham, Sister Thomasine said. We know a little about nursing.

Why, yes, ma'am, Myra said.

Why, yes indeed, Beckham said. She's a fine little girl—but she's just a pretty sick little girl!

I'm sure she's a fine little girl, Mr. Beckham, Sister Thomasine said.

Tom and Myra took them into the room where Nora lay in the crib; and Sister Thomasine said: My, what a lovely spiritual face, Sister Magdalena. It reminds me of the painting of Our Lady in Detroit. Now, Mr. and Mrs. Beckham, won't you go out and eat your supper and let us sit by your daughter's bedside for a little while?

Tom and Myra went back to the table.

Did you hear that, Myra? Tom said in a bluff, hearty whisper.

The Catholic sister said she had a lovely spiritual face. By Jesus Christ, that is a compliment from a Papist!

Sister Magdalena came out of the bedroom first and began talking about the weather and the drought; and then Grandma Hanks took her to the kitchen to show her some preserves she had put up. Tom got up from the table and walked to the bedroom door:

Sister Thomasine was kneeling beside Nora's crib with her beads in her hand. Tom saw her lips moving. He walked away and went silently out the front door. The late afternoon sun fell on the glazed leaves of a cottonwood tree; they were not moving at all. Nothing was moving. The sun stood, a great red ball, on the straight horizon.

Well, by God! Tom said to himself. She was a-praying for the child. He suddenly felt ashamed that he had brought that book, *The Jesuits in Our Homes,* with him from Philadelphia.

After that evening Sister Thomasine came three times a week to the house and prayed over Nora while Tom and Myra were having supper. She never knew that they knew she did it. Tom and Myra left her alone with Nora; and Sister Magdalena sat near the supper-table as if to stand guard. When Sister Thomasine came away from the child's crib, her full lips were wet, her blue eyepupils dilated and her white cheeks underlaid with a tinge of coral.

What lovely spiritual beauty! she said again and again, as if she were still praying. . .

One December day when a light snow was blowing around the rattling windowpanes, Myra came into the bedroom from the kitchen and heard the child Nora chirp Papa! from the crib.

My, my! she said and walked over to the cribside. She's calling for Beckham. She looked down—and there was a smile on the child's face as bright as a dollar! Well, Nora, honey, she said, you're all well!

Mamma! Want Papa! Nora said. She was thin, but her eyes were shining—not like with the fever—and she was smiling the same smile she had smiled six months ago. And she was talking!

Myra rushed to the door and who-whooed at Mrs. Stacy and asked her if she wouldn't send Billy over to the store to tell Beckham to come right home—that Nora was calling for him.

Is she worse, Mrs. Beckham? Mrs. Stacy said.

No, no, Myra said. She's ever so much better. She's well, but don't you let Billy tell Mr. Beckham. I want to surprise him. You know how he idolizes that child.

Well, that's just fine and dandy, Mrs. Beckham! Mrs. Stacy said. I'll do just as you say. And if Mr. Stacy isn't there, I'll have Billy tell Mr. Beckham to close the store!

Beckham came home without his overcoat or hat, his whiskers and his hair white with snowflakes. He was puffing when he burst through the door. He must have run all the way.

What's the trouble? What's the trouble, Mamma? he said, a deep frown on his face and darkness in his eyes.

Now, Beckham, Myra said, you didn't wear your coat and hat—and it's snowing and cold!

What's the matter with that child, Myra?

You go in there and look, Beckham, Myra said.

Tom was already leaning over the crib.

Papa! Nora said. Papa!

Well, you just bet your Papa's here! Tom said in his big bluff voice. Nora put her arms up to him, and Tom swung her up from the crib. She laughed and clucked happily, taking his beard in her hands.

She was a-calling for you, Papa, Myra said, smiling. I came in here a few minutes ago and she said, Papa, and smiled just as big as life!

Well, well, honey, Tom said tickling her chin with his beard, she knows who's her Papa's girl, don't she? You just bet she does.

Nora clucked and put her arms tight around Beckham's neck.

Mamma, Beckham said to Myra, his voice breaking a little, Mamma, I just knew she'd get well. She's got just lots of spirit in her like her Grandpa Hanks.

There, there, Beckham, Myra said. You mustn't tire the child. She's been too sick to be wooled around like that.

She don't care, does she, honey? Tom said, but he put the child down in the crib. Mamma, I'm a-going back to the store and get my hat and coat and ask Mr. Stacy for the rest of the day off.

When Beckham came back he had the biggest doll in the store for Nora and a little wagon for Harry, who was still at Grandma Hanks's house, and a lovely piece of silk for Myra. Myra cooked him chickenwings for supper; and they gave Nora a little bits of a piece of chickenmeat along with her broth and milk.

And when Sister Thomasine and Sister Magdalena came, Beckham whispered: We won't ever let on we don't think they done it, eh?

Myra smiled and said: No, we won't, Beckham.

And do you know what, Myra? I jist found out Doctor Vogel was a surgeon to a rigiment of Dutchmen in the Army of the Potomic!

CHAPTER XLII

THE years of weariness, cynicism and despair had begun to eat at the edges of Tom Beckham, the hotelkeeper. The money Mr. Stacy had lost in wildcat currency, the subsequent loss of Tom's job at the store, the proud building of the Beckham House, the death of Captain Hanks and the birth of Ellen, all long gone, nonetheless weighed upon Tom's back. He felt himself growing older and heavier. Three children —plenty of hostages to fortune. Things looked black.

He had once thought of going back to Philadelphia and trying to read law as his father had wanted him to do when he came back from the war, before he remembered that he had disregarded Pa's wishes by coming west, that he was older and that the malaria and dysentery—to say nothing of the ball—which he had picked up in the swamps around the Chickahominy and the James had done him no good. He didn't get anything from the government; and he and Myra had saved only about three hundred dollars. They didn't even own the little house in which they lived.

Beckham had written to Brother Joe back in Philadelphia and asked him to lend him some money, but before he got an answer, he got a letter from Joe saying that Pap had died and that Pap's estate in Philadelphia and in Lancashire would be divided between his children. So Tom had borrowed two hundred dollars from Ernie Stewart on the strength of that and had built the Beckham House. It was a flimsy frame building with about a dozen rooms for bullwhackers and drummers. Myra and a hired girl did most of the cooking—but Tom helped, for Ma had taught him and all his brothers to cook. He was pretty Goddamned proud of the Beckham House, especially the big red-lettered sign he had painted on it—and it began to get a reputation for good grub and clean comfortable beds too.

One day a drummer came along and put up at the hotel and sold Tom a tintype camera outfit. This was just after the Keland gallery had closed. The drummer was a gangling redfaced Irishman from Pennsyl-

vania who had been in the Army of the Potomac and could gas all
night about the battle of Gaines's Mill. When he found Tom had been
captured at Savage's Station, he let Tom tell him about the lice and
maggots on Belle Isle—and how he almost starved there. And then they
talked about Philadeffy and how there was space between the houses
and how the doorsteps were white—and about how Pennsylvania had
trees and was green, by Jesus.

Tom told the drummer that he was a Pennsylvania Dutchman, all
right, by Jesus, even if he did live way to hell and gone out here in
Kansas. And then Tom told him how Pa had died only a little
while ago back in Manayunk.

But mostly Tom liked the drummer, Flaherty, because he made
over Nora. Nora was now a pretty, plump little goldenhaired girl
with snapping brown eyes—and just her papa's girl. She looked archly
and flirtatiously at Flaherty.

Have you got a beau? the drummer said.

My Papa's my beau, Nora said smiling.

You just bet he is! Tom said.

And a fine, pretty girl she is too, Mr. Beckham, the drummer said,
opening one of his telescopic cases and taking out a pair of little white
shoes with tassels on them. See if these'll fit that dainty foot of yours,
Miss Beckham, he said.

Nora took off her little black shoes with scuffed toes and put the
new white kid shoes on laughing and chirping all the time.

What do you say to Mr. Flaherty, Nora, honey? Tom said.

Thank you, Mr. Flurry, Nora said and ran to show Mamma her
new white shoes.

My, oh my! Mamma said. Where *did* you get those new shoes?
If they just ain't the swelldom!

Mr. Flurry gave 'em to me, Nora said.

Well, well, he did? Mamma said. Now you just run and take them
off. We'll just have to save those shoes for *good*. They're real
pretty.

By that time, Flaherty was showing Tom some Brady and Tyson
Brothers photographs of Civil war scenes and the camera was as good
as sold to Tom.

When Mr. Flaherty left, Nora kissed him goodbye on the cheek.
But Mamma didn't like it very well because Papa had bought the
camera outfit.

Beckham, she said, I just don't know what you want to spend money on a picture takin' machine for. There ain't anybody around here that wants their faces taken. That other old picture-man had to move away.

Now don't you worry, Mamma, Beckham said. It'll pay for itself in no time.

Nora had lots of fun making mudpies and baking them in the sun and playing Mamma to her dolls Papa had got for her at Mr. Stacy's store—and to Ellen, her little sister. And the Indian who tried to buy Mamma from Grandpa Hanks for a whole herd of ponies and some squaws to boot came riding up to Papa's hotel one day on a pretty white and tan pony all painted up with red and blue and yellow paint. And the Indian was all painted up himself and had feathers and a blanket and buckskin pants and red rags braided in his hair— and some colored stick candy braided in his pony's mane.

Papa came out to meet him, but Nora and Ellen ran into the house shouting: Indians! and hid under the bed in Mamma's room.

Nora got out after a minute with her heart beating fast and peeked out of the window and saw Papa walk up to the Indian chief.

How d'ye do, Chief? Papa said, his head thrown back and his beard pointing at the chief.

How, the chief said holding up his hand. Takum horse picture, the chief added sullenly and kind of grandly.

You just bet we takum horse's picture, Papa said.

How much? the chief said.

That will be two dollars, Chief, Papa said, holding up two fingers.

Ugh, the chief said and nodded, yes.

Papa brought out his new camera and made the chief stand and hold the pony. Papa put his head under the black cloth and it was funny if Nora hadn't been a little bit scared of the chief still. The Indian had a tomahawk hanging at his belt and something that looked like hair, so Nora dived under the bed again.

Is he dawn? Ellen whispered.

No, Nora said. He's got a tommyhawk, but Papa's making his picture. My Papa's not afraid of any old Indian.

He's my Papa too, Ellen said out loud.

Nora dearly loved going to Grandma Hanks's. One day Uncle Ream drove over in the buggy and took her and Ellen and Brother

Harry, who was the oldest and quietest, Mamma said, over to Grandma's. It was a nice warm day toward the end of May and the tall Lombardy poplars were stirring just a little in a little breeze and the quince bushes and the silverleaf maples looked all green and silver and full of sap and beautiful. Nora just thought she would like to get out of the buggy and run along over the dirt and lie down in it and hug it up to her.

Brother Harry kept asking Uncle Ream if he could see Grandpa Hanks's sword that he carried in the war. And Uncle Ream said: Well, I don't know. Grandma's fixing to give you to them Osage Indians. She says they want a white papoose that'll take the war paint better when he grows up. They offered us a couple of mangy ponies, but Grandma said she didn't want to cheat the chief—so they could have you free.

I don't believe it, Uncle Ream, Harry said, and he threw back his head like Papa did, Nora thought—so much like Papa that she put her arm around his neck. But he shook it off a little bit roughly and looked at her with Papa's wild look in his eyes. She wanted to kiss him, he looked so much like Papa then—but she didn't dare, because he thought kissing was kind of silly.

She noticed that Ellen, who had black hair like Mamma's and was a little bits of a thing, was pouting jealously. Why, Ellen, she said, what's the matter? For she could understand how Ellen felt, being kind of left out of it. She put an arm around Ellen's neck, but Ellen turned away and moved over on the buggy seat, not saying a word.

Pretty soon Nora saw that Ellen's dark eyes were standing full of tears and that Ellen was trying not to blink her eyes, because if she did the tears would fall. And that made Nora sorrier for Ellen, because she could feel her little sister's stubborn pride.

They drove into Grandma Hanks's yard and Old Ring ran out to meet the buggy and stood barking at them a little. Ellen got so excited over seeing Ring again that she blinked her eyes and smiled and the tears spilled down her cheeks even while she was smiling at Ring. Nora took her handkerchief and quickly wiped Ellen's cheeks so Grandma Hanks wouldn't see and inquire what was the matter.

I can see Grandpa's sword, can't I Uncle Ream? Harry said and then added: Papa was in the war too, but he wasn't in the same company. He was with the Pennsylvania soldiers.

Grandma Hanks came out to the buggy and lifted Nora and Ellen down to the ground. So they came to see their grandma, did they? Well, I bet they smelled their grandma's cookies from way over there in Sedan. And Ring frisked a little and then went over and lay down under the pecan tree.

Cookies, Grandma? Ellen said.

Nora went and got Old Ring around the neck, and Ellen had him by the tail—and Ring was trying to lick Nora's hand and looking at her with a pair of eyes that were a little bloodshot and watery.

Harry went out to the barn with Uncle Ream to help him unhitch the horses—and Grandma said: Now, you kids come into the kitchen and wash your hands. Now, now! let Ring alone! You can worry the life out of the poor old dog later. Dinner's ready now and your grandma and your Aunt Hettie and Aunt Ellen don't like to be kept a-waiting. And besides it isn't mannerly for little girls to keep their grandma a-waiting.

Going to give Brother Harry to squaws, Ellen said.

To the squaws! Grandma said. Whoever heard of such a thing! Who's been telling you such a story?

Uncle Ream, Ellen said darkly.

Oh, Ellen, Nora said exasperated with Ellen's credulousness, you know Uncle Ream was a-fooling.

Well, that's what he said, Ellen said sullenly.

Now, Ellen! Nora said. You know Uncle Ream would never do any such a thing.

Ellen said nothing, but her dark eyes got a hot wet look in them again and her lower lip stuck out as if she were thinking about that bad place Papa talked about when he swore.

Come, come! Grandma said. You two git! Get in the house!

Aunt Hettie came to the screendoor of the kitchen and looked out. Hello, you kids! Aunt Hettie said. Hello, Ellen! Hello, Nora.

Nora knew that Aunt Hettie liked Ellen better, but she didn't care. Aunt Hettie was kind of pinched around the mouth and her face looked sharp like Grandma Hanks's—only Grandma Hanks's was like the face of some keeneyed bird, but Aunt Hettie's face was just sharp and cranky except when she looked at Ellen—and then it got kind of soft. Aunt Ellen was pretty and laughed a lot and had beaux and didn't pay much attention to them.

Auntie Hettie! Ellen said and took hold of Aunt Hettie's apron.

Aunt Hettie will sneak her an extra cookie later on when I'm not looking, Nora thought. But she didn't care. She squinted her eyes a little in the sun and looked at the stable and the orchard and gave Ring an extra pat. The sun just soaked into her fair skin and shone on her golden hair and she felt happy and warm and nice. And a little black hen walked proudly across the backyard and the sun shone purply on her feathers.

Look, she said to Grandma, the hen's like Mamma's and Ellen's hair. Ain't she beautiful? She smiled up at Grandma.

Yes, and like your Grandpa's, when he was a young man, Grandma said.

When is Grandpa coming back, Grandma? Nora said.

Grandma looked funny and said: Maybe not for a long long time.

They went into the kitchen and Nora washed Ellen's hands and face and then her own and Ellen grumbled.

Grandma had chicken for dinner, and it was good, and Nora took the neck, because even if the meat was hard to get off, it was *so* good and tender. And Aunt Ellen was pretty as could be and Grandma Hanks said: I do believe Nora looks like her Aunt Ellen more than she does her own mother. And Nora thought that was nice because Aunt Ellen was so pretty—but not any prettier than Mamma.

That afternoon she and Ellen took Ring and went up to the pasture. There was a big round wooden watering trough there, and when they got tired of trying to ride Ring, Nora said: Let's take off our shoes and stockings and go wading.

Oh, I don't know, Ellen said.

Oh, come on El! Nora said impatiently. One of her shoes was already untied. You make me sick!

Well, Ellen began indecisively to pull at the laces of her shoes. Nora had both hers off and her stockings too before Ellen had one shoe off.

My, you're helpless, Nora said in Myra's tone of voice, fussing at Ellen's shoes. *She* had them off in a jiffy.

Ring was sniffing disinterestedly at the pile of shoes and stockings, and they were climbing into the tank. It was deeper than Nora thought, and she didn't pull up her skirt quite quick enough. It got all wet, because the water was up above your knees. She grabbed Ellen's though, and made her hold it up out of the water. They both began screaming and splashing. Ellen was scared for a minute or two, because the water was up above her knees, but she forgot about that because it was so much fun and walked around the big tank with her sister. There were little wiggly tadpoles in the water and some green scum on the top and a water-skipper or two all purply.

Nora and Ellen tried to catch tadpoles and skippers and forgot to hold up their skirts and then it didn't matter any more, because they were all wet anyway. Trying to run in the water was funny, because it drew at your legs and you couldn't run fast at all—and it made your legs feel funny and heavy. After a while they began splashing water at each other and screaming because it was fun—except that Ellen had begun to look sullen.

Here, you little rascals! Git out of there! I suppose you want to drownd and have the tadpoles eat you up!

They hadn't heard Uncle Ream come up. He lifted them out of the tank and made them walk back to the house over the rough pebbly pasture in their bare feet.

CHAPTER XLIII

A NOTE of Mr. Stacy's which he had endorsed, the restiveness of Myra, who missed the illusion of permanence and respectability she had felt in her father's house, even in Kansas, and complained of the hardships and disadvantages of living in a little prairie town, and Tom's own needs to try once more to Make Good—a need to feel, see and hear some definite, perhaps mechanical, orgasm, indicated outside of him in the manner that a safetyvalve blowing a whistle on a steam engine indicates that a full head of steam is up—something which would say: Tom Beckham has Turned the Trick, He's Pulled It Off and is Now A Success, all forced him to make the next move.

The note which he had endorsed for Mr. Stacy, because Mr. Stacy had once been his employer and because Mr. Stacy was from Pennsylvania and had fought with a regiment of Pennsylvania Reserves, was for only two hundred dollars. It could have been paid by borrowing from Grandma Hanks—but Tom was unwilling to lay himself open to the years of nagging which he knew would follow such an admission. For had he not heard the thousand recriminatory references to that old Clint Belton, whose ingratitude and duplicity had come to be traditional in the minds of the Hanks women—had he not heard it now for enough years always to know when Myra would bring it up again? Any deal in money—whether it involved notes or not—in which even someone who was known to Myra only as a friend of one of her friends, a name only, perhaps with the most vague background of residence or none at all (Mrs. Lozer's great friend back in Illinois was done out of his property in just sich a way; or that man Mrs. Stacy's always talkin' about, back in Ohio, lost his money just the same—always foolish—way. You know, a fool and his money!), would be an occasion for Myra to refer to that old Clint Belton's ingratitude. And although Myra's father had escaped the ignominy of his daughter's baldly calling him a fool for being so soft as to be taken in—done—by such as that old Clint Belton, who, though he had several other titles such as Brevet Major-General and Mr. Secretary, was now never distinguished by Myra as anything but That Old, which meant that she did not approve of his principles, but granted him a womanly but unspoken admiration because of the successful acquisitiveness which had raised him to his position of wealth and power before he fell, he, Rome Hanks, did not escape his daughter's estimate that there had been something unaccountable and faulty in his character, to have allowed a falsefriend to beat him out of his home and business and force him to bring his family to the awful little one room house in this flat violent country.

Tom was aware of this residue of emotion in Myra, and, therefore, did not tell her of the note on which he had greatheartedly scrawled his name for Stacy, because he was remembering the days in Philadelphia when, as a corporal, he first put on his little blue Zouave's jacket, his baggy red trousers and his white gaiters—and not remembering that he had been promised a commission by a friend in another regiment but never got it.

Tom had no desire to hear, That Old man Stacy, the rest of his life, for he knew, without the need formally to admit it to himself, that Myra did not love him enough—as she had her father—to spare him the ignominy of letting him know that she considered him a fool and an easy mark, if she found out what he had done. Therefore, he allowed her to believe that her desire to be away from the tedious prairie town and his need to find something with a future had led him to make the decision to sell the hotel and move away from Sedan.

Flaherty, the Pennsylvania veteran, the drummer who had given Nora the little white shoes with tassels, had acquired some business property in Fork City, which was up toward the northeastern part of the state, a "thriving," if "rough" little town near Fort Davis, a cavalry post. Flaherty liked Tom and remembered the brightness of little Nora. He was lonesome for someone who could talk to him of Philadelphia. So he wrote Tom a letter and offered him the job of "head book-keeper" of the "enterprises" he had acquired: a "trade" in ice, a lumber-yard, a stockfarm and a small brewery.

Tom showed the letter to Myra, commenting that while it was no great shakes, it would give him a start and a chance to look around for something else—maybe an opportunity to go into business for him-self, keep hotel, or open a photograph gallery.

Well, Beckham, Myra said, I just don't know. That travelling man may be all right, but there's mighty few of 'em got any principles—

But he's an A number one man—and from Philadeffy too. Why, Myra, honey, you used to like him. He's just boss. He gave Nora that little pair of white shoes with the tossels!

Now lookee here, Beckham, there's no usea you jumping into some-thing that you may regret all your life. Just look at Papa and what that old Clint Belton done to him!

But Jesus H. Christ, Myra, I'm not a-going on Flaherty's note. Why, by God—

Ah! Ah! Myra said sharply. Beckham, why must you swear so?

I tell you, Myra, it's the best proposition a man could get. It's bully. It gives us a chance to get away from here and look around in new pastures.

Now lookee here, Beckham, neither you nor I know that man at all well! And that old Fork City! From what I hear it's wide open—soldiers and all sorts of things and (here Myra blushed and her voice equivocated) bad houses. We'd do better to stay here for a while until we get a real good chance.

Good God A'mighty! Tom shouted. Good God A'mighty, Myra! What, in the name of God, do you call a good chance? Why, by the gods, I came out into this country with ten dollars and a carpet sack. Why—

Now, Papa, Myra said, just control yourself and stop that old swear-ing. We've got the children to think of!

But, Mamma! Tom said in infinite exasperation and wonder at womankind. You've been waiting to get away from here for years!

Now, Beckham, Myra said, I have not! I only said I hated to leave home—Ioway. I don't want to go to any old soldier town.

A week later Myra was in the full fret of preparing to leave. She was telling Mrs. Prescott, the wife of the man to whom Tom had sold the Beckham House, what a nice place she'd heard Fork City was, and what a nice situation Mr. Beckham had with Mr. Flaherty, who came from Philadelphia where Mr. Beckham was born.

Mamma gave her fifty dollars. And she told Mamma and Sister Hettie and Sister Ellen and Brother Ream goodbye. Harry and Nora and little Ellen cried over leaving Ring and the pecan tree.

Thus, one spring morning in Eighteen eighty-one, Tom Beckham and Myra Hanks began their last important migration. Myra, looking back at the row of Lombardy poplars, the silver leaf maples—for they started from the Hanks farm—and at the pecan tree, the orchard which Papa had planted with his own hand, Old Ring and the Hanks house itself, which had grown from the horrid tear-bringing beginning of the one room shack to a bigger house than any in the county, forgot that it had been her desire to leave this lonely country for the vague social benefits of a town and again burst into tears, saying brokenly to Tom: My, oh my, Papa, I just hate to leave home!

For a moment, Tom, whom Myra had led to believe that her real home was Knoxville, Iowa, and that she was an urban soul who could not bear the life of the Kansas prairie, was amazed and confused. But only for a moment. For, looking back at the pecan tree and the poplars, he remembered the day that he had ridden into the yard of the Hanks house for the first time, which was the first time he had met Myra—a Myra of whom a part sat beside him now on the wagonseat— and how he had begun to love her that first day he had seen her. And these thoughts so touched him—perhaps in part because the Myra beside him was not the Myra Captain Hanks had introduced him to that day in sixty-nine, or perhaps because Captain Hanks himself was dead— that his throat muscles pulled taut and tears came into his eyes. But Myra did not see them, for she was too busy with her own.

At Sedan Tom did not even stop at the Beckham House, which was already in the possession of the Prescotts, for it was as much as he could do to look at the fine big red letters of his own name.

Nora, standing in the small empty space in the wagonbed, where the canvas cover was rolled back, her feet tingling through her shoes with the jiggle of the splintery board-bottom, her nostrils moving like a proud doe's in the cool air, smiled and shouted, pointed out rabbits, and the queer shapes of clouds and trees to Harry. Harry, being two years older, could not expose his dignity to her infantile enthusiasm; and Ellen, frightened by the unusual act of riding in a wagon with things which should have been in a house and envious of the enthusiasm which Nora seemed to have at instant command, sat sullenly on a tarpaulin covered roll of quilts and blankets, her lower lip protruding and her eyes glazed with the half-smothered tears of a misunderstood soul.

They were four and a half days on the journey, the last night of which, though they were but ten miles from Fork City, they chose to spend at a crossroads called Scrabbleton, a place with a general store, a hotel and a post office all in one frame building which already appeared old, though it had been built perhaps one year.

Here there was a boy of twelve, who, upon seeing Nora, stared and blushed heavily and began to talk importantly to himself or the thin air, outfaced and stunned by the quality of her beauty and her amazing golden hair and the little ring of woven golden wire (like her hair braided into a tiny band), which, being a present from Papa on the night before they left Grandma Hanks's, she wore on the heart finger of her left hand.

The boy was up early in the morning to see Nora off, and, though he hardly said a word to her, Nora could see that he liked her—so she smiled and waved goodbye to him. Thus, all through her life, there stayed in her memory, the animated picture of a boy of twelve, dressed in long pants thrust into boots, a shirt with a hard collar and a little black cowboy style felt hat, jumping up and down and waving, the foreground of which was a crossed white sign, which said: R. R. Crossing; Look Out For The Cars.

CHAPTER XLIV

A LITTLE station on the plains is something that the mind can grasp, Lee thought. Fork City, Sea Level 987 Ft.

On a sunny day with the gravel shining in points and the engine chuffing as the train pulled up and a car or two waiting and the town above say on a Sunday lying quiet and in the sun just under the rimrock of the little valley.

In the World there are many things: Mother's hairpins, the *Works of E. P. Roe* in the bookcase, the oak newel post on the stairrail at home, the harpwoman on the door, another like her at Anne's house in Lawrence, prisons, whores, almanacs, old letters, corners of rooms, sabretaches worn by the Officers of Crack Russian Regiments, copies of *Uncle Vanya* and *The Cherry Orchard,* the selfsame single stones in old buildings (say the Parthenon) that have been there for thousands of years and seen thousands of people doing thousands of things.

But a little station on the plains is something that the mind can grasp. It is a little gravel island in time, neat, with goldenpoints of Green River, Wyoming, gravel (gold content $1.25 per ton) in the sun where the train chuffs and steams and stopping, strains.

Nothing is beyond the station. Even Mamma, waiting in the old car, now getting out of it—even Mamma, holding her head proudly and smiling—does not exist, except as a painted figure in a sun-bemused landscape.

And all the nightmare-sea of what has happened and when and where and how and why is now a pleasant lake without a ripple on the surface: The Emperor at Waterloo and Wellington at Windsor when he was an Etonboy eating strawberry messes and those shops in Brussels with steel engravings of cavalry in shakos and the shakos themselves and all kinds of swords and even hussars' jackets with only one sleeve for wearing picked up there they said out there on the field lost, pillaged: 1815. Lord Byron. And even Mamma's tobacco samples and the houses in Lawrence and Quantrill's Raid and the scars on the houses he left and even now there must be guns he used in the houses. But a little station on the plains is something that the mind can grasp.

Inside the roundbellied stove and the clicketyclick of the telegraph instruments in the flyspecked wooden hoods and the racks of flyspecked tickets that lead you out into the Great World where the things you think about really happen and Mr. Wally Hughes with the green celluloid eyeshade around the slick baldhead and everything tranquil and lazy and the sun falling on the brass of the telegraph keys and the old Oliver Visible Typewriter and the most interesting gum and chocolate machine that doesn't work and the drinking fountain. Union Pacific. Fork City. The Overland Route. Elevation 987 Ft. Above Sea Level. Denver 487 Mi.

But you never go to the station unless you're going away and then as soon as you get to the station the station is an island again and the town is no longer there with all the castiron hydrants in the backyards of the Oldsoldiers who were in the Civil War you don't look back but look at the train and smell the train and feel the plush on the seats and look at the bugs in the lightglobes and wonder about the girl across the aisle and look at the shine on the conductor's blue serge coat and the leather binding around his punchpocket and you begin to go away from what the mind can grasp as you see Mamma standing with tears in her eyes beside the track the gravel pointing up beside her in the sun and the train puts out toward the plains and desert or the hills and mountains or just toward the Great East with a capital E where everything is more confusing than thought and History waits or crouches ready to spring.

So suddenly but without shock you see yourself riding the bicycle Papa bought for you after you came back from California sick to the Death and the Negro helping you to ride in the sun and Dee Given and Breezy Gortz standing in the street asking for a ride and the maple trees in the frontyard all tranquilly you think of these and of Grandma's house and Grandpa coming home in the snow and of Anne in the snow saying it's so crisp and of the buffalo ranging the plains in the early day and coming to scratch at the streetlamps on Pawnee Street and of the West You Never Won with a Colt's singleaction revolver.

And who in God's name Won the West anyway and for whom and for what did they win it was it James Butler Hickok and the Railroad up at Abilene was it Buffalo Bill's Wild West show was it General George A. Custer and the Seventh or was it Grandpa Hanks and the Hundred and Seventeenth Iowa Ninety-seventh Pennsylvania Eighty-sixth North Carolina all present or accounted for sir we're only half-strength like Rebel whiskey All's Quiet on the Potomac Everything's Peaceful at the Bloody Angle the High Watermark of the Confederacy's recorded in *The War of the Rebellion Official Records of the Union and Confederate Armies* in seventy volumes, one hundred and twenty-eight books, 138,579 pages, 1,006 maps and sketches in the Atlas, edited by Lieutenant-Colonel Robert N. Scott, Colonel H. M. Lazelle, etc. and published at a cost of $2,858,514.67 and now in company front on the shelves with Napoleon's Campaigns and Early Americana.

Everything's neat now. A little station on the plains is something that the mind can grasp.

Fork City lies in the great Free State once known as Bleeding Kansas, an epithet, it is said, which was misunderstood by a strayed and

lonely Cockney, who, in the eighteen-fifties, found himself set down
from a bruising stage ride in a treeless, homeless prairie and told by a
laconic driver that this dusty horizon of grass was Athens, Carthage,
Troy, New London, or whatever inflated label the real estate agent had
whimsically printed in the Town Company's Brochure, which also contained a steelengraving of a Little Jewel of a City—A Very Utopia—in
full blast, complete with steamboats on a limpid river, great ladies
smartly turned out for church, city parks, amusement centers, tree-
arcaded Residential Streets, school buildings being entered by happy
children, happy men going about their daily business in avenues where
not a bawdyhouse or doggery was visible, but only everything to make
the place A Settler's Dream.

Bleeding Kansas, the Cockney said sadly. Suits the 'orrid plice—it
bloody well does. And that bit of a picture cost me two shillin's and
bloody sixpence! But the legend tells that the Englishman stayed and
founded his own town, which became in time as bustling as a Cockney
shopkeeper. From that legend, perhaps, grew the other that Fork City
—although the country in which it lies could not be called prairie, could
not be called prairie but in the wildest perjury—was founded by an
Oxonian, who wished to retire from the Great World and build an
unspoiled community on the frontier. Now, however, both the Cockney
and the Oxonian are nothing more than words in the mouths of a few
of the Oldest Settlers—and even the realities are so nearly forgotten and
obscured by time and wishes that the origins of the town are shrouded
in the mysterious opacity of dates and pompous sentences illspoken in
Memorial Addresses and published in Historical Collections.

On the day when we see the covered wagon of the Beckham family
nearing the Town which had seemed to Myra Hanks to be so desirable
in contrast to the Trading Station community where she and Thomas
Beckham had had their Young Love and married, the Town was still
the county seat of Breckinridge county—a name which had been
allowed to stay on the map through inertia and ignorance, for it was
that of a Pro-Slavery Vice-President of the United States and as blackhearted a Secessionist Brigadier as ever mounted an overbred hunter
and delivered himself of sententious speeches about Chivalry and the
Noble Cause, before he led his men to the Very Cannon Mouth. To
aid in transforming him from an abstraction with plumes, horsepistols,
firegilt buttons, goldbraid galons and the Noble Eagle Light of the

Confederate General's Eye to something near a man, perhaps it would be well to say that he rode over the muddy roads and through the cold, spring rain to Shiloh before Romulus Lycurgus Hanks, with his bunch of raw Iowa boys, arrived there on the Steamboat *Die Vernon*—and that he, Breckinridge, was doubtless within a mile of Rome himself on the battlefield of Shiloh. But nobody knew anything about this in Fork City, even in Eighteen eighty-one; and the town was still a satellite of Fort Davis, named for—so help us God—Jefferson Davis, the President of the Confederacy, himself. Fork City is the Whore of the Plains— the Troopers' Trollop!

Thus, in a state whose counties bristled with such Union names as Grant, Rawlins, Sherman, Sheridan, Meade, Thomas, Wallace, Sumner, McPherson, Sedgwick, Butler and even Lincoln, Fork City remained the seat of Breckinridge county and the satellite of Fort Davis. How then was this possible?

Perhaps many of those men who came to Kansas with Sharp's rifles and copies of the New York *Tribune* in their pockets and loud protests against Human Slavery upon their lips to help Old Osawatomie Brown free the Black Man, came only because they were younger sons from New England (where paupers were auctioned off) with no inheritance, or opportunist young men from anywhere who needed a Cause, or cynics of any age who saw wealth was to be gained in this new territory.

In the archives of Fork City there is a memoir by Major (Forty-seventh Kansas Cavalry) Albert H. Prentiss, who came to Kansas from Massachusetts in 1854, teaching at points along the way to gain enough money for the journey. In Knoxville, Iowa, Albert, a tall bleak boy who already had a lean cadaverous jaw, and, who, even then, had the hard polishedup look of avarice and rapacity on his eye, scraped up an acquaintance with a little man, one James Forster, of electric energy and gimleteyes, who was about to run a consignment of Sharp's rifles and a Napoleon gun into Kansas for the Free Soilers.

They met in a barbershop—it must have been not far from Lieutenant Romulus L. Hanks's (late of the Mexican war) livery stable— and talked cautiously of the Great Cause they would be furthering by the fletching in of these arms, most of which were later sold to Pro-slavery men, negro-stealing syndicates which preyed on the passengers of the Underground Railroad, and horsethieves, though these facts are omitted from the memoir, no doubt because of Considerations of Space. Looking at each other from eyes narrowed by cunning, they praised their mutual Mission against Slavery. Major Prentiss later wrote in his memoir of how he had said to his mother: I feel, Mother, that I must go to the Kansas Territory. I cannot bear to see those noble Free State people overrun by the Border Ruffians. Perhaps he quoted this speech to little gimleteyes in the Iowa barbershop; perhaps little gimleteyes matched him in kind.

Whatever followed, they began to understand each other, and when the Forster wagontrain crossed the Skunk river on the Lane trail the next day, Albert Prentiss was walking along beside one of the wagons on long rubbery legs. All the way to the fork of the Smoky and Shejaw rivers, Prentiss and Forster watched each other stealthily, for each was armed, and the caravan—considering the time and place—was worth a good deal of money.

It was this trip which made them feel at one. Both having survived a trek on which a man might have died in any number of ways without a soul to blame, they came to respect each other's cunning—and besides to feel such warmth as each was able for each other, because of the tribulations which they had endured together while crossing the plains.

It was the Forster & Prentiss Mercantile & Grain Company & 'Army Sutlers who were the prime movers in securing a town charter for Fork City in the year Eighteen sixty. And it was Albert Prentiss who became president and James Forster who became vice-president of the First State Bank of Fork City in Eighteen sixty-one. Experts on mortgage law, they owned a good slice of the property along Pawnee street and a fine parcel of bottom land farms. They are almost forgotten now, but there was a day when the town was theirs. Their influence was still heavy in Eighteen eighty-one.

Nora looked at this camp at the edge of the plains, this no-town, this microcosm of an American city as Papa drove the wagon down Pawnee street from the south: Houses began to appear, small square frame houses with chimneys in the middle of the roofs, stiff twostory stone houses with stiff porches, big frame houses built like logcabins (or Nora's own drawings of houses), frame houses built with cupolas, gables, scrollwork, tin combs and cockades on the roofs, a stone house or two built with ungainly towers and perhaps picture-windows. There were white wooden picketfences and here and there an iron fence and perhaps an iron effigy of a little negro or a little man or dog holding out a ring in which to tie a horse.

It was spring, and where the lawns weren't cut well, fringes of weeds and sunflowers stood rank and green at the edges of yards, sometimes almost hiding the effigies and the ordinary castiron hitching-posts, sometimes bursting up through the sidewalks of limestone slabs or wood and the dried mudruts in the streets.

There were often not over two or three houses in each block—and sometimes only one. Around even the smallest house there was a good-sized open space, yet Nora, the prairie-born, looking at these many dwellings, felt cramped and shutin.

Papa, she said, why are the houses so close together?

Why, honey, Beckham said, this is a real town. This is Fork City.

The houses kept getting closer and closer together until there was a little woods with a path through it and a funny little open kind of a house in it. The grass under those trees was green and smooth and even. And there were some ladies in calico dresses—one with a sun-bonnet—spreading a cloth on the grass and taking dishes out of a basket—and some men standing around as if they were waiting with their hands in their pockets.

It's a woods, Nora said.

Naw, Harry said. That's a park.

Yes; that's just what it is, Harry, Mamma said.

It was about noon and the sun was high overhead, but it couldn't come down through the trees much, because they were pretty thick and close together. Nora hadn't ever seen so many trees.

Mostly ellums, Papa said. Some maples. But they have honest-to-God trees in Philadelphia.

Oh, Mamma, Nora said. Let's get out and have a picnic!

Mamma said there wasn't a thing to eat in the wagon—and Papa drove on past the woods. And there was an awful big brick hotel—an awful lot bigger than Papa's big hotel in Sedan—and then a lot of stores and a lot of spring wagons and shiny buggies in the street and plows out in front of the stores and piles of dress goods that were so pretty. And most of the stores had porches out over the sidewalk and big windows—and the stores were all so close together you couldn't see between them.

There were lots of people on the street, but Harry was the first to see the soldier. He shouted: Papa, there's a soldier! And the soldier turned and waved! And Papa said: You just bet! This is near one of Uncle Sam's forts. He's a calvaryman.

A fort! Harry said. Papa, can we see it?

You just bet! Papa said.

So many things, Nora thought. So many things! How the light shone on the yellow stripes on the soldier's trousers and on the shiny new plowshare in front of the hardware store and on the star on the marshal's coat and on the glass that had pictures of people behind it that Nora wanted to see close up. And then all the bottles with colored medicine in them in that drugstore window. And the swinging doors that Papa wouldn't answer any questions about.

When they came to a low frame building that looked kind of like a farmhouse and had a windmill in the backyard, Papa stopped the horses and helped Mamma and Nora and Ellen down from the wagon and Harry got down just like Papa did. There was a hot, greasy smell of cooking coming from inside the house; and Nora saw a dirty red-checkered tablecloth through the window.

Here's the rest'runt, Mamma, Papa said.

Mamma wrinkled her nose. Peevou! she said. It looks and smells dirty.

A goldengreen fly circled the dirty amberglass sugarbowl and settled once on Ellen's nose. The room was stuffy and hot and dark. Nora wanted to get back in the street where the sun was on the soldier's stripes and the plow—she wanted to go right close up to the glass that the pictures were behind and stare through it at the people there who were flat and had only one way—always the same—of looking back at you.

The table was next to the window anyway, and she could look out at the rutty gray street that was beginning to be powdery. There was a whiskeybottle with a bright label lying in a rut catching so much sunlight that it blinded her when she looked straight at it.

The woman with the dirty motherhubbard came up to the table and looked at Mamma and said: We got potroast and ham'neggs.

Well, Beckham? Mamma said.

I'll just have some of that potroast, Papa said, brushing the little greenfly from his nose.

I want potroast too, Harry said quickly.

I'll just have some of that potroast too, Nora said, looking proudly at Papa.

Ellen looked down at the tablecloth, her lip hanging. I want ham'neggs, she said.

Mamma ordered three orders of potroast and a half one of ham and eggs, her nose wrinkled all the time she ordered. It did smell bad, so Nora kept her face turned to the window and kept looking at the whiskeybottle in the street and the Fairbanks Morse scales with dry horse manure on the planks. No soldiers—not even anybody—passed for a long time. And then she heard the boardy rumble of a spring-wagon going fast—Nora could tell what it was before she saw it.

By Jesus, Papa said, *those* horses are running away.

There was a man jostling from side to side on the wagonseat—and then he fell down over the wheel and hit his head on the hub. And the wheel broke the whiskeybottle. And the man fell on top of the glass.

The horses broke into a hard gallop and dragged the wagon out of Nora's sight. The man lay there in the street in blue denim trousers and a bluechecked hickory shirt—not moving at all. His brown greasy hat lay a few feet from him.

By the gods—Papa began.

Tch, tch, tch! Mamma said. He's had too much of—you know what.

A skinny man in a funny little black cap and short black whiskers came out of a store across the street and loped through the dust to where the driver lay. Papa started to get up.

Just you stay where you are, Beckham! Mamma said. It serves that old fellah right. Just disgusting!

But Mamma, Papa said, the man's hurt—

Well, he wouldn'ta been, if he let—if he was a-doing right. I tell you, Papa, I never in the world should have consented to come to this old town. I knew just what it would be like with all them old soldiers and all—

Mamma stopped and looked at Nora and Ellen and Harry.

The man in the skullcap and a soldier carried the man over on the wooden sidewalk. And Nora could see that the top of the man's head was all red and his face was a kind of dried puttycolor and he had a short stubbly growth of gray whiskers stained with tobacco. They laid him down in the sun near·a patch of weeds growing between the rocks and the soldier took off his blue cap with the crossed brass swords on it and fanned the man a little.

Stinko, said the soldier, grinning.

The man in the skullcap—Nora could see it was black silk now—shook his head as if he didn't approve.

A man in a black buggy with red wheels said whoa to his pair of horses and wound the lines around the whip. He was short, a little plump with lots of curly, dark hair. But he stepped up on the front wheel lightly and jumped down into the road with a little black grip in his hand. He ran over to the man on the sidewalk.

Well, that just beats all! Mamma said. There's the doctor.

Nora could see that there was blood on the sidewalk boards.

The man in the silk skullcap looked up and said in a hard, flat voice, How d'ye do, Dr. FitzGerald. Mr. Dantzig's had an accident.

Well, well, the doctor said. Looks like Greg's got a nasty wallop on the head. How'd it happen?

Well, the man in the skullcap said, I saw him jiggle around as he was a-driving across the street—and it looked to me as if he fell off the seat and caught his head on the wheelhub of his spring wagon. They went on down toward the deepo.

Stinko, the soldier said, grinning.

Yes, I saw them, the doctor said, ignoring the soldier. They stopped to graze in a lot. They'll be all right.

The man on the sidewalk moved a little and sat up, feeling his head. Hat? he said. My hat.

Still grinning, the soldier brought the dirty brown hat from the middle of the street.

Here, V. P., the doctor said, give me a hand, and we'll see if we can't get him in my buggy.

The soldier helped too; and the man got up, swaying a little. He looked at the doctor as if there was no one where the doctor was standing. Then he put his hand down and started to unbutton the front part of his pants.

Piss, he said. Jus' take good piss now.

Before the doctor and the man in the skullcap could catch him, he was tottering toward the window where Nora and Papa and Mamma and Harry and Ellen were sitting—and unbuttoning his blue denim pants. He was looking right their way, but he didn't seem to see them.

He had his pants open now and he began to take part of himself out when the doctor and V. P. got hold of him and turned him around.

Stinko, the soldier said, laughing.

By God! Papa said and started to get up.

You just sit still, Papa! Mamma said. Don't you go out there and get mixed up with them old drunk men. Nora, Ellen, Harry, look the other way!

As they turned the man around, Nora saw the blood was running down his forehead and his face had turned a kind of red-purple. She didn't look away like Mamma said, but she felt her own face get warm and a funny feeling tingle all through her—she felt scared and as if she were having fun at the same time. Just as the hurt man was getting himself out of his pants to wet, Mamma reached up and pulled down the shade. I told you to look the other way from that nasty old man, Mamma said.

Nora didn't say anything, for she felt queer. Papa didn't say anything either, but kept looking down at a greasespot on the tablecloth.

The waitress set a big platter of stringy meat and salvy looking potatoes in the middle of the table. There was some watery gravy with spots of tallowy-looking grease floating in it.

Cawfee? the woman said.

No, Mamma said, shutting down her lips tight.

Why, that old stuff ain't fit to eat, Mamma said when the woman went away.

Papa got up and went over to a little counter in the room and laid down a silver dollar on it. Come on, Mamma. Come on Nora and Ellen and Harry. We'll go back to that hotel, by Jesus!

Nora got up and they walked out of the dark, little room and away from the greasy smell. And oh, it was *so* good to get back into the sun and air that she forgot to look in the street and see if there was any blood there.

Beckham, Mamma said, as they got back into the wagon, I told you and told you that I didn't like the idea of us a-coming to this old place. No, sir! What's the very first thing we see? An old drunk man a-getting ready to show himself off before decent women. That dirty old fellah oughta been killed when he fell off that wagon. And if them horses hadn't had more sense than he had, he *woulda* been too. I declare, I don't know what possesses men to get themselves into sich a condition. And that old rest'runt! If I was you, I just wouldn'ta paid one cent!

I'm hungry, Ellen said.

And the children! That was a fine sight for them to see, wasn't it? Oh, I wish I'd put my foot down and not let you move. It's just like Mamma always said, never move until you're sure of where you're a-moving to. A bird in hand is worth two in the bush. If Papa hadn't gone on that Old Clint Belton's note, we'da never had to leave our home in Ioway. I just don't know what gets into you men sometimes—

Oh Christ A'mighty, Papa said under his breath. But Nora heard him.

They went back to the big brick hotel. And there was a big wagon with a humpback top with four horses on it and pictures on the side— and Papa said it was an omnibus to take people to and from the train deepo. And there was a *big* diningroom with ten tables all with white table cloths—and Nora and Papa and Harry had fried chicken. And Ellen wouldn't even eat her ham and eggs that were all right.

They rented a house right away from Mr. Prentiss at the bank and Papa and Mr. Flaherty brought the things in out of the wagon and set up the bedsteads.

Nora and Mamma swept the house and made the beds; and Harry brought in some wood for the cookstove so Mamma could get supper with the groceries that Mr. Flaherty brought them from the Forster & Prentiss Mercantile and Grain Company that Nora had seen right across from the restaurant but didn't remember on account of the drunk man who tried to take himself out of his pants.

Mr. Flaherty said to Papa: Be Jaysus, Beckham, I didn't know you'd be here so soon or I'd a been a-setting at the end of Pawnee street a-waiting to welcome ye, I'd been. And this fine young lady! he said to Nora, laying a big, red-freckled hand on her shoulder and looking down at her with a round red face and a bluewild Irish eye. She'll set the young-feller-me-lads agin each other, she will!

Mamma, who looked tired and dusty from getting the house ready, looked at Mr. Flaherty with a don't-like-you look, but didn't say anything. Mr. Flaherty said: Well, Tom, I'll just give you folks time to get settled. So don't think about coming to work until Monday morning! I'm sorry that trouble caught you and Stacy both—but Sedan's loss is my gain. And he went out and drove away in a little lowbacked Irish buggy with only two wheels.

Stacy? Mamma said. I didn't know any trouble caught *you,* Beckham.

Papa didn't look at Mamma, but she stood there still with the broom stopped where it was on the floor. She didn't say anything for a long time. Then she said:

Beckham, did you go on a note for that old Stacy? Did you, Beckham?

Papa didn't say anything.

So that's why we had to come to this awful old place? Mamma said her voice almost breaking. Papa mighta had some excuse for going on that Old Clint Belton's note, but there wasn't a bitta use for you to get us put outa house and home. Oh my God, Papa.

Now, Mamma, Papa began.

Don't you now Mamma me, Beckham. It happened to my mother and now it's happened to me. I never knew it to fail. Mamma began to cry.

Well, Beckham, Mamma said after a while, to my dying day I'll regret a-coming to this old town. You just oughta have known better than to get mixed up with that old Stacy.

Now, Mamma, Papa said, he was my friend. He let me off when Nora was sick—

And you just oughta known better than to get mixed up with that old shanty Irish fellah, Flaherty. Don't you ever darest to lend him a thing—don't you ever even sign so much as a littlebittova piece of paper he asks you to! It's just like Doctor Purvis use' to say back in Knoxville: The shanty Irish are all the same, they'd rob their own mother.

Ellen came in crying from the weedy yard, a red lump on her nose.

A bee bit me! A bee bit me! she screamed, but Mamma didn't understand what she said.

Now quiet, Ellen! Mamma said. Quiet! Then she turned back to Papa. And this old house too! Twenty dollars a month!

A bee bit me on the nose! Ellen screamed.

Oh my, oh my! Mamma said.

Harry came in from the backyard with an empty wooden bucket.

Papa, Harry said, there ain't any water in the well.

Mamma took Ellen to the kitchen and put some lard on her nose and Harry went to borrow some water. Nora and Papa went out on the front porch and the boards cracked a little under Papa's feet. But there was a flame colored and blue sunset just starting.

Across the street there stood a stone schoolhouse with a wooden belfry in the middle of the top of it—and there was a great big bell in it. Papa was pulling at his beard and looking so kind of worried as he sat down on the steps that Nora was worried too. For a minute Papa didn't say anything and then Nora said:

Is that the schoolhouse where Ellen and Harry and me'll go to school, Papa?

Eh? Papa said.

Nora asked Papa again.

I expect it is, honey. Papa expects it is.

But Papa didn't talk like Papa did to her usually. He didn't say: You just bet! or Don't you forget it! And he looked awful sad.

Papa, what's the matter? Nora said. What's the matter?

Why, nothing, honey—nothing. Papa just set down here to rest a bit. Don't you like to light after travelling all day? Why, you just bet you do.

But though he said you just bet, it didn't sound like Papa. She got up beside him and put her arm around his neck, and he put his arm around her. Suddenly she began to cry.

There, there, honey, Papa said softly. Then she put her face into his beard and cried as if her heart would break.

Thus, Nora Beckham came to the place in the world which she was to call home—Fork City.

CHAPTER XLV

Nora's lips were bright and red and full, but her face was chalky and little crystals of coldsweat lay under her nose and on her forehead. One hand was holding tight to the wooden bedstead. Her long honey-brown hair showered over the pillow. Even in the dim yellowcarbon-light—even in the spasm of pain, she looked pretty and young and pert.

WHY, I can see my mother, drying her eyes as she looked at her son's pale face and dark eyes and his almost trembling lips. Why does he treat me this way? From the unanswered question her memory would leap wordlessly to a search of her own youth and she saw

herself moving through the years wherein there had been little pause
from toil, as a woman waiting for her lover in a museum on a rainy
afternoon moves through the silent glassed-in passages.

She saw herself as she leant against the screen door at dusk in the
house on Third street in Fork City, waiting for Wilfrid Hincks's
horse and buggy to clump up to the curbstone. She heard the cicadas'
burr and the somnolent slap of screen doors as Old Man Pearson took
the ladder from his buggy box, placed it against the iron cross-bar of
the street lamp in front of Mrs. Brown's, climbed up and touched his
torch to the wick. The light flickered yellowly on the weeds in the
street; she felt the hot summer wind at her tightly wound up golden
hair. She had mistaken Old Man Pearson's buggy for Wilfrid's.

Like so many other Sunday nights in summer, it was a relief after
a week at the Bee Hive where she sold turkey red and figured calico
from Mr. Hincks's stock and listened to the German farmers' wives
gabble in their queer tongue. *Sehr viel Geld! Sehr viel Geld!* Always,
no matter what the price, the calico was too expensive.

When Mr. Hincks had raised her wages to six dollars a week, she
could pay Mamma and Papa three dollars a week for her room and
board. She was tired, for she had ironed all day, and on Saturday she
had stood behind the counters of the Bee Hive from seven-thirty in
the morning until that night with a half hour off for dinner.

As she leant on the screen door waiting for Mr. Hincks's son she
thought that she would work hard; she would pull herself out of this
mire that Papa's easy-going improvidence had brought them. She
would hold up her head. Why, pshaw! She could be *somebody*! All the
young fellows liked her, and she wasn't fast either. Her straight spine
straightened the more; she moved away from the door a little, disdain-
ing to lean, and with a well-guided young hand, smoothed the stiff
white linen of her only linen dress. Oh, if she were a man, she would
make a lot of money and see life—and travel. What a lovely time she'd
had in Riverside, California last summer—and how much fun it had
been when the tracks were washed out at Flagstaff and the railroad
company had had to feed all the people on the train for a week. That
singer from New York was a fine looking fellow. He could sing classical stuff as well as ragtime.

Well, she didn't have any trouble about fellows. She always had
one, you bet. And she didn't let them get fresh with her either. Why
even the boss's son, Wilfrid, who'd been to college—Nora hadn't got

through high school for she'd had to go to work—came to see her. He was coming tonight, but he was late.

Mamma, Nora said to the dark, hot cavern of the house, what time is it?

A quarter of eight! said Myra's voice from the kitchen. Are you a-waiting for that Hincks boy?

Yes, Mamma, Nora said.

Well, I'll just tell you right now, I don't think much of him.

Mamma, how many times do I have to tell you he's all right?

Mamma complained thinly, as she walked from the kitchen to the living-room—the parlor. Wilfrid was no good: runnin' around with Laura Webster and that gang that was always actin' so sweet, but if the truth was to be known—

Why, Myra said hotly, she's hardly any better than someone from Eleventh street. Why, if the truth was to be known, I'll bet old Wilmer— Wilfrid, Mamma! I don't care what his name is—it's all the same—that old Wilmer Hincks goes down there to those bad houses his own self! Why, Mamma, Nora said quietly, her young rage pent in her, Mamma, I don't know what makes you talk that way. Wilfrid Hincks's one of the finest fellows I know, and I won't have you say another word against him—no sir, not another word!

Now, Mamma, said Tom Beckham from the dark porch, the boy's all right. He's a fine boy—a jim dandy boy.

You shut up, Beckham! You stay outa this. I'm goin' to say what I think. I don't think that fellah's decent company for Nora! You just bet I don't!

Mamma, I'm paying my board and room in this house, but I can pay it somewhere else. I'm sick and tired of you telling me who I can go out with! Mamma you make me so darn mad I could—I could— Nora's vocal cords tightened and her voice came, intensely concentrated, through her teeth—I could bite a nail in two!

Oh Jesus Christ, Tom muttered and started for the back yard, his hand on a plug of Tinsley tobacco in his hip pocket.

Oh, I just don't know what will happen, Myra wailed.

Clump, clump-clump, clump-clump, clump. It must be Wilfrid driving up the street, Nora thought.

Mamma, she said, will you please keep still?

Quickly Nora went into her bedroom and smeared some medicinal rice complexion powder on her nose. Myra left the room talking to herself as she walked carefully on her sore leg. There was a knock. Nora hesitated a moment, set a smile on her well-formed lips and went to the door. It was almost dark now, but she could see that it was Wilfrid, even though there was no lamp lighted in the house.

Good evening, Wilfrid, she said.

Hello, Nora, he said, taking off his new pearl gray derby from the East. I hope I didn't keep you waitin' long. The time I had gettin' here was the limit.

Oh no, not at all, Nora said. I just finished dressing. What's the matter, Wilfrid?

Can you go for a ride? Wilfrid said, with a cubbish smile. For all his clothes from the East he seemed a little self-conscious.

As the buggy moved through the hot dark of Fork City's dusty summer streets, Nora's heart still beat rapidly from the anger her mother had set up in her breast. Nora, though she knew little of the earth but the town at the edge of the prairies and what she had seen on her trip to California, thought: If I could only get away from here: this heat and snow and slush, Mamma wrangling and nagging, Papa making no money now but his Civil War pension, Ellen, her younger sister, nagging, that awful store where those fast women buy those towels to use in those houses on Eleventh street . . .

Nora, Wilfrid said, I'm going East.

Going East? For how long?

I guess I'll be gone for a long time; I'm going into my uncle's printing and engraving business, Wilfrid said.

The rig, a high two-seated trap, jingled a little, rolled through the stifling night out of Fork City into Rawlins Avenue towards Fort Davis. Over Grand View hill above the Smoky river a great moon hung under the visible stars. The rig passed a cavalryman walking back to the post with a little stagger in his gait. He's going home from those old saloons and houses, Nora thought. He's coming back from those women on Eleventh street, still drunk. Up there on Grand View hill I can see the lights of that old man Wintersteen's wine garden. Booze and soldiers and Doc FitzGerald breaking the mirrors in the saloons and Mamma nagging—oh, if I was a man! She felt her freshly ironed white linen mussing beneath her and her sweat trickling down under her corset stays. Oh, if I was a man, I would see the world! I'd leave this awful, little old place.

That's just fine, Wilfrid! she said. That's just fine! You'll get to see all those places—you'll get to see a lot of sights and travel! That's just wonderful!

But it wasn't so wonderful. No, Wilfrid had been just about her best beau. There was Tom Zorn and Abel Gortz and Charley Given and a lot of others and even that new fellah Robert Harrington who'd bought Papa's picture gallery. Just about all the fellahs in town came to see her. Why, she'd taken Wilfrid away from that Laura Webster who worked at the Bee Hive. She uses face paint and she's fast, Nora thought. Why she laughed when that old Frank Weston said that about a piss ellum club in the store the other day. But now that Nora had got Wilfrid away from Laura, he was going away.

When you going, Wilfrid? she asked with a bright, chirruping voice that had reminded Rome Hanks of Little Ream. She held up her dimpled chin and smiled.

Tomorrow, Wilfrid said. Dubiously, he stopped the horse and tentatively wound the reins around the buggy-whip.

Tomorrow, Nora's bright chirrup said. You won't be with us long, will you Wilfrid?

Nora was sitting still and straight. The staggering soldier moved past toward the post. The leaves of the cottonwoods rattled. She felt Wilfrid's breath on her cheek, his hand on her thigh—on her— Ecstatic shivers scurried over her skin. Oh Lord! It was a discovery.

Trembling, she moved away from him. With a great effort of will she brought back her bright, chirruping voice, though it sounded false: Wilfrid, she said, we must go home. I have to work tomorrow.

She felt her breasts against her stays, Wilfrid's breath going away from her cheek. She thought of the women in the fast houses on Eleventh street; she thought of Mamma; she felt ill. She moved as far away from Wilfrid as she could: she could hear herself breathe above the rattling of the cottonwood leaves in the hot breeze. She felt as if she might faint.

What's the matter, Nora? Wilfrid said, his voice strained.

Nothing, Nora said, nothing. Then with the great intensity of will which was to remain at her command for many years, she said in the voice which was always a falsity:

My, it's terribly hot. What's that over there? Is it heat lightning? I just hope we don't have another one of those old thunderstorms. Well, Wilfrid, that certainly is fine for you! I'm so glad!

It is to be noted that Nora said nothing to Wilfrid about his ad-

vances. Perhaps her emotions and her will had been called on enough
for one evening. Now, Wilfrid is going away, she thought, and my
chances are less. And to the dim caverns of her mind she took the discovery that had come with his touch, for that inexplicable ecstasy she
thought indecent—and she remembered with dread her mother saying
that Wilfrid visited the brothels on Eleventh street.

But it had not been heat lightning. As Wilfrid set her down from
the buggy, a large splashy drop of rain fell on her face, as if it were
the only thing but them in a dark, windless world. The night was dull
and still, and Mr. Pearson's lamp burned fitful in the darkness. Wilfrid
and she groped to the porch, and he, suddenly and awkwardly, leant
over as if he were about to kiss her. She moved her head away and with
a false laugh, said:

Goodness me, Wilfrid, you'll have to hurry or you'll be soaked and
catch your death of cold.

Oh, I'll be all right, Nora. Will you write to me, Nora?

Nor-uh! It was Mamma's voice calling petulantly from the inside
of the house.

Yes, Mamma.

Is that you? My, my! I didn't think you'd ever come—with that old
lightning a-going on. Oh, Myra paused standing in the light of the
doorway. Oh, good evening! she spoke to Wilfrid grudgingly.

I'm all right, Mamma, Nora said quietly. Mamma turned from the
doorway before Wilfrid answered: Good evening, Mrs Beckham.

As Wilfrid's horse's hooves beat down Third street, which would
soon be a swamp of loblolly mud, the rain started to fall slowly in
great splashing drops. Nora went inside the house. She hooked the
screen door and leant against it listlessly, listening to the rain. She
hardly knew that she was crying until a hot tear fell on her wrist.
Quickly she wiped her eyes and went into her room . . .

She lay in bed listening to the drive of the now heavy rain on the
roof and the bumble of the midsummer thunder, and thought (and
thought it strange that she thought) that it's raining on Old Man
Wintersteen's wine garden and the staggering soldier and the fast
houses on Eleventh street and in the Smoky river and on Grand View
hill and on Wilfrid who's going away.

Noh-rah, Mamma said from the doorway of the bedroom. What
was you and that old Wilfrid Hincks doin' buggy riding so long?

Oh, Mamma, Mamma, do be quiet. Nothing, nothing.

Well, I jist don't like you doin' those kind of things—out ridin' till all hours!

When Mamma moved away from the door, Nora was crying again. But it was dark, so she didn't stop. She didn't have to exercise her will. She cried herself to sleep.

But, Lee thought, I would have had it happen as it did happen. It is well that she married the boy who came from Gadkin County, North Carolina, to look at the bleakness of Kansas on a Century camera ground glass.

It is well that she knew the Spanish cannon in the park, and the saloons on Pawnee street all her life, for, God help me, I should not have wished to have been born anywhere else but there—and I would not have had any one else for my father whose eyes had dazzled when he saw the silver and the collodion and the actinic rays, the boy who built the gallery on Pawnee street.

CHAPTER XLVI

Doc Gaines got back from the call in the country after dark; and gave his mare the oats in the manger. After ten years' practice, he was still in a state of wonder about himself. He could stand off and watch himself putting the small black instrument and medicine case into the buggy and see his own fine Burnside whiskers (he knew how they looked: there was a mirror in his private office and a fine one at home—and the big mirror in the barbershop where, in the shaving-mug rack there stood the cup with Dr. Z. W. Gaines in goldleaf Old-english letters). A wonder and a delight it was to be Zachary William Gaines, Medicinæ Doctor, a physician, a man of some consequence in the community. To be able to know all the little frobles (this was the way he pronounced foibles) of human nature, to meet all kinds of people, and to practice the Noble Art of Healing (he used those words to himself).

Boy and man, he had wanted to be a doctor; boy and man he had longed to be A Gentleman of the Old South: There was the book which had the paragraph at the beginning (a book written by an adjutant of the First Virginia Cavalry—and written after the war was over at that—who should have known better, but could not break the regimen of a lifetime): Having returned to the seat of my family at ———, Virginia, and hung up a dingy gray uniform and a battered old sabre, for the inspection of my descendents, I propose to employ some leisure hours in recording my recollections, and describing, while they are fresh in my memory, a few incidents of the late War Between the States.

The doctor was born at a Kansas crossroads called Thebes; and Gentlemen of the Old South—except for the Medicine Show Man, who came through Thebes in a painted wagon and told how he had studied (and felt obliged to give to the world—at cost) the esoteric secrets of the Indians, who, by his bounty, occupied a part of his Old Virginny Plantation—remained men who hung up dingy gray uniforms and battered old sabres, told Old Tom to fetch a julep and look sharp, while under the magnolia-bordered Greek portico, they began to record their recollections of blood with a quillpen.

Perhaps the quack, speaking in the smoky flare of pineknots, gave the doctor the Soft Southern R's which now—in all the wrong places —slurred his Kansas speech; perhaps the Medicine Man, speaking of the deep, dark, obscure, esoteric secrets of the Indians, had led him through the miles and hours and boredom which made him a small-town frontier doctor with Burnsides (by some mistake, or ignorance, or reflex, he had chosen the whiskers of a blundering Union General, instead of the beard of a Jackson, or a Hampton, or a Stuart—or even the fictional goatbeard of thousands of colonels and majors who must have been somewhere sometime in the South, or somewhere posing for whiskey advertisements) and a patriarchal bedside manner at forty.

Perhaps he had come to believe that his father had been on General Lee's own staff and that somewhere in a ruined South there was an ancestral home, an Old Southern Mansion, which, in his mind, had been old as soon as the architect's ink was dry. This stuff, mixed with an earnest, priggish boy, had become a man, who, as his novel-reading in slack moments increased, and he laid up a store of phantom Gentlemen of the Old South, became party to a conspiracy with himself.

For the sugary Doctors of the awed smalltown women and the farmers' wives, he had heard Colonels for a good many years. And though he was not as awesome to the Kansas Negroes as Dr. Fitz-

Gerald, who kept a string of polo ponies of sorts, many of them came to him, the Colonel Doctor, because, if he did talk roughly to them and call them niggers to their faces now and again, he could be counted on not to make them pay. They never knew that when they came into his office, they became Negroes on the plantation of Colonel Doctor Gaines, Surgeon of the Army of Northern Virginia, who, though he had read a good many novels which must have differentiated, did not know the difference between a house Negro and a field hand. Even before he became a doctor, while he was still teaching in the little country school—walking five miles a day in brutal weather with no overcoat, the money being necessary to get the M.D. behind his name, so that he could translate the awed obsequious, worshipful, even loving Doctors into Colonels—he began to mush his R's; he began to indulge a taste for words unusual and obscure to him and Latin and Greek derivatives whose pronunciation (and often their meanings) he decided for himself, and which always sounded twice as juicy and sententious as the correct but empty shells of them which he tossed away once and for all when he had heard himself articulate his own pronunciation once.

You'd better leave your bag in the buggy, his wife said from the backdoor. Somebody called—a woman. Maybe you ought not to go though. Maybe you won't wanta go when you hear the address.

Who was it?

It's one nineteen East Eleventh.

Oh. What name?

Maizie Smith—but it wasn't her that called. It was that Belle woman. She said she was bad.

I'll have some supper and then go.

Do you think you'd better go down to one of those houses at all. Ten chances to one it's something bad. Those women don't deserve—

Look heah, Lucy, I can't deny anybody medical treatment because of their *mores* (he pronounced it as if it were the English comparative plural). You must undahstand that I am not a judge of human frobles and idiosignócrasies. I am a physician.

I know—but those women—those houses— If anybody was to see you go in one, they might think—

Well, they'd be incórrect. I'm not any more anxious about going to such a place than you are to have me go, but I took the oath of a physician.

But he was. He had never been in one of the houses. He was timid and his stiff manners were not calculated for those of a whore's physician. But he knew the girls by sight. Some of them were pretty: juicy fatbreasted women, he thought. Perfumed vaginas. Where had he heard that? And when you went into one of the houses to do your business, you did it as if you were eating your victuals in a restaurant and paying your money—and no bashful nonsense about virtue. But still there were always the clap and the syph.

He hurried through the ham and eggs, not enjoying them, but thinking with a coldthrill of the visit to Morro Castle and the juicy membranes and curved cuticle which was offered for rent. Entrance and friction, the winking of a muscle. For two dollars I will wink a muscle for you—I will relieve you.

His wife watched him from the kitchendoor as he drove away. The streetlamps had been lighted and the city park pointed in the thickhot leaves with small yellow lights. The wooden bandstand and the bronze Spanish cannon which the Fifty-fifth Kansas brought back from Cuba and gave to the city. She could see them all as she listened to the dustmuted hooves of her husband's mare.

CHAPTER XLVII

THE DOCTOR saw the lacebacked glasspanel in the door glowing red with the guildbadge of whoredom. He tied the mare to the hitchingpost as a cannoncracker exploded in Pawnee street. She stomped and nickered as an unsteady soldier shuffled past. Tomorrow was the Fourth. He took his bag from the buggybox and started toward the redlighted door, simulating boldness. He turned the bell. Heavy unhesitant steps marched doorward. His pulserate rose as the thicklace drew back behind the glass and the eyes looked out. The door swung open and he saw the madamedignity before him.

Good evening, Doctor, Belle said, as if she were any smalltown married woman. Come in.

Good evening, the doctor said stiffly, dividing up the word ev-en-ing into resonant pompous syllables. A Miss Maizie Smith was not feeling well. You rang me up on the teluffone.

Yes, Doctor, the Madame said. She's sick in bed. Up in the tower.

Now, the doctor said, what's the trouble here?

I hurt, Doctor, the girl on the bed said.

Belle whispered to him.

A knitting needle, eh? By God! Bleeding, eh? Not now, eh? Hummm!

He threw back the kimono and looked at the goldenred pubichairs on the *mons veneris* under which there had already begun a green discoloration of the white bellyflesh.

Madame, he said, phone up Holzer's drug store for an ice bag— and the ice plant for some ice.

Yes, Doctor, Belle said. There's ice on the beer. Is that all right, Doctor?

Ice is ice, Madame.

Right away, Doctor, Belle said. All *her* Doctors were easily translated into Colonel.

The girl on the bed. Nineteen or twenty. Fine grained white skin, smallfine turnedup nose, red golden hair—even the pubic—vacant blue eyes. Maizie Smith. Prettier than Lucy.

Doctor, she said.

Yes, Miss Smith.

The widevacant, Maizie-eyes swung open, fringelashed. Doctor?

Now just take it easy, Miss Smith. We'ah goin' to do all we can foah you.

There reely ain't much chance, Doctor, is there?

Now, I wouldn't say that, Miss Smith.

But there ain't. I seen a girl that done it once with a crochet needle. She was the same as I am. She said she thought it was the hook thing on the needle—and she oughta used a knitten one like she done before. She died—all swollen up. It began like me. I used a knitten one. I know what's gonna happen.

Now, Miss Smith, theah ah cases of septicæmia which recovah— and a good healthy guhl like you—you've nevah-ah-had anything—ah —have you?

No. Doctor. I always been clean. Doctor—?

Huhm?

You look like Poppa. He had whiskers just like yours.

Um? the doctor said. Ah—did he? He took out his watch and reached for her pulse. Maizie took his hand tightly in hers with a warm shameless womangrip, closed her eyes.

Yes; just like Poppa. She ran her hot feverfingers over the brown hairs on the doctor's handback.

Wheah is youah fathah? the doctor said.

He passed away when I was twelve, Maizie said.

Oh, the doctor said, looking at the red in the slopjar. Excuse me, Miss Smith.

The icebag's on the way—and I ordered some more ice, Belle said from the doorway.

Keep her packed in it all the time, the doctor said. I'll be back tomorrow morning.

Maizie again swung open the bluevacant eyes. Goodbye, Doctor, she said. What time tomorrow?

Not too eahly, the doctor said.

Belle walked down the hall with the doctor.

She's bad, ain't she, Doctor?

I'm afraid so, Madame. I'm afraid so. Knitting needles!

Yes, I know, Doctor, Belle said, but when them pills won't pull it off—

Well, Madame, keep the ice on huh abdómen.

They had reached and passed the pinkglobe on the newelpost. The doctor's hat was in his hand and his olfactory nerves were shocking once more to the incense-perfume of the brothel. And his libido was busy scurrying through the bedclothes of the women of the stews. In this house, he had heard it said, there were twenty women of all complexions. They came and went all the time: They came from Kansas City, Omaha, Chicago, the Islands, Mexico, Dallas. Incense, perfume, whoretowels from the Bee Hive—Lucy used to sell them. Long thighs, short thighs, broad hips, boy's hips; big breasts, little tits —roundstretched, warmdowned cuticle. Two dollars a crack. Probably cost less than to keep a wife, providing, of course, you didn't have to pay for repairs.

Maizie's a nice girl, ain't she? the Madame said. Pretty ain't she. One of my best girls too—like my own daughter to me. Come here from St. Joe. Real reefined too.

Ah, yes, Madame. She is very pleasant.

She won't—

I can't promise you anything, Madame. I must be getting home now. I've had a hahd day. I delivahed a baby this mawning.

Yes, Doctor, I know it ain't easy being called out at all hours—I know how it is. I have a lot of girls almost as nice as Maizie.

Eh? Oh. Madame, I am a married man—and besides—

Oh well, Doctor, no offense. The invitation still stands.

A thick buffalo-clumping crossed the porch; and the doorbell rang hard. The Madame opened the door and two soldiers shoved inside.

Hello, Belle, the sandyhaired one said, we decided, by Jees, that fi' dollars ain't enough for the f—in' dawg—a genuwine Mexican hairless Chiwow oughta rank a free piece.

Yeh, Belle, the darkhaired one said, a free piece. Look, we spent a good deal of money with you—

And we're gonna have a free screw, by Jesus Christ, the sandyhaired one shouted as his dilated eyes suddenly perceived the doctor. Who's the old bastard with the whiskers?

Deftly, Belle picked up a small roundlegged Grand Rapids chair, swung it above her head and down on the sandyhead. Rungs cracked; the sandyone's knees gave way. That'll teach you respect for the Doctor, you son of a bitch! Belle said in loving righteousness. Then modestly apologetic, she turned to the doctor: I hope you'll excuse us, Doctor. It ain't often anything like this happens.

Warm with pride Colonel-Doctor Gaines closed the door on the redlight and got into his buggy.

CHAPTER XLVIII

As IF Time were on his back with a knout, Robert came down the staircarpet over the hardpine, highpitched staircase, turned through the dark diningroom, his flatfooted tread tinkling the wedding-present and Christmas-present dishes in the Grand Rapids chinacloset. He bumped his head on the doorframe, lit a match on his trouserseat, twisted the hardrubber fingergrip on the socket of the carbonbulb before it engaged and he stood blinking in the forty candlepower yellow light. The telephone hanging on the wall beside the kitchencabinet stared at him with two belleyes.

He turned the crank hard and set up an uneven ringing, looking down at the patternless spot on the linoleum where his feet rested. He turned the crank again—harder.

Central, he said, Central, git me Doc Gaines's house quick!

He watched the old alarmclock eating up the time as it stood on the twoinch pineplank which held the squat iron cisternpump over the sink. Twelve-thirty. He took a cigar from the breastpocket of his brown shirt, bit the end off it and thrust it under his wideblonde Chester Conklin moustache. His light blue eyes under the cold oval-rimmed spectacles stared with fear. His right hand groped for a match in his trouserspocket, dragged the sulphurhead over the seat of his trousers, broke the stick.

Pshaw! he said mechanically. Daggone!

He grasped the stub and dragged it over the hardwool trousers again—trousers which would hold their shape and not shine soon—holding it to the cigar, puffing until the match fell on the kitchen floor and burnt the squaretipped pyrocolored fingers.

Doctah Gaines speaking, testily said the Gentleman of the Old South voice into Robert's ear.

Doc, Robert said, I guess you better come over here, Nora's—well, she's havin' pains pretty bad. I know you said it wasn't her time, but all this noise—all these big crackers is gittin' her bad.

All right, Robaht, I don't think you'll requiah me tonight, but I'll be ovah directly. His voice was testier, for he was always annoyed (though all the men of Fork City did it) when called Doc. It could not be translated into Colonel.

Right away, Doc! Robert said.

There was a grunt in Robert's ear.

The yellow carbonlight shone on the oily dometop of his baldhead as he drew at the cigar. Down from the direction of the park a great buhloom! rolled out of the darkness. A highthin shriekscream cut through the walls from the backbedroom upstairs. A few faraway phut-snaps of Chinese crackerbraids answered weakly. Robert started in a flatfooted trot, his arms waving, his shoulders bent forward exaggerating the coffinstoop, he went, heedless of the chattering china-closet, through the diningroom. Swinging hard on the ornamental oak-knob of the newelpost, he felt the finish nails give way and heard a cracking of wood. But the newelpost did not give way. He gained the staircase and went up the fourteen steps in three clumsy leaps. The backbedroom was quiet when he got to the top.

Nora, he said, what's the matter?

It's all right, Robert. It's all right now. Those awful old firecrackers made me hurt worse. I'm in a cold sweat. Did you 'phone up the doctor?

He's on the way now, Nora.

Robert.

Yes, Nora.

Call Mamma and Papa.

I was goin' to when I heard you holler. But I think I better stay here—Mamma!

Oh, Robert, 'phone up Mamma and Papa. And as soon as the doctor gets here, you better hitch up Old Kate and go for Mrs. Krause. She'll never get here, if she has to hitch up her own horse at this time of night.

You sure you'll be all right, Nora, while I ring 'em up and go?

Nora's lips were bright red and full, but her face was chalky and little crystals of coldsweat lay under her nose and on her forehead. One hand was holding tight to the wooden bedhead. Her long honey-brown hair showered over the pillow. Even in the dim yellowcarbonlight—even in the spasm of pain, she looked pretty and young and pert. A lipbite and a nosegrimace did not spoil her face as she held harder to the veneeroak of the bedstead.

Hurry, Robert—'phone up! she said.

Robert ran down the steps, swiveling on the newelpost again to turn through the dining-room, stopped, ran back, turned on the light in the downstairs hall, saw his white face with a gone out cigar under the Chester Conklin moustache as he opened the groundglass door with the harpwoman on it and turned on the five candlepower porchlight for the doctor. With hardly a break in his motions, he resumed his trot to the telephone.

The clockface beside the cisternpump said twelve thirtyfive. Cannon crackers blammed on Pawnee street. A desultory whoop or two proclaimed the Insanefourth to the fourthousand who lay bedded in the valley.

Brrling! Brrrrrllling! Robert rang. Hello Central, he said. Gimmie forty-seven as quick as you can, please.

He stood waiting again, his teeth sinking softly into the cigarend, the wisp of Sunny Jim hair on his baldtop sticking up in the carbon bulblight.

Hello, hello! said the ghost of a hearty voice into Robert's ear.
Thomas Beckham's house.

Mr. Beckham, Robert said, I jist 'phoned up Doc Gaines. Nora's—

Eh? She is, eh? Well, by Jesus, Mamma and I'll be there just as
fast as ever we can! Mamma! Mamma! Robert could hear him calling.
Nora's— Oh, Robert, you just tell Nora Mamma and I'll be right
over there. Goodbye!

The front door bell rang as he hung up. That would be Doc
Gaines. Robert trotted through the chinaclatter. He put his hand on
the knob and the nightlatched Oriental harpwoman swung back past
the pierglass into the hall. In the five candlepower light Doc Gaines
stood uncollared, the Burnside whiskers stirring in the hot night-
breeze. Collarless, his neck was white and puckered with the beginning of age.

Hello, Robaht, Gaines said. By God, I hope you haven't got me
up on a false alahm. That child of youahs is due to arrive next week—
acccading to Hoyle. How is Mrs. Harrington?

Pretty bad, Doc. All that noise—

Yes, I know, Doc said. Those Goddamn' sons of bitches. Soldiers
and grown men too. They fired off that Spanish American Wah cannon in the pahk. And some Goddamn' ignorant fellow—a buck private
from Fort Davis—threw a cannon crackah undah Mag's heels. Now
then, wheah's Mrs. Harrington?

Up in the backbedroom—head of the stairs, Robert said.

The sirocco fanned through the door which Robert had left open;
a few insects beat at the screendoor; the maples in the frontyard
rattled their drying leaves; a long doghowl went up as the braided
fuse of a packet of Chinese crackers led fire to the powder.

Robert led the doctor up the staircarpet; the darkhaired and sandyhaired soldiers squirmed in the haytickle of the mow on Eleventh
street; Maizie Smith awoke with her forehead and lips burning hot
and fire on her belly, put down her hand to find that the fire was the
rubber icebag which Big Belle had put there a few minutes before, sat
up in bed and saw the greenblue swelling on the delicate white hide
between the redgold hairs of the *mons veneris* (my poor, hot stummack, she said, a few hot tears washing down her hotdry cheek);
Madame Belle opened the frontdoor to admit Louis Kuhn and Henry
Monkhouse (whose wives had gone shopping in Kansas City). Ah!
Ah! Madame said. Naughty! Naughty! Naughty but nice! Henry

said, snidely, shaking the round beginning of an amplebelly; Dee Given, two years old, stirred in his childsleep, as a mosquito dug its syringesnout into his light olive hide; Albert Herbert Mullin, assistant to the Boots at Sinsegraves College, Oxford, rose early in the thirdfloor bedroom of his mother's house in Long Wall street to help her with the boots and breakfasts of the New College gents who were staying up for the long vac (ostensibly to read for greats but with lustful eyes on the daughters of a tobacconist and tailor)—but he did not have his mind on his task. He was thinking of his new Oxford City blazer and cap and how that afternoon he would join the batsmen at the cricket ground against Henley. Poets awoke with hair awry and psychoneurotic eyes, with stubpencils set down firstlines, whole stanzas, notes only. Lovers curved into each other, enjoying the smooth tickly beginning of tactile pleasure as Robert Lee Harrington stirred in his mother's womb, about to be snatched into Thisworld by Colonel-Doctor, Gentleman of the Old South, Gaines, who had never been below the Mason-Dixon Line, was an indifferent obstetrician, very tired and fed to the teeth with spasms, orgasms and reactions of human cellular material—after which he always had to clean up.

Bob, the doctor shouted downstairs, wheah the hell you goin'?

After Mrs. Krause, Doc, Bob said. Nora wants her.

Oh! Well, put me a good big containah of watah on the stove to boil before you go aftah that midwife. Humph! A good big one!

All right, Doc.

The doctor went into the back bedroom and looked down on the sweaty face of Nora, Well, Mrs. Harrington, how ah you?

Oh, Doctor, Nora said, I just don't know. I just guess, as the old darky says, I could be worse. Did Rob—Mr. Harrington go for Mrs. Krause?

Theah, theah! Mrs. Harrington. Mr. Harrington went for the—hum—midwife, Mrs. Krause. Now everything's going to be all right. Wheah's an old sheet I can get, Mrs. Harrington?

There's one in the top drawer of that chiffonier right there, Doctor —under those towels.

The doctor walked across the oakstained, shinyvarnished pinefloor to the veneer chest of drawers, which stood, bulgefronted with brass pulls like the frogs of a musical comedy leftenet, in the corner between two windows. He pulled the wornsheet from the drawer, shook it out into bluewhite billows of cotton and began to twist it up.

Here's something to get your teeth into, Mrs. Harrington, he said tying it across the bed on the slat supports,—and to pull on too. How do you feel now?

I haven't had a pain for a minute or two, Doctor, Nora said, taking hold of the tornsheet which Mamma had given her when she got married.

Downstairs the springbell buzzed flatly, slowly running down. That's Mamma and Papa, Nora said. Where's Robert? Why don't he let them in? Her hands tightened on the sheet.

I'll let them in, Mrs. Harrington, the doctor said.

Robert ought to've left the nightlatch off, Nora said. Then she screamed as the child kicked inside her ripe belly.

Hold onto the sheet, Mrs. Harrington, the doctor said. He hopped downstairs, the beginnings of the look of an old man on him. The whore, he thought, redgold Maizie, with the beautiful bellydown. She didn't want hers. A knitting needle for two lives. Maybe all for the best. Who'd want a chippy for a mother? I'm a bastard and my mother was a chippy in Madame Big Belle's house in Fork City, Morro Castle, on East Eleventh street. She screwed several regiments of cavalry to say nothing of the Town Boys and the militia—but no Indians or niggers, by Jesus. This is a strickly White, strickly twodollah house. No two bit Chinee here, me fine bucko!

The doctor swung back the Oriental harpwoman, who sat among the *fleur de lis* with a hookah at her feet, and Myra Hanks Beckham stood in the fivecandles which traveled all the way up from the dynamo at Mr. Hogarty's mills on the river.

How is she, Doctor? Myra said. How's Nora? Are we soon enough? We came just as fast as ever we could. Where's Robert? Is Mrs. Krause here? I told Nora to have Mrs. Krause. You always need a woman, don't you, Doctor?

Now, Mamma—Tom said putting his hand up to his beard which looked sablesilvered in Mr. Hogarty's fivecandles.

Is she all right, Doctor? I heard her, Myra said cutting Tom off.

Now, Mrs. Beckham, you mustn't excite youahself. Mrs. Harrington is behaving quite noahmahlly.

Phut-blang! Phut-blang! Blang, blang, blang! Buhloom! the vasthot nightmorning said.

Oh my, oh *my!* Myra said. Those nasty old firecrackers. If it isn't one thing it's another. This is an awful time to pick—

Now, Mamma, Tom said, Nora can't help it. She didn't pick—

You keep still, Beckham. I'm a-going up to see Nora. What can I do, Doctor?

I believe Mr. Harrington put on some hot watah to boil. If you'll see to that—

Beckham, you go to the kitchen and see to that water, Myra ordered. I'm going up to see what I can do for Nora. I do hope Robert gets back with Mrs. Krause in time. Poor thing—leavin' her here without a soul.

Yes, Mamma, Beckham said, taking off his broadbrimmed black Stetson Old Soldier's hat and tramping through the chinachatter of the diningroom to the cookstove. He poked the fire, which Robert, in his hurry had choked with coal, filled two more kettles.

He hummed *The Girl I Left Behind Me* and turned to look at the telephoneface on the kitchen wall. Well, by Jesus, Nora was a-going to have a boy (he thought of it as a boy already). It'd be a fine boy; and this day and age was a great one to live in, all right. Why there was the telephone: you could talk into the damn' thing and talk to someone miles away. And there was those fellahs flying around in flying machines—and all the books that Frenchman, Verne, wrote were coming true. By the gods, he was glad the boy was coming to live in a world that was new and full of inventions. Why, if he'd got that job in the Baldwin Locomotive Works, he might've invented something himself.

Here he was going to be a grandfather; and the big world going on; and men inventing things; and the country just through whipping those Spaniards; and all kinds of great things happening—and by Jesus, it was the Fourth of July at one o'clock in the morning. Oh, by the gods, he felt trembling to be doing something—to be in the great big business of this world—

Buhlang! the night said.

Now, by Jesus H. Christ! he said grinning to himself, that sounded like a cannon—that wasn't a cracker. He remembered the guns at Gaines's Mill, forty-odd years ago.

A padded clop and a dustgrind on steeltires came from the driveway. Tom saw Robert pull up the horse and part the wheels so the old midwife in wide flowing calicoskirts and petticoats could step on the buggystep. She got down and took her black witch's bag from the buggy, groaning in an oldwoman voice.

Just come right in, Mrs. Krause, Tom said. And go right upstairs. The doctor's already here.

Doktor? Mrs. Krause said. Doktor? Her eyes, hard chinablue in the carbonlight, rolled, more expressionless than patent doll's eyes. Doktor? Vot Doktor?

Between the chinablue eyes a deep, oldwife, frownfissure, clogged in middlecourse with a hairtimbered wart, contracted and deepened with displeasure. Doktor! The two tightstretched applecheeks fell and the lips wrinkled around the empty maw worked like a sphincter muscle drawing the tongueclicks out into the hotair.

Doctor Gaines, Tom said. You jist go right upstairs, Mrs. Krause. Mrs. Beckham's up there too. And fetch us a fine patriotic boy.

He ain't gifen die snoof yed, is he? Mrs. Krause said.

Hey? Tom said.

Die snoof—it gemacht eassier. Mrs. Krause went through a rapid pantomime of sniffing snuff. Die Copenhagen—die schneeze brings die baby.

Oh no, Tom said. He ain't done that that I know of.

Gute! I bring it.

The polished blue eyes rolled across Tom ignoring him and toward the diningroom door. She pointed a knobknuckled finger at the door: Ja? she said.

Yah, Tom said. I'll fetch you to the stairs.

He led her to the newelpost and pointed up the stairwell. The hylo light in the hall was going on high. The first room to your right, Tom said. And tikeer the stairs!

Eh? the old woman said, cupping her knobknuckles, as a cracker banged outside, over an ear hung with a gold gypsy circlet.

Tikeer! Tom said loudly. Tikeer the stairs!

Beckham! Beckham! Myra stagewhispered from the stairhead. Shut-tup! Not so loud! You'll disturb Nora and the doctor!

All right, Mamma! Beckham stagewhispered back.

Shut-tup, Beckham! Myra said frowning. Oh, Mrs. Krause, I'm so glad you're here.

Jesus H. Christ! Tom said in a real whisper and stroked his beard.

Mrs. Krause vanished up the stairs in a flatplod—for many years she had had nurse's foot, and now she wore men's shoes with bulldog toes half-laced and half hooked.

Tom went back to the kitchen, hearing his own battlelimp on the floor and the chinachatter which can be heard in a million middleclass houses of America when a foot is set upon the diningroom floor.

Mrs. Krause, the mediaeval midwife, was now by Nora's side, with the Colonel-Doctor. Puerperal fevers hung about her like an aura; she had had many a little one born blind—with second sight, she said; many a pinkrump she had thwacked; and many a first bewildered wombhunting cry had she heard. She tied an umbilical cord as if she were an Eagle Scout grown up into an old woman; she provided the attended mother with a set of birth superstitions which served as maxims for the rest of the mother's life and hounded the child to his dying day: Pretty in the cradle, ugly as a man; rain on the baby's face, freckles on the man's—

Tom heard Robert coming up the wooden walk from the barn in the nervous trot he had been using for twenty-four hours. When he threw back the kitchendoor and came leaningforward into the kitchen, his Sunny Jim wisp standing up on the slickdome, the unlighted cigar still sticking out from under the Chester Conklin moustache (still a proud relic of the days when he played the guitar on the respectable frontporches of Fork City to the girls in crispshirtwaists and corsetcovers), he saw Tom sweating over the damper of the cookstove.

Hello, Robert said. How's Nora? Is—

Well, Tom said, I don't know. Your mother-in-law wouldn't let me git within twenty foot of 'em. They haven't been after me fer the water yet.

Buhloom! the Watches of the Night said.

By Jesus H. Christ! Tom said. You can bet your bottom dollar that's the cannon in the park. Some crazy son of a bitch—

Two loudhigh longscreams cut through the frame house, the windowglass rattled faintly. Quick footbeats fell on the upperfloor. Robert ran to the stairfoot, started up. Myra stood in the yellow hylolight at the top. She shook her head, frowned, lifted the warning indexfinger. Robert paused, his hand on the wrenchedloose newelpost. Myra tightened her lips, frowned again and shook her head. She pointed to her lips and then at Robert and shook her head.

Robert felt for his mouth, his pyrostained fingers closed on the cigar. Oh, yes, Mrs. Beckham didn't like smoke. He took the cigar to the door and threw it past the hookah-smoking harpwoman onto the burnt-brown July grass that lay in the dark around the maples.

Myra, the oldwoman sentry at the lifeportal, still warned from the stairhead. As her head shook sideways again, a whimper and a whah, whaaah, whaaaaaah came from the backbedroom door. Mrs. Krause's head came out. Wasser! Vater, it said. Bitte! Hod vater!

Water! Myra said. Hot water, Robert!

Robert trotted through the chinaclatter to the kitchen.

Hot water! he said. They want it! I heard him cry.

A boy, eh? Tom said. You jist bet!

I don't know, Robert said. Sounded like a boy.

Yes, sir, Tom said. I heard him hollah. By the gods, I'll jist bet you it's a boy.

Each took a kettle and a bucket from the stove and walked through the protesting chinaclatter.

In the backbedroom (the two front ones were rented to two brakemen who later became conductors and Thirty-second degree Masons) on the lefthand side of the bed there lay a small pinkwhite mannikin, squinting its eyes and whimpering querulously. It was two o'clock in the morning of July Fourth, Anno Domini 1904, the one hundred and twenty-eight anniversary of the Independence of the United States, the Forty-first anniversary of the Confederate retreat from Gettysburg and a Glorious Fourth for the Town Boys, two regiments of cavalry, one battalion of artillery, eighteen whorehouses, fifteen saloons, and some thousand-odd small boys—in Fork City alone.

It's a boy, Myra said.

What'd I tell you? Tom said.

A boy! Robert said. How's Nora?

Well, I don't know, Myra said. Them old crackers!

It's a shame to see him so pooty in die cradle, Mrs. Krause said. He'll be ugly before die grave.

Robert went up the steps in three jumps again. How's Nora? He said. How's—

Doc Gaines came out of the room and went into the bathroom across the hall. His shirtsleeves were rolled up and he was sweating. Well, Bob, he said, it's a boy—a fine boy.

Thus Robert Lee Harrington came into the world, but he was not so well-fitted up as the Colonel-Doctor suggested: He had in him a pair of weak lungs perhaps from some North Carolinian, whose father had been kidnapped in London and sold in Virginia, the seeds of various dermoid cysts, a slight lateral curvature of the spine—perhaps the Colonel-Doctor's forceps slipped, for it was a hard delivery and he got the forceps down farther than the head before he saw what he was doing, perhaps the birthgift of Robert, the coffinmaker's apprentice, a high wild yardarm temper from a Cornish Lord turned pirate, and the small tics and hitches of a thousand years' gifts from a thousand careless, idle, wretched people. He was the same as the storeroom of dubious items in a museum.

From his great grandfather, Romulus Lycurgus Hanks, (spelt variously, Hengist, Hawks, Hengs) the Roman Saxon, Lee may have got nothing. For the weakness of the bowels, the pellagra and the broken constitution which Rome had brought back from the bivouacs, battlefields, marches of the Army of Tennessee and from the prisonpen at Andersonville, Georgia, to lay down forever in Eighteen seventy-nine, had never touched the seed which begot Myra. But there were enough of halt, blind, lame, warped, fey, incestuous, mad, howling, ignorant ancestors to saddle the boy with a carcase and cranium full of a hundred weaknesses, doubts, fears, little quirks and troublesome tricks, thirsts, fears, hungers, obsessions—a mind dark and obtuse, melancholy and curious.

CHAPTER XLIX

YES, Lee said to the four sonnets, there have been a good many women in the world—a thousand battalions of them, who have walked through the lives of as many men; nay, marched through their lives in a sort of Iambic squad drill: Guinevere, Katherine Theron, Helen, Laura, Grosse Margot, Florence Nightingale, Mrs. Bracegirdle, Nell Gwynn, a probable Dark Circe, and Beatrice Portinari. Not all, said Lee softly, could count themselves onlie begetters of sugared sonnets, even when they were sung as chamber music for the beguilement of most private friends.

I had never written a sonnet, Lee thought curiously, until the adrenalin of Christa's stripéd hair and child's lips and her face and her voice had shot through me that day at the Memmingers' house. And then perhaps the night in the coupe when her stripéd hair lay fanned out behind her head; or it might have been on a cold morning, walking on a country road in Missouri. Perhaps she may have said something like this: I believe in form myself. If one, say, could write a perfect sonnet—that is all one would ask.

I believe I brought these verses to her, one by one.

I see her sitting, pouring tea, in a most easy attitude—oh, much more regal than little Beatrice, in subdued and goodly crimson gown —perhaps under the Venus de Milo, near the set of Goethe, looking almost exactly like the lovely chocolate box drawing.

Lee picked up the four sonnets, and began to read them to the photograph:

I

If in this impermanence I love you more
Than all the other shadows of my days,
This is my permanence—there is no door
For me—swung outward from these darkened ways:
This ancient prison of the stripéd hair—
This donjon of each sweet-swift curve of light
That is your face, has forced me now to bear
The sore indenture of your lovely might.
Chance is that I shall see the sky again
Through golden gratings hiding half my stars—
But I shall wander cell-less and insane,
And still be held by your strong loveless bars.
I only heard your jingled gaoler's key
Along the corridor—I am not free.

II

Eternal things which wound me to this day:
Each minute action that I learnt of yours
Are now companions of the lonely way
I walk, where nothing but the ghost endures.
The instant's edge whereon we rode a while
Lies, ticked-out, in the neverness of mind—
Tramped on by all the foolish single file
Of slug-like seconds arrogant and blind.
But on the empty moments always go
The distant turnings of your golden head,
Your lashes lying on your cheeks below

Your sleeping eyes, your voice and what you said.
And as I lie remembering in the night,
I rise in fear and pain, to strike a light.

III

Since I am done with pretty compliment,
And this brief ardor is my first and last,
Then you shall always light my firmament
As one white star from cinders of the past.
I know the universe shall burn as black—
When your last kiss falls on my eager mouth
As ancient cities laid by fire and sack,
Or forests after centuries of drought.
Then time, commingling with the cosmic dust,
Shall dull your star—and April's urgent need
Dissolve in ravaged moments all my lust—
Through petty things perhaps I shall be freed.
Then I shall love you not, but look upon
Your star with grateful eyes—my ardor gone.

IV

Finding you also transient, and the sky
But empty space unfilled by any blue—
Well, I shall make me maxims by and by
Which I shall use in loving such as you.
You see, I looked up with my lips apart,
And saw, unguarded, that your hair was gold:
Thus, tongue on strings of my most treacherous heart,
I spoke—not then so frightened of the cold.
Forever prone am I to think the sun
A constant warmth—and love a constant rule—
And yet I know the sum of one and one
And all dull maxims that I learnt in school.
Oh no, I do not call all loving vain,
But I shall never people space again.

Thus, Lee said sententiously to the photograph, love ends in a
joining, even if it is the bittersweet couplet of a fourteener to which the

bard gave his name. There is no Christa now, she has been transubstantiated by a quadruple dose of Miss Austen's antidote for love.

A most sterile Dante, Lee said.

He picked up the sonnets and began a little tear in one edge—
but he knew he could not tear them up before his hands began the motion. It was a bootless and unwitnessed gesture. He watched the spider
climbing up the wall over his desk toward an engraving of Friar
Bacon's study over Folly Bridge.

Outstanding books from Second Chance Press
All titles come in $16.95 cloth editions and $8.95 trade paper editions unless otherwise noted.

Bloom, Harry. TRANSVAAL EPISODE. "Fiery and admirable, with power, passion and a controlled savagery that makes it uncomfortable but fascinating reading." *London Daily Telegraph.*

Broun, Heywood Hale. A STUDIED MADNESS. "The most ruefully articulate, inside book on the American Theater in years." *John Barkham.* "A highly entertaining memoir that could be mistaken for a novel." *Milwaukee Journal.*

Conrad, Earl. GULF STREAM NORTH. "A graphic recounting of five days at sea. The crew is black, the captain white, but all are bound together in the mystique and commerce of fishing. A first class reissue." *San Diego Union.*

Degenhard, William. THE REGULATORS. "This six hundred page novel to end all novels about Dan Shays will not let you down. It manages to endow the uprising known as Shays Rebellion with all the sweep of a minor epic." *New York Times.* (cloth $22.50: paper $11.95)

deJong, Dola. THE FIELD. "An overwhelming tragedy of refugees escaping Europe during World War II, this novel can tell us more about history than do books of history themselves." *St. Louis Globe Democrat.*

Goodman, Mitchell. THE END OF IT. "A classic of American literature; the single American masterpiece about the Second World War." *The Nation*
"Philosophical, poetic, it says something new about war." *Norman Mailer.*

Laxness, Halldor. THE ATOM STATION. An American offer to lease an atomic base in Iceland allows this Nobel Prize winning author to serve up a black comedy peopled with Brechtian characters.

Levy, Alan. SO MANY HEROES. "Alan Levy lived through the Russian-led invasion of Czechoslovakia in 1968 and has written about it with an intimacy of detail and emotion that transcends mere journalistic reporting. A large book about a tiny nation's hope and tragedy." *Newsweek.*

Lortz, Richard. LOVERS LIVING, LOVERS DEAD. "The sort of subtle menace last evinced in Henry James' *The Turn of the Screw.* This portrait of innocence corrupted should keep a vast readership in its terrifying grasp." *San Diego Union.*

Lortz, Richard. THE VALDEPEÑAS. "The story begins with a seemingly realistic depiction of a group of vacationers summering off the coast of Spain . . . then becomes progressively surrealistic. Suspense builds to a chaotic ending making this a one-sitting, hard-to-put-down book." *Library Journal.*

O'Neal, Charles. THREE WISHES FOR JAMIE. "A humorous, sensitive love story with adventure, laughter, tears and a sprinkling of Irish folklore." *Los Angeles Times.*

Pennell, Joseph Stanley. ROME HANKS. "Such a picture of the Civil War has not heretofore been painted. A fantastic and utterly original book." *Philadelphia Inquirer.*

Salas, Floyd. TATTOO THE WICKED CROSS. "An extraordinarily evocative novel set on a California juvenile prison farm. One of the best and most important first novels published during the last ten years." *Saturday Review.*

Schuman, Julian. CHINA: AN UNCENSORED LOOK. "It is appropriate, timely and fortunate for those who wish to know how it was in China during the momentous years from 1948 through 1953 that the *Second Chance Press* has reprinted this book. Its time has come." *Foreign Service Journal.*

Shepard, Martin. FRITZ. The definitive biography of the founder of Gestalt Therapy. "A masterful yet loving portrait that goes far beyond biography, offering a Fritz Perls to whom few, if any, were privy." *Psychology Today.*

Singer, Loren: THE PARALLAX VIEW. "A tidy, taut and stylish thriller that functions as a political chiller as well! Breathtaking suspense." *New York Magazine.*

Stern, Richard: THE CHALEUR NETWORK "A brilliant fusing of the themes of a father's attempt to understand and exonerate his son with a plot of wartime espionage." *Richard Ellmann* "Brilliant . . . authentic . . . exciting." *Commonweal.*